GRAVE DANCING

on two
left feet

ESSENTIAL PROSE SERIES 191

**Canada Council   Conseil des Arts
for the Arts   du Canada**

ONTARIO ARTS COUNCIL
CONSEIL DES ARTS DE L'ONTARIO
———————————————————
an Ontario government agency
un organisme du gouvernement de l'Ontario

Canada

Guernica Editions Inc. acknowledges the support of the Canada Council
for the Arts and the Ontario Arts Council. The Ontario Arts Council
is an agency of the Government of Ontario.

We acknowledge the financial support of the Government of Canada.

GRAVE DANCING

on two
left feet

Raphael Burdman

GUERNICA
EDITIONS
TORONTO • CHICAGO • BUFFALO • LANCASTER (U.K.)
2021

Michael Mirolla, general editor
Lindsay Brown, editor
David Moratto, interior design
Rafael Chimicatti, cover design
Guernica Editions Inc.
287 Templemead Drive, Hamilton, ON L8W 2W4
2250 Military Road, Tonawanda, N.Y. 14150-6000 U.S.A.
www.guernicaeditions.com

Distributors:
Independent Publishers Group (IPG)
600 North Pulaski Road, Chicago IL 60624
University of Toronto Press Distribution (UTP)
5201 Dufferin Street, Toronto (ON), Canada M3H 5T8
Gazelle Book Services, White Cross Mills
High Town, Lancaster LA1 4XS U.K.

First edition.
Printed in Canada.

Legal Deposit—Third Quarter
Library of Congress Catalog Card Number: 2021933308
Library and Archives Canada Cataloguing in Publication
Title: Grave dancing on two left feet / Raphael Burdman.
Names: Burdman, Raphael, author.
Series: Essential prose series ; 191.
Description: First edition. | Series statement: Essential prose series ; 191
Identifiers: Canadiana (print) 20210145730 | Canadiana (ebook) 20210145749 |
ISBN 9781771836128 (softcover) | ISBN 9781771836135 (EPUB) |
ISBN 9781771836142 (Kindle)
Classification: LCC PS8603.U7328 G73 2021 | DDC C813/.6—dc23

For my late sister Raya
and
my loving daughter Riel

SOME MEN HEAR voices. I have visions.

Don't get me wrong, I'm no believer-in-past-lives-new-age-nutjob but, to survive, my parents buried their childhood traumas so deep in their psyches they kept trying to appear in mine.

Few families escape the carnage of history unscathed. At some point, however distant, our ancestors have been victims. Some have been victimizers. Perhaps, in different epochs, both. Not only is our ancestral past hidden deep inside us—though there may not be clear emotional through-lines that connect us across time—there are often fine strands of twisted emotion that gnaw at us, tug at our hearts, threads that link us to pasts we may not know, haunting us in ways we cannot fathom.

As a child I didn't know what to make of my visions or the characters that peopled them. Not until adolescence did it become clear to me: I'd been reliving scenes from my parents' childhood. Their unhappiness permeated our home with such powerful all-pervasive persistence, it must have seeped in through, if not the pores of my thin skin, the membranes of my frail ears.

I'd often hear my father wailing, lamenting with such plaintive power, he could have been a cantor pleading for mercy from the Almighty. But the brutal end to his boyhood had removed God from the picture.

Forced to flee their native countries as children, as adults my parents carried the scars of that exodus. Ensconced in a safe Montreal suburb from birth, still neither my sister nor I escaped unscathed. In fact, we both felt like fugitives: my sister, from my parents, I, from their past. Their torment led me to play life safe. My sister to risk hers.

I'm an old man now and my parents are dead. But when the ordeals of their youth were followed, a lifetime later, by blows even more unbearable, not only did it destroy them, I too wanted to die.

But I'm getting ahead of myself here. Way ahead.

GRAVE I

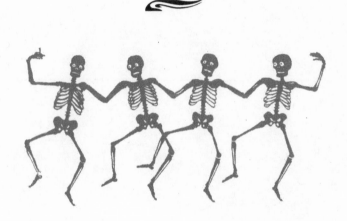

LIFE FOR JEWS in early twentieth-century Russia, above all in the Ukraine where most of them lived, had always been precarious.

You might ask, what could cause a bunch of armed Russians to attack a group of unarmed Jews? Well, in Russia, pogroms didn't need a reason. Resentment of the Jew had been an integral part of Russian life since there were Jews to resent.

Accordingly, a reign of terror against Jews would take place every decade or so. However, trying to predict one, like trying to time the Russian stock market's ups and downs, was not for the faint of heart.

By 1914, there had not been a single slaughter of Jews in almost a decade. At least none large enough to make the news. Complacency in the Jewish community began to set in. Filled with a false sense of security, Jewish defense organizations had largely disbanded. Those which hadn't were largely dormant. There appeared to be nary a black cloud in sight. Until the storm struck.

* * *

My father's father never did own a legitimate business. All his buying and selling was on the black market. Nevertheless, he was not what you would call a criminal. Nor was he considered one. His lawbreaking was a way of doing business for a whole swath of Odessa citizenry.

The port of Odessa was a gateway for goods from Turkey to Greece, from eastern Europe in the west, and the rest of Russia to the east. Indeed, the Orient was its oyster. And not only figuratively. Shellfish was a delicacy one could enjoy right there at the Odessa docks. A delicacy my grandfather refused to deal in.

"I don't do perishables," he would say. "Especially foodstuffs. Someone gets sick maybe they can't sue me black market there's no paper trail, but for sure they can shoot me. I don't need someone should shoot me."

Little did he imagine he could suffer worse.

Other than food, my grandfather would buy whatever he could, wherever he could, from anyone he could, as long as they were willing to sell to him at well below wholesale. As often as not they may have been stolen goods. But my grandfather never did the stealing. He just did the dealing.

"Far as I know the goods are on the up and up."

It was none of his business where his sources got their goods. As it was none of their business to whom he sold the goods. As it was none of the business of those to whom he sold those goods from whom he had bought them.

"If those I sold knew where I bought why would they need me?"

Eventually, those connections became sacrosanct. So that even if he knew a seller's sources, it was forbidden for him to cross that line, take a shortcut, cut out the middleman. Once a buyer or seller had been another's connection for a long enough period, it became an unbreakable bond, one you were not allowed to circumvent. Or rather, you circumvented it at your peril, especially if you were a Jew. And your source was a Gentile.

What kind of goods did my grandfather deal in? Anything and everything. From piece goods, that is, rolls of fabric left over from clothing factories, to clothes themselves, to tobacco and alcohol. Anything he could get his hands on, with the exception of unlawful goods like guns and drugs. Stolen, he'd look the other way. Illicit, he couldn't take a chance.

With snitches everywhere, both the Cossacks and cops had a pretty good idea what came into Odessa and what went out, who had what and how much. And as far as my grandfather was concerned he was a law-abiding businessman, one forced to bribe Cossacks and cops to keep real criminals at bay.

Should a black marketeer refuse to pay while trying to remain in business, most likely he would then lose not only his business but his life. And what good is a business without a life?

* * *

On this bleak Odessa morning, Lance Corporal Dimitri Alexandrov Illytch senses an approaching storm. He has a nose for such things, can sniff clouds in a clear blue sky. And this is a day he's been dreading. Summoned to his Cossack commandant's office.

As a Cossack, Dimitri makes almost a living wage, certainly more than he would with any other kind of steady employment that suited his skills, or for which his skills suited him. Which are very few. For he has little formal education, can barely read or write. But he is handy with his hands.

This means that, as a Cossack, he can put money in your pocket and, before you can blink, pull it out, leaving you wondering whether you'd pulled the wool over his eyes or he over yours. Of course this was a skill you were either born with or had to learn if you weren't brought up with a silver spoon in your mouth. But the only spoons he'd been raised with were rusted, which left him with a bad taste in his mouth. For being born so poor and lacking in privilege, even those accorded other peasants, Dimitri was determined that, when he grew up, nothing would get in the way of his being able to afford sterling silver cutlery and a set of fine china.

To become a Cossack you had to be born into it. And Dimitri was born as far from it as a Zhid in the Pale. He'd begun making a living begging on the Odessa docks. He'd save those kopecks until he'd accumulated enough to buy goods on the black market from those he'd once begged. After several years, his profits allowed him to bribe his way into the Cossacks.

On their own, Cossack wages are not enough to make him a man of means. But the money he makes on the side, using his status as a Cossack, will ensure his children won't have to bow before anyone, except maybe the Tsar. Nor will they have to bootlick like their father.

In the hall mirror of his home, he glances at himself. How elegant he looks, how important he must make his family feel, their father charged with helping to keep order in this dangerous chaotic world. But at home he's filled with uncertainty, with fear. Yet he dare not show it, not to his family. Never.

Ready to exit his house with the usual morning fanfare, he kisses his children's cheeks, hugs his wife, bids them a hurried goodbye, then steps proudly out the front door, eager to exhibit his uniformed self for all the world to see, *surtout* his neighbours. Yes, he often throws a little French into his conversations, even when talking to himself while indulging in his many internal monologues. Just to keep *au courant*, remind himself that he's not just another simple Russian peasant but part of an elite, a royal guard. Despite that, he's never guarded a royal in his life. In fact, he's never seen one in person, not even from a distance.

He missed being assigned to Moscow, where most royal sightings and parades take place. Albeit not so much of late, he's heard, not since the 1905 uprising. Now most of the Romanovs are afraid to leave their *chateau*. There, he did it again. Just like a member of the intelligentsia. He knows enough French he could almost pass for one, at least among his Cossack peers, who were easily impressed by his casual bandying about *quelque* phrases *en Français*. On the other hand, since he doesn't have as much formal schooling as most of them, he has to be careful not to push it too far. Flaunt a French word or phrase once too often and he could easily be made to look like a fool if one of the officers should overhear and begin conversing with him in that language of the educated elites. He'd be tongue-tied. He must be more sparing with his use of the little he knows. For the little he knows can go a long way in impressing those that know less, but those that know more may easily thrust open a most embarrassing door.

He turns, waves to one of his neighbours, then, paying too much attention to her, almost trips over a street stone, manages to catch himself, regaining his balance just in time to turn back to the neighbour and smile again, proud that, at the end of the day, he may be remembered more for his athletic agility than for his initial awkwardness.

* * *

My grandfather was a buffer in his community, a *shtetl* suburb consisting of a series of unpaved streets filled with colourfully ramshackle wood houses, haphazardly juxtaposed. Some had land between them, some seemingly part and parcel of a single-storey apartment complex. In reality they were separate houses that, with complete disregard for property boundaries or privacy, had expanded willy-nilly with the size of their families.

Trained neither as a notary or lawyer—he'd barely finished grammar school—my grandfather often served as one. *Shtetlers* would come to him to mediate their disputes—mostly business—or help settle who owed what to whom, where, when and why. A *kluger farshteyt fun eyn vort tsvey.* 'A wise man hears one word and understands two.' My grandfather was considered a *kluger,* the wise man of his small *shtetl* community and the *shadchan* of its synagogue, not one who made marriage matches, but one who could take a couple of men with irreconcilable business differences and show them where their interests overlapped, where they clashed and what to do about it. He frequently managed to turn business competitors into partners.

Russian Gentile and Russian Jew didn't mix. Certainly not socially, unless extremely wealthy. Or when it came to business and the law. The Jew breaking the law and the Gentile giving him the business.

But my grandfather not only pushed the boundaries between Jew and Gentile but those of his business and the law, often crossing the thresholds allowed to him and his fellow black marketeers. Neither a Bolshevik nor Menshevik sympathizer, nor one of those who agitated against the Tsar, he had a penchant for politicking, arguing what was fair and what not. In the end, maybe that was his downfall.

* * *

Inside his commandant's office, the single small window, set close to the ceiling, lets in so little daylight the place looks more like a cell than an office. The commandant's enormous grey metal desktop was disconcertingly bare without a single paper, pen or pencil on it. Everything must be stored inside its drawers or in filing cabinets lining the vacant, colourless walls. Not a family picture, painting or poster in sight. There is no life in this office, Dimitri thinks. No light either. Everything is in shadow.

With an aura as austere as the office he inhabits, the commandant is as thin as a rake, as stiff as one too, with a demeanour that could be summed up in one word: mean. Somewhere between 50 and 60, his brush-cut reddish-brown hair just beginning to grey. Standing in the shadow against the wall beneath the only window, he looks like an apparition. Dimitri wonders if he's planned it this way, the better to hold sway over those of lesser rank.

Yet he seems as dismayed as Dimitri by this encounter. In a very different manner. He's furious that he's been forced to chastise his subordinate about a business he'd wished he'd never heard of. Preoccupied with the most pressing of Cossack matters, such as being prepared to wage war, maintain the peace, protect the royal family and mother Russia, he was above such dirty business. If his personal coffers were being filled by his underlings, it must appear to be without his knowledge. But now this Lance Corporal and his recalcitrant Zhid are threatening to wreak havoc with this carefully-maintained image.

Dimitri knows that this *baksheesh* business is the proverbial elephant in the room, a subject his commandant never allows to sully his soul. Dimitri's probably earned the man's eternal resentment for making him get his hands dirty. His commandant doesn't have to say a word. Dimitri can feel his fury as the man just stands in the shadows, staring at Dimitri who cannot see his eyes, only the speck of light reflecting off them, like some animal about to pounce upon him.

Finally, the commandant breaks the silence.

"You cannot control one insubordinate Zhid."

"This Zhid is not your normal obedient Zhid, sir."

"Settling disputes among Zhids is one thing, confronting us, another."

With a sinking feeling, Dimitri is certain he will never see a promotion now, no matter what he does. He'll be lucky to maintain his rank. How low can he go and still call himself a Cossack? He must find a way to defend himself. He opens his mouth but before he can find the words to begin his defense, his commandant resumes his offense.

"Zhids refusing to play their part in a tax system which has worked so well for generations is tantamount to a Menshevik uprising. One such insurrection was enough. This Zhid's intransigence threatens our whole way of life. Which Cossack can afford to live on his meagre state salary?"

Again, Dimitri opens his mouth ...

"Right, none. This system of informal taxation has worked so well for so long we cannot allow it to be upended. Understand?"

Dimitri nods. But his eyes have a faraway look. He's thinking how he will have to deal with my Zhid grandfather, Beryl Blittstein.

"This is not an office in which one daydreams, Lance Corporal. This is not an office in which one does anything but one's duty. Since you're closer to him than any of your colleagues would dare to get, for fear of contamination, I expect you to put an end to this pestilence. If need be, an end to this pest. Dammit, Lance Corporal, do your duty or, I swear, I will do mine. And you will not like it. I can assure you of that. Do I make myself clear, Lance Corporal?"

"Yes sir."

"Good. Now get the hell out of my office."

* * *

In the hallway, Dimitri finds himself somewhat shaken. He hadn't expected kudos. But neither had he anticipated such condemnation. They'd saddled him with Blittstein because they knew how tough it was collecting from him. He'd felt proud of how well he's handled things so far. But now, for some reason, they're pushing him to push Blittstein too far. They're pushing all Zhids too far. Even a dog you can only push so far before its bark turns to a bite.

This has become more politics than business. Both his commandant and Blittstein have made it so. Blittstein's the kind of man the commandant himself should be handling. Or at least call in someone more than a lance corporal. So why doesn't he? Because if I fail they can blame it on me?

Maybe they think I've encouraged him to stand up to them, that I'm trying to kiss up to the Zhid. On the other hand, willingness to sacrifice yourself for your colleagues is at the core of the Cossack code. As is the will to kill. Perhaps they're testing me, to see how I cope. My days as a Cossack may be numbered. I'm not long for that world. Maybe this one, too. But neither is Blittstein. I've got to be blunt. Unless he does his duty I'll have to do mine.

Having decided to let Blittstein be his lamb, sacrificed on the altar of Dimitri's ambitions, on the altar of both their ambitions, the Cossack feels little relief.

* * *

My grandfather knows Dimitri is on his way. While he doesn't like where their recent haggling is heading, can't see how it's going to end, he still likes the man, doesn't fear him. Dimitri's superiors, that's another story. He wishes he and Dimitri could go back to the beginning, before those above him started raising the stakes. Those days seem so far away. Especially that first day. My grandfather had just finished delivering a couple of dozen cases of Turkish tobacco to the back door of the Evgeny Onegin Tobacco and Liquor Emporium, not far from Plisetskaya Square.

'Not far from Plisetskaya Square,' part of a poster for a once-posh Odessa hotel, had become a common tongue-in-cheek expression among Muscovite tourists. My grandfather would hear them bandying the expression back and forth, comparing the majesty of their Moscow to the mediocrity of his Odessa. Yet these same hoity-toity tourists would gobble up his Turkish tobacco like it was the best beluga caviar. He could barely keep up with the demand, wishes he had—now—something that sold so well. There's nothing like having an exclusive on something everybody wants. But that exclusive didn't last. Nor did the Onegin emporium. Driven out of business by bootleg competition, competition protected by the Cossacks.

However, back then the place was bustling. Among the throng of shoppers coming and going my grandfather couldn't help spotting this awkward-looking Cossack. He stood out, appeared out of place. Rather than leaning forward to read labels like other shoppers, he remained rigidly erect. If it hadn't been for the uniform, he could have been a guard, employed by the store, surreptitiously keeping an eye out for shoplifters. Perhaps that was what he was pretending to do. But Cossacks didn't do that kind of work, not in uniform. He just didn't fit—in his uniform or in the emporium.

As my grandfather began to make his way out the back exit of the emporium, Dimitri barrelled by him, turned and blocked his way. Now my grandfather knew: this was the Cossack chosen to replace the one who'd died a few months before. He'd known he couldn't get away forever without paying his percentage. His sources had told him that someone had been chosen. But they wouldn't say who. They probably didn't know. And if they did, they wouldn't divulge it. Not for just a case of corn flour, the most my grandfather was willing to pay. All he'd wanted was an inkling of when he might have to start greasing palms again. He didn't necessarily need to know to who. When it came to politics the only thing that interested him was whom to pay to look the other way.

But his informants had told him that, to settle on who should be rewarded with this position, it had taken weeks of wrangling among the more powerful and prestigious Cossack families. In the end, rather than choose a man from one of those families and thereby ruffle the feathers of the others, they had to come up with a compromise, a real nobody.

And so my grandfather wasn't surprised when the Cossack blocked his way. Yet his wary, uncertain, somewhat nervous glance gave the man away. Instead of feeling intimidated, my grandfather was relieved. Finally, the wait was over. The uncertainty too. And this was someone he could handle.

Sensing he was losing his initial leverage, Dimitri tried to regain the upper hand, transform himself back into an assertive presence to be reckoned with: "I've come to collect," he growled out the side of his mouth. "Six weeks worth."

"You think this is the time and place?"

"We choose the time and place."

"Why do I get the feeling we're getting off on the wrong foot?"

Dimitri had tried to maintain a tough façade, but my grandfather could sense a soft-heartedness in him. And, when they discovered that, not only were they *"landtsmen!"* from the same small town but had known each other as young boys, they immediately developed a rapport. Born on the outskirts of Tulchin, 250 miles northwest of Odessa, my grandfather in a *shtetl*, Dimitri, on a tiny peasant farm, sporadic and clandestine as their interactions had been, they could hardly have been called friends. But from time to time they'd kicked a soccer ball back and forth.

Nevertheless, it was a secret they shared only with their spouses. For they knew, if Dimitri's superiors found out, he would be reassigned, and could imagine the increased taunting from his peers: "Consorting with a Zhid as a kid, eh?" followed by a slap on the back, one that would feel more like a slap in the face.

Dimitri's vulnerability, along with their boyhood bond, makes it all the more difficult for my grandfather to see that he feels trapped between the greed of his superiors and the profit margin he, my grandfather, needs to maintain. Still, today should be no different than all the others. But it is. My grandfather knows it is. He also knows that Dimitri is merely a flunky and is surprised that they keep assigning him to collect now that they're squeezing him—squeezing all of them—so hard. You'd think that, as spokesman for Odessa's Jewish black marketeers, he'd warrant someone more senior, someone with more clout, someone my grandfather can talk turkey to. But, most likely to show him that he's not as important as he thinks he is, they've stuck with Dimitri.

He could go to them. But at best, they'd laugh 'we don't take *baksheesh*, and don't believe their men do'. More likely, they'd have him arrested for denigrating their good name, thrown in jail for making false accusations. They could even have him killed.

Anyway, another Cossack would certainly be tougher to deal with. But at least he wouldn't have to care about him, the way he cares about Dimitri. Care about him?! Why should he care about him? They're all the same: leeches who, once they latch on to you won't let go. But there's a limit. And it's been reached.

* * *

On his way to meet Blittstein, Dimitri Alexandrov is a bit anxious as always. Usually it's a pleasant sort of excitement. He loves bargaining with him. At least he used to. But now there's little joy in it, even less in the relationship. In fact, it's beginning to get ugly. And bound to get uglier.

Still, he's fond of the Zhid. Prefers his company to that of his own Cossack colleagues. In spite of having to twist their arms, he's managed to stay on the good side of most of the Zhids he collects from. Mostly because he takes a smaller cut than his colleagues. However, not as small as he lets on. Sometimes he feels like just blurting it out.

"I get more than you think!"

No, he dare not. His life as a Cossack would hardly be worth living. It's barely tolerable now. He hates having to keep up a *façade*, act tough, when deep down all he feels is fear, not only of harming his Zhid targets more than usual, or being sent to fight at the front should war break out, but of being demoted or dismissed for not living up to the Cossack code.

He's doing better than he discloses when it comes to *baksheesh*, well enough to save for a rainy day. But the storm has come sooner than expected. Too soon. He doesn't yet have enough savings to quit. What will he do? Go back to selling fish? Partner with one of the other Zhids who grease his palm?

Before things began to go from bad to worse, his fellow Cossacks were already accusing him of being a bleeding heart, letting these Zhids get away with murder, lose respect for the whole regiment. And they may have been right. After all, most Zhids are Bolshies. Don't hold the Royal family in high regard. Don't respect mother Russia. A nation unto themselves, at heart they're not true Russians. The only loyalty they have is to themselves.

No matter, Blittstein's his buddy. Even if he is a Zhid. How can you hate a man with twinkles of laughter in his eyes haggling how many kopecks he can't pay, then, when you insist he has to, he gives you a big jovial bear-hug like you're joking. Yet, when you talk heart to heart, he listens, with a warm caring look, not a forced smile like other Zhids, trying to stay on your good side, then cursing you behind your back. Or maybe he does and I don't know it. No, he wouldn't dare.

* * *

Beryl Blittstein and Lance Corporal Dimitri Illytch Alexandrovitch meet, as they often do, in the cramped horse, wagon, office and storage barn behind the Blittstein home. Lately, since the demands for an increase in payments, their encounters have become quite cantankerous, bitter. Usually, no matter how heated the haggling over the number of kopecks constituting a fair Cossack share, negotiations never spilled over into outright enmity. Now their encounter not only has crossed that line but has taken on a tone of do-or-die desperation. You might expect the despair of the one who's being ordered to pay to be greater than the one who has to collect. But you'd be mistaken. Being forced into doing something he does not wish to do—by someone who refuses to listen to what he considers reason—Lance Corporal Alexandrovitch feels himself a victim of both his Cossack superiors and this Zhid inferior who insists on maintaining his high and mighty moral ground.

"Some in this black market business don't have to bother with such strenuous activities as buying and selling goods," Blittstein says. "They just blackmail those that do."

"We're paid to protect you from gangsters."

"At the same time look the other way as they break the laws we work around. Anyway, I still have to pay the police."

"You think I'm not being squeezed?"

Blittstein had been hoping that his best schnapps and the presence of Mendel the horse could melt the icy barrier that has developed between him and Dimitri, or at least rekindle some of the camaraderie they had once enjoyed. But it isn't working. Still, seated opposite one another on stooks of hay, another one between them serving as an unstable table, Blittstein keeps pouring and Dimitri keeps drinking.

The Cossack savours the sharp nectarous flavour, not too sweet, not too bitter. Yet it does have a bite. And is not heavy on the head like his cheap vodka. No wonder he can never resist Blittstein's schnapps. Not that he wants to. Not after he's had his first taste. He could never splurge on such expensive stuff. Blittstein probably didn't. It's probably black market trade, all the way from Austria. He can tell by the taste.

Doesn't have to look at the label. Won't give Blittstein the satisfaction of looking at the label.

"More schnapps, my friend?"

Without waiting for a response, Blittstein pours.

"You consider me a friend?" Dimitri asks.

"Of course," Blittstein replies.

"Don't you do favours for friends?"

"When you needed a few kopecks to tide you over I wasn't there?"

"You were. And I'm grateful."

"And I'm grateful you paid me back. You didn't have to."

"I keep my word."

"That you do."

Blittstein continues pouring and Dimitri continues drinking. Along with his ire, the Cossack's voice rises with every round. The thin shed shelves, stacked with bags and boxes of all sorts of black-market goods, including roll upon roll of colourful silk, cotton and wool fabric, alternate between shaking with the rage of the Cossack's shouting and holding steady with the angry calm certainty of his host. Moreover, one moment soothed by the self-righteous indignation of his master, the next, stirred by the exasperated raving of the Cossack, Mendel the horse, usually an unflappable old nag, on this afternoon, chomps at the bit with the exclamations of each man. He can't stand still.

"Be quiet!" Blittstein vents his frustration on his unruly horse.

Mendel is not used to his master raising his voice at him. Not inside the shed. Outside, another story: it's how his master gives him instructions, especially when it's wet and windy, this horse's hearing not being what it used to be. Usually, a jerk of the reins is all that's needed. But Mendel is old and sometimes becomes confused. So the shouts serve only to supplement the reins. Never in anger. This upsets Mendel. Particularly in his home. The anxious undercurrent between the two men has become so substantial the horse's fear is bordering on frantic. More than anything, he's afraid for his owner.

Like Blittstein and Dimitri, he'd rather be out rambling along a beautiful Black Sea beach. Instead, all three feel like climbing the claustrophobic walls of this shed. Mendel has been through a lot in his long life and looks it. On his last legs some would say. But he's looked that way for years and has always managed to do what is asked of him: lug goods from seller to buyer and buyer to seller.

Not the richest Jewish black market businessman, however, as their spokesman, Beryl Blittstein is the most influential. And for him, Cossack greed has gone amok. Some speculate it is due to a turf war between the Odessa constabulary and Cossacks, the latter trying to drive out the competition for commissions. And men like Beryl Blittstein have been caught in the middle. As is this Cossack who, however reluctantly, can't stop himself from being seduced by Blittstein's charm. Or is it his schnapps? Dimitri's not sure. He never has been.

From the beginning he didn't trust Blittstein's friendliness. He didn't trust any Zhid, even if they were nice to him. Especially if they were nice to him. Why should someone be nice to you when you're bleeding them dry? Because they're afraid of you. And one of the perks of the uniform is the ability to instil fear in others. Especially Zhids. But this doesn't give Dimitri the satisfaction he'd anticipated. And any fear he's been able to arouse in others has been diminished by the fear he feels of his fellow Cossacks, especially his superiors. They know he bought his way into the regiment, that he's not really one of them, and they never let him forget it.

"Here, have some more," Blittstein says, sensing that the schnapps is finally beginning to subdue the Cossack. It takes longer each visit.

"You trying to get me drunk?"

"Definitely."

"You know, I like you. I've always liked you."

"And I, you."

Blittstein refills his glass. Dimitri raises it, toasting: *"Za ná-shoo dróo-zhboo!"*

"Za ná-shoo dróo-zhboo!" Blittstein responds, raising the whole bottle.

Dimitri downs the liquor in one swallow and Blittstein refills it.

"Don't think I don't know why you don't drink with me," Dimitri says.

"I save it for the Sabbath, when I can share a glass or two with God."

"That's good. That's very good. Share a glass or two with God. Next time she asks why I drink I'll tell my wife I'm sharing a glass with God. Speak of the she-devil, I should be going. More schnapps and I won't know whether I'm coming or going."

"Then one for the road. To give you a sense of direction."

Blittstein knows Dimitri has a hard time turning down such expensive schnapps. And Dimitri knows Blittstein knows that. Dimitri feels a twinge of anger at Blittstein taking advantage of him. He's also angry at himself for not having the will to refuse. For not having the pride.

He tries to compensate with a firm: "Not a *kopeck* of your surtax goes into my pocket."

"It doesn't feed my family I don't care where it goes," Blittstein responds, just as firmly.

"You don't like it find another business."

"Why don't *you*?"

"Believe me I've thought about it."

"Meantime you hide behind a gang of armed thieves. Thieves with fancy uniforms. Behind who can I hide?"

No sooner have these words left Blittstein's lips than he regrets saying them. He tries to compensate for his peevish words by refilling Dimitri's glass.

His drunken fury mounting by the moment, Dimitri tells himself the more he drinks the more he'll be taking from Blittstein's pockets, and besides, soon he'll be too tipsy to care. Still, his mind rages.

Why should I pretend I've had enough, I've got to go, when I don't? Try to impress him how important and busy I am, that I'm a somebody when he knows I'm a nobody. He's just a Zhid. And I'm a Cossack. Not many can say that. As long as he keeps pouring I'll keep drinking. He wants to get me drunk, it'll cost him. I'll make him spend, drink another bottle if I have to, let's see the Zhid start to sweat when I don't stop. He thinks all we do is drink. That we're all drunks.

Not bothering to raise a toast, he downs another schnapps in a single swig.

Seeing Blittstein screw the bottle top tight, raise it and, with an exaggerated decisiveness, toast "*Za ná-shoo dróo-zhboo*!" intensifies Dimitri's seething. How dare he! Like he's telling me I've had enough. Who does he think he is?

"Remember I took you for a sleigh ride you drank a whole bottle to stay warm?" Blittstein asks. His tone is so gentle and smile so warm it's like they're sharing a fond memory and begins to dilute Dimitri's anger.

Bloody Zhid. Can't even stay angry at him, Dimitri thinks. "How could I forget?"

"And how can I forget you dropping under the seat soon as you spotted another Cossack?"

"They don't understand it's easier to collect if you're cosy. Anyways, only reason I went for that ride, you were so eager to show off how fast you could go from summer wheels to winter sleigh I didn't want to disappoint you."

"Snow or no snow I have to make a living."

"Sober or not, so do I," Dimitri mumbles as he unsteadily stands. "But at least it's not snowing. I don't like snow."

"Neither does Mendel. Right Mendel?" Blittstein says, stepping over to stroke the horse's head.

"Stop giving me a hard time," Dimitri says, pleading. "Please stop giving me a hard time."

* * *

As Dimitri reaches his house, still somewhat tipsy, afraid to face his wife this way, he turns and, as though he's suddenly realized he has to be somewhere else, rushes away from his house. Halfway down the block, he stops, turns, starts back towards his home. But when he reaches it, same story: he slows, hesitates, steps onto the stoop to reach for the door handle, decides against it, turns and, as though he's again suddenly realized he has to be somewhere else, rushes away, in the opposite direction. He's being watched. But he's so drunk he doesn't notice.

Then, as he turns back toward his house, determined to enter this time, he spots his neighbour across the street watching from his front porch, a big smile on his face. More like a smirk. That bastard Burmistrov, always on his porch, sucking his pipe. He should be embarrassed his wife forces him to smoke outside. Instead, I'm the one embarrassed, caught skulking around my own home. Enough is enough.

On the front stoop, he reaches for the doorknob, gently turns it and ever so slowly slides open the door, hoping against hope he can slip into the house without being heard. Then he tiptoes across the hall to the bedroom, carefully closes the door behind him, then just stands there, teetering ever so slightly, before collapsing onto the bed.

* * *

Blittstein's eight-year-old son Chaim and Dimitri's nine-year-old son Alexei had often eyed one another on the street or at their secret soccer field. The Cossack had always spoken so highly of the Zhid, appeared in awe of him, envied his courage and the respect his community had for his wisdom, something the Cossack could never imagine himself having even from his own son. Because of this Alexei was drawn to the Zhid's son. But he could never show it, had to hide it if he wanted to maintain his 'true Russian' upper hand.

Likewise, Chaim had been drawn to Alexei, but he too must hide it. He'd yearned for a 'real Russian' friend like him, one whose father rode, not behind an old wagon-pulling nag like Mendel, but atop a real horse, carried weapons, went to war. He might sometimes make fun of the man, but Chaim knew his father feared him. And Chaim envied Alexei being the son of a man who could instil fear in his father.

Chaim wonders what it would feel like to be one of them: Not having to be afraid of one's shadow, of being attacked for living where you weren't supposed to live, playing where you weren't supposed to play. He's tried to imagine how good it must feel to be the son of a Cossack, how safe a boy must feel. There was something in the Cossack boy's bearing, the way he carried himself, a kind of arrogance, afraid of no one and nothing, something Chaim couldn't imagine. Yet his own father seemed fearless and the Cossack treated him with respect, with a kind of reverence.

But recently their relations appear to have soured, at least on his father's part. Chaim can't understand how his father could begin to talk so disparagingly about the Cossack when the man has always been so kind to him. The past few weeks he's heard his father refer to the Cossack as 'the goy'. He'd never used that disparaging phrase about anybody before. And the last time his father had uttered those words, his mother had tried to defuse his anger, begged him to not let it get the better of him.

"After all, the man is a Cossack. And could make trouble for you."

"He's not making trouble already?" his father responded.

"Well, you want more?"

They bickered until his father stormed out of the kitchen. Chaim was scared to see his father so angry, not only at his mother, but at the Cossack. A Cossack, it was rumoured, could kill a Jew with impunity. That night Chaim had trouble sleeping. And the next day couldn't concentrate on his studies.

* * *

The Russian and Jewish primary schools in this Odessa district are almost directly across from one another. It's as though the powers-that-be decided that they would build their school there, if not only to let the Jews know they were keeping an eye on them, then to clearly set a limit to their community, beyond which they dare not expand.

Jewish children made sure to stay on their side of the street separating the *shtetl* from the rest of the city. No matter what their age, they rarely walked that street alone, especially at night. Going to or from school, they had to be accompanied by a parent or schoolmates. Their teachers rarely kept them after school, no matter how badly they'd misbehaved, unless they punished a whole group so that no one would have to walk home alone. The early darkness of short autumn and winter days made it especially dangerous for a Jewish boy to be out on his own.

But one fall day, Chaim did stay after school, a favour from his favourite teacher. To show his students how interesting history could be, the teacher had brought boxes of 1882 and 1905 newspapers he'd obtained from the estate of a man who'd collected them from across Russia. The teacher passed the boxes around the class, challenging his pupils to find accounts of pogroms.

According to his teacher, pogroms were as inevitable as the business cycle, often coinciding with its bottom. He never did explain what the business cycle was, except to talk in terms of good times and bad, always adding that for the Jew times were never truly good.

Thus, after the failed 1905 revolution, Jews were blamed for that uprising, and in 1882, for the assassination of Tsar Alexander II. Encouraging the Russian poor to believe Jews were Christ-killers who used the blood of Christian children to make their matzos turned Jews into convenient scapegoats for Russia's less fortunate, rather than the royal family.

For Chaim's teacher, organized attacks and the slaughter of Jews were in the marrow of Russian life; as unpredictable as the dreadful weather.

"So we should all beware."

It's hard to say if it was the newspaper stories themselves or simply the excitement of the search but Chaim was so taken by the task, shaken too, that he asked his teacher if he could search for more after class. By reading accounts of pogroms, he could almost imagine what it was like to live through one.

Delighted that one of his students had taken such an interest in the subject, the teacher agreed to his request as long as he could arrange to have other boys wait to walk home with him. Chaim claimed he'd walked home alone so often it had become a habit. He hadn't, of course. But at Chaim's self-confidence in uttering his white lie combined with his enthusiasm for the subject of pogroms, his teacher couldn't resist.

* * *

Alexei and a few of his friends spotted Chaim strolling home from school alone, past what they considered to be 'true Russian' turf, i.e., theirs. For a while, they just silently followed him. The more he quickened his pace the more they quickened theirs, without saying a word, always keeping the same short distance behind him. Chaim considered running but was afraid it might change the whole dynamic. They might let him go, content that they'd scared him off. More likely, they'd simply race after him. The faster he ran the faster they would.

He decided to slow down, see what would happen. And they slowed too, still saying nothing, keeping the same distance behind him. Now, not only were they beginning to scare him, they were making him fear for his life. Growing up, he'd heard so many stories about Jewish boys being badly beaten—some to death—by gangs of Russian boys, you never knew which tales were true and which were merely *shtetl* myth. But they were enough to instil fear in every *shtetl* boy. Unable to control his trepidation, he chose to face it, and stopped, just stood there, his back to the other boys, who'd stopped too, still keeping that same distance behind him. The same silence too.

Slowly, one by one, still mute, they surrounded him, all the while making sure to keep their distance from him, their facial expressions and body language clearly communicating they were afraid of being contaminated if they got too close. Yet each time he tried to step through a space between boys, they'd close ranks there, blocking his way. Fearing that bumping into, or worse, trying to force his way by them would trigger a beating, Chaim would quickly stop and, as a pair of boys inched toward him, step back, scared that if he didn't, the contact would spark a drubbing. At the same time, he had to make sure he didn't retreat too suddenly, without giving the boys behind him time to step back and avoid contamination. He knew the game. He'd heard about it often enough, had seen it enacted from afar.

Finally, Alexei broke the silence, teasing and taunting him, adopting a boy's conception of big-man bravado, as though he was a Cossack or cop.

"Zhid, what are you doing on Russian soil?"

Taking Alexei's lead, the other boys immediately joined in, emulating his tough-guy manner.

"Have you forgotten your place, Zhid?"

"Don't you know this street is out of bounds for you?"

"You want to soil it with Zhid blood?"

As they kept verbally taunting him their small circle kept moving ever so slightly this way or that, forcing Chaim to keep carefully moving with them to avoid touching or being touched by them. They kept at it until Chaim was on the verge of tears. Not only did Alexei do nothing to divert or stop the other boys, when they started to slack off and lose interest, he retook the lead, taunting Chaim more intensely than before. And Chaim understood.

Because their fathers did business together and were friends—as much as an ordinary Gentile and Jew could be friends—and these boys were drawn to each other, Alexei felt he had to go out of his way to prove his anti-Semitic credentials, be tougher with Chaim than the other boys, until Chaim finally broke down and cried. Satisfied that they'd accomplished their task, humiliating a Zhid, the boys started to disband. As they did, Alexei took one last shot at making his anti-Semitic mark.

"Better catch your tears, Zhid. Don't you dare contaminate our street!"

Cupping his face with his hand, Chaim started running back toward his *shtetl*. He didn't want to give Alexei a chance to see through his tears, sense the true source, not fear, but a feeling of betrayal by the son of a friend of the family, a boy he'd become fond of from afar.

Chaim would try to imagine what it might be like if he lived under an assumed name, converted to Christianity and attended church. But it would always be obvious that he was not one of *them*, didn't really know their liturgy. Not only was this a frequent daydream but a fantasy Chaim's psyche would often flirt with asleep. This usually turned into a nightmare in which, stripped naked in a church school playground by a bunch of much bigger Russian boys, Chaim was exposed as circumcised.

Accused of being a Jew, he'd be tarred and feathered. Chicken feathers plucked from a live bird were poked into him like pins till he fainted from the poison and pain.

* * *

After this encounter, Chaim and Alexei established a clandestine kin-
ship, limited in the beginning to their soccer field. Not a public park,
but a piece of vacant land bordering the northern edge of the *shtetl*,
separated from the Gentile section of the city by several abandoned
single storey-warehouses. Rumoured that dangerous gangsters kept
stolen goods in these buildings, no boy dared break into them.

Divided in two, the much larger, more level field was reserved for
'true Russians'. Jewish boys could kick the ball around on the much
smaller lumpy lot, but the line between the two fields was one they
dared not cross. God forbid that one of them should kick their soccer
ball with enough force and inaccuracy to propel it onto Russian turf,
that ball and that boy, without the most profuse expression of exaggerated apology, might trigger the Russian boys' piling on and pounding
the excrement out of the perpetrator, punishing him not only for that
sin, but for the litany of transgressions perpetrated by his people on
theirs, including their betrayal of the Lord's only son. One wayward
kick was all it took.

However, to separate themselves from those who cowered in the
face of Gentile intimidation, once, a few foolhardy Jewish boys, filled
with Maccabean bravado, decided to play Russian roulette with their
soccer ball. And that is when the bluster of one of these bigger Jewish
boys was truly tested and found wanting. Abandoned by his peers, in
the ensuing pile-on by bigger older Russian ruffians, he was badly
beaten, his nose broken along with two of his teeth. After that rarely
did another Jewish soccer ball stray.

Yet that is precisely what lent such a special aura of excitement to
playing there. Stray Russian balls, erred either by accident or on purpose, were always returned with the appropriate deference, even when
done to toy with the Jewish boys.

But such taunting and beatings were rare. The Russian boys knew
the land wasn't public and didn't belong to any of them. For all they
knew it belonged to some rich *shtetl* dweller. Or the gangsters who hid
their stolen goods in the rundown buildings. But as long as they were
allowed to play there and the Zhids knew their place, they didn't care.
In fact, both groups of boys knew that, if they could keep the peace,

their secret soccer field would be safe with them, and they'd have a place to play. A place Jew and Russian could share, only not together, at the same time, on the same turf.

Like Chaim, a loner by nature, Alexei often kicked a soccer ball around by himself. Chaim had often sat there and watched but, though it might have been more fun for both of them, had never dared to join him. He knew the law of this Gentile versus Jew jungle.

One afternoon, a few weeks after Alexei and his friends had taunted Chaim on the street, Chaim had been at the soccer field kicking the ball around by himself. Alexei arrived and, perhaps feeling he'd not only clearly established his bona fide anti-Semitic credentials for his friends, but his ethnic superiority for Chaim, instead of, as was the custom, simply stepping onto the field, a signal that Chaim had to immediately leave it or stick to his bumpy corner, he'd just sat there and watched, his exaggerated body language making clear he didn't really feel like playing just yet. So Chaim kept dribbling and kicking the ball around by himself. A Russian boy's failure to promptly establish his entitlement to this turf was rare. And should word have got around that Alexei let this happen he might have become, if not a pariah among his peers, a convenient target for teasing.

* * *

It began quite gradually. For a while, each of them playing alone, just watching the other. Then, one day, fed up with playing by himself, Alexei decided to cross the line and kicked his ball directly to Chaim who'd been standing there watching him. And it evolved from there, each looking forward to finding the other there, not having to play alone, or with their own group of friends. There was something about teaming up that felt different than being with their usual playmates. Better. More fun. While you couldn't tell from the grim, sometimes grudging, look on Alexei's face, or from the silence between them, there was an edge to their play. An excitement that in all likelihood emanated from its forbidden nature.

When just the two of them there, often as not they took turns playing in goals while the other took penalty kicks. The goal boundary was demarcated by the boys' jackets and one of the abandoned buildings' walls served as a backstop. This way, the one playing goals wouldn't have to chase the ball too far when the other scored. They would play until it became too dark to see the ball. They confined their game to the area closest to the *shtetl*. This way, if some of the other Slavic boys showed up, Chaim wouldn't be caught "contaminating" their turf.

Alexei, without his Russian buddies, and Chaim, without his Jewish ones, could be friendly contemporaries, temporary friends. But as soon as Alexei spotted his friends their game was over. He became a different boy, taunting and acting tough along with his peers when a Jewish ball was kicked too close to Slavic turf.

The two had hardly spoken before being "formally" introduced by their fathers. On the soccer field, they'd either pass the ball back and forth in silence or, if taking turns on penalty kicks, stick to calling out the score. They used a primitive shorthand for keeping it, as though they spoke different languages and could only communicate by numbers and such simple gestures as pointing to one or the other to indicate who was ahead.

It could have been shyness on Chaim's part and, on Alexei's, maintaining distance between them. But they both understood that their relationship was—and had to be—limited. They could not jabber or tease one another as boys tend to do. That sort of intimacy went beyond the pale of their inter-ethnic soccer play.

Still, every once in a while, a laugh, smile or shout—even an exuberant expression of delight—might slip out. That would usually be followed by an embarrassed silence, at least from Chaim. Alexei usually managed to maintain his grim determined demeanour.

* * *

One day, sensing an edge in Chaim's attitude, as though something significant was going through his mind and would soon make its way to his mouth, Alexei steeled himself. If it had to do with why Chaim's father had to pay Alexei's to stay in business, he would be ready. But it wasn't. Instead, Chaim brought up the time Alexei and his gang had taunted him, Chaim blurting out words that had been on his mind since they'd first started kicking the ball around together.

"How come you chased me that time?"

"We were just having fun."

"It wasn't fun for me."

"We didn't hurt you."

"You might of."

"Nah. Not with me there."

Suddenly overcome by shyness, Chaim didn't know how to respond to that touch of intimacy, so he just stood there, staring down at the ground.

* * *

On this Sunday morning, to get out of going to church with his wife, Dimitri insists it was the best time to catch Blittstein at home, to discuss urgent business.

"I'm taking Alexei. Show him what his father has to do to make a living in this world."

His father's favourite—his brother was his mother's—Alexei was bored by church. His younger brother loved it, or pretended he did. Alexei didn't bother pretending.

But Dimitri's meeting with Blittstein hasn't worked out as he'd hoped. It began to go downhill right from his opening salvo as he strutted into Blittstein's barn: "If you don't pay the piper you'll have to face the music."

Dimitri had thought it so pithy and clever, had been planning it for days. Instead, he was left feeling awkward as Blittstein ignored it, turned to Alexei with a warm, ebullient "Welcome!" before lifting him up in an exuberant bear-hug. Setting the boy down, he bent close and with a soft smile shifted to an intimate whisper.

"Maybe someday you and my Chaimeleh will be friends your fathers get along so good why shouldn't you it's never too soon to start. For men like your father it's more important to be fair than rich. Same for me. Hope you two can learn a lesson from how we do business here."

Dimitri felt outmanoeuvred, frustrated and furious at how quickly the Zhid had taken advantage of the boys' presence.

Now, as he struggles to match Blittstein's big beaming smile with his own sheepish grin, he pledges to never forgive the Zhid for humiliating him in front of his son, not to mention the other boy.

Still, Dimitri can't let Alexei sense his humiliation. Perhaps he shouldn't feel slighted. It's only Blittstein's way of going about his business, charming buyers and sellers alike, putting on a show. But now, how is Dimitri going to begin bickering with Blittstein, have his son watch Blittstein try to get the best of him? He cannot. So he turns to the boys with a burst of false confidence meant to match Blittstein's bluster, exclaims: "This business could take quite a while. Why don't you go outside and play?"

Blittstein senses he's gone too far. He hadn't mean to exploit the presence of the boys so blatantly. His intention was simply to soften things between him and Dimitri ever so slightly, start with some diplomatic nicety. But the only way to deal with Dimitri's aggressive entrance was to ignore it, countering his insolent tone with a more amiable one, one aimed straight at the Cossack's son. Yet he knew from the way the first words had come out of his mouth how it would look and sound to Dimitri. Now it might be harder to get him to acquiesce, convince him to talk sense to his superiors. So, to compensate for overdoing it with the Cossack's son, Blittstein decides it best to go along with the boy's father.

"He's right. As usual, your father's right. There's no point keeping you boys cooped up here when you could be outside."

* * *

Unsure what their fathers might make of it, Chaim and Alexei had avoided mentioning that they'd met. Each, in his own oblique manner, had indicated that they'd seen each other, without acknowledging any more than that. They hadn't had to. Both fathers had long ago learned not to bother trying to fathom their sons' indecipherable responses to the simplest of questions.

Nevertheless, once outside the barn, Chaim and Alexei don't know what to say to one another. Alexei, usually cocky, seems unsure of himself. In fact, staring down at the ground, his back hunched up against the barn wall to be as inconspicuous as possible, he looks a little lost.

"We could go back in if you're afraid out here," Chaim said.

"Been out here a bunch of times."

"Not with me."

"So what?"

Now there's another prolonged awkward pause during which Alexei kills time by clearing some soil and small stones to the left with his right foot and then, with his left foot, the same pile to the right, over and over.

As the voices inside the barn reach a fevered pitch, the boys continue to stand, looking somewhat flustered. It may be because they're face to face, away from the soccer field and, unable to just silently kick a ball back and forth, they now have to talk to one another and don't know what to say. But more than anything, they're embarrassed not only that they're eavesdropping, but that they have to hear what they're hearing: one of their fathers threatening, the other being threatened. From the tone of their voices and through the thick barn wall, who's intimidating and who's being intimidated is not clear.

Like his father, Chaim is trying to understand precisely what the Cossack is now demanding of him. He seems to have a choice. His first option is to increase the lump sum he pays every month from ten percent of what the Cossack estimates he earns to fifteen percent.

"An increase of five percent?" Dimitri insists with a plaintive whine.

"I don't know where you went to school but from where I went it's fifty percent," Chaim's father responds.

"Anyway, it's time all you black market buyers and sellers begin keeping an account of everything you buy and sell on paper, receipts and bills so we can keep track of how much cash is exchanging hands, where and when, and be able to check if the figures add up."

"Sure, we could find a way to finagle our books. But it would take too much from what's a strictly cash business. Keeping paper would take too much time, it would make too much of a dent in our margins. Worse, it would scare off those who take advantage of our port to dump goods they get from god knows where, from god knows who, god knows how and be the beginning of the end of the advantage we have over other cities. This makes us like a business that pays taxes to the state. What has the state ever done for us?"

Without waiting for a response, Chaim's father continues.

"You want to cut off my nose to spite your face, be my guest. You'll regret it."

"I regret it already but it's not up to me. Please?" Dimitri pleads.

Recognizing his father's plaintive tone, an embarrassed Alexei has had enough of the harsh sounds.

"They're shouting in there."

"I can hear."

"Don't like shouting."

"Me neither."

Chaim glances around, wondering what his friends would say if they could see him now, talking to this Russian tough. But none of his friends are out. No neighbours either. Highly unusual for a Sunday morning. A few younger boys are playing at the far end of the block. But at this end, nobody. Considered worse than police, it could be that seeing a Cossack scared them off. Just looking at one the wrong way and you never knew what could happen. It was better to stay out of their way.

Yet there's old Mrs. Popavitch, in her finest floral-patterned dress, the same one she wears every Sunday, strolling down the street like she owns it. Queen of her community, she's afraid of nothing, certainly no Cossack.

As soon as he spots her, Chaim turns away. Not that he's embarrassed to be seen with this son of a Cossack. He's proud of it and hopes word will get back to his friends. It probably will because Mrs. Popavitch has a big mouth. In the community she's what's called a *yenta*. What Chaim doesn't want is for her eyes to catch his. If that happens she'll come over and begin bending his ear, quizzing both boys to get any gossip she can out of them. And if he responds to her questions, she won't let it interfere with her train of thought, the train of her unstoppable tongue.

Hoping against hope she hasn't seen him looking her way—and, since her eyesight is failing, she probably hasn't—Chaim turns to Alexei and looks him in the eye, focusing the full force of his attention on him. All he intends is to look so engrossed to Mrs. Popavich that, if she spots him he can ignore her, his attention so totally taken up by his friend.

Quite certain she's passed far enough down the road that she no longer poses a threat, as if he's still afraid she might hear or read his lips, Chaim's hand cups his mouth as he whispers: "My dad always sleeps after synagogue."

"So what?"

"We could have the whole barn to ourselves."

"What for?"

"I don't know. So we don't have to worry about rain."

"I don't mind rain."

"Anyway, weekends, too many other kids kicking the ball around. Here we can just play. Sometimes I do my homework here or bring my books, just read. Mendel's good company."

"Who's Mendel?"

"Our horse. My mother won't let him into the house. So I play with him in here."

"You're nuts."

"What do you say?"

"I'll see."

Dimitri storms out of the shed.

Chaim murmurs: "I'll be here."

Alexei doesn't respond as his father whisks him away.

* * *

That night, his wife snuggles close to Dimitri, tries to slip her head over his arm. Too antsy for such affection, he slides it away. She persists, then realizes that he's not up to being a husband, feeling beaten down as a man and that her first touch was too intimate. He might be more comfortable being mothered. As though checking for a fever, she runs her hand over his forehead.

"Maybe you could get another job," she whispers.

"What do you want me to do, go back to the black market, all controlled by Zhids and criminals now? And they'd never let me quit. They'd kick me out but they'd never let me quit. Not knowing what I know, doing what I've done. They wouldn't trust me."

"They don't trust you now."

"At least now they can keep an eye on me."

Lately, their nightly routine has gone like this, his wife trying to soothe Dimitri so he can sleep. But all it does is upset him. Yet she has such a sweet voice. Before they met, hearing her solo in the church choir made him fall in love with her voice. But, believing himself not good enough for such a woman, he was reluctant to approach her. He was still eking out a living on the black market. Or had he already been a Cossack? He can't remember. All this stress is affecting his mind, his memory. Everything's become confused because he's not getting enough sleep. He's got to get more sleep.

* * *

In an ornate office filled with plants, plush chairs and a sofa, the Cossack commandant looks rather sheepish sitting opposite the self-assured, smartly-uniformed chief officer of the Odessa constabulary. This office, in stark contrast to the commandant's, is bright, with French pane windows on all four sides. The hustle and bustle of uniformed and plain-clothed police seen coming and going through the pair of intra-office windows is another stark contrast to the gloomy sense of isolation of the commandant's workplace.

Seated behind his desk, the white-haired police chief picks up and scans one sheet of paper after another, shakes his head. There is an aura of war-weary ennui about him, both in his slow motion movements and manner of speech, which peters out in exasperation out at the end of each sentence.

"This is not good. No no, this is definitely not good. For you, for me, for any of us. And I must tell you, I am being forced, albeit most reluctantly, to consider a complete reversal of our forces' roles in this matter. Though our duty is to make sure the law is being obeyed, and yours, to maintain order, right now neither of us are doing a good job. Would you rather have the constabulary become the primary agency of collection?"

"Of course not."

"If you cannot adequately begin collecting for us, we may have to continue doing so for ourselves."

"Paperwork may be as much a part of the problem as money."

"Without a proper paper trail could we trust you are paying us our fair share? Could you prove we are asking more than is actually owed us?"

"You think with paper that you can't cut corners?"

"Indeed you can."

"Then ..."

"It makes it more difficult."

"It makes collecting more difficult. Specially since we've been doing it for decades without paper ... without a problem."

"My dear man, we have been doing many things without there appearing to be a problem. That does not mean there has not been one. In any case, times have changed. And so must we.

"The Tsar has decided that there are simply too many rubles floating in and out of this port without anyone keeping proper track. He wishes us to track the movement of each and every kopeck coming into or leaving this city, one of the worst in all Russia when it comes to under the table business."

His formerly pale face now suddenly crimson, the Cossack commandant struggles to contain his fury. How dare this lowly cop use the Tsar's name. As though he and his crooked crew are the true royal representatives in this town. Cossacks are this country's most loyal patriots, the true protectors of the Romanov family, not only in Odessa, but throughout mother Russia.

The commandant has never met a member of the royal family, yet he considers himself part of it, protecting them from anyone who might mean them harm. Among those, he considers Zhids to be the most threatening. To him Zhids and Mensheviks are one and the same. At best, Zhids are Menshevik sympathizers. At worst, they are actively working to overthrow the Tsar.

That is why, no matter how much he resents this cop's attempt to upstage him, he knows they must not quarrel, must pretend to get along, focus on keeping this black market thing from getting out of hand. If he has to swallow this bastard's bullshit, so be it. His time to deal with this crooked cop will come.

The Cossack commandant's torrent of thought is derailed by the police chief: "Both the mayor and governor agree with our Tsar. And since all three of these honourable gentlemen concur, who among us might deign to differ? Believe me, I do not like having this dirty business work its way down to me."

"You think I do?"

"Hence we must sort this out. And quickly. It does not look good for the constabulary to be engaged in seemingly corrupt practices. Citizens lose respect for the law. You Cossacks, on the other hand, are not saddled with upholding the law. Maintaining order, maybe, but not upholding the law. Certainly not in this city. In any event, the powers that be have insisted—in the most polite manner, I might add—that neither I nor any member of my constabulary indulge in further off-the-book collection of commissions. Hence that concession is now solely in your hands."

The Cossack starts to speak but the police chief cuts him off.

"As far as this administration is concerned there will be no further clandestine collections. Nevertheless, it is understood that our men cannot adequately sustain themselves on the salaries they receive from government coffers. Waiters in the best restaurants receive tips for their service, why should not public servants?"

"You'll get no argument from me there."

"However, unlike waiters, our tips must be accompanied by the appropriate paperwork. What can be more uplifting than knowing one is playing a small part in a much larger political process aimed at beginning to rationalize the business procedures of this land? In any event, it is time we renew respect for the law in this city at the same time as we maintain fear of it. Perhaps if you were to let our clients know that our constabulary will be phasing out its collections, some may not be so recalcitrant."

"It's never a good idea to feed carrots to these Zhids. Specially since sticks is what they best understand. Besides, like snakes, they can smell weakness."

"Then I can trust you will put your house in order?"

"You can."

"And soon."

"Rest assured."

As he exits the constabulary office the commandant's mind is reeling. At one time Cossacks were top of the food chain in this town. Now they're talked down to by some lousy cop. Made to take orders from some lousy cop. On his high horse who does he think he is? I'm a Cossack for Christ's sake. A goddamn Cossack. Why should I kowtow to him, pretending he's been anointed by friends in high places? We Cossacks fight wars. What do police do besides put pressure on petty criminals? Well no cop's going to pressure me.

He clutches his side. Then his stomach. Goddamn cop getting my ulcer to act up. He'll pay. We'll make the bastard pay.

With this thought, the commandant begins to feel better.

* * *

Chaim looked forward to the Sabbath, his favourite day of the week, the day he accompanied his father to shul. His father had stopped holding his hand while walking anywhere when Chaim was five. But strolling to shul was a different story. Some boys Chaim's age would be ashamed to be seen holding hands with their father. But not Chaim. On *Shabbos*, he was proud to be seen holding his father's hand.

His father called it their *Shabbos* handshake, a sacred one, more a bond between male equals than between man and boy. The link between a father and his eldest son was a special one in the *shtetl*, one deemed so by the Almighty. As Chaim's father would say: "His is the unseen hand we share." And to Chaim it sometimes felt that way.

The synagogue, a small back room in the home of the *rebbeh*, was always packed on *Shabbos*. The place would not pass any fire code but the inspectors didn't bother the *shtetl*. And the *shtetl* didn't bother the fire inspectors, even when there was a fire. The *shtetl* had its own volunteers.

Inside the synagogue, Chaim loved watching his father clutch the edge of his prayer shawl, kiss it to express his love for the *torah* and its teachings and touch the velvet-covered sacred scrolls with the tip of his *tallis*. His father's well-worn wool prayer shawl, black stripes on white—now yellowed with age—had been handed down to him by his own father. He in turn had it handed down to him by his father. Slightly frayed at the edges, some fringes missing, Chaim knew that, as the oldest son, he would one day hold the shawl. After his father passed away. But he couldn't imagine life without his father. He didn't dare

When the voices of Chaim's father and the cantor soared above all the others and the congregation chanted in ecstatic union, it could be mistaken for some great cathedral chorus. Sometimes the two of them appeared to be competing, other times, complementing each other. Chaim's father was considered good enough to be a cantor and when the cantor was ill or otherwise indisposed—vocal cords coarse from too much vodka—Chaim's father would be asked to take over. Eyes closed, body swaying back and forth, his voice exuded a rapturous blend of joy and sorrow.

But the ritual doesn't leave Chaim spellbound on this *Shabbos* morning. From time to time his mind wanders, wondering if the Cossack's son will show up that afternoon.

After the service everyone wishes each other "Good Shabbos!" and takes part in a *kiddush* with wine and appetizers. Then, hand in hand, Chaim and his father start for home. On this Sabbath, Chaim can't wait to get there.

"Why you so walking so fast, you got ants in your pants?" his father asks.

"I'm hungry."

"You just had a bunch of *bublitchkis*?"

"Just two."

"Two is one too many. You'll spoil your appetite you want your mother sweating over a hot stove for nothing?"

"But I'm hungry?"

"Doesn't matter."

Sometimes their conversations went in circles like this, especially after his father'd had a glass of *kiddush* wine followed by a shot or two of *Shabbos* schnapps.

* * *

Back home, together with Chaim's younger sister and baby brother, they sit down to a hot *Shabbos* meal. It begins with the blessing and breaking of his mother's fresh *challah* bread, followed by gefilte fish, his father's favourite. Chaim's too, especially smothered with horseradish. And on *Shabbos* his mother doesn't stop him, doesn't say a word, doesn't give him that stare. *Shabbos* is special and she won't spoil it. Both parents go out of their way not to spoil it, above all by avoiding arguments. Not that they argue that much.

Beryl Blittstein may be a big affectionate bear of a man, but his wife wears the pants in the family when it comes to the children's behaviour. She's the disciplinarian, he the buffer between her short fuse and the ensuing tirades.

But on Shabbos it's a sin to raise your voice, to use harsh words with anyone, especially other members of the family. So one day a week Chaim's mother defers to his father.

Yet, as happens every Shabbos, Chaim's sister asks: "How come Chaim gets to put so much *chrain* on his fish and we don't?"

"Because you get tears in your eyes when you try copying him," her mother answers. "Or do you forget?"

"She asks the same question every week," Chaim says, a touch of impatience in his voice.

To which Chaim's father responds: "If you don't have something nice to say don't say anything, just smile. It's important to smile, especially on Shabbos. The rest of the week too. Though you don't want to overdo it, or you'll look like a lunatic. But on Shabbos you should be beaming. In summer we're closer to the sun than in winter, so on Shabbos we're closer to God than the rest of the week. In fact, the rest of the week He can be crabby, but on Shabbos, even the Almighty's all smiles. So smile Chaimeleh, smile. Besseleh, you too."

A little Shabbos wine and schnapps and nothing can stop his father's cheerful philosophizing.

* * *

After lunch Chaim retreats to the barn, sharing his hopes and fears about his newfound friend with Mendel the horse. He often spends time confiding in Mendel, usually while feeding, brushing or hitching him to his wagon. But sometimes, when there's no one else, he just sits in the barn beside Mendel, carrying on a one-sided conversation.

A light tapping on the barn door brings delight and relief. Once again the first moments are awkward. Something is gnawing at them, a mirror of the tension they'd felt between their fathers. They know that something bad is brewing there. Initially the two men had wanted to have their sons meet. Now there might be hell to pay if they found out the boys were doing so behind their backs. This added thrill was based on a lie. Both fathers had sensed something was up between the boys, and hoped against hope that the budding relationship might help smooth over their own ragged one. A faint and, perhaps, futile hope.

Chaim watches as a wide-eyed Alexei glances around the barn.

"Look at all this stuff! Your pa sure has a lot of stuff! He must be rich!"

"Not after he pays off your pa."

"He protects you."

"From who, Cossacks and cops?"

"Why you always wear that cap? You got a bald spot?"

Alexei tries to grab Chaim's skullcap. But Chaim is too quick, grabbing Alexei's one hand with both of his.

"You ever do that again I won't be your friend."

"Why you making such a big deal? It's just a cap."

"Want me to yank that cross off your neck?"

"I'd kick your ass."

"Mendel would bite you."

"That nag looks more like a donkey than a horse. Let's take him for a ride."

"He's too old. Gets tired easy. We have to save him for work."

"Just a short one."

"My dad'd be mad. Besides, it's too much trouble hitching him up."

"On top."

"He's not used to it."

"We hang on to his mane. Horses don't feel it."

Alexei climbs up on Mendel. Mendel whinnies.

"See?"

"He doesn't like it."

"He's okay."

"I hitch him up every morning. Feed him too. He only sounds like that when he's unhappy."

"You unhappy there, horsey?"

Mendel snorts, rears back.

Chaim shouts: "You're gonna bump your head!"

"Ow!"

"Told you."

* * *

Once a year Cossacks are allowed to bring their families to the Cossack soccer stadium to celebrate family day. The rest of the year, unless a Cossack club is practicing or playing another team, the stadium remains empty, enclosed by a high chain link fence. Knowing there'd be hell to pay, no kid would dare trespass here. Yet it must be tempting. Few soccer fields in the city are so well-groomed, white lines so clearly etched.

Stretching for forty meters on one side of mid-field, slatted-wood stands reaching six benches high are filled with clusters of precinct families, each dressed in their after-church Sunday finest.

On the top bench of the spectator stand, Dimitri sits alone. Watching his son dribble the soccer ball past one of the older boys then immediately pass it over to one of the younger ones, Dimitri is filled with pride. His son is good, as good as some of the older boys, yet is kind and generous, doesn't hog the ball like some of them.

From the time Alexei was two or three, Dimitri loved nothing better, was rarely happier, than kicking a soccer ball back and forth with his little boy. And Alexei relished it as much as his father. Until he was old enough to wander off on his own, and discovered his neighbourhood's makeshift soccer field, where he could play with boys his own age and, because he was good enough, older ones. And he's right at home on this soccer field. He's so fast, so nimble on his feet, he's earned the respect of the other Cossack sons, especially the older boys, the ones who usually look down on the younger.

Dimitri's eyes shift to his daughter, with other girls her age helping their mothers set the long white-linen-covered lunch table between the soccer field and the stands. Lined with a colorful array of platters, each family has brought its favourite dish.

Dimitri takes a deep breath, savours the aromas wafting his way. The women get along so well together. His wife looks right at home, all smiles, though he knows she feels no more at ease with her peers here than he does with his.

* * *

It's hard to know what draws one boy to another, above all when their friendship is more taboo among their peers than a similar rapport would be among their parents. That their fathers had a relationship probably helped draw Alexei and Chaim to one another. Before the new Cossack payment edict, both fathers had shared stories about their sons. And now, both sons began to share stories about their fathers.

Not only were the boys' shared accounts of their fathers' exploits exaggerated, some were thoroughly made up. Each boy strived to impress the other without so straining credulity as to lose credibility.

When Alexei did so Chaim wouldn't say anything. True or not, he loved the tale, was grateful Alexei would take the trouble to tell it. However far-fetched, he wanted to believe. But when Chaim tried to match Alexei in outright exaggeration or lies, making up ways his father had outsmarted Alexei's, pretending to be poorer than he was, hiding how much money he'd managed to make on many of his deals, unable to handle that this might be more truth than fiction, Alexei would subject Chaim to prolonged put downs, dismissive daggers that hurt.

Still, Chaim sometimes fantasized about being a Cossack like Alexei's father, and Alexei a highly-respected black market businessman like Chaim's. Both fathers and sons made strange bedfellows, the relationship between the sons as odd and twisted as that of their fathers': enmity on the surface, a precarious intimacy beneath it. Perhaps this, as much as the element of risk and danger, drew Alexei to Chaim. For some boys there's nothing like breaking a taboo. For others, intimidation may be the sincerest form of flattery. And tough little Alexei certainly intimidated Chaim. Yet Alexei's eagerness to be his friend blinded him to the boy's bullying.

Neither of them could let himself be seen fraternizing with the other, above all not by their friends. But they took every opportunity to meet, usually in the Blittstein barn, which became their clandestine clubhouse. Alexei loved Mendel the horse. Mendel, on the other hand, was not fond of many people. Especially Cossacks or police. He was one fussy horse. But for Chaim's sake, he made an exception.

For a while it became a weekly after-synagogue ritual: Chaim and Alexei in their adopted clubhouse, a place they could be alone, away from the prying eyes and ethnic enmity of their peers.

* * *

Chaim's father wondered why a Gentile boy, the son of a Cossack, would spend so much time, most of it in the barn behind the house, with the son of a Jew. Were they ashamed to be seen together outside it? Or were they afraid? God knows what the two of them did in there all day. Maybe the Cossack boy was studying his stock. Thought he was doing his father a favour. Or his father forced him. No. The Cossack had been there often enough to keep an eye himself.

Anyway, the relationship between the two men was coming to a head. In one meeting after another they simply couldn't come to terms. At work, not only from his commandant, but from his peers, pressure kept building on Dimitri to take the bull by the horns, one Cossack going so far as to warn to him: "If you can't handle your Zhid, one of us will show you how."

And, though Dimitri hadn't yet warned his son to stay away from the Blittstein boy, Alexei could hear his father's constant complaining to his mother: "That Zhid Blittstein's going to be the death of me. The death of us all. Starting a war between them and us."

Alexei didn't have to be told who 'us' were and who 'them'. All he knew was that it might be better if he stayed away from the Zhid's son.

* * *

And, early one weekday evening in the Blittstein barn, the rupture between fathers comes to a head. As the wind shakes the barn rafters and seeps through the wall cracks, one moment the lantern casts crazy shadows and the next an eerie glow. Alternating between shouting to be heard and speaking more softly to save their voices, like some demented duet, the sound of both men rises with every gust and falls with each ensuing calm.

Blittstein again argues the Cossacks are going too far in their baksheesh demands and Dimitri again pleads Blittstein is going too far in his refusals. It seems that no progress has been made since their last encounter. The only difference is that Dimitri is more desperate. That only serves to make Blittstein more obstinate.

"And if I take from my own pocket and make like you're paying?"

"I'm not asking you to—"

"You're forcing me!"

"You think that would stop me from speaking out for others in the business? Besides, how long before you couldn't afford it we're back where we started?"

"Upsetting the whole applecart you'll get yourself killed!" the Cossack shouts. "Please, if not for your sake then for mine. After all I've done for you."

"And I haven't done for you?"

"What good will your death do? What purpose will the deaths of dozens of you serve? Turn their families and yours into beggars, their breadwinner gone. And for what? A few kopecks? Please Blittstein, please. Don't bury yourself for a few kopecks. Don't bury your friends. Don't bury me!"

"If we don't stand up now when will it stop? Already they're taking such a slice out of us, anymore and there won't be enough left for us to put food. Besides, I've laid down the law to my peddlers, how you think it'll look I start backing down now?"

"Like you've come to your senses. Like you prefer living to dying. Like you want to watch your children grow up and have grandchildren."

"I do. And I will."

"Not if you don't come to your senses."

"You're afraid to stand up for yourself I'll stand up for you."

No sooner are the words out of Blittstein's mouth than he realizes his mistake.

"I mean if you're afraid to stand up to them by yourself I'll stand up with you."

"I know what you mean you're all the same you Zhids! Think you know better than us! Think you're better than us! Well, you can't see farther than the end of your nose. Your long stubborn nose!"

"There's only so low a man can let himself sink and still call himself a man not an insect. Only so low. Looking down on us like we're leeches is one thing, treating us like it is another."

"Then let the corpses fall where they may."

Dimitri charges out of the storage shed, leaving a somewhat shaken Blittstein behind. Filled with angry apprehensive emotion instead of his usual calm reserve, Blittstein's head has succumbed to his heart. He is hurt. His honour has been offended. As far as he is concerned the Cossacks are bent on crushing him and his cronies. Because they can. Because they think they can. Because as Jews they're just cockroaches in Cossack eyes.

Livid, yet somewhat scared, what has he done? He reaches for his horse, tries to soothe himself by stroking its head. But it doesn't help. He's frightened his horse with his shouting. He's panicked himself. He's not used to shouting. Specially at someone with whom he has to do business. Well there's no turning back now. There was no turning back from the beginning.

* * *

Outside the barn, Dimitri's head is spinning. He simply has to tell his boss, he couldn't talk Blittstein out of it. The bastard will hit the ceiling, but once and for all he has to tell him, it's a *fait accompli*. Blittstein knows there'll be hell to pay, not only for him, but for Dimitri, above all for Dimitri. Well now he has to betray Blittstein as Blittstein is betraying him.

* * *

A grey day. It's going to rain. He's supposed to go grocery shopping with his mother, help look after his sister and brother. But if it rains they might wait till it stops, or not go if it doesn't. He hopes the rain starts soon. So he can keep tabs on the meeting in the barn, his father's business office, warehouse and showroom. You can usually tell who's there by the horse and wagon tethered outside. His father rarely has more than one customer at a time, and therefore just one horse and wagon out back. He's not sure how many men are there now, but it's more than a few. Yet there's not a single horse and wagon outside.

Only on the Sabbath or high holy days would they all come on foot. But it's just an ordinary Sunday. And though there might be a *minyan*, they're not *davening*. His father never davens in the barn. Sometimes in the house. Like when Chaim's grandfather died, or somebody from the shul, whose home is too small. Either they all left their horses and wagons at home because there wasn't enough room to tether them all out back or they didn't want anyone to know they were meeting. Normally his father doesn't want the competition to see what he has in stock. Yet now it doesn't matter enough to hold the meeting in the house. If they're not meeting in the house then his father doesn't want his mother to hear. So Chaim knows something's up. He also knows he shouldn't be eavesdropping. But he can't help it.

He leans his head against a crack in the back of the barn door. There's a collective singsong, a chorus of everyone arguing at once, but in confused whispers. Chaim swivels his head, removing his ear from the crack and replacing it with his eye. He sees his father and seven or eight men, some standing, others sitting, some muttering to themselves, others to the man next to him, everyone talking at once. A veritable tower of Babel. Finally, his father, like a cantor, his high tenor voice rising well above the others, shouts a prolonged legato "Shahhhh!" shushing the other men.

"You want somebody should hear?"

"Who's going to hear here, the horse?" Grudging hoarse laughter followed by a short coughing fit from the most obese of the men. A man Chaim's never seen before. He must be one of his father's competitors.

"First thing Monday morning, two weeks from tomorrow, Plisetskaya Square, I'll make a speech. If anyone else wants it's up to them. But at least pass the word. We can't do this alone. We have to do it together. Bring the corruption out in the open."

"They'll make our lives a living hell!"

"It's not hell already we can't make a living?"

"It's too much like politics. I don't like politics. Maybe you like politics. I don't like politics."

"This isn't politics, it's business."

"Well I don't like this business."

"You think I do? But what choice do we have?"

"Chaim?!" Chaim hears his mother shout for him just as it starts to pour. He races to the house where his mother, little sister and brother are standing on the stoop, its roof sheltering them from the rain.

"Where were you? I've been looking all over for you?" his mother asks, lips clenched, shaking her head from side to side to make clear to her son that he's never where he's supposed to be.

* * *

Events between their fathers had brought the friendship between Chaim and Alexei to an apparent end. Chaim missed Alexei, and would go out of his way to encounter him. Alexei also missed Chaim. But he would go out of his way to avoid him. Since Chaim knew Alexei would not let himself be seen stopping to talk to Chaim on the way to or from school, and that he could not go to Alexei's home, the best place to bump into him was their soccer field. As usual, if Alexei was with friends, Chaim wouldn't approach him, wouldn't even acknowledge he knew him, let alone that they were friends, albeit friends who'd had a falling out because of their fathers. But if he was there alone, kicking the ball around by himself, Chaim would bite the bullet, beg him to still be his friend, no matter what happened between their fathers.

Alexei would try to ignore him. But Chaim would persist. Then, raising a fist to him, Alexei would warn Chaim if he knew what was good for him to get away from him. And Chaim would back away. For a while. Then the battle of wills would begin again. Why one or the other wouldn't leave it was hard to say. In some ways they savoured each other's company, even if it was fraught with their fathers' turmoil. Finally, Alexei became the first to cave in, and stay away from the soccer field.

Every afternoon, for over a week, after school and on the weekend, Chaim stood by the soccer field and waited. Watched but never played. Other boys came and went, but Chaim never joined in, even when his friends asked him to. Nor did he bring his own ball to kick around by himself as he often had when no one was there. He was there, for one reason and one reason only, and he was determined to stay focused, wait forever if need be.

Little did Chaim know that not only was Alexei as upset over what was transpiring between his father and Chaim's as Chaim, he was as tormented by having to snub Chaim as Chaim was by being snubbed. Should he tell Chaim what was in store for his Zhid father? Or would he be betraying his own father if he divulged what he knew?

* * *

The following Monday afternoon, the wind blowing something fierce, as he approaches their soccer field, Alexei is startled to see Chaim, just standing there, staring at him like some kind of apparition, transfixed by another. At first Alexei tries ignoring him. Or pretending he is, acting like he's angry, and isn't going to quit playing just because of one Zhid.

He keeps his kicks short, mostly dribbling this way and that. But it isn't much fun. Usually, when he's there alone, he imagines himself playing for a Cossack team, dribbling past one opponent after another, his father on the sidelines, cheering him on. But now, with Chaim standing there staring at him, he can't daydream. He should just take his ball and go home. But that wouldn't end it. Chaim would keep plaguing him.

Not wanting to antagonize an aloof angry Alexei, Chaim makes no advances, physical or verbal. Just stands there, hoping something might break the ice. But Alexei keeps his eyes glued to the ball. Yet he's always aware, not only that his former friend is there, but precisely where.

Finally, Alexei has a brainstorm. He'll pretend to have one of his kicks go awry, towards Chaim. In fact, he'll kick it straight at Chaim, hard. That should scare him. And so, what Chaim had been hoping would happen, does. But Chaim chooses to not merely block and bounce the ball half-heartedly back toward Alexei, or pick it up and throw it, but to stop it by stepping on it, then intently take aim and kick it right back at Alexei, hard. After that, keeping a wary eye out for the arrival of other boys from Alexei's neighbourhood, and with an undercurrent of edginess more pronounced than their initial encounters, they keep silently kicking the ball back and forth.

For a while this is a convenient way to avoid looking at each other, saying something, anything to confront their estrangement. Finally, Chaim musters the courage,

"How come you've been going out of your way to avoid me, be so mean?"

"Cause your dad's being mean to mine."

"My dad?!"

"He won't pay like he's sposed to!"

A half-missed angry kick by Chaim, and the back and forth with the ball comes to an abrupt halt, the ball just lying there, mid-way between the boys. Each standing their angry ground, neither makes a move to retrieve it as Alexei keeps trying to convince Chaim that it's the black marketeers' duty to pay tax taxes to cops and Cossacks. Who else can protect them? Without them the whole business would be taken over by gangsters. Real crooks with guns and knives. Chaim insists that cops and Cossacks are the real crooks.

Unable to hold back any longer, not only with words, but with a firm fingers-cross-the-neck gesture, Alexei shouts what's in store for Chaim's father. Chaim knows Alexei's a bit of a braggart, likes to play the big man and make his father out to be more than he is. But he looks as scared as he is angry, says because he's nice to him, always has a big smile, he likes Chaim's father. He begins pleading with Chaim not to let his father force Alexei's to do what he doesn't want to do, what, if he doesn't do, the Cossacks might do to him. With Alexei now close to tears, Chaim is truly terrified. His father's life is definitely in danger.

Shaken, his mind racing, Chaim thinks that maybe if he tells Alexei about the meeting, Alexei could talk to his Cossack father. As Chaim's friend, convince him to back down. He'd do the same for Alexei. He is doing the same for him.

He exclaims: "They're going to have a meeting, in public, to embarrass the Cossacks and cops."

"Where?"

"Plisetskaya Square."

"When?"

"Next Monday!"

From the frightful look on Alexei's face, no sooner have the words left Chaim's mouth than he realizes he's made a mistake. A terrible mistake.

* * *

Next morning, as he helps his father hitch Mendel to his wagon, Chaim keeps obliquely circling the connection between the Cossacks, Tsar and police. His father, hands busy arranging the horse's harness, remains silent and unresponsive, as though not hearing his son. Rather than preoccupied with what his hands are doing, his mind seems elsewhere. Or is it that he doesn't want to hear what his son's saying? Chaim can't tell. No matter what he says, he can't manage to engage his father.

Maybe he's exaggerating the danger, maybe he's overreacted to Alexei's firm fingers-cross-the-neck gesture, but his friend had been so emphatic, so fearful too. And, though he tries to hide it, these days, his father seems desperate. Chaim can tell by the way he now talks about the Cossack. That he can no longer trust him, trust any of them. Not that he ever could. Ever did. A goy is a goy. But he'd thought this one was different. Not cut from the same cloth as other Cossacks.

Despite his father being filled with righteous indignation whenever he spoke of the Cossack, Chaim could tell he was more scared than angry. Children can tell when their parents are afraid. And it frightens them. But Chaim couldn't lie. Not to his father. He couldn't live with himself if he did. He couldn't live with his father, look him in the face. Determined to get his father's attention, he tries a more direct yet still circumspect tack.

"Have you ever been through a pogrom, pa?"

That gets his father's attention.

"What kind of question is that?"

"Our teacher brought a bunch of old newspapers to school."

"Well, he should know better than to scare young boys."

"I'm not scared, pa."

"Good. You shouldn't be. It's something from which, God willing, you should never have to know."

"Are you going to pay what the Cossacks want?"

"Another crazy question?! It's not your business to poke your nose into your father's business. Your business is to study and do well in school you shouldn't have to do what I have to do."

The horse now fully hitched to the wagon, Chaim cries out: "But you could be killed, pa?!"

"Who told you that?"

"I heard!"

"You heard where? From who?"

"I heard."

"Rumours are always running round this shtetl! You want to become a yenta like old Mrs. Popavitch?"

Chaim is about to protest but, since his father has never done so before, when he raises his hand as though ready to slap him, it startles Chaim into silence.

"You're not the only mouth I have to feed in this family! Are you going to feed your brothers and sisters?"

"I help?"

"Hitching Mendel on days you don't have school, I want better for you."

"But ..."

"I don't want to hear another word, hear me, another word! One more word out of you and I don't know what I'll do!"

In tears now, Chaim cries out: "I'll plead with Alexei ! Beg him to talk to his father! If that fails, I'll go straight to Alexei's father, plead with him!"

"That's who started this. I should have known. Using his son to get to mine."

Shaking, he glares at Chaim tapping the boy's chest firmly with his finger as if to accentuate each of his words. "I'll take a stick to you if I have to. You're not too old."

His father rarely raises his voice. Now he's shaking and shouting so it scares Chaim. Not because he's afraid of his father, but because he's afraid *for* him.

* * *

There are no more words out of Chaim's mouth that morning. But his mind won't stop spinning. All of eight years old, wracked with fear, not knowing which way to turn, who to turn to, Chaim contemplates talking to his mother, telling her what he knows, how he knows. Maybe she can talk sense into his father.

But that might infuriate his father more. He's already afraid telling his father what Alexei told him was an even bigger mistake than telling Alexei about the meeting. For now, enraged that the Cossack would stoop so low as to have his son scare Chaim, his father might become more resistant and antagonistic, take greater risks, threaten the Cossack, stirring up more of a hornet's nest.

Chaim once did that, with a stick. The stings sent him to the hospital, in shock. He almost died. His mother was so scared for his life she didn't even yell at him for doing something so stupid. Maybe if he told her what Alexei told him she wouldn't lash out at his father for being about to do something so stupid because she'd be afraid for *his* life.

But he's afraid of his mother. She has a nasty temper, can fly off the handle at the slightest provocation. And the last thing he wants to do is set his mother against his father.

* * *

On his way to pick up a shipment of cigars, it feels hotter than usual for this time of year. This time of morning too. Yet the pedestrians his wagon passes appear dressed more for fall than summer. Some with sweaters or light coats. With just a light shirt, Blittstein is dressed for the sun. But it has disappeared, and white clouds have gradually given way to dark gray. He feels a slight chill, yet only a moment ago he was sweating. Maybe he's getting sick.

His right hand takes hold of the horse's reins, his left feels his forehead. It doesn't seem hot. For sure no fever.

Why all of a sudden should his son ask about pogroms? Since when do they teach such things in school? It brought back memories Blittstein would rather forget. He may not have been a Bolshevik back in '05, but he was a sympathizer. The unarmed workers marching to petition the Tsar may have been led by a priest, and some of them participated in pogroms after, yet when he heard that troops had fired on them he was furious. If it wasn't for his wife, he would've joined the revolution. But they'd only been married a year. And she was adamant.

"We'll soon have a newborn. Now's no time to be a hero."

"You want our son should grow up his father a coward, Ida?"

"Better he should grow up his mother a widow?"

And when the pogroms started she refused to let him join a Jewish defense group. He's never forgotten cowering behind the house with his wife, never forgiven himself. His wife either. Well, he's not going to make the same mistake again. Anyway, pogroms are a thing of the past. The Jewish defense groups have disbanded. It's time to take a stand. If he backs down now he'll lose face, both in the *shtetl* and black market. As fond as Blittstein has been of him in the past, like some beast of prey, who won't stop stalking him, Dimitri's become more than a pest. And Blittstein is losing patience. He's not going to let some Gentile nobody make a fool of him. A coward either. If he can't stand up to Dimitri who can he stand up to? If Dimitri can't stand up for himself, why should he have to pay?

"Move, Mendel move!" he cajoles his horse, followed by tongue-clicking noises, a futile attempt to encourage the nag to speed up. The horse is feeling the heat as much as his master.

* * *

This office appears more dimly lit than the last time Dimitri had to face his commandant, the man thinner and more austere than the phantom that bedevils both his day and nightmares. Dimitri knows there's going to be hell to pay, not just for Blittstein, but for him. At least he has something concrete to report, something more than mere refusal to cooperate.

Dimitri hesitates, tries to clear his throat, but instead cough ups some phlegm, just enough so that his first words sound like he's gargling.

"They're going to ..."

Dimitri stops, clears his throat again, this time succeeding in swallowing before speaking.

"They're going to have a meeting. An open one. In public."

"Where?"

"Plisetskaya Square."

"Plisetskaya Square?!"

Dimitri nods yes.

"How do you know?"

"His son told mine."

"Your sons know each other?"

Dimitri nods a sheepish yes.

"You and this Zhid are such good 'friends'?" The last word uttered with a sarcastic sneer, as though such familiarity is not only impossible, but an illusion of fools.

"I thought if my son befriended his it would help Blittstein bend."

"Well, he will bend now. They will all bend. For as you know my dear Dimitri, except for the richest of the rich, not only are there certain areas of our fair city in which Zhids are not allowed to live, and others in which Zhids are forced to live and no others allowed—though who among those able to live anywhere would want to live among Zhids?" The commandant's vocal rhetorical inflection and facial expression infer this should be obvious.

Since, to Dimitri it is not, he holds his breath, maintains a safe silent grin, followed by a slight sigh of relief he's not been given a chance to respond.

"Certain areas of our fair city, though not formally deemed unfit for a Zhid to pass through, may be informally forbidden for them to do business in. At least at certain times of the day, and certain days of the week. Left more to *our* whims, what these days and times are may never be completely clear. Still, these black-market Zhids develop a nose for where they can go and when, why and why not."

"That they do, sir."

"Outside the pale of settlement Zhids may be vulnerable as individuals. Whereas inside, they are more prone to collective punishment."

"Those who wish to attack or incite attacks against them know where they may be found," Dimitri says, straining to show his anti-Semitic bona fides.

"And if it is known where they may be found outside the pale con-gregating where they are forbidden to congregate?"

"They also make themselves prone collective punishment?"

"Precisely. And you will take the lead. Or you will see no end of grief from your fellow Cossacks. I've had it with you and your Zhid. With all your Zhids. Holding a meeting in a place as public as Pli-setskaya square is meant only to embarrass us. Well, we will make them pay. We will make them all pay."

* * *

As Dimitri approaches his home's front entrance, he slows, hesitates, steps up onto the stoop to reach for the door handle, decides he can't do it. One second sweating, the next shivering, chilled to the bone as though he has a fever, his stomach feels like it's been harnessed, and someone's pulling on the reins. Afraid to enter his house, be confined by its four walls and the faces of his family, especially his wife, his heart's beating so he's out of breath. Yet the last few minutes he's barely moved, just stood there, anxiously shifting from one foot to the other.

He became a Cossack not to kill, but to be seen as a somebody, a man of stature, not just a simple farm boy, beggar or black marketeer.

To become a Cossack you had to be born into it. And Dimitri was born as far from it as a Zhid in the Pale. The youngest of twelve chil-dren, eight boys and four girls, Dimitri was the last born but the first to leave the bosom of the family farm to seek his fame and fortune in the big city by the Black Sea: Odessa.

They lived less than a long day's horse-drawn cart-ride from the city and its sea, yet Dimitri was the first of his siblings to set foot in either. The youngest too, soon after his voice began to change and his chest sprouted its first hairs. At such a young age, it took courage for him to relieve his family of the burden of having to feed one more mouth by bestowing upon them the good fortune of having to feed one less.

He started making a living begging on the Odessa docks. He'd save those kopecks until he'd accumulated enough to buy goods on the black market from those he'd once begged. After several years, his profits allowed him to bribe his way into the Cossacks.

Yet, once in, he could never seem to get his way within the pecking order. Just a rung above a private, he's still treated like one by his colleagues, most of whom hold higher rank.

Still, he wants his wife to have a real house, with fine furniture, in a better part of Odessa. But his Cossack salary is barely enough to make ends meet. Only the elite officers make enough to support their wives and families in the manner he'd imagined. So he, like so many other Cossack regulars, has to find a way to skim spare kopecks and rubles, fleecing Russian citizens who themselves are too poor to have the influence and power to fight back. Then Beryl Blittstein comes along. And threatens to put a wrench into the whole works, the Cossack regulars' whole way of life.

Yet Cossacks are there to protect the Zhids' way of doing business. Without men like Dimitri to act as intermediaries there would be chaos. The black market would be a free for all. They'd be at each other's throats.

As it is, from time to time some of the bigger black marketeers will start cutting prices in order to drive their smaller competitors out of business. Eventually, one of them will end up in a bag by the Black Sea, their bodies dumped on the docks.

Still standing there on his front stoop, he keeps telling himself he can't let his job interfere with his home life, his feelings with his work. He must do whatever being a Cossack demands, and not let it hinder his roles of father and husband. But, in keeping him from facing his family, it already has. And will continue to do so. Yet he's going to do this for them. He has to.

With that thought he musters enough courage to open his front door.

* * *

At this meeting, the blinds on the windows to the other offices are down. It is not quite as bright as the last time these two met. And the mood is more tense.

"You're wondering why I've asked for this meeting," the Cossack commandant says, leaning across the police chief's desk."

As if recoiling from the commandant's aggressive movement, the police chief leans abruptly back, uttering: "When you have yet to put your house in order."

"Well, we're about to."

"Have I not heard this before?"

"We've now received precise information about our troublemakers' tactics. Which will allow us to put a stop to them. There's nothing like the combination of disturbing the peace and ethnic animosity as covers for cleansing ..."

Without looking at him, the cop raises his hand to cut off the commandant. But, feeling cocky, at the same time fearing that the cop is about to reject his scheme, the Cossack keeps talking.

"Like surgeons, our Cossack scalpels are going to remove the Zhid cysts quickly, quietly, and efficiently."

"Be careful lest you kill the geese that lay our golden eggs."

"Only a goose or two. Just enough to scare the others into producing more eggs."

There's a prolonged pause as the police chief contemplates what he's just heard. Finally, his decision made, the cop raises his eyes, stares directly into the Cossack's.

"I have not heard this. I have not heard you."

"My lips are sealed."

"Your lot too should they not remain so."

* * *

It's like a dream, a bad dream, a nightmare from which he can't seem to wake, a dread he can't seem to shake. He's not really sure that, in confronting Blittstein, he's made himself clear. He thinks he has. But he can't remember how. He takes another sip, straight from the bottle. This vodka will be the death of him. Good thing his wife's not home. And the kids are in school. He should be at work. But his nerves are wreaking havoc. And the alcohol doesn't help. The more he drinks the worse he feels. Yet he can't stop, doesn't know what else to do, how to deal with killing someone he feels close to. Strange that he should feel so close to a Zhid. Maybe he has some Zhid blood in him. God forbid. He couldn't be so cursed. If that Zhid refuses to help himself, insists on making himself a target, why should he, a Cossack, care? One moment determined to do what he has to, the other struggling to find a way out of this hell, his back against the wall, he knows there's no way out. He keeps trying to get too drunk to care. But he can't.

* * *

Beryl Blittstein is having trouble getting to sleep. He's always slept like a log, until lately, but has never had a night of tossing and turning like this. Not that he can remember. He knows it's come down to the crunch. He also knows there is little he can do about it. It's in God's hands, more than his or the Cossack's. Still, this morning he davened like a dead man, like his life spirit had already left him. And all this turmoil has upset his wife. Their bickering has begun to get him down, more than his clashes with the Cossack. He was never one to take his business troubles home, at least not burden his wife with them. But lately it's been written all over his face, saying nothing's been worse than saying something.

As if she's heard what's going on in her husband's head, his wife whispers: "Beryl ..."

"Don't start, Ida, please don't start."

"I can't sleep."

"You think I can?"

"We can move. Start over somewhere else. The letters we get from your cousin Karmelit in Canada, how much she loves it there. Once and for all why don't we move where a Jew can live like a human being? What've we been saving for all these years?"

"I'm too old to start over."

"You wouldn't be starting from nothing. The family has a business there."

"And I have a business here."

"You see what this business is doing to you here. What it's doing to our whole family."

"I don't take handouts from anybody. Family or no family. Here at least I'm my own boss."

"Your own boss? Your own boss? You're no more your own boss than the Cossack is his!"

Regretful that in insulting his status she's hurt him, she softens her voice, embraces a more intimate tone.

"We used to talk about having our own little minyan."

"We used to talk about a lot of things."

"Now you turn away from me."

"I have a lot on my mind."

"I don't want you to go to that meeting."

"Without me there's no meeting."

"Then there's no meeting."

"Do I tell you how to cook and take care of the kids."

Before she can answer—

"No. Because I trust you. Why can't you trust me?"

"Because you're too stubborn for your own good. Too stubborn for all our good."

He turns onto his side, away from her.

"I have to get some sleep. At least try."

"Then we'll talk in the morning."

He twists back to her.

"The time for talking is over. It's time for action."

"And to hell with your family."

"This is bigger than our family."

"You're making speeches to me now? Don't make speeches to me. I'm not one of your black market cronies."

He turns away again.

* * *

Groggy at first, Dimitri wakes filled with fear and anticipation. He has not slept, only in fits and starts. And those few moments, filled with flashes of what was to come, were anything but deep restful repose. Instead, they felt like bits of silent Stenka Razin film clips, without musical accompaniment either, resembling ones he still remembers, but adapted by his unconscious imagination. For he was Stenka Razin (the great Cossack leader who led a major uprising against the nobility and tsarist bureaucracy in the17th century) leading the charge, shouting for his subordinates to fight, yet never making a sound. The vignettes were so short, and the scenes so vivid, yet he'd kept dozing off between them. Or was it during? It seemed like one long battle scene, and each time he awoke or dozed off, the scene had moved on, jumped to another setting. At least that's how he remembers it.

Strange. No matter. This is no time to reminisce about a dream. Or was it a nightmare? He's so stuporous he's not sure. But as he slips on his britches, he starts to feel better, awake at least, though still filled with fear. Once he pulls on his boots he'll feel better. He always does. They make him feel like a soldier. Whereas he's never really been in battle. Never killed anyone. This will be his first time.

* * *

On this morning, the man chosen to silence my grandfather looks in the mirror, decides he must trim his moustache a bit more. Make sure it doesn't mask his lips. Full lips make him look fierce. And his eyebrows need trimming. He doesn't want to look uncivilized when descending on the Zhids. Not a peasant in Cossack's clothing but a man bred for the role, one of elite upbringing. An officer to be. Born to it. Bound for it.

Moments later, as he dons his Cossack uniform, he's not sure what he's going to do when push comes to shove. All he knows is that there's going to be an attack. And he has to take part in it or be persona non grata among fellow Cossacks for the rest of his days. Be seen as a potential traitor, one they could no longer trust, one who, if push came to shove, might be forced to point fingers at his fellow Cossacks, perhaps identify the key instigators.

But why is he worrying? Nobody cares what happens to a bunch of Zhids. Certainly nobody in government. Attacks on Zhids don't need excuses. Or they need only the most flimsy of excuses. Attacks on Zhids are justified just by the fact that they're Zhids.

Anyway, in this uniform I'm no longer Dimitri Alexandrov Illytch. I'm part of the Cossack corps. Cossack to the core. And to wear this uniform is a privilege for which others would be willing to kill. A privilege for which I must be too.

He struggles with his boots. He always struggles with his boots. First the left, then the right. Always from left to right. If these boots were on *his* feet would *he* betray me?

Once both boots are on, he feels better. He always does. They're the hardest part of his uniform to get on, reaching as they do almost to his knees, at the same time, being a half size too small for him. At least for his left foot, which is slightly longer than his right. But he didn't want to make a fuss, be forever mocked for insisting that his boots be made to order instead of as-is off the Cossack shelves. He feared being seen as a pretentious peasant who, instead of feeling honoured to be given the privilege of becoming a Cossack, was too arrogant to accept a pair of boots that weren't a perfect fit. He should have opted for the larger half size rather than the smaller. But he didn't want his boots to look too big for the rest of his body. A big mistake which, as soon he realized he'd made it, he was reluctant to retract. He didn't want to be seen as indecisive.

Well, today is the day he proves he isn't. Short as he is, once he dismounts he must stand tall, show he is ready for the kill. To help add to his stature, he's tried adding a millimetre or two to the soles of his boots. But it was murder on his toes. He couldn't wiggle them. Not even on his shorter foot. Just a tad too tight for circulation.

He closes his eyes, imagines himself engaged in a contest with his colleagues, each one upping the height of their heels until they lose their balance, making utter fools of themselves and becoming the laughing stock of the city. All except Dimitri who, his heels back to their original height, sits atop his white stallion, watching his fellow Cossacks and smiling.

Feeling better about himself, he opens his eyes, decides that keeping his britches properly tucked in is the key. The creases can't look random, like he's just gotten out of bed, slept in his uniform, which he never does, never has done, would never dare do. He has too much respect for his outfit, is always careful to hang it up, over the back of the same chair, so they'll be fit to wear in the morning.

Knowing he'd need to look his best today, his wife pressed them last night, borrowed that steam iron from a better-off neighbour, that busybody Natalia Borodin. He couldn't quite bring himself to tell his wife why they needed to be pressed again. Only that they might have to do battle. Thank god she didn't ask him against who when, where, or why. She knew better. She didn't have to ask. There was no war, so for what else could it be? Maybe mass arrests.

And sometimes they help the cops when it comes to dealing with gangs, out and out criminals who kill. They and their cronies, as well-armed as the army who, like the Cossacks and cops, are as wary and afraid of them as they are of uniformed officials. From time to time the two sides do slip into out and out war. Still, sooner or later their leaders meet and one way or another manage to make peace. Make crime pay for both sides.

Compared to these hardened criminals these black market Zhids are harmless. Still, they have to be put in their place. And it's up to us to put them there.

His wife knows this is a special occasion for him. He's sure she can sense it. Making soup for breakfast, He can smell the beets. Hot borscht. He's lucky to have such a wife. One who gets up a half hour ahead of her husband so that he can have a hot healthy breakfast.

On this morning, the most momentous of his many in uniform, he wants anything but for his family to see him so uncertain, nervous, shaky, his mouth and throat so dry he can't seem to swallow a spoonful of hot soup. He tries again, but something seems caught in his throat, blocking the way.

Finally, he gives up, decides to cut his breakfast short, skip it altogether. Dropping his spoon back into the soup, he mumbles: "You know, for some reason I'm not hungry this morning."

"You don't look well," his wife says. "Maybe you should stay home today."

"I can't. Not today," he responds, a nervous edge to his utterance. His wife stares at him. He looks away, abruptly springs up.

"I should go. I don't want to be late."

He's thinking she knows. How could she ask him to stay home today? Of all days. His life wouldn't be worth one kopeck if he dared do that. No matter how sick he was supposed to be. He could have a heart attack, the others would still be suspicious he drank rat poison on purpose. He could never look any of them in the eye again. He'd be ostracized, mocked, made a fool of by his fellow Cossacks, humiliate him in public. They've done it before. To others who let them down.

No, he dare not not show up today. He has to go through with it, with enthusiasm, feign it lest they find out how fearful he feels. How sick too. Like he's going to throw up. Yet he didn't eat a thing. He better get out of the house, get to work, before he collapses here. From sheer fear. He probably feels as much terror at the thought of what he's going to do, what he's going to have to do, as Blittstein will when he sees him. If only he knew he probably would, if not forgive him, at least understand he's just doing what he has to, to make a living, to stay alive.

He stands there, his family staring at him, waiting for him to say something, break the silence, perhaps just leave the table. But he doesn't move. He's afraid to.

"Dimitri, don't just stand there. Either go or stay. Better, sit down. And finish your soup."

"I don't have time."

"You look terrible."

"I feel terrible. But what can I do?"

He dons his Cossack coat.

"You can do something else if this job is going to kill you sick like this. You can do something else. You're handy with your hands."

"I have to go."

She gets up, follows, tries to hug him. He pushes her away, abruptly. He knows that if he doesn't go now he'll never go and what kind of life would be left for them?

"I'm sorry. I'm not myself today. Please, just let me go."

"Go."

He mutters a somewhat sheepish "I'm sorry," as he steps past her, opens then steps out the door, saying: "I'll feel better after all this is over."

His wife stands there shaking, tears in her eyes. The two children rush over to her.

"What's wrong with papa?" the youngest asks. "What's wrong with papa?"

"Nothing. He's just tired. Works too hard."

She shunts them back inside the house, slams the door shut.

* * *

Outside, Dimitri's mind keeps torturing him with whirlwinds of what might happen. After he disposes of Blittstein, other Zhids might kow-tow before him even more. But only if he stays on the force. Should he quit, they'd avoid him like the plague. And who could blame them? But if he resigned on principle, refused to participate in this pogrom, maybe they'd slip some business his way. But would his superiors let him get away with it? Maybe if he quit first, fast, before it's too late, without making a fuss, saying his health has been going downhill. No, they wouldn't buy it. And his life would be a misery.

But how will he live with himself, killing his friend? His only friend. No Cossack comes close. He'd never confide in any of them. He should have consulted his priest. But he couldn't trust him, not when it came to betraying Cossacks. Word would get back. They live in as much fear of his Cossack superiors as he does. He'd sooner seek advice from Blittstein. If it concerned anybody else he would. No man gives better advice. He should warn him at least. But he has. Maybe not in so many words but ... the man's not stupid. Stubborn, maybe, but not stupid.

His superiors aren't stupid either. They know the Zhid's his friend. That's why they've put the onus on him. If he doesn't go through with this his life won't be worth a kopeck. And if he does how will he live with himself?

"Lord forgive me, I live more in fear of my fellow Cossacks than most Zhids," he mutters just as he bumps into a neighbour, one he doesn't get along with, one he's never got along with.

"Watch where you're walking!" the man shouts.

"Sorry. I didn't see you."

"I'm sure you didn't. You were too busy talking to yourself."

"I'm a little preoccupied lately."

"Wife giving you trouble or work?"

"N-neither," Dimitri mutters, then rushes to get away.

"Then it must be money," the man mutters back, before he realizes Dimitri's out of hearing range.

* * *

The closer Dimitri gets to Plisetskaya Street the more anxious and excited he becomes. He can't tell if it's anticipation or revulsion, but his stomach is beginning to cramp. Christ. Not now. Of all times. Good thing he didn't eat this morning or he'd really be sick. Maybe that would have been better, not coming into work like his wife wanted.

He should never have married her. But she had a cousin who had a cousin who helped him buy his way into becoming a Cossack. If it wasn't for her he might never have become one, wouldn't have to put up with all this.

Still, the children are the loves of his life, a gift from his wife. So he should be grateful. But he's not, not at this moment, forced to kill a man who's been so kind to him, so kind to everyone. Several times he's spotted him giving away goods to one street urchin or another. He could have arrested him, it's against the law encouraging kids to beg. But it was the constabulary's duty, not his. As it was they complained that Cossacks were encroaching on their turf. But Cossacks can do whatever suits them, whenever it suits them. One of the bonuses of being one, having to kill Zhids, one of the curses. A Cossack who can't kill a Zhid would be deemed worthy of derision.

Well, after this there'll be no looking back. He'll be one of them. Once and for all he won't feel like an outsider. Won't be one. Who's he fooling? He'll always be one, always feel like one. No matter what he does, how hard he tries, it's just not in him to be truly one of them. No matter how many Zhids he murders.

Maybe they all feel the same way. No, couldn't be. He can tell. Most of them enjoy the job, love it, especially the status, the stature, the uniform. He does too, if it weren't for his fellow Cossacks, and days like today.

Dimitri feels like throwing up. Not here. Not now. Not so close to Cossack headquarters. Someone might see. But he can't help himself. He rushes over to a large leafless tree, bends over, trying to hide behind the large chunk of black and gray bark hanging loose off the tree's trunk. Some kids must have been trying to peel it off, got caught by a cop, and had to run for it. Well he can't run anywhere. He's got to vomit. But nothing comes out, nothing but sour saliva dripping down his chin. Thank God he didn't eat breakfast. Hope no one saw him, drooling like some idiot. He glances up and down the street, the few pedestrians appear too far to have seen him.

Relieved, he leans against the tree, wheezing, coughing to clear his throat. His mind's a blank. But his body feels better. A little spitting up is all it took. He's no longer nauseous. Or as anxious. He better keep going, before the anxiety starts eating away at him again.

* * *

Odessa is the Russian city with the largest percentage of Jews, roughly half its residents. Here Jews live mostly on the city's fringes, what in a later time might be seen as suburban slums, but now are simply referred to as *shtetls*, tiny tight-knit Jewish enclaves, centred around synagogues.

Here, Blittstein has always felt safe. Outside the *shtetl*, not so much. Still, the more affluent areas of Odessa, especially the most central ones, are well lit by gas light and well-patrolled by police, so they should be safer for Jewish businessmen than less well-patrolled ones, especially during the day, filled with people. Of course, the police are just as likely to blackmail a black-market businessman as to protect him and, whether amidst a throng of pedestrians in the light of day or a deserted square in the dark of night, nothing would save a Jew once a pogrom was underway.

But it's been so long since there's been one it doesn't enter Blittstein's mind there could be another, let alone that he might trigger one. Nevertheless, he knows he's putting himself in harm's way.

Outside, in back of his barn, it is a breezy cool—but for the smattering of high cumulus clouds—clear morning, much like the morning before, and the morning before that. But for Blittstein, this day is different. Does he truly think that, to keep the conflict under the table, the Cossacks will back down, come to some compromise?

Well, negotiation is a way of life for him, part of the very fabric of his being. He lives and breathes deals. And the Cossacks won't indulge him. He's not one to accept orders. From anyone. He won't be bullied. He has to raise the stakes, force them to negotiate. Even if it backfires.

As he struggles to complete hitching his horse's harness to its wagon, he finds his fingers trembling ever so slightly, so that, instead of being able to snap each of the harness's back buckles quickly into place without thinking, his fingers miss. Sensing his nervousness the horse neighs, pulls away.

"Whoa!" Blittstein shout-whispers. "Simmer down. Today's no different than any other day."

But he knows it is. And his horse knows it too. As sensitive as children, horses read and react to the mood of their masters. This horse may not have understood the meaning of its master's words, but from his anxious undertone, it could sense him compensating for his fear. Truth be told he's not used to hitching up the horse alone. For months Chaim has been his helper. But this morning Blittstein insisted he'd do it himself.

"But I want to go with you. Just today," Chaim had pleaded.

"I told you no. How many times do I have to tell you, no means no? I don't want you missing school. You want to end up a peddler like your father all your life?"

Normally, Chaim knew when to take no for an answer. Specially when the no came from his father. When he didn't want his son exposed to certain shady dealings, done with certain shady characters. But on this day it was not certain shady characters nor certain shady dealings that Blittstein feared exposing his son to, but a warning to all Jewish black-market businessmen to stay away from Plisetskaya Square.

These warnings had been in the air for more than a week, had been building for days. Until yesterday Blittstein had taken them with a grain of salt. But something had happened then, an incident that shook him to his core. He'd seen the son of one of his competitors beaten and bloodied by a policeman's truncheon right in front of his father. What's worse, in spite of a crowd gathering to watch, and the boy's father pleading with the policeman, the cop wouldn't stop. Not until the boy, unconscious, could no longer move, just lay there in a heap, his father draped over him, tearfully trying to protect his son from further blows. For a few moments, ominously waving his truncheon, the cop hovered over them.

Not a single soul, including Blittstein, dared lend a helping hand. They knew what would happen to them if they did. When the cop shouted "What are you staring at?" the small crowd, with the exception of Blittstein, silently dispersed. The cop glared at Blittstein. Blittstein stared back. A prolonged silent standoff. Finally, the cop uttered "Let this be a warning!" and casually walked away.

Blittstein jumped down from his wagon and rushed to the peddler. When the man tried to shoo him away with "I don't need your help. I don't want your help," implying Blittstein was responsible for this incident, Blittstein, as if defending himself, responded with "This could have been my boy! This could have been my boy!"

But that incident only served to confirm that what he would do the next day would be done without his son. Until then he had considered having Chaim accompany him, to let him see how a man stands up for himself. But now he knew: he could risk his own skin, but he would not risk that of his son.

"Stand still!" Blittstein shouts to his horse, as though still angrily addressing his son earlier that morning.

Startled by the shout—Blittstein hardly ever raises his voice to anyone, not even his horse—the horse stops moving. The shout helps steady Blittstein too, just long enough for him to get both ends of the harness hitched to the wagon. But once this crucial bit of business done, as he tries to untangle the reins, his fingers again begin to shake. He must be *farshimmeled* to let the reins get caught under the harness trace. And he's tied the girth too tight. This horse likes it loose. But in his hurry, his anxiety, he got carried away. No matter, most horses accept it like this. His son's helped spoil this one.

"Besides, leave it too loose and it chafes your belly. Then see how you like it."

He's talking to his horse. He rarely does. But now he finds it calms him, lets him catch his breath, stop breathing so hard. He keeps talking and, before either he or his horse realizes it, he's talking to himself not his horse.

"You keep on like this you'll have a heart attack. You decided and there's nothing you can do about it now. There's nothing *they* can do about it. Not if you get peddlers to pool together. Neither Cossacks nor cops want word to get back to the mayor, governor or, god forbid, the Tsar there's trouble on the streets. It doesn't look good for anybody, least of all their ringleaders."

As he succeeds in straightening out the reins, his mouth stops moving and his monologue shifts to his mind. No one wants trouble. Least of all himself. But you let these people keep pushing and soon you can't pay your rent, can't put food on the table. This has to stop somewhere.

As he shuts the barn door, slides the latch and locks it, the horse is chomping at the bit. So is Blittstein. There's no turning back now. There's no backing down now.

* * *

As Dimitri turns the corner onto Plisetskaya Street, his heart skips a beat, then picks up speed as he spots the regiment headquarters ahead, a bunch of Cossacks clustered on the front steps. Usually, they're in the back, readying their horses. But now they're waiting for him, like he's some kind of hero, big smiles on some of their faces, some sort of leer on the fatman's. Dimitri feels he's going to be sick again. He can't be sick now. God, don't let him be sick now.

His nose is dripping. His nose always drips when he's nervous. Drawing a forearm quickly across his face as though saluting or waving to his Cossack co-workers, he discreetly wipes his nose with his sleeve. Now, to make sure he doesn't look scared, that he looks like he's on top of the world, he starts to strut. A swing of the arm, one final nose wipe hand combined with a hand wave and he picks up the pace, moves into a marching rhythm.

But, as he approaches the headquarter steps, in spite of his strenuous efforts at looking suave, his strut starts to stiffen. For the first few steps he manages to strut tall and straight—ramrod straight—but then, in spite of his best efforts not to, he starts stumbling up the stairs. His body's fleeing his brain, refusing to take orders from it, to take orders from him.

Still, Dimitri can sense the excitement of the regiment. As he limps up the stairs, they give him a huzza. An actual cheer! They're cheering him! It goes straight to his head, like a shot of adrenaline. He straightens up, smiles, his head gives a few token nods of acknowledgment along with a bit of a bow. But it's also a way to avoid their eyes. He doesn't want them to see the fear in them, the shyness too. He's going to be sick again. He's definitely going to be sick again. He's got to get to the bathroom.

But the man referred to as the fatman is in his way, won't let him get by, grabs him in one of his headlocks, the usual arm around the neck that Dimitri so resents. Showing off his superior strength, his superior stature too. A real pig of a man. Dimitri tries to pull away, slip out from under the man's grip but the fatman won't let go.

"A fine day for hunting," he says out of the side of his mouth then laughs, a hearty har har followed by a round of wheezing that turns into coughing. All the while the man manages to keep smiling and staring at Dimitri, as though stubbornly awaiting some response.

The fatman is so overweight and unhealthy he should be an embarrassment to this regiment, Dimitri thinks as he struggles to return a smile, albeit one that looks more like an angry grimace, matching more what Dimitri truly feels. The fatman was his first partner, the one who showed him the Cossack ropes. He should be grateful. But he's not. He can't stand the man. So gross in every way.

The fatman flings his arm around Dimitri's neck and pulls him close as he whispers: "Today Dimitri's going to lose his cherry, huh huh har har!" More laughter followed by another fit of coughing, spittle sprinkling Dimitri's face. Dimitri tries to pull away. But the fatman is too strong, holding on too tightly, using Dimitri to keep himself from keeling over as he continues his coarse laughter and coughing.

* * *

His father was usually accommodating when Chaim felt like skipping school to help him. Chaim was a good student. So his father didn't have to worry about him failing. And he loved to have his son by his side. But when Chaim persisted, pleading with his father to let him go with him, his father became more adamant and angry than Chaim had ever seen him.

Nevertheless, Chaim continued to beg. His father threatened to punish him if he didn't stop. Since he was not one for making threats, certainly not to his children, nor had he ever raised a hand to them, his father's harsh words only confirmed to Chaim how much danger the man faced. All the more determined not to leave his father—indeed, afraid to—Chaim stood his ground. His father grabbed both the boy's arms, spun him around and shoved him so harshly he nearly fell. Startled by his father's hostility, Chaim turned and shuffled away.

"Look after your brother and sister! As the oldest I'm counting on you!" his father shouted, his words both ominous and apologetic to Chaim's ears.

Tears in his eyes, Chaim turned to his father. But the man's firmly pointing finger, pursed lips and stern look said all he needed to say. Reluctantly, Chaim pivoted and headed toward school.

* * *

As he makes his way toward school, he is joined along the way by his usual friends. But, unlike them, intensely silent, his mind elsewhere, he has no patience for their usual pranks or boisterous banter.

"What's the matter?" one of the boys asks.

"Nothing," Chaim responds in a brusque manner.

The boy doesn't pry any further. Neither do the others. They know something's up between his father and the Cossacks. But they're not sure what. Rumours have been swirling around their small *shtetl*. And from Chaim's grim demeanour, they know it must be serious. By the time they reach their schoolyard the silent gloom has spread to the whole group.

As they enter the yard, Chaim lags behind ever so slightly, then, before his friends have a chance to ask what he's doing, where he's going, he spins and starts running, the long way around the school block, taking him farther from Plisetskaya Square. His father had been so firm in forbidding Chaim from following him to Plisetskaya Square, it has not only increased Chaim's determination to do so, but also enhanced his fear that, to make sure he was securely ensconced in school, his father might be following him. At least pass by Chaim's school before proceeding to Plisetskaya Square. It's not like his father to mistrust him. Certainly not to go as far as to follow him. But this morning is unlike other mornings. And Chaim is not thinking straight. His mind is all over the map.

What does he think he'll see in Plisetskaya Square? What does he think he'll do? He doesn't know. But he simply can't see himself sitting in school while his father is out there risking his life. He has to be there.

On foot he can take the shortcut across little Plisetskaya park. Horses can't cross there, not when pulling a wagon. His father would have to take the long way around. If he can get there before his father, he can tell them the Cossacks are coming, beg them to stop the meeting. But will they listen to a boy like him?

He's seen his father make speeches at meetings, shaking his fists as he spoke, everyone all ears. He may not be a man, can't speak like one, with the same authority as his father, but he could howl and cry. It might scare them. Or he could find Alexei's father, plead with him in front of the others. Maybe that'll stop them. The Cossacks must be nearby.

Soaked with sweat, a sharp pain in his side, head spinning and heart beating so he can barely catch his breath, he's afraid if he stops his father might die. But what chance does a boy have against a bunch of Cossacks? What chance does his father have? Yet hoping against hope, he keeps running.

Filled with fear, suffused with guilt for betraying his father, revealing what he'd overheard to Alexei, he keeps trying to console himself. It was a mistake. But he did it to save his father. He didn't know what else to do. He should have known there was nothing he could have done to stop his father once he had made up his mind. He was a wilful man. A stubborn one too. If his mother couldn't stop his father, no one could.

He passes a string of shops, some with shopkeepers standing in their doorways, waiting for customers, others, outside their shops, serving the odd customer there. Half the shops have the same faded greyish green awnings. As he runs, his surroundings float through Chaim's head like some daydream, fleeting images emanating from his own mind. Everything seems strange. Everyone too. Their faces blurred, Chaim's vision distorted by tears.

Here and there a few heads turn towards him as he races by. Others, perhaps wondering why he's running so, looks so desperate, pretend not to notice. Maybe he stole something. No one's chasing him. No one's shouting after him. Best to stay out of it. Mind one's own business. Don't bother with Zhid kids. They only mean trouble. Who knows what are running through these Odessans' minds? But such speculations are rushing through Chaim's, as if, unable to tolerate his anticipated anguish, his mind keeps spinning off in all directions, filled with one fleeting rescue fantasy or another.

He could ask for help. No, it might only make things worse. Adults wouldn't listen to a young boy. No one will listen. No one ever listens. The shopkeepers will think he's coming to steal. That he's stolen. That's why he's running. But he's not carrying anything. His pants have no pockets. And who would help him? How could they help him?

One moment in the middle of the street, the next on the side, he zigzags to avoid bumping into the few pedestrians, bicyclists, and the one passing streetcar. He should race to catch up to it before the next stop. Not having the kopecks to pay his way on to the tram, he could slip through for free, use the rush hour crunch as cover. To ensure they weren't late for work, every morning, crowds would jostle, go through the same push and shove process to make sure they got on their chosen trolley and not have to wait for the next. But there's no rush hour now. No one's in a hurry but him. He sniffs, struggling to stop his dripping nose, get another gasp of breath. A strange scent permeates Plisetskaya street.

As Chaim approaches Plisetskaya Square, the entire area appears more empty than it should be this time of day, much quieter too. Odessans have a way of anticipating trouble. It has been years since any pogrom, at least one of any size, especially one perpetrated by the Cossacks, yet locals could sense one was coming. Peddlers and Cossacks converging on the same area at the same time had to be a recipe for upheaval. No one wanted to get trapped between the two of them.

Chaim reaches the end of the narrow alley he's used to slip into Plisetskaya Square and is struck by the sight of line after line of mounted Cossacks, a dozen or so horses wide, ominous in their slow and steady—almost ceremonial—pace entering the square from all sides.

At the square centre, dozens of peddlers, their wagons and horses surround an elevated monument of some Crimean war hero, or perhaps Peter the Great. Chaim could never remember. But, as what is about to happen hits him, he is suffused with fear.

Most of the black marketeers are not on their wagons, but in front of their horses, clutching them by the bit, standing in semicircles several wagons deep. Somehow, through all the chaos and distance, Chaim sees his father spot him, or thinks he does. For, his mouth in mid motion, eyes aghast, he suddenly stops shouting to his crowd of black marketeers, glares at Chaim.

Chaim is so far from his father that, though he can clearly hear his voice, he can barely see his mouth moving, read his lips, let alone make out what his eyes have to say. Yet he's sure he can. And is jolted by that ominous 'What are you doing here?' look in his father's eyes. That rage. He'd warned him not to follow. Yet he must have known his son wouldn't listen. Just as a father can sense when his son is in danger, so a son can sense when his father's in peril.

Now, terrified of turning Cossack attention to his son, Chaim's father quickly looks away, resumes his speech.

Chaim's head and heart are beating so, his whole body shaking, he's as out of breath now as when he was running. But now he feels no pain in his side, in his whole body, nothing. He can't even cry, let tears relieve some of the hurt, help him feel anything but a suffocating numbness.

* * *

Above the collective bass beat of the pounding horses' hooves and higher-pitched clippity clop of their metal shoes, Chaim can now hear the frenzied shouting of the Cossacks and see the crazed commotion of the crowds through which they charge, swords swinging this way and that.

It seems that part of the appeal of this pogrom for the Cossack perpetrators is the terror being inflicted on the throng into which they swarm. For, apparently not yet aiming to slaughtering anyone, but simply to scare the life out of them, they stir a hysteria that betrays such distinctions as some black marketeers struggle to hold on to their horses, others hoist themselves back on their wagons, and still others scatter every which way.

But the sadistic see-Jews-run Cossack game abruptly ends with a command from their leader: "Kill these Zhids!! Now!!"

That prompts the howling horde of Cossacks, some now on horseback some not, some with bayonet rifles, others with swords, to begin the slaughter. Frozen with fear, Chaim spots his father stubbornly standing atop a set of monument stairs in the centre of the square, shaking his fist, seemingly admonishing his colleagues to stand their ground, not be scared off.

Then, through all the tumult, as though just one fearless man, swept up in the emotion of his own rhetoric, can withstand the momentum of a massacre, he hears his father, in a booming voice, seemingly echoing from on high: "We have to make a living! We have to *live!*"

As though his feet have been freed by his father's voice, Chaim scurries over to a set of basement stairs, slinks under its railing and slips down below ground level, still outside, in a recessed area that leads to a washroom. But it is locked. A large padlock probably meant just for this occasion. To keep peddlers from hiding here. At least that's what races through Chaim's mind. His head is spinning. What is he doing here anyway? He can't help, can't shout for help, do anything to intervene. He should have stayed home like his papa told him to.

But hoping against hope Dimitri would intervene, do something to save his father, protect him if possible, he had to be there, as if his mere presence, his being a witness to what was happening, might be enough to stop it. Now his only fallback plan is one that tells him to stay as close to his father as he can, keep him in sight at all times, until he can think of some way to save him. But at the moment, his mind is a blank. He doesn't know what to do: to run, keep crouching, stay hidden or stand for all to see. He's shaking so he can barely stay on his feet. His hands have to grasp the cement wall ledge to keep him from collapsing.

His legs bent, ducking as low as he can, making sure to keep his head down, he swings toward the front of the stairwell, facing the square, the source of the unearthly shrieking. But, as hard as he tries to stealthily raise his head to see what is going on, he can't. It's as though some force, perhaps some benevolent or demonic deity, is conspiring to keep him from witnessing the worst sight any son can see. He can hear his father's voice. He's sure he can hear his father's voice, separate it from all the others, raised above all the others. His cries like a knife in his young son's heart. No matter how hard he tries, Chaim cannot straighten either knee. The pain is too great.

But he persists, still crouched, slowly straightens his legs, until his eyes are elevated enough to peer over the cement wall of the stairwell. He's startled to see his father making himself more of a target, taunting the Cossacks closest to him, going out of his way to maintain their attention, doing anything he can to divert them from spotting his son. Does he know his son's still there? Can he sense him? Out of the corner of his eye did he catch him disappearing down these stairs? Having spotted his son, afraid for him, so his son can escape unscathed, is he going to let himself be slaughtered. If Chaim weren't here might his father try to escape? A split second, but a blink, and Chaim imagines his father's eyes saying all they have to say. Run, son. Run now. While you can. Before they kill me, run. Run, son, run!

* * *

And what of the man ordered to execute Blittstein? A small man, slight of build, with an equally ordinary mind, he has a uniform to make him feel enormous, add power to his otherwise unimpressive persona. Nothing puffs him up more than donning that uniform. Yet, surrounded by his fellow Cossacks, swept up in the fervour of this pogrom, the fever-pitched pace through which they swoop through the square, watching peddlers desperately trying to scurry to safety, he experiences none of the elation the other Cossacks seem to. In fact, he feels as much fear as his victims. One of the few Cossacks still on his horse, not only is Dimitri afraid of toppling off and being trampled, he's scared to dismount and meet the same misfortune. But most of all he's terrified of confronting Blittstein.

Maybe he can just stay on his horse, let one of them do the deed. Or dismount, lose himself in the chaos, let himself be trampled to death. Then he wouldn't have to be tormented anymore, by Blittstein or Cossacks.

A pair of officers ride up on either side of Dimitri shouting: "Come on, get that Zhid, Illytch! Get that goddamn troublemaker!"

Startled out of his fleeting escape fantasy, for the first moments after dismounting, eye to eye with Blittstein, transfixed by the man's gaze, Dimitri must now face the music, the terrible discordant sound he's so feared, the agony of his closest friend's death.

To make sure he cannot escape, a slew of Cossacks encircle Blittstein.

* * *

Hidden, unable to move, cowering beneath the set of basement stairs, his head just high enough so that he can see, Chaim cannot keep from recoiling, trembling as, again and again, Alexei's father slashes away at Chaim's with a sword. As though the sound of his father's screeches—so distant yet so loud—has destroyed his eardrums and deafened him, all Chaim can do now is watch, transfixed. He can no longer hear anything but his own heart, his own head, beating in unison. Like distant thunder.

* * *

If one didn't know better one might think that Dimitri was tormenting Blittstein with near misses rather than actually striking him just to entertain his colleagues. For one hit to Blittstein's head with either edge of the sword—the blunt or sharp—and Blittstein would be dead, instead of rolling and writhing this way and that, wailing each time Dimitri's sword just manages to avoid hitting him.

Perhaps somewhere in the deeper recess of Dimitri's unconscious—his conscience perhaps—he's trying to keep Blittstein alive as long as possible, hoping against hope that he won't have to kill him. Something will intervene to save both of them, put a stop to this insanity. Meanwhile, the closer Dimitri's sword gets to grazing Blittstein, the more frenzied Blittstein's cries, and the madder more terrifying the scene. It's as though the two of them are engaged in some perverse prelude to a dance of death, one composed by some crazed choreographer.

A few seconds later, frozen by a failure of nerve, flooded by a cascade of conscience, try as he might Dimitri cannot move.

Then, triggered by the Cossack commandant's fierce shout to "End this charade now!" Dimitri's sword finally strikes its target. Blood spurts all over his Cossack uniform, hands and face. But he does not let it stop him from hacking away at Blittstein. Perhaps if he stops to favour his eye, to cleanse it, he would not have the wherewithal to continue with the killing.

As Blittstein lies in a pool of blood, the blunt edge of Dimitri's sword hits the side of his head, tearing a hole right through his temple. Then, the sharp edge of Dimitri's sword strikes Blittstein's neck. Well before Blittstein is brain dead, his head severed from his body, he has choked to death on his own blood. Yet Dimitri keeps hacking and hacking till he can do it no more. Spent, his arms limp, he collapses beside Blittstein. But not before hearing the faint sound of clapping from his fellow Cossacks.

* * *

Distorted not only by tears but by the sheer agony of seeing his father hacked to death, his eyesight as hazy as his hearing, Chaim is dazed, dizzy, feels he's going to faint. They'll find him if he faints here. He's got to go, get away from here. If they knew he'd witnessed what he just had, his life would be worthless. Without his father what's his life worth now?

He crouches, as low as he can, slips up the stairwell, one slow step at a time, then, after slinking along the side of the street for several seconds, he starts running.

Everything hurts. His head feels like it's splitting in two, between his eyes and his ears, as though that sword has gone through his head along with his father's. He wishes it had been his head and not his father's. Then why didn't he say, do something to stop them? Against his father's wishes. He'd done it before. He couldn't bear his father being angry at him. But that look in his eyes, not only angry and defiant, but sad and lost. He'd never seen him like that. It broke his heart. Before the blows.

His senses, distorted all day, feel like they'll never be the same again. Nothing will ever be the same again. Not for him, not for his family. The whole business is but a blur, a bad dream. Maybe he's been making it up. It's all in his head. His father's not dead. But he is. And he did nothing to save him.

His knees are about to give out. His whole body hurts. He doesn't have to run anymore. He's safe now. Far from his father. A few blocks at least. He looks around. Feels lost. Nothing looks familiar. He's not sure where he is.

* * *

Chaim reaches the edge of his *shtetl*, but he's afraid to set foot there. How could he have come so far so fast? And no one stopped him. Asked him what was wrong, why he was so distraught. Perhaps they knew. They must have known. Well, he can't go home. Face his family. Tell them what has happened. He needs to think. But where? The barn. No. Without his father it will be too empty. There's nowhere to go. He has nowhere to go. His soccer field! He'll be safe there, can rest, think.

No sooner does he set foot on the soccer field than Chaim's mood shifts, from unmitigated anguish to a mixture of fear and anger. What if Alexei shows up? No, it's a school day. Alexei never skips school. Well, neither do I. Only to help my pa. Maybe he was in Plisetskaya Square helping his. Or just watching. Just watching?! Chaim feels a surge of rage. Followed by fear. He wouldn't dare come here. Not today. If he does he'll have to kill him. And if he doesn't, he knows the route Alexei takes home after school. He's taken it with him, that Sunday, to show off he wasn't afraid to be seen "consorting with a Zhid." I can catch him on that last leg when he's alone, sneak up on him and, before he knows what's hit him … No, he doesn't want him to die. Not without knowing who did it, watch his face, see his eyes, the shock. He shouldn't be thinking like this. God'll punish him for thinking like this. He's punished him already.

He better go home. He has to. He's the oldest now. But what's he going to say to his baby brother and sister? To his mother? That he watched his father die and didn't do anything about it? Couldn't do anything about it? He can't pretend he doesn't know. But he can pretend he didn't see. There was a commotion, a bunch of Cossacks, he couldn't see. No one must ever know what he saw. What he did. What he didn't do. What didn't he do? He couldn't have saved his father. His father didn't want him to. But he can't tell them that. They wouldn't understand.

He spots someone entering the far end of the field. Alexei? Couldn't be. But it is! Kicking a ball, hard, as if trying to hurt it, putting all his anger into each kick. Oscillating between fear and rage, Chaim is shaking, scared, not of being hurt by Alexei, but of what he might do to him—what he might *have* to do—if he kicks the ball any closer.

Alexei's so close now, and his next kick so hard that, before Chaim has a chance to duck the ball bounces off his head. Turning his back to Alexei, Chaim runs toward the ball and, about to pick it up, spots a sharp fist-sized stone against which the ball has come to rest. But before Chaim can grab it, Alexei is on top of him,

They wrestle frantically, clinging to each other, a tug of war and test of wills, both afraid to let go.

Desperate to prevent Alexei from doing any damage to him with his fists, Chaim squeezes Alexei's head as hard as he can, struggling just to maintain a grip as much as trying to hurt him. He knows how truly tough he is. He's seen him beat boys bigger than he.

Stuck beneath Chaim's headlock, Alexei seems to be half-consoling himself with his bear-hug, as though clinging to Chaim's body is helping him forget what his father has done to Chaim's.

For a few moments, Chaim too, consoled by Alexei's closeness, feels a little less forlorn. Lumped together, they roll this way and that on the ground. It's as though in struggling to both console themselves and cripple the other with their grips the two are locked in a single heap, each terrified of letting go, not only for fear of the pummelling that might follow, but for the feeling of aloneness and vulnerability their fathers have wrought for them.

But, alas, this strained moral support does not last as Alexei, squeezing Chaim's stomach for all he's worth, breaks free of Chaim's grip and begins flailing away at him with his fists, a loose cannon lashing out, perhaps as furious with himself as with Chaim.

"Didn't I warn you what would happen?"

Chaim tries to counter Alexei with a mad flurry of his own. Alexei, the bigger and stronger of the two, manages to twist and get Chaim in a headlock. Clutching Chaim's neck in the crook of one arm he pounds away with his free fist. Chaim bucks like a mad bull, trying to shake Alexei. But the boy is gripping Chaim's neck so tightly he's making it hard for him to breathe.

As desperate to put an end to this battle as Chaim is to breathe, Alexei shouts: "You stop I'll stop! You don't I don't!"

Gasping for air, barely able to muster enough breath to communicate he's choking, Chaim is afraid he's going to be beaten to death and no one will care, certainly not the Cossacks or cops. His father knew what was going to happen to him, but couldn't avoid it. Now Chaim feels he's going to suffer the same fate. Recalling his father's last words to him, Chaim is determined not to leave his family not only without a father, but without their oldest son. With a burst of will, he struggles to stretch his arm out, reach for and grab the sharp fist-size stone beside the soccer ball and, with one fierce blow to his temple, Alexei goes limp.

Spent, struggling to catch his breath, Chaim stumbles to his feet. One moment so scared he's shivering, the next in a calm cold sweat, nothing seems familiar. Nothing feels the same. It's dark for this time of day. As if night's come too soon. Before it's supposed to. It smells different too. Like blood. He should get Alexei to a hospital. To a doctor, at least. Or a doctor to him. But what good would it do? He's dead. He's sure he's dead. And if he isn't, if he doesn't die, he could tell who tried to kill him. Better to make sure he's dead. But he doesn't have the heart to hit him again.

No Jewish boy can kill the son of a Cossack and get away with it. Even if they can't prove it was Chaim, they're bound to suspect him, bound to suspect all Jewish boys.

He's got to run. Convince his mother they have to go. Go somewhere, anywhere. They're probably going to come after his whole family. Specially when the Cossack finds out what's happened to his son. He'll know who did it. For sure he'll know.

* * *

Her home crammed with *shtetlers* trying to calm and console her, my grandmother struggles to express what she wants for her husband, but can only stumble over her words. Someone hands her a glass of tea with a cube of sugar. She drinks it slowly, but can't swallow. As gently and discreetly as she can—showing she still has some dignity left—she lets what's left in her mouth roll back into the glass.

Chaim's two younger siblings look more stunned than sad, more lost than mournful as, her mouth barely able to utter a consoling word or sound, my grandmother's hands try to soothe them. But, as though spastic, her hands won't stop shaking. She feels like she's going to vomit, but can't let herself, lest leaving the two youngest for a few moments to rush to the kitchen sink will upset them too much. And, even if she wanted to move she can't: for her legs seem to be suffering some sort of paralysis, struggling to move, but unable to. Cloistered as the three of them are in a cocoon of mutual consolation, all Chaim's mother can do is cling to the two little ones, as though, without their support, she would keel over.

* * *

Outside, trembling as he reaches for the doorknob, Chaim inches open the front door of his home. A strange sense of relief comes over him: at least he doesn't have to break the news to his mother. What's more, he doesn't have to tell her he's witnessed what happened. But how to explain his torn shirt, bruised and bloodstained face?

As the front door closes my grandmother feels a cold wave of fear in the pit of her stomach, a cold wave of fear through her whole body, as though the angel of death has just entered. But it's her son. Her head is spinning, dazed by his dishevelled appearance alongside a fleeting image of the angel of death. As Chaim steps into the room, it goes quiet. But the quieter it becomes the more it feels filled with fear.

Chaim has never seen his mother so distraught. Teetering between struggling to hold herself together for the sake of her two youngest and lapsing into a state of complete despair, she looks like a mad woman. She may not be able to contain her short bursts of sobbing but, to reassure Chaim's little brother and sister as they cling to her, she manages to quickly stifle them.

The instant she throws her arms around him Chaim begins weeping and she too feels a brief sense of relief that she doesn't have to break the news to him. He seems to know. Rumours spread as quickly as tuberculosis among schoolchildren.

* * *

That evening, the house not quite so full of *shtetlers*, the atmosphere, though sombre, is more serene, at least on the surface. Now my grandmother is much more matter of fact, not only aware that she has to deal with her situation, but determined to do so.

Hugging Chaim, she can feel his fear. He's not sobbing, just shaking ever so slightly. Maybe he's afraid what happened to his father will happen to him, or her, or all of them? No, why should he think such a thing? He probably doesn't know what to think.

But something keeps troubling Chaim's mother, something, in shock, she did not have the wherewithal to cope with earlier. And then, as though thinking aloud, wasn't prepared for her own question, the words pop out of her mouth:

"How did you get all those marks on your face? And your shirt?"

Taken aback, Chaim doesn't quite know what to say, starts to cry. He got into a fight at school, then on the way home from school, he keeps changing his story. To his mother it's obvious he isn't telling the truth, certainly not the whole truth. Finally, unable to hide both horrible experiences, and desperate to divert his mother from what he feels is the more terrible, that he'd watched his father being hacked to death and was too scared to say or do something to save him, between spates of sobbing he manages to weave a coherent white lie about the events leading up to the fight with Alexei.

Knowing something terrible was about to take place, he and Alexei had decided to skip school, hide together on their soccer field. But while there they'd got into an argument over who was responsible for the trouble between their fathers. Chaim was never one to start a fight, but Alexei kept piling insult upon insult, and when he called Chaim's father a dirty crooked Kike, that was the last straw. He warned Alexei to take it back. But he wouldn't. So Chaim jumped on him.

Finally, Chaim wails out the truth: "I killed him! I killed my best friend! It was an accident but he was choking me, had me gasping for air, and I was afraid I was going to die so I reached for a stone and hit him on the head! I didn't know what else to do!"

Everyone in the house is horrified. Those who'd earlier been trying to calm my grandmother are now frantic and, along with other *shtetlers*, expressing fear for their lives. Adamant that it's no use having people there who only exacerbate her family's fear, Chaim's mother raises her voice: "If you can't help better you shouldn't be here!"

That manages to silence the other *shtetlers*. She then struggles to comfort Chaim. How can she know that he may be crying not for what he's done to Alexei, nor simply for the death of his father, but for what he didn't do to try to save my grandfather. Chaim can't be sure himself. In such an all-consuming state, how can he be? His mother keeps reassuring him and his little brother and sister that as long as they have each other, they'll be all right. And, since Chaim is the oldest, the man in the family now, he has to act like one, help her take care of his siblings. There will be time for more tears. But not now.

"That will just keep upsetting the little ones," she whispers in Chaim's ear.

Chaim feels somewhat relieved. Somehow he's managed to summon the wherewithal to conceal one shame with another, use a half truth about one to keep from having to out and out lie about the other.

* * *

However, this pair of deceptions would take their toll. Had my father been able to confess to his mother, she might have convinced him that whether he'd confided in the Cossack's son or not, whether he'd used that angry admonishing long distance look from his father as an excuse to hide instead of crying out to spare him, there was nothing he could have done. Hell bent on freeing himself from the grip of those determined to squeeze the life out of his business, his father had sealed his own fate.

Instead, by the time my father was old enough to understand this, the feeling he was at fault had been with him so long, been driven so deep, it couldn't be uprooted. Assigning blame may be the result of rational deliberation in a court of law, but the court of individual conscience may not need true cause. A minor, though deemed not mature enough to be tried in an authentic tribunal may, in his own private one, judge himself more harshly than any jury. And so it was that my father the boy sentenced the man he would become to the prison of despair for life.

* * *

Next morning, only a handful of *shtetlers* remain in the Blittstein home —all women—cooking breakfast, clearing the table, cleaning the kitchen, taking care of the youngest children. In the living room, Chaim sits watching his mother search through a box of her husband's papers when, without knocking, a group of male *shtetlers* burst into the room, among them a notorious gossip-peddler. They'd missed this massacre—or, more likely, because no one could talk 'sense' into Chaim's father, they'd turned a blind eye and deaf ear. Still, *shtetlers* had a grapevine, a way of keeping their ear to the ground for gossip that helped them survive. And this man was its key practitioner.

"We have good news and bad," the breathless intruder exclaims.

The others gather round him like he's a messenger from the Almighty.

"The good news is, though he's been badly beaten, the Cossack boy is alive, and going to be okay."

As though someone has just let the air out of the enormous balloon in which they've been encased, there's a deep collective sigh of relief.

Whether it's a boy's macho code you don't snitch or go whining to your parents when you lose a fight, or that he was embarrassed to admit he'd been beaten by a Jew, or that he felt so badly for what his father had done to Chaim's, the Cossack boy had refused to betray his friend.

Suffused with shame, Chaim tearfully confesses he'd been confused. He'd thought he'd killed Alexei, left him there for dead, but maybe not. Yet he didn't know what else to do! He couldn't run for help, a Jew beating a Gentile, specially a Cossack's son, they would have killed him on the spot, come after his family!

"The bad news," the messenger announces, "is they refuse to return Beryl for burial. And if you ask they'll ask 'Are you accusing our Cossacks, the most dear loyal protectors of the Tsar, law and order?'"

"There must be witnesses? Some who've survived?" one of the *shtetl* elders asks.

"You expect witnesses? There's no witnesses. And there won't be any witnesses. There may be survivors but survivors aren't witnesses. And they won't be. Not if they want to keep surviving."

"If I don't claim his body he'll be buried in a mass grave, or worse, cremated," Chaim's mother says moaning.

"Better you should remember him as he was," a *shtetl* elder says. "As you'd like to remember him."

"The least I can do for him, for our family, is have a funeral."

The *shtetl* elder warns she'll only be making more trouble for her family, for the whole *shtetl*.

"There's already been a burial," the gossip-peddler says. "All the bodies together. What're you going to do, ask them to dig it up? How're you going to identify him, in pieces? You want to pick through a bunch of bodies which pieces are part of your Beryl and which not?"

Responding more to their mother's state than the man's words, clinging to each other as well as their mother, Chaim, his brother and sister now form a protective ring around her, as though they're consoling her rather than the other way around.

Chaim's mother keeps trying to cover her children's ears with her arms. But, determined to bolster his case, the rumourmonger keeps up his verbal barrage.

"They wanted to send a message, they sent a message. To the black market it's loud and clear. They made sure it was loud and clear. But to the rest of the world it never happened. The message is it didn't happen. You poking your nose in you want them to send a message to you too?"

Pushed over the edge by the gossip-peddler's words, Chaim's mother can't hold back.

"Better it should have been your body, than my Beryl's!"

Oblivious to her insult, the gossip-peddler continues: "They can do with you what they want too. You want your children should be without a mother it's not bad enough already they're without a father? Like they'd just butchered a bunch of birds for pooping in the plaza, to make sure it couldn't come back to haunt them, they've whitewashed it clean as a whistle. Even if orders came from the Tsar, there's nothing to investigate. They swept up all the bird-poop and blood. Don't think they'll hesitate to butcher you too, chop you into little pieces and feed you to the pigeons."

Trying to moderate the mood in the room, one of the elders pleads:

"Enough. Please, for your sake, for you family's sake, for the sake of the children, for the sake of all of us, let sleeping dogs lie."

"My husband's not an animal. I won't let him be buried like one."

"We have a minyan here we can say Kaddish. We don't have to have the body to say Kaddish."

"If the Almighty let this happen to my husband why should I pray to him, praise him with Kaddish? To hell with the Almighty He should let such horrors happen to my husband!"

Some of the *shtetlers* are horrified, emitting a collective gasp.

My father's atheism only really took root later in life, a delayed reaction to what he'd heard and witnessed that day. But my grandmother's angry impiety had put the first nail in the coffin of belief handed down to my father by his. Especially when some of the other *shtetlers* began blaming my grandfather for leading his black market lambs to slaughter. The shame Chaim felt for doing nothing to save his father or friend was promptly overshadowed by the fury he felt at these *shtetlers*. His mother was even more furious. The last thing she needed were these grovelers blaming her husband for the massacre! In front of the children no less! Now, not only did she feel they had to get out of this miserable *shtetl,* they had to get out of this farshtunkene country!

* * *

No Russian Jew ever felt safe or secure. They knew they were at the mercy of their Gentile neighbours. Thus, even those barely able to make ends meet always saved for a rainy day, when the Russian climate for Jews would take a turn for the worse, force them to flee for their lives. So, to add to the kopecks they'd saved in a jar hidden under a kitchen floorboard for just such an occasion, my grandmother began selling off their family's personal belongings and my grandfather's black market merchandise at bargain prices. She accumulated just enough money to pay the family's way out of Russia and, in the ensuing fog of war, through the southern Balkans before embarking for Greece. Eventually, after another long torturous and tortuous route, they crossed the Atlantic ocean to Ellis Island, and from there made their way north to Montreal.

His family would escape Russia, but my father would never escape the fingers pointed at his father by fellow *shtetlers*. His faith in the small world of the *shtetl*, along with the bubble of belief in its God, had burst, punctured by those *shtetlers'* black marks of blame. Even as he refused to believe in him, for the rest of his days my father would hold a grudge against God. As would my grandmother. She'd refuse to let her son have a bar mitzvah. Knowing how his father would feel, my father would experience twinges of regret.

While his boyhood belief that both his father and God would always be there for him had died, and he no longer had faith in either to hold on to, their absence would haunt him.

GRAVE II

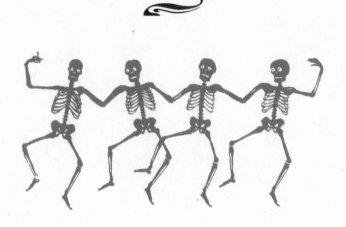

Chapter 1

INITIALLY, LIFE IN North America came as a shock to my then eight-year-old father, his mother and two younger siblings. But they soon adjusted. My grandmother not only ran the home and raised the children, especially the two youngest, she worked full time selling fabric on Montreal's 'shmatah strip,' St. Lawrence Boulevard, also known as The Main. The area surrounding it was the first immigrant stop in their step up the steep socioeconomic ladder to the suburbs.

My grandmother didn't speak English or French. Fortunately, most of the store's customers were immigrants who spoke Yiddish. With someone who spoke only English or French, she used her hands, facial expressions and emphatic Yiddish exclamations and somehow managed to understand and make herself understood.

"When there's a will there's a way," she would say. In Yiddish. And though it loses something in the translation, it was never lost on her that hard work would pay off, her children would finish school and go to college, become doctors or lawyers.

Unfortunately, she died of a stroke the year after my father started high school and he had to go to work to support himself and his younger brother and sister. Raise them too. He'd been looking after himself, his younger brother and sister while my grandmother was working, and now became responsible for them full time, a father more than a brother.

The cousins who'd given my grandmother a job did the same for my fourteen-year-old father. Not only that, they 'took the children in.' That meant renting their one bedroom basement suite to my father and his siblings at a 'bargain price' and looking in on them every once in a while. Mostly leaving them on their own.

Desperate to survive, support his siblings and free the three of them from their cousins' yoke, while still working at the store my father began to build up a business, selling quilts made from store 'leftovers of leftovers' on the side. These textile remnants were too small a quantity to be worth taking up shelf space in the store. At least so my father convinced his cousins.

What he didn't say was that they could be used to make quilts. And that my father had hired a couple of other young immigrants to do just that. Soon, business was booming. My father couldn't keep up with the demand and had to hire more young immigrants. Before you knew it he had his own little sweatshop that sold to specialty stores.

Without emotional support and despite the anguish he still suffered—perhaps because of it—he was driven to succeed. And over the ensuing decades he did.

Marriage and children may have provided my father with some solace. But they also allowed him to indulge his anguish. And this is where my story truly begins.

Chapter 2

FOR MOST OF my life I've had to battle a debilitating sense of despair. Stemming from the grief in my home growing up, but amassed over so many generations of bloodletting, it's been embedded in my bones.

Now, one generation's emotional legacy though strictly-speaking not genetic, may be passed down to the next with just as powerful and certain an impact as if embedded in DNA. Indeed, emotional heritage may be more deeply planted in our bodies than any double helix, parents affecting infants before they're able to protect themselves.

From diffuse anxiety to straight-forward fear, sinking spirits to flat out despair, mild amusement to ecstatic joy, my father was a veritable maestro of unchecked emotions. At times it was hard to discern his state: oscillating from elation to despair, he seemed suspended between the two. Unlike typical manic-depressives my father was most manic when most depressed, expressing his deepest despair with real flair: crying, wailing, beating his chest with the fervour of a mad euphoric, emitting such high-pitched wails dogs next door would respond with their own.

My first encounters with my father's confusing complexity of emotions must have been as an infant. When a parent suffused with anxiety picks up his newborn, his newborn picks it up. Granted that both the parent and baby's bodies may pacify each other, but an unbalanced transference takes place: at the same time as the undeveloped infant's agitation is eased, it absorbs some of its father's more firmly entrenched turbulence. You can't fool an infant with false smiles or fawning words. It can feel the fear behind the facial mask.

My father would often feel a desperate a need to cling to my twin sister and me, to hug us, not only because he loved us so, but because holding us seemed to help keep his demons at bay. When we were babies, he would often snuggle in bed with us. Cradling my sister and me in his arms, he'd sing us to sleep. Then he'd fall asleep.

Now and then, holding my little sister or me, tears welling up in his eyes, my father's joy seemed to trigger his sorrow. I could tell from the way he clutched us, at times squeezing so tight it hurt, his sighs of relief fading into fear that something might happen to us, take away his fleeting happiness.

* * *

As a young child, I was sometimes shocked out of my sleep in the middle of the night by a shriek so high-pitched and piercing, the first time I heard it I was sure my sister was having a nightmare. But she wasn't. It was my father, in the voice of a child, shouting for his father in Yiddish "Tateh! Tateh!" with the power only an adult could project.

Neither my sister nor I were yet of school age, too young to know the significance of our father's cries, but we did understand that our father had been crying out for his. When you're young you rely on your father to be some sort of rock, a fortress protecting you against the vagaries of this world.

Oh the harsh disappointment when you discover that the closest thing to god here on earth, your father, is flawed, and filled with fear, so filled with his own he can't assuage yours.

* * *

From the moment my daughter was born I was at the beck and call of her every emotion. When a baby cries what can you do but console? Evolution has programmed parents to put the emotional well-being of their infants above their own. Because my father seemed unable to, I tried to make sure I was.

From the time she took her first baby steps, my little girl and I seemed to have a reciprocal agreement: whenever she felt sad or afraid she would reach her arms up for me; whenever I was either unhappy or anxious, I would reach my arms down for her. Was I using my daughter? Transferring my anxiety to her? I don't think so. I certainly hope not. Was she using me? I certainly hope so. What are fathers for? Perhaps parents and children have been put on this planet to pacify each other.

In my sometimes frantic need to find sanctuaries of affection with my daughter, might I have emulated my father's grasping for straws of solace, clinging to someone too young to cope? If so, could I have planted anxiety in my daughter as my father did in me? And would that lead her to avoid danger like I do or, like my late sister, chase it?

Once again, I'm getting ahead of myself here. Way ahead.

* * *

Because my father never made clear what part he did or did not play in his father's death, and all his efforts to avoid the subject—evasions that began the moment the horror happened—my family history has always felt like an unfinished film, one missing key pieces, trying to complete itself in the dim editing room of my unconscious.

We all have blacked out parts of the brain, creepy crawlies of the unconscious buried so deep they only surface asleep. And, while dozing, my dreams have always been as randomly nonsensical bits and pieces as most people's. Awake, though my visions are as real and intense as any nightmare, they are neither random nor nonsensical. In fact, these snippets of scenes, however short, always make sense, seem to be part of a larger linear narrative. And I'm never more vividly conscious than when they materialize.

Fortunately, as with dreams of one's own death—above all murder —that one can never quite contemplate to completion, so, when it comes to the most horrific of visions, terrifying scenes of incipient mutilation, I've been confined to the anticipation, the split second before the fatal blow. No matter how hard I tried not to, I snapped out of them. My father couldn't face his father's final moments. Neither, it seems, could I.

To try and figure out what made me tick, my parents sent me to see a shrink. Lest he think I had a screw loose or worse, refuse to believe me, I was determined not to let him know where my mind went when it wandered. I let him think I just liked to daydream. Which was true. Or half true. I wasn't nuts about these trances. In fact, I was afraid I might be nuts period.

As these short vivid visits to another epoch became more frequent, breaking through the present with such power from the past, I became terrified. Was I actually losing my mind, suffering from some kind of aberration? Afraid to share my trances with anyone but my sister, she'd listen intently as I recounted them to her.

"Boy, you really are a nutcase! But a lucky one! I'd love to be in such great company! The company of the greats!"

She then rattled off the names of what she referred to as mystical geniuses. Alas, unlike Joan of Arc, Moses or the others whose names she so enthusiastically cited, I never experienced gods or angels. But at least she sympathized with me, and supported me in my insanity, convinced me that lapsing into these transcendent states was nothing to make a big deal about. Everybody had their idiosyncrasies. I was just your normal neurotic who, ill at ease in this world, from time to time found solace in another.

"You don't have to be here if you don't want, you just have to pretend to be." Words of wisdom from a precocious eight-year-old to her late-blooming twin.

And that was all the approval I needed.

* * *

Shy and introverted though I was, I used to blurt out family secrets to strangers, in stores, on the streets, everywhere. My father never seemed to mind. I'm not sure if it was because he wasn't bothered by the impropriety or, preoccupied with whatever was on his mind, was oblivious to it.

My mother, on the other hand, face flushed like it had just been dipped in a bowl of borscht, would turn and, with a sheepish smile, give the stranger an 'Oh-what-nonsense-the-imagination-of-young-kids-can-concoct' shake of the head.

Then, embarrassment unmitigated, she'd whisk me away with an angry: "You have a big mouth for a little boy."

My sister was the only one who knew how to handle me. In a store or the street, whenever we were about to pass strangers, should she hear me inhale, getting ready to spout, she'd beat me to it with a playful: "Our lips sealed, little brother, our lips sealed."

I'd never been officially diagnosed as such, and curse words were never part of my vocabulary, but my sister decided I had a G-rated touch of Tourette's Syndrome.

How'd she know about such an exotic disease at such a young age? The same as other esoterica: *Encyclopaedia Britannica*.

· I doubt either of my parents ever opened a single one of the set's books. But they looked good lining the living room shelves along with the complete collection of abridged *Reader's Digest* novels.

But that was not the reason the salesman had convinced my parents to buy the set. Nor was his pitch that it was essential to their children's education. No. The sales-clinching coup de grace came when the man pulled out pictures of his children. Filled with sympathy for a don't-take-no-for-an-answer negotiator like himself, my father pleaded with my mother: "How can you not have *rachmones* for a man who, to support his family, is forced to go door-to-door like a poor peddler?"

As a child, Maya so often used knowledge from the encyclopaedia to provoke my parents, I'm sure they rued the day they bought it.

* * *

Gradually, as I learned to let go of my fear, the brief flashes began to give way to longer interludes. During these lucid daydreams, I was aware of where I was, that, neither awake nor asleep, I'd simply lapsed into a state I could snap myself out of if I so wished, whenever I so wished. But I rarely chose to do so. I was conscious of my 'real' surroundings, yet immersed in my apparition, more intense and iridescent than material reality, as though I was under the influence of some powerful hallucinogen.

As I grew older, these spells became rarer and less pronounced. Still, a little ADD can go a long way. The line between so-called reality and dreams has always been blurry for me, but I've learned to navigate it so that, though I may be out of my mind, I don't appear out of place. I don't mutter to myself or drool. Casually, as though nothing untoward is happening, I'm just the preoccupied absent-minded professor.

My mother used to say she could tell I was a dreamer while still in her belly. She never used the word womb. Too risqué. Too risky too. Excessively close to conversations that to her were taboo. I tried to pin down not only how she knew but when. Was it before or after I was a fully formed foetus. That word rattled her more than womb. The messy business of giving birth appeared to offend her prudish sensibilities. Had she not been Jewish she might have tried to convince me I was the product of an immaculate conception.

No matter how stubbornly I persisted in trying to pin down how she knew, all she would say was: "I knew. Don't ask me how, I knew. A mother knows." Her mantra to most questions my sister and I put to her as kids. The tenses might change, but the essence remained: a mother is infallible, blessed with a form of maternal omniscience, one beyond questioning.

My sister and I learned early on that, even if we could puncture holes in her claims, there was little we could do to convince her, not without her lapsing into a state of exasperated silence, as though we were calling into question not only her authority as our mother but her integrity, intelligence and, above all, intuition. Intuition didn't need explanation. It defied and transcended reason. What she knew she knew in ways my sister and I wouldn't understand. Neither would her husband. She used the same tactic on him as often as she did on us.

Anyway, though others may have seen my daydreaming as a way of escaping this world, over the years I've begun to realize that it may be a means of immersing myself more deeply in it, going beyond the present to some lingering residue of long ago to which it is linked. Sucked into such time warps, I'm not so much dreaming as remembering.

Early on family and friends learned to accept that I was a bit of an oddball, someone whose attention might suddenly wander. Where, they didn't know. Nor why. Neither did I. Some relatives thought it a trait I'd inherited from my father. My uncle Izzy would often say: "The apple never falls far from the tree." Others: "The boy marches to a different drummer." And I did.

Still, it was no secret that my father often appeared distracted. It used to upset me that whenever I talked to him, his mind elsewhere, his eyes had that faraway look. But he wasn't having visions, intensely immersed in another reality. As someone well-versed in the latter, I knew the difference.

It must have tormented my father more than it did me, but he refused to relive his past. I couldn't avoid it. My relationships with women later in life might have lasted longer had I been more forthright about my visions. But afraid of scaring them away, I kept them hidden. Of course, sooner or later that secretiveness, along with my many other idiosyncrasies, scared most of them away. My teenage sweetheart being the exception—I ended that relationship.

Some of my most awkward moments with women occurred on first dates when, in the midst of seductive chit chat, I'd suddenly have a powerful flash from that other period. What could I do but surrender to it? It overwhelmed the present, obliterated it. Sophia Loren could have been seated opposite me, my psyche simply didn't give a shit.

Once, while clinking glasses of Chateau Latour with a winsome graduate student I'd had my eye on for a long time, out of the blue I was back in Odessa, watching my father wrestle the Cossack's son. Was this my unconscious wreaking havoc on my love life, sabotaging the relationship before it started, subjecting me to a lesser pain now than the one I would experience breaking up after a co-dependent bond had been established? Maybe there was method to my madness, a wisdom in my unconscious. Because the same thing happened on several subsequent first dates. Perhaps that's why, in old age, I'm still single.

Anyway, I never told my father about my daymares. They would have shaken him to his core. Some of them certainly shook me. As did my father's bed-ridden moods.

* * *

A bright autumn afternoon, leaves in peak multi-colour bloom, just beginning to fall. Orange, red, yellow and magenta everywhere. Cool, crisp, not a cloud in the sky. Or me. Skipping home from school, all of six or seven, I'm floating on my feet, feeling elated. Must be the hint of frost, the slight whiff of winter in the air.

I love winter. Always have. Fall too. Soon as it turns cold. I'm not much for hot sweaty summers. Must be my Russian roots. My father was a cold fresh air fiend, often drove with the convertible top down in the middle of the Montreal winter, and always kept his driver's car window open, no matter how frigid the air outside. Same story in his bedroom at night. My parents slept with the window slightly open all winter. It could get so chilly in their bedroom snow would accumulate on the inside window sill and not melt until the window was closed in the morning. So I thought my father would have been feeling pretty good on such a brisk fall day. He loved the cold. And it was close to freezing outside, specially in the shade.

But, as I stepped through the front door of our home, I could hear my father's oy yoy yoy yoy yoy yoy yoy, sobbing ever so softly to himself, helpless sounds of sadness.

I immediately got that sinking feeling, the butterflies in the belly. So much for feeling good. I could tell my mother wasn't home, and my father didn't yet know I was. I peeked into his bedroom: the middle of a weekday afternoon, and he's in bed!

"What's wrong, dad?"

"Nothing, son. Just a little blue today."

* * *

Whereas I struggled to make sense of my father's remorse via endless rumination, my sister, determined to experience life straight, no chaser, kept flinging herself body and soul into the middle of its maelstrom. Until she became its casualty.

Biologically, we may have been twins. But by the age of ten my sister could pass for twenty, older with lipstick and eyeliner. My face a parade of pimples and peach fuzz throughout my teens, I couldn't pass for twenty till I was thirty, and still get asked for ID at bars.

Growing up she'd tease me. "You're my baby brother, and I'm your big sister."

And she was: born ten minutes before midnight, I, ten after, we celebrated our births on different days. She insisted.

The reason for the twenty minute hiatus was never clear, other than there were complications with me. What they were I never found out. I'm not sure my parents knew. In those days doctors didn't feel compelled to elaborate.

But my Aunt Bessy did. "You were afraid to leave your mother's cozy whatchamacallit. Maya couldn't wait to get the hell out!"

Alas, I was a misfit the moment I exited my mother's womb. My sister took much longer. Since she could read like a second or third grader, she was allowed to skip kindergarten, go straight to first grade. And in third grade, because her reading, writing and math were superior to her peers, she was allowed to skip to fourth.

Expelled one year for drifting off in class and not doing homework, I was still a high-school sophomore when my sister went off to college.

* * *

For my father, like most upwardly mobile old-country Jews, education was the passport to success. And my expulsion from school alarmed him.

How serious was the offence that lead to my banishment? Did I steal from the school library? Spew obscenities at my teacher? Beat smaller boys?

No, the closest I came to making waves in school, a stark contrast to my sister's enthusiastic shit-disturbing there, was to arrive late almost everyday. My circadian rhythm just didn't mesh with the school clock's. And once I did arrive, I'd retire to an alternate universe.

Flashbacks to parental history aside, my mind's always been prone to meandering, being anywhere but where I was. It's not that I refused to let the straightjacket of school stop me from daydreaming, it's that I couldn't.

It began when I first encountered the pearly gates of that prison, those dark brown doors at the bottom of a short set of cement stairs down which, as though it was to death itself, I feared descending.

Crying, kicking and screaming, I refused to enter that kindergarten basement. At that age I could not have articulated my fear, but I certainly sensed that once those doors shut behind me my days of free all-day play would be over. Ensconced in the drudging discipline of school meant being sentenced to a life of constant supervision by authorities who'd forbid me from fantasizing. And I'd die if I couldn't. In a sense, I was fighting for my life.

I'd have nightmares in which, unable to move, barely able to breathe, my body encased in cement, metal bars running through me, I was not merely in prison, I was part of its wall.

After staying home for weeks, with neither my sister or kids my age to play with, I got bored and gave in. Of course, once I started school I wasn't allowed to stop. So I got used to it, the way one gets used to living with elephantiasis. But I never learned to like it. Or stop daydreaming. Which got me into constant hot water with teachers. Wishing I could sleep till noon like my father, all I wanted to do was anything but what I was doing. How could my father be allowed to log Z's as long as he liked and I couldn't? He had a business to run, I didn't. It didn't seem fair.

Nevertheless, with my teachers complaining that I wouldn't pay attention in class and the principal expelling me for being late everyday, my father was at his wit's end.

In those days corporal punishment of your kids was not a crime. In fact, it was quite fashionable. But only that once did my father ever hit me, chasing me round my bedroom, wildly swinging at me with his belt, crying and shouting: "It hurts me more than it hurts you! I don't know what else to do! It hurts me more than it hurts you!"

He kept aiming for my buttocks, the traditional spanking spot. I may have been passive, but I couldn't stand pain, and refused to hold still long enough for him to hit me where he wanted. Unlike my sister, who'd take our family's internecine warfare into the streets and, out of embarrassment, force my parents to back off, I didn't have the heart to humiliate my father, wouldn't even force him to chase me round the house.

Perhaps I thought I had to take my punishment like a man. Or, unlike my extroverted sister, I, an introvert, preferred to keep my humiliation within the confines of my own bedroom. Still, I refused to stay in one spot. So as I rolled this way and that on the bed, darted round the room, more often than not, he'd miss my backside, strike my arm or hand. But I was so quick and adept at scooting out of harm's way, and my father so blind with rage and tears, his strap would hit the wall, bed or chest of drawers as often as it struck me. Yet when it did, even if it was just the tip of the strap, it would sting. Oh how it would sting.

Yet what hurt most was seeing my father so beside himself, not only with anger, but sorrow. I could deal with his anger. But his heartbreaking mixture upset me more than the beating. I could tell he didn't want to hurt me, that his heart wasn't in it. But he didn't know what else to do.

Finally, he stopped trying to hit me, broke down sobbing, striking the mattress with the strap, over and over, as though attempting to exorcize both his anger and hurt. Wheezing like he was having an asthma attack, gasping for breath, his tirade had come to an end. Crouched below a window against the farthest wall, my heart still pumping full speed, I kept watching as my father caught his breath then, without saying a word to me, without looking my way, as though sleepwalking, just stared into space as he slowly made his way to the bedroom door. It seemed as though, to escape the hurt of striking me, his mind had slipped away, to somewhere else.

But, after stepping into the hall, he stopped, slowly turned to me and, tears in his eyes, said: "I built up a business you shouldn't have to go through what I went through, please don't waste it sleeping through school." He looked so forlorn as he shut the door, it stung.

* * *

I don't know which was more humiliating, the spanking, my father's subsequent crying in front of my teacher, pleading "My Velvel's a good boy," or winking as he pulled a can of pipe tobacco out of his coat pocket to help convince my school principal to take me back, not expel me.

Taken aback at the blatant bribery, the principal reacted to the tobacco like it was some kind of too-hot-to-handle contraband. But my father would have none of it. And so I watched, half mortified, half amused as, like a couple of drug dealers, each trying to foist cannabis on the other before the cops burst into the room, they pushed the can back and forth. As the poor can seesawed back and forth between them, my father's sales pitch in favour of me kept escalating in volume.

"My Velvel's a smart boy, maybe too smart for his own good. He likes to daydream, what can you do? He's better off here than at home. Believe me the boy's better off here. At least here he absorbs. Even he's dreaming he absorbs. Believe me he absorbs. He makes like he doesn't but he does. At home what's to absorb? Here, he absorbs. "

Finally, to stop the physical contest of wills along with the torrent of repetitious phrases from my father, the principal agreed to take me back, along with the can of pipe tobacco.

Fear of further embarrassment by my father caused me to pay attention in class, at least try to, for a little while. But it wasn't long before I fell back to my old mind-wandering ways. I could no more stop daydreaming in class than my father could stop weeping in front of strangers.

* * *

Diagnosed with borderline dyslexia, ADD, depression and an IQ in the low 80s, I didn't perform well under pressure. Forced to read some inane story aloud in class I'd stutter and stumble. However, alone at home I could devour a dozen-page chapter on Darwin in minutes. Nevertheless, consumed by anxiety, I couldn't concentrate on homework or cram for exams. I'd fall asleep or read other stuff, everything from fantasy fiction to popular science rags on relativity and quantum mechanics which, though meant for a lay audience, I could hardly wrap my head around. I still can't. Yet I'd savour every sentence.

Not forced to memorize what was in these pieces, deal with details, do calculations, come up with right or wrong answers, the joy lay in just getting a general feel for the material, dreaming big, imagining universes other than our own. Grand theories I could grasp. Simple equations I could not. My math skills began and ended with simple arithmetic, at which I was a whiz.

Teachers couldn't tell whether I was brilliant or a dunce. Neither could I. Forced to take part in class, like some asleep-for-a-century Rip Van Winkle, I'd snap out of my stupor with non sequiturs that on the surface might seem related to the subject matter, but had little connection to the specific question.

Instead of a straightforward response to a calculation concerning Newton's third law—for every action there's an equal and opposite reaction—I asked how we know the whole universe is not some kind of net, strings pulled by forces we can't begin to fathom.

When it came to evolution, I argued the world wasn't old enough for a random series of accidents to lead to something as complicated as us. There must be powers pulling the strings that shape us. My loony string theories were so far out in left field they must have reinforced the belief that I was some sort of best-disregarded religious nut.

I didn't know what I was talking about, but it certainly wasn't god. Biblical time lines made no sense to me. Not when taken literally. Literarily, that's another story.

* * *

During my father's breakdowns—and in between too—my sister became my harbour, though not always a safe one, especially when we were little.

As a young boy, I was scared of the bogeyman under my bed. My mother offered to leave a light on till I fell asleep. But when I woke during the night to pee, too afraid of the dark to get to the bathroom, I'd wet my bed.

My parents tried putting in a night light, a tiny bulb that plugged directly into the electricity socket. But that only made the room more eerie, and it was still dark under my bed. The bed-wetting continued.

Finally, my sister came up with the solution. All we had to do to was leave a tiny light on *under* my bed.

"Just like we're afraid of the dark where we live, bogeymen are afraid of the light where they live. Under beds."

Her world as skewed as mine, and she elaborated with such conviction, I was convinced. My parents were not.

"It's crazy! Who puts a light on under the bed? It could catch fire!"

The bed-wetting persisted, until finally my parents paid an electrician to "hook up something safe."

Still, light or not, I never got over my fright. But knowing my sister was in the bedroom next to mine made the fear bearable. Yet with the following fire game, my sister burnt small a hole in that security blanket.

* * *

A late autumn morning. There are few leaves left on the trees. My sister and I are out chasing them as a cold winter-heralding wind whips them round our backyard. The sky is clear blue, the air is so crisp I can almost taste the coming of snow. The happiest time of year for me. For my father too. The Russian in him loved the cold. A big fur and leather Ushanka hat on his head, its flaps tied over his ears, he'd take long winter walks with my mother. Ice cold air and freshly fallen snow seemed to be the one true love they shared. Other than my sister and me. The two of us loved winter too, not only because our parents would take us tobogganing, but because they seemed almost happy doing it.

Of course, we'd have more fun playing in the snow alone, just the two of us, sans supervision. Freed from parental warnings that we'd take an eye out, we could fire snowballs at each other's most enticing targets, the face.

On this particular fall day the wind was blowing so, to hear each other, my sister and I had to shout. While she chased after leaves, I chased after her. Then, out of the blue, she stopped, turned, looked me in the eye and asked: "Who's the one person in this world you'd run into the house to save f'it was on fire?"

Now, we were all of five or six, old enough to know that was the kind of question kids should avoid. Most likely why my sister decided to pose it. She loved testing the boundaries of taboo. Perhaps too, she was trying to see just how much she meant to me. Not that she didn't know. But from time to time she liked a little reassurance.

I knew the question was rhetorical. That she was the obvious answer. But she'd so often monkey with me I'd long ago learned to monkey back. I took so long, pretended to be thinking so hard, that she impatiently shouted: "How can you take so long?"

"I'm thinking."

"In a fire you don't have time to think."

I could tell she was irritated. But I wasn't ready to give her what she wanted. Not right away. It was my way of conveying the unfairness of the question, and showing her I could stand my ground.

"But there's no fire now."

"If there was?"

"I'd call the firemen trucks."

"You can't call the firemen trucks."

She was getting angry now. I feared her temper, yet I enjoyed inflaming it. It was like playing with fire.

"Why not?"

"Cause the phone's in the house."

"So I'd run in."

"There's no time."

"Why not?"

"Cause the house is on fire, stupid. You've got to save one of us before it's too late."

"Why can't I just shout 'Fire!' And you all run out?"

"Cause we're all sleeping, stupid."

"I'd shout so loud I'd wake you all up."

"The game is you can only save one of us. You want to play or not?"

"Nah, not really. I don't like this game."

"Ah, you're no fun."

She started walking away from me. Afraid she was abandoning me, might refuse to play with me anymore that morning—at that age, a couple of hours is an eternity—I shouted after her: "You!"

She stopped, slowly turned back towards me and, her eyes again staring into mine, emphatically mouthed the word: "Sure?"

I nodded my head.

She shouted: "I can't hear you!"

I shouted: "Sure!"

She shouted: "Who?"

I shouted: "You!"

That's when the nightmares in which our house was on fire started. And I couldn't decide who to save. My dad was the breadwinner and I loved him. But my mom did the cooking, cleaning and took care of me. And what would I do without my sister? Who would I play with? I was too shy to make friends myself.

The flames were blocking me from all three bedrooms yet, not knowing what else to do, I kept racing up and down the hall, back and forth between each, frantically shouting "Fire!" But the crackling flames were so loud no one could hear me. And I was losing my voice, coughing from the smoke. It kept getting hotter and hotter, the flames burning higher and higher until they reached the roof, which started collapsing around me.

I'd wake from these nightmares in a cold sweat. My first inklings my parents and sister weren't immortal. I'd never dreamt of their deaths before, never imagined they could die. And rarely had nightmares asleep. Confined to my waking hours, they always took place in the remote past, never the present or future. Now, thanks to my sister, my bad dreams took on new tenses, new tensions.

And so the bed-wetting began again. Albeit not as frequently as before. My sister was forcing me to grow up.

> *My dear dear baby bro,*
>
> *I've never felt so alive. Don't think having a baby could beat it. Seeing the walls and roof of our communal bakery finally up and the ovens working would certainly be a close second. I laughed and cried and got drunk on the scent of fresh bread. Never tasted anything quite as satisfying as that first loaf.*

Yes, this is my true tribe, my big fat extended family. Think I've finally fallen in love, found the real thing, with this whole community, every last one of them. This barrio's going to become a model for others. Oh baby bro, I'm so blessed. Doing what I love, where I love, with those I love. What could be better? By the way, getting laid too. But my true love lies not with the man of the moment but with all the men, women and children in my life here. Even the ones I don't get along with. I find a way. We find a way.

I feel truly at home, truly at peace, yet I hardly get a moment's peace. The left wing guerrillas against the bakery on one side (we're co-opting these poor campesinos with a few crumbs, making a bakery the be all and end all of their politics, undermining the likelihood of a real revolution) and the right wing death squads against it on the other (it smacks of socialism) with pa's little girl in the middle. All the blood, sweat and tears it's taken to get it built, our little barrio bakery has been riddled with so many bullets some of us have begun jokingly referring to it as Panaderia Bala.

Well, these people taking control of their lives—and me taking control of mine!—is just the beginning. Feels so good, it's scary. My skin literally glows with all the sun and sweat, putting in pipes for the sewer, pumps for the well, hands raw from laying bricks. Driving that backhoe. A big toy. On the run from morning to night. From one crisis to another: pipes bursting, tools missing, families feuding.

Feels like I'm back on the kibbutz. Only better. I'm no longer a dilettante. The bullets make the stakes deadly serious.

Love you, baby bro, love you,

Maya

Nothing would snap my father out of his self-absorbed stupor, lift his spirits, however short-lived, the way my sister's shenanigans could.

She could evoke the beginning of something resembling a grin from my mother. Of course, afraid she'd only be encouraging my sister's mischief-making, my mother would quickly stifle it. Not to be outdone by my father, my mother fretted over us, but in a slyer more subdued manner.

Affection and anxiety were so intertwined in our family it was hard to tell where one began and the other ended. Embedded in that deep and desperate love, a deep and desperate fear.

And that fear was something my sister fought, would fight all her life. It showed up while she and I were wee ones, the pride she used to take in teasing our parents, pretending one of us was lost, better call the police. We were probably all of four or five the first time. And our hiding places were obvious. At least mine were. My sister's, not so much.

Our parents may have been overly protective of us, but my sister kept pushing the boundaries, insisted on expanding her horizons. It became easier to acquiesce than to try and keep her confined to the front porch or back yard. Inside the house was out of the question.

After weeks of being stuck with me constantly whining "Why Maya can play out there and I can't?" my mother finally gave in, as long as I promised to stay close to my sister and off the street. I got my way by snivelling, my sister by shrieking. She liked being deemed mature enough to be responsible for looking after me. Nevertheless, to make my mother feel indebted to her, she pretended to resent it. She was a manipulative one, certainly more so than my mother, and saw through my mother's "You're such a grown up little girl" to convince Maya to look after me. She knew it was in her interest to agree, but only after initially arguing.

Knowing how much of a daredevil Maya could be, why my mother trusted her with me is still a mystery. She probably figured it was easier to keep an eye on the two of us playing together than separately, and was glad to get me out of her hair.

She might peer out the kitchen window or appear on the front porch every once in a while, but other than that my sister and I were on our own. The sidewalk, from one end to the other of our short block, was our limit. Of course, my sister didn't like limits, or having me tied to her apron strings, but she now had a partner in petty crime, a straight man for her mischief.

Our neighbourhood was considered safe, so much so that the word unsafe simply didn't cross most parents' minds there. But our parents weren't most parents. No place was safe enough for their children. Our own home was seen as hazardous. Shocks loomed at every electric outlet. Childproof plugs were screwed into each. They couldn't be pulled out without using both a screwdriver and pair of pliers. Cupboards containing cleaning chemicals had locks on them. Medicine cabinets, same story. Bath-time meant danger of drowning. We weren't allowed to be in there alone, unless we kept singing the whole time. The second we stopped one of our parents would appear.

That is precisely what happened when my mother saw me pacing back and forth in front of the house without my sister. She immediately rushed out of the house shouting: "Where's your sister?! What're you doing without your sister?!"

My sister popped up in front of our front lawn bushes shouting: "I was tying my shoelaces. Why're you shouting? Can't I tie my shoelaces?!"

My sister had planned it. I didn't know it then but in retrospect it was obvious. She'd convinced me that, while she took the time to retie her shoe laces tighter, I should pretend I was alone.

"For who?" I'd asked.

"For you," she'd answered. "You want to feel like a grownup, don't you?" Before I could respond, she'd added: "As grownup as me?"

I didn't really understand what she was getting at. But the word grownup sounded good to me. And the idea of being like her better.

"But you're still too little to play down the street. So you have to start just walking back and forth in front of the house. So mom can see you."

That should have given me a clue what she was up to. But I was so taken with the idea of being able to play alone outside just like my big sister that it didn't.

"And you can't talk or look at me or it's not like you're playing alone."

"But you're here?"

"Want to play or not?"

At that tender age she knew how to intimidate and manipulate me, manipulate me by intimidating me.

"Sure."

"Then just pace up and down in front of the house as if I'm not here. If it's too hard to pretend then close your eyes."

Not wanting to overdo our first foray into hide and seek games with our parents, eager to leave room for escalation, she was making sure I didn't look like I was looking for her. It's hard to fathom how, at that young an age, she could extrapolate so far into the future, think in such an abstract, yet concrete and calculating manner. Yet she could. And did, taking forever to tie and retie her laces, finishing only when she heard my mother's shout.

Had I kept that incident and similar ones that followed in mind I might have realized what my sister was up to playing hide and seek with me the next summer. I could believe in the boogie man, but conspiratorial minds like my sister's were beyond me.

She'd kept upping the hide-and-seek stakes a little each time, until one day she disappeared for what must have been an hour, but to me seemed like much more. I searched high and low for her, hitting every one of her favourite hiding spots, in neighbours' backyards, underneath their stairs.

Finally, freaked out, I started running up and down the street, shouting her name. I should have known that the more frantic my voice the more excited my sister would be that our hide and seek had hit such a fever pitch, and that would only encourage her to stay hidden. The higher the stakes the more she savoured the game.

Hearing me, one of the neighbours came rushing out of her house shouting: "What's wrong, Velvel, what's wrong?" I was too out of breath to speak, and too scared to stop running. Had I stopped, I'd have had to tell her I'd lost my sister, she'd tell my mother and we'd probably be prohibited from playing outside without her supervision for a whole week. I should have realized that by not stopping I'd be causing more consternation, and that would only make it more likely that word would get back to my mother. And that's what happened. The neighbour immediately phoned my mother. And she too came running shouting: "What's wrong, Velvel, what's wrong?"

Somehow, perhaps subliminally, she must have heard the neighbour, for she used the exact same words, but with a more frenzied inflection. Of course, it could have been coincidence. What else could she have said in such a situation? She might have just shouted: "Velvel! Velvel?!" Or simply called for me to stop, using my name so some other pedestrian or passing car wouldn't think she was shouting at them. Something like: "Velvel stop!" Or: "Velvel?! Stop!"

A lot to be running through a little boy's head. By then all of five or six, my mind already had a tendency to run away with itself.

At first I was afraid to say anything lest my mother get angry at me, and worse, at my sister. My sister never backed down. She could throw a tantrum that not only scared me, but my parents too. Yet what else could I do?

Breathlessly, I told my mother: "We were playing hide and seek but then Maya got lost and maybe some bad man kidnapped her."

I must have been blinded by both my fear and the tears in my eyes, for before I'd finished my confession, my sister had crawled up behind my mother and startled her with a short staccato "Boo!" Nervous wreck that she was my mother was easily startled. Before she was out of diapers boo had become one of my sister's favourite words. Eventually, mine too.

This one word, delivered with appropriate surprise, gave my sister her first taste of the power of the prank. And soon, I jumped on the boo bandwagon. No matter how often we did it, our mother always seemed startled. Still, after absorbing the initial shock, she'd always resort to her aggravated look, in some perverse way she seemed to savour the rush. A relief from an otherwise humdrum day. Like my sister, but in her own subdued way, she too may have been an adrenaline junkie, albeit, a reluctant one.

Anyhow, on top of the consternation caused by the neighbour's phone call, my frantic shouting and having to run so far so fast, the added surge of stress from my sister's scare tactic seemed to do the trick. It certainly took the steam out of my mother. So out of breath she could barely manage a long-suffering sigh, she'd lost the wherewithal to scold my sister and me. With a single word my sister had enabled us to escape punishment while providing my mother with relief from her worst nightmare. Her children were safe. And so, in silence, the three of us strolled home.

* * *

While I was the considered the dreamer in the family and my sister, the doer, she could dream up games that I, in my wildest nightmares, would never dare imagine, let alone be a part of, if it wasn't for her.

Bored with beating me at checkers one Sunday morning, she came up with a brainstorm.

"Want to play hide and seek?"

"Not that dumb anymore. Know you're gonna try'n scare me into shouting for you. Anyway, don't wanna play."

She thought for a few seconds, hesitated, then leaned close to me and whispered: "Not just me and you this time we'll get mom and dad."

Right then I knew she was up to something. But my curiosity got the better of me and I asked: "Mom 'n dad?"

"Shh," she said, leaning closer, whispering: "We don't tell them they're playing. They have to figure it out themselves."

"They'll think we're lost?"

"Shhh, that's part of the fun. If we tell them we're playing, they won't. They're not the kind. Dad's almost an old man now."

And, by the standards of the day, she was right. My father was almost fifty.

My sister persisted: "They won't know we're playing till they find us. But once they do it'll be just like that time you and mom were really scared you lost me and then were so glad when you found me."

We were still single digits age-wise, yet my sister could speak with such certainty and conviction that she seemed like an adult to me. In any case, it didn't take much to convince me. As usual I was afraid to disappoint her. Her approval meant so much to me. More than my parents'.

Besides, I was curious: How was she going to involve our parents in the game without doing what she did before? She knew I wouldn't fall for it again. Moreover, something felt different. I didn't have a clue what it could be, but I felt part of a plot rather than a patsy of it. And couldn't resist. My sister had hooked me, sucked me in to her excitement.

And so, without telling them, the two of us slipped out of the house and hid away, not only for the whole day, but an entire night too. This was so daring I could barely deal with it, couldn't deny it either.

Frantic, my parents called all our friends. When that didn't bear fruit, they called the police. Cruel stuff. Were we a couple of callous kids or just oblivious to the agony we'd caused our parents? Well, I don't think I was either, but I'm not sure about my sister. I think she valued her independence above all, including the anguish of our parents. In fact, she resented their fear, and in her naive way sought not only to free herself from it, but from our parents, by pushing them to their limits.

Her explanation was that, though we knew how precious we were to our parents, we simply wanted to test their love, at the same time remind them how much they treasured us. At least that's what she used to convince me to play along, and the excuse she used to disarm our parents when we showed up the next morning none the worse for the wear for having slept outside overnight. A pretty precocious justification for a six-year-old. And she was to come up with many more as she fought to lengthen the leash to which she felt tethered.

Instead of being pissed off and punishing us, my father was so relieved he broke down crying, hugging and kissing us as though he'd never expected to see us alive again. My mother contented herself with quietly seething, angrily shaking her head with an enhanced I'm-at-my-wit's-end-with-you-two look that lasted for weeks.

That she again managed to get off scot-free with one of her capers certainly didn't help rein in my sister. Her persistent attempts to burst the bonds of family woe frequently had her up to no good.

And though it was not the first time blameless little me—trouble-maker-in-training and reluctant but easily-recruited accomplice—had felt the same sense of intoxication as she, it had to be the last. I couldn't keep up with her. I was afraid to. If she wanted to live dangerously, she was on her own. Of course, I couldn't think in those terms, but I could feel their equivalents, especially in the form of pity for my poor parents.

From the time she was a young child, my sister was always taking chances, pushing the envelope of what was permitted: riding her bike on the busiest of streets before she was allowed; taking the bus alone when she was too young to buy a ticket.

She'd talked the bus driver into letting her on by telling him her mother was taken to the hospital and there was nobody home to look after and feed her so she was going to her aunt's. She knew how to get there by bus because she'd often gone there with her mother. Her father was no longer alive. He was killed in a car crash when she was too young to remember. She was so convincing that one of the other passengers offered to pay for and look after her till she got to her stop. She was all of five when this happened.

You can imagine what such antics did to my parents. They were at a loss at how to handle her. And who can blame them? She was a handful.

A wilful child, if she didn't get her way she could throw a tantrum, and then, look out. There was no holding back. As temperamental as any diva, she could out-shriek Maria Callas, throw a tantrum that not only the next door neighbours could hear, but the whole damn block. Which would embarrass my mother no end, and my sister knew it. This gave her the upper hand, especially in winter. With the windows shut tight, to make sure the neighbours could hear, my sister would run, open the front door and holler blue murder. She could really make it sound like someone was trying to kill her.

Embarrassed the neighbours might think she beat her children, my mother would rush to the door and beseech her to come back in with "You're wasting electricity!" After a few more surges of screeching from my sister and a few more You're-wasting-electricity threats of locking the door from my mother, they'd both back down. My sister could only stand so much cold, and my mother only so much embarrassment.

Still, when it came to a tug of war between a long suffering stoic and a short-fused volcano, it was no contest. My sister not only had the will, but the ways. And with my father, hysterics weren't my sister's only weapon. When they didn't work, girlish giggles would. Even at a young age she knew how to manipulate men.

* * *

Children are born with a vulnerability and primal innocence we as adults can't help find fetching: i.e., we're genetically programmed to love and protect them. As they grow older, the attachment, now laced with hopes for achievement and social status, becomes less pure and primordial, and the physical affection one feels for one's children gradually sublimates into something less fierce. But not with my father. Especially for my sister. His earliest feelings for her never seemed to diminish.

At the age of eight or nine my sister had to cope with having the body of a fully developed young woman while her psyche was still that of a little girl. But as she matured into her body, rather than resort to tantrums, she increasingly learned to use her charm, becoming so sweet she could tickle the tusks off an elephant. She knew that, if the carrot of her pizzazz didn't work she could resort to the stick of her shriek. But her sweetness was so seductive, especially with men, that she rarely had to. Above all, not with my father.

And while my father's affection for my adult sister was more powerful than anything he felt for me, I didn't mind. I too was mesmerized by her. Every time I thought of her I would start to smile. Her bebop body language, her impish grin, as if she were up to something. And she usually was, trying to get a laugh or smile out of me.

My father once said to me: "She can make you feel lucky to be alive." This, from the king of melancholy. But he was right on the money. Why does one love another? Because they make you feel alive, that life may be worth living. One lives for that love.

My father would take my sister to Broadway musicals, buy her record albums he pretended he didn't want my mother to know about. But of course my mother knew. How could she not? My father never tried to hide it. He'd just pretend he did. So he could share a wink and a nod with my sister. One of my mother's pet phrases to my father was

"You spoil her. You spoil that girl." The older my sister got the more my father seemed to 'spoil' her.

* * *

My mother may have been jealous of my sister, the way she could make my father smile, cheer him up when he was down, something my mother couldn't do. Or, bogged down by his relentless demands of her, gave up trying to.

In any case, while down was the default mood of both my parents, my mother's despair never appeared as deep or debilitating as my father's. She certainly wasn't as flamboyant in expressing it. In fact, within the family, she maintained a consistent face, expressing a steady state of disappointment, one which rarely wavered, certainly never fluctuated like my father's. In that sense, she was the rock of the family, but one anchored in some dim shallow sea of dashed hopes and dreams.

While more emotionally erratic than my mother, my father was also more exuberant, even upbeat, if only in brief outbursts. Should my sister or I say or do something he found endearing, he might smile, laugh or simply throw his arms around us exclaiming: 'A leben ahf dein kepele!' His joy so unrestrained his hugs sometimes hurt.

But should some similar shenanigan of ours catch my mother off guard and she should then, god forbid, find herself starting to smile, controlling emotional pilot that she was, she'd instantly make a midcourse correction, shifting the smile into a grimace and the start of a laugh into a sad disappointed sigh. I think she feared that, if she let her guard down, showed the slightest happiness, she risked losing what little sway she had over us. Perhaps she also feared jeopardizing her emotional equilibrium, leaving herself vulnerable to ups and downs like my dad's.

Some schoolteachers use fear to maintain classroom discipline, my mother employed disappointment to manage us at home. Outside the family, she was always cheerful. Inside, rarely. Gloom was the glue that held our family together. Yet if a phone call disrupted her otherwise depressing day, she would cheerfully chat with whoever was on the other end of the line, unless it was my father, sister or me. For us she would revert to her exasperated tone. Which I resented.

If my mother could smile for strangers why couldn't she smile for us? Well, of course, strangers were merely passing through, so she could afford to put on airs. While our family was a permanent fixture, she couldn't afford to paste a smile for us. It was too taxing.

Yet in some sense she did posture for us, her stoic exasperation being just that. I never saw her cry. Still, when she thought no one was home, I often heard her. But even sure no one could hear, unlike my father, she simply could not let go, not completely, struggling to stifle her sobs.

It would cross my mind that I should try and console her. But then I'd be invading her privacy. She wanted to hide her tears. I shouldn't intrude.

* * *

My parents met through a Jewish immigrant organization's matchmaking service. Both were well into their thirties, my father closer to forty. The matchmaker convinced them it was time to take the bull by the horns, that is, take what they could get as a marriage partner and make the best of it. Love would come later. What they wanted was a family and, the one promise she made my prospective parents swear to before she would let them meet was that, by hook or by crook, come what may, they would stay together for the sake of the kids.

She must have known from her long experience that they wouldn't get along. They were such different types, each stubborn in their own way. Anyway, in those days you didn't get divorced just like that. Especially if you were an immigrant. Scandal could undermine your standing in your newfound community. And divorce was the supreme scandal of all, even if it didn't entail infidelity. The implication was always there. So separation was to be avoided at all costs, even if it meant the health and happiness of your whole family.

Before my parents married my mother worked as a bookkeeper and managed the office of one of the biggest electrical supply wholesalers in the city. But after they wed my father insisted. "No wife of mine is going to work. A woman's place is in the kitchen, with the kids. My mother killed herself trying to do both. I don't want the same should happen to you."

"When the kids are born we'll see."

"Before they're born we'll see."

Their first major argument. But certainly not their last.

* * *

Before I go any deeper into my parents' miscarriage of a marriage, I should show a little humility and describe one of mine. Not my first. Too far back. But my last—though it lasted only two years, and ended nearly a decade ago—it's so fresh it still stings.

Some men like to make love just so they can fall asleep. At my advanced age, I'd rather read! I've always been an avid reader. My last wife was an avid reader too. In fact, our favourite thing to do in bed together was read.

No, we didn't meet at a book club. I was not one to leave my lair on the off-chance I might meet a woman there. My method was more direct: a NUT SEEKS SQUIRREL ad in the *Montreal Gazette.*

On our very first date, I knew I'd stuck gold. Telling me about her family, she cried. Instantly, I was smitten. I'd found a tormented soul mate! Tears in my eyes, I told her my tragic tale. I'm sure that's why she took to me. What man weeps on a first date? But being intrigued by an eccentric is one thing, living with him, another, and my eccentricities gradually lost their lustre.

Once married, boredom and anger became her primary domestic moods. She blamed me for both, hated being home alone. Since I was now a permanent fixture of the place, like the furniture, I didn't count as company. Retired too young, she was at loose ends when she wasn't playing bridge, attending art exhibits, the theatre, 'cinema' (she never used the word movies) or simply socializing. Each of which I detested.

What I loved was snuggling, strolling or just sitting on a park bench watching dogs and kids play. She had no patience for any of this.

Thus, but for reading ourselves to sleep, we rarely shared the simple contentment of being together.

In my mid-sixties, all I wanted was peace and a place to write. Nearly ten years younger than I, all she wanted was adventure. She always needed someone with whom to hobnob. At the latter she was a master, charming and ebullient. She came alive in company, thrived on it, performed for others as she would never bother to do just for me.

Seeing herself as some sort of artist, actress or flamenco dancer manqué, she tried her hand at all three as a Jewish Community Center amateur. And did have some talent. What she didn't have were the training, skill, confidence or perseverance to pursue them as a career.

All her life she'd thrived on her sex appeal. As did most of the men she met. Constantly propositioned by one man or another—even while married to me, though far as I know she didn't take them up on it—she loved it. You could tell by her good-natured girlish laughter followed by an if-I-wasn't-with-him wink. Then she'd shrug and was off to flirt with some other jerk. So much for merging marriage and art with the cock-teasing of cocktail parties.

She'd been in the picture-framing business, so was always being invited to one art gallery opening or another, dragging a reluctant me along. I hate openings. Detest the chitchat you have to make. Especially when compelled to comment on the dreadful art, and can't think of a compliment that won't sound like an insult.

I've never been comfortable with 'normal' people. Just can't seem to relate to them. Or they to me. Maybe that's why I didn't get along with this wife. On the other hand, maybe what drew me to her was what drew her to the less fortunate of her fellow human beings.

For as much part of her everlasting sex appeal as her shapely body and beguiling smile, she had an élan, a joie de vivre, an enthusiastic openness to anything and anyone, especially the oddball.

A long lost friend of hers had been looking after his brother, a middle aged man who'd miraculously come out of a coma he'd been in for years. The moment he was introduced to me and my wife at his rebirth day party, he went straight for her, humming, arms out, enticing her to dance. There was no music. And no one was dancing. Yet, without a moment's hesitation or recoiling reflex at someone so childlike and slow-witted as to seem retarded, humming the same tune as he, she slipped into his emaciated arms.

His drool dripped on her but, entranced by this out-of-the-blue chance to dance, she didn't seem to notice. This incident was no accident. Once, some wretched soul came up to her in the street, started talking gibberish. She simply smiled and started spouting gibberish back to him, slipping right into his world. She embraced the offbeat, the more offbeat the more enthusiastic the acknowledgment.

Except when it came to her husband. For as open as she was to exotic incidents, within our marriage she was conventional to a fault.

Her niece's wedding was one of these occasions. For the afternoon ceremony, I'd worn the tux my wife had rented for me along with a pair of shiny black patent leather shoes. In all that dark formal attire I felt like I was attending a funeral. But what the hell, if my wife felt she had to compensate for her relatives' image of me as an oddball, who was I to deprive her? After all, I was merely the most recent in a long line of colourful husbands. Albeit the first Jew. That didn't stand me in good stead for long.

I thought wearing my white sneakers with my black tux for that niece's nocturnal wedding party was more than a let's-have-fun signal. It was so my wife and I could dance up a storm. Rather than calmly explain that she was terrified my sneakers would embarrass her, or give me a chance to say I'd bring them in a bag, and wait for the after-dinner dancing to put them on, my wife hit the ceiling.

It was like having another mother, but one who, rather than suffer in silence, could, like my sister, shatter fine crystal with her shrieking. Fortunately, I was never the object of my sister's ear-piercing ire. Unfortunately, I was frequently the object of my last wife's.

Although this particular evening's ear-shattering outburst may have stemmed from a need to control me, it was also an expression of fear, of being embarrassed in front of her family. I knew that. And it broke my heart. But I couldn't let her break my balls. Not by bullying me that way.

I'd tried jesting. "The night is young! Pace yourself! Save your performance for the party!"

She didn't find it funny. Neither did I. But I had to try. Once into shriek mode, she was on automatic pilot. Nothing could switch it off except acquiescence: immediate and unequivocal collapsing in a heap before her vocal shock and awe onslaught.

While she did trigger a primal response in me, a perverted form of fight or flight, I wasn't going to give her the satisfaction of fleeing. Moving out was too inconvenient knowing that after a few days I'd be begging her to let me move back in. At the same time, I was too stubborn not to stand my ground.

And stand my ground I did. The way I always did with matrimonial warfare: hostile silence. Humour can be as hostile as silence. But not as long lasting. I could never stretch facetious remarks out for a whole week. With hostile silence, there was no limit. But that took will. And after a week or two I'd usually run out.

Hence my response to her high-pitched harangues was usually the six-day silent treatment, sometimes stretched into seven, especially if the shrieking had started on a Saturday or Sunday. A symmetry that allowed me to keep track of the length of my passive aggressive punishment. Once in a while I'd get it up to ten or twelve days, sometimes two weeks. But that was tops.

Hostile vindictive silence my push-button backlash to her shriek attacks, each of our actions only encouraged an equal and opposite reaction from the other, an elegant Newtonian equation unbefitting our inelegant behaviour.

I thought my tactics would curb hers, perhaps cure her of her outrageous behaviour. Of course, she presumed hers would do the same to me. Sad to say, we were both wrong.

Her niece's wedding party turned out to be an embarrassment for both of us. Yet, in a sense, she'd won. I didn't wear my white sneakers. Neither did we dance. We didn't even talk.

Yet that didn't stop her from flirting with younger cousins, dancing with the few who had the courage to ask. They'd glance at me, seeking my approval. Stubbornly, I stuck to my stony silence, stupidly refusing to let anything break the ice.

Not only was I, in old age, a one-woman man, I was a one-trick pony when it came to punishing my wife.

The irony is that the one marriage in which my bitter half flirted with every male who came within inches of her erotic orbit was the only one in which I remained faithful. Less because of genuine fidelity than waning interest and will. I'd ridden on that merry-go-round often enough to know that all it does is get you dizzy.

(An aside: when I was an adolescent I used to speed-read through novels to get to the erotic action; an old man, I skip the latter, flipping pages till I get back to the pure plot.)

Since flirting bored me more than bitter silence, I couldn't retaliate by asking my wife's female cousins to dance.

Irony number two: if I so much as glanced at another woman, especially a younger attractive one, *she*'d hit the ceiling. Once, she locked me out of the house for days and, when I tried to climb in a window, called the cops.

On another occasion, to stop her from flailing at me with her fists, I had to resort to the same weapon I employed as a boy to keep other boys from hitting me: a headlock. In court, I referred to it as our wedlock. The judge didn't find it funny. Neither did my wife. But she refused to press charges. Thus went this couple's crazed carousel.

Neither of us wanted to enter our twilight years alone, but the vicious cycles of shrieking and silent treatments took their toll, and we separated. Rather, she threw me out, changed the locks on the doors, and I didn't have the will to climb in through a window again.

It's sad how our whole lives we search for islands of affection to help us feel at home amidst the hostile seas of this world, then, when we find one, we do everything we can to demolish it with our demands.

Anyway, since our divorce, we get along better than we ever did. In the decade since we split up we've had several clandestine—hush-hush for her, she's married to a very jealous man, I have no partner—dinners. We carry on civil conversations, share a laugh or two, including the occasional intimacy, without getting each other's goat. During these trysts—her tongue in cheek term—she flirts with me as though I'm a fresh face.

Alas, for some of us, divorce may be the closest we can come to wedded bliss.

* * *

Unfortunately, my parents never got to experience the delights of divorce.

Still, it's not as if they never shared a good time. At least tried to. When they were younger they'd go ballroom dancing twice a week. On cruises to the Caribbean they'd win prizes for best dance pair. My father loved to be the centre of attention. My mother, not so much. If you only followed their feet as they strutted their stuff, you'd think they were having fun. But their faces betrayed them: taut-mouthed grins more like grimaces, pretending to have a good time—*struggling* to have one—rather than truly having one.

No. No open-mouthed bare-toothed expressions of unadulterated delight. Not for this couple. Not as a couple. But there were times when the joy on my father's face matched that of his nimble feet.

When I was just learning to ice skate—my sister was already quite adept—my father would take the two of us to an outdoor rink that encircled a narrow island with logs that served as benches and open-topped metal barrels as wood stoves. As smooth a skater as he was a dancer, there were no tight-lipped smiles from my father gliding round that oval rink, hand in hand with my seven-year-old sister, swinging her round the narrowed ends of the rink, she too all smiles, though with a few missing front teeth.

The two of them cut quite a swath: my sister in a short pink skirt, matching jacket and long white leggings, her long braided ponytail reaching halfway down her back; my father with his huge Ushanka hat, long fur-collared black coat and large padded leather motorcycle police-man's mitts the size of hockey gauntlets.

I rarely saw him radiate such unadulterated joy, look as alive or elated as he did skate-dancing to the amplified music with his 'little girl'.

At six I could barely stand on skates without frequently falling.

Bored with my being unable to keep up, cramping her style, my sister would insist my father skate with one of us at a time. And to please her —to appease her—he'd acquiesce.

Sitting there like a bump on a log, I'd feel cold and left out. Watching and waiting my turn, I'd be angry my father had left me behind, envious that my sister and father were having such a good time. But eventually my father would glide over, let go of my sister's hand, and she'd slide right up onto the island, into me and, beaming, give me a big hug accompanied by: "Your turn!"

My father would then sweep me up in his arms and start skating around in time to the music. And I too would be in heaven.

Wish I could say I felt the same when, in my early twenties, I'd arrive home from graduate school in New York, unannounced, usually in the middle of the night. I can still picture him flinging his arms around me in unadulterated elation, thrilled to see me. More accurately, relieved that something hadn't happened to me, that I was home and, as he liked to put it, "In one piece."

In Manhattan, I'd tell myself that I was just going to go for a little drive, get a taste of nature, breathe a little clean country air. I'd pack a small bag, just in case I decided to stop at a motel in the Catskills or Adirondacks. But I'd keep driving, until I got so close to Montreal I couldn't resist continuing on. I knew I was fooling myself, but some part of my psyche, unwilling to deal with the darkness at home, couldn't quite acknowledge that I was going to go all the way to Montreal. Yet a part of me ached for home, for a respite from the lonely hustle and bustle of Mad Hattan.

I'd play this game with myself: see how close I could get to my home town without feeling too down. Guided by some strange compass, one powered by an equally eerie emotional magnet, one moment I'd feel a powerful force pulling me towards Montreal, and I would accelerate, perhaps eager to get the agony over with. Moments later, I would feel a resistance, as if my beat up '54 beetle was facing a severe headwind. The car would start stalling at high speed, and I'd be forced to slow down. The beetle's way of telling me: *Don't go there.*

But I couldn't help myself. It seemed simpler to keep going than to make the hard choice of turning around. By that time reversing directions seemed like a defeat. Of course, so did staying the course. But inertia always overcame momentum. Rather, like some kind of neurotic alchemist, I could turn momentum into inertia, and going forward into going back.

Once, just as I crossed the Jacques Cartier bridge into the city, the butterflies in my belly beginning to go to my head, the engine caught fire. To this day I'm convinced it was caused by the emotional upheaval.

By the time I reached home it was four in the morning. Yet no sooner had I unlocked the door and stepped into the dark hall of my parents' home than, like some psychic sensing my arrival, my father came rushing out of his bedroom, threw his arms around me and hugged me so hard he dislocated my acromioclavicular joint.

"Son, you're here!" he cried. "Oy son you're here!"

Then to my mother: "Millie, he's home! Our Willy's home!"

Back to me, hugging and crying: "You're home! Tanks god! Oy, tanks god! You're home!"

It was as if I'd been kidnapped and, to my father's astonishment and relief, had been suddenly freed.

Tears of joy and sorrow are never far apart, inextricably linked in the heart and soul of any man who allows himself to fully feel the fragile contradictions of life, death and the disasters in between. Still, not only did my father wear his heart on his sleeve, his whole being was stitched together with strands of it. Our home may have been lacking in laughter, but it was never lacking in love.

Maybe there is no such thing as sheer happiness. Not in the Russian psyche or soul. Not in any soul sensitive to the suffering in life. Perhaps true happiness only belongs to the truly oblivious. Or maybe it involves an ability to forget, to turn off the hot tap of tears, the cold faucet of fear and, if not embrace, face each moment with all its flaws, immerse oneself in it, find blissful forgetfulness.

Anyway, with my sister, homecomings were more melodramatic. For after she finished graduate school, she was always much farther away than I. Thus her arrivals, more infrequent than mine, were filled with more tears of joy.

* * *

But rarely had there been tears at our dinner table. Either of joy or sorrow. Such emotings were always reserved for between meals. Eating was a serious business in our family, and my father's grumbling about business made sure it was.

Some families begin meals with a prayer. We began them with prolonged anxious silence. All the stresses of the business day or, in my mother's case, of coping with my father, sister and I came home to roost with our chicken soup.

In our house soup was sacred. Each afternoon and evening meal began with it. My mother considered it the key to keeping us healthy. We'd probably have had it for breakfast had my mother not considered cream of wheat an equivalent.

Afternoon and evening soup was always followed by, as my father put it, 'a piece fish,' most often, 'a piece carp' or pickled herring. My sister and I would skip straight to the main course. We couldn't stand the smell of fish. We couldn't stand most of what our mother made, usually salt and spice-free bland, boiled beyond anyone being able to tell the look or taste of one species from another. But for the sake of family peace, and with the help of the humane folks at Heinz, we did our duty.

To be fair to my mother, I couldn't get enough of her cookies, laced as they were with loads of sugar. Seeing her son scoff down dozens with glass after glass of milk evoked almost audible sighs of satisfaction from her, as though she and I were sharing some transcendently sweet symbiosis. To this day I can hear my mother sigh from on high as I stuff myself with strudel. But such delights were relegated to dessert and between meal snacks.

When it came to the main course, stuck between pleasing my mother and my deprived taste buds, I found a way of accommodating both: quantity. The less tasty each morsel the more desperate my grasping for gustatory satisfaction. The more I would eat in search of some totality of taste, the less morose my mother. For both of us, my bloated belly became a path to contentment from bland meals. Having stuffed myself to feel satiated, I'd feel like I was pregnant, my mother, like she'd been nursing me. A strange symbiosis for sure, but one not unfamiliar to many families.

Anyway, I could eat without end. And never gain an ounce. Nor was I one of those unfortunate souls who had to shove a finger down his throat to continue gorging himself. Uncle Izzy used to say: "Keyn a hora, the boy's got an empty leg! He must have an empty leg!" An extrovert's version of what my mother felt but, lest she lose her moody leverage over me, would never express. Certainly not in such an exuberantly upbeat manner.

Of course, I prefer delicious dishes. But my gourmand appetite didn't grow into gourmet until I left home. And by then the damage was done. Overeating had been embedded in my psyche.

In any event, there's a catch with tasty nutrition that you don't have with its opposite: the more scrumptious each morsel the more you want to keep savouring it. Yet flavour has a shorter life span than a mayfly. The experience is so ephemeral, a few seconds and poof, it's over. You just have to take another bite. And another. Never wanting the instants of ecstasy to end. So, superb cuisine or second-rate, I can't help pigging out.

Fortunately, my two wives were terrific cooks. But they could barely afford to feed me. Nor could they endure the embarrassment of taking me to dinner at friends' where, purring like some contented kitten, I would feast till our hosts ran out of food. Or hid what was left. Then had to lie that they hadn't.

The one activity I find as gratifying as eating is breathing. You can savour the sweet scent of cedar forest without ever feeling full. But indoors or out, ah the charcoal aroma of seared steak as it wafts its way up your olfactory apparatus, those rare filet juices flooding across your tongue, the thrill of the taste flowing down the sides of your neck till your shoulders start to tingle.

No doubt about it, food's one of my favourite pastimes. One of my favourite ways to pass time. But the letdown when the last meal of the day comes to an end can be unbearable. My antidote for postpartum after-dinner depression? Don't stop. Why stop when you can stretch desserts such as Sarah Lee or bowls of Ben & Jerry's all the way till you hit the hay? The sugar helps keep the blues at bay. And makes for sweet dreams.

Yes, nights are Nirvana, mornings, misery. Before breakfast. After, life begins worth living again. Such is my circadian rhythm.

* * *

Push come to shove, as a boy, mealtimes were mostly misery for me, for the rest of the family too, especially dinner, when my father would host a meeting of his day's money demons. My mother would just sit there, sadly sipping the odd spoonful of soup or chewing the odd bit of boiled chicken while my father would use the slightest lull in the sound of chewing to turn to the main course of the meal, between bites bemoaning his business woes: the bank asking him to bring in more paper; his accountant telling him he was in arrears on his taxes, in over his head on his investments.

"Millie, I'm going to have to take a loan on my life insurance, to pay the taxes on this place. It's twice what it should be we shouldn't have built on a corner."

"Who's we?" my mother would ask.

"You didn't want this house?"

"All I ever wanted was some peace and quiet. Not a mortgage we couldn't afford."

"When we sell we'll make it back in spades."

"Did you build to sell or live?"

"Both."

My father had expensive taste, without the money to match. But that didn't stop him. My mother didn't drive and my sister and I were too young, nevertheless, we had two cars: a Buick Roadmaster convertible—my father would drive with the top down in winter—and a sedan, both cars equipped with the only remote garage door control in the neighbourhood.

Each house he built had to be finished with expensive stone on all four sides, rather than the usual cheaper brick on sides not visible from the street. Wealthier men used brick there. But not my father.

Yet when it came to clothes, furniture, appliances or anything cheaper than a car or house, it was always: "We can save I know somebody!" Meaning, he could get it wholesale. My mother couldn't buy hair curlers without going through his 'connection'.

Still, for his castles he would spare no expense. They were his fortresses. There he could forget the world he'd once had to inhabit, try to fend off the forces eating away at his insides. But it never worked. While he was in the process of building he'd manage to maintain some semblance of emotional balance. He was making his mark, constructing something permanent, a bulwark against the past, a monument to the present.

However, once built, the financial burden of maintaining his mansion would dismantle his emotional defenses. The stone walls he'd worked so hard to erect, once finished, rather than keeping those malignant spirits out, seemed only to shut them in, so that, swept up in torrents of panic, he'd have to get away, go somewhere, anywhere, just to get out of the house. His dream homes, rather than protecting him from old nightmares, seemed only to rekindle new ones.

Our family's migrating patterns, induced as they usually were by a cash crunch, one manufactured by my father as an excuse to move, or brought about by the bank threatening to foreclose on his mortgage, wreaked havoc on my ability to maintain friends. Once I had to switch elementary schools twice in the same year.

Because my father couldn't afford the extravagant houses he'd built, he'd be in such a hurry to sell he'd have to dispose of each house at a loss. The pattern kept repeating itself. Until finally he could afford to lose no more. Or build. With no castle to contemplate, he could barely get himself out of bed, rising later and later each day, looking after his business less and less, until finally it failed.

My theory, for what it's worth, is that his inner turmoil led to restlessness. To cope with it he had to keep moving. And getting in over his financial head forced him to. He used money troubles to take his mind off other troubles, worse torment. In reality, he couldn't escape either.

From time to time financial pressure would lead to longing for the simple *shtetl* life.

"We might not have had a pot to pee in but long as we had what to eat we didn't know we were poor."

"So that's why you built so many bathrooms?" my mother would say, her explanation morphed into a question merely by tacking an upward inflection on to the sentence's end.

"You can't have too many toilets."

That would silence my mother.

"If it was up to me we'd have twice as many," my father would persist.

Knowing my father's way of dealing with anxiety was to stir up an argument, my mother's best weapon was implacable silence. My father would simply circumvent that strategy by responding as if she'd spoken.

"I should feel guilty five bathrooms?"

Her silence rendered ineffective, my mother couldn't resist.

"There's only four of us?"

"And the cleaning lady, you don't count the cleaning lady?"

That would evoke a prolonged aggravated sigh from my mother, just long enough for a quick follow-up from my father.

"Back then we had to go outside! We didn't have indoors!"

"You keep spending like this we'll *end* up on the street."

"You like to wait?"

"I don't want to talk about it anymore."

"One word, yes or no, you like to wait?"

"The table's not the time."

"Thank god no one in this family has to wait. No one in this family will ever have to wait. For that I would think you'd be a little grateful. Just a little. But no, you have to rub it in. You don't mind splurging on china when it suits you but when your husband spends hoo hah you hit the ceiling!"

Hoo hah was one of my father's favourite expressions, one he could fit into any phrase, tack on any sentence, to give it a heft it might other-wise not have.

My sister and I would watch, as in back and forth slow motion, our parents, seemingly oblivious to the consequences of their bickering, indulged in another indigestion-inducing grievance match. I still have knots in my stomach before every meal, especially dinner, and binge on sugar-laced biscuits after. Nothing gives me that sense of satisfaction, that feeling of fullness, of fulfillment in life, like a pound of pecan cookies. My sister, on the other hand, enjoyed an abbreviated life of anorexia.

The seeds of the difference in our eating disorders was most likely planted in our polar opposite ways of dealing with those dinner table dramas: I, a passive participant in those sad stage shows, grew into an aggressive gorger; my sister, a feisty performer in them, became a reticent eater.

* * *

The dramatic dye was cast in how she'd begin her performance, in a low key, pushing her plate away with a simple: "I'm not hungry."

"You don't have to be hungry to eat," my mother would answer, sliding the plate back towards my sister.

My sister would again push the plate away, this time a little farther.

"I spent all afternoon sweating over a hot stove the least you can do is eat," my mother would insist, shoving the plate back.

For a while my sister would just pick at her plate, exaggeratedly going through the motions, cutting and mashing without actually eating. Anxiously attacking our food, the rest of us would try to ignore her, at least pretend to, hoping she wouldn't provoke a scene.

"It's too quiet. I can't eat when it's so quiet. How d'jou expect me to eat when it's so quiet?" my sister would ask.

"Stop talking and eat," my mother would admonish. Lots of admonishing went on at this table.

"I can chew and talk at the same time why can't you two?"

"I've had about enough of you, young lady," my mother would warn.

"Why don't you put me up for adoption then? There's tons of parents who'd love to have a smart talented daughter like me. Why don't you put us both up for adoption? I bet lots of parents would love to have a couple of smart kids like us. Right, baby brother?"

To me it seemed like a lose lose so I'd remain silent, stoic. Without a smile or the slightest movement of my head, I'd just keep eating. But before long my sister would have more to say.

"This house is too unhappy for my taste. Soon as I'm old enough I'm gonna find a happier home."

For her second act, knowing it was futile trying to cheer us up, my sister would try to spice things up, concoct some shit-disturbing stuff she'd done in school that day, just to catch our parents off guard, so that when she did some truly taboo stuff, it wouldn't seem so terrible. And her hijinks only added to their anxiety. They never knew what she might say or do next. She knew how to shock my mother. My father, not so much. Even when the subject of sex came up. Actually, it wouldn't just come up, my sister would spit it up.

"Mom, would you mind if Bobby Allrod and I had hymeneal relations? He's so cute."

Often as not she might mispronounce them, but from the time she was little, not long after she learned to talk, my sister had loved big words, liked to play with them, pull the wool over adult eyes, watch them glaze over when they didn't know the meaning but didn't want to let on that they didn't. She would lie in bed reading the dictionary like other kids comic books.

With his lack of familiarity with the English language, especially with the slang or street vernacular—Russian and Yiddish being his two mother tongues, and French the first language he learned when he came to Quebec—I'm sure my father didn't know what hymeneal meant. But he got the gist of it. My mother's reaction helped. And before she could say anything he leaped to his little girl's defense.

"Millie." In a tone meant to admonish my mother not to bite, make an issue of it, aggravate him and spoil his meal. One word, my mother's name, pregnant with so much meaning.

My parents knew how distinguish between my sister's true stories (few and far between though they were) and stuff made up just to tease and taunt—even titillate—them. They had their own kind of collusion, which was to lapse into the safest stance, silence. When my sister would persist, as she was wont to do, my mother, as she was wont to do, would mouth one word "Enough," which meant that a full-fledged argument was to follow.

My sister: "He's such a sweet boy. If I was going to lose my dingle-berry with anyone it would be with Bobby Allrod."

My mother: "Enough."

My father: "Millie."

For the next few moments all you would hear would be the sound of the four of us masticating louder and more energetically than either normal or necessary.

Then, as if to fill the void, "Who's Bobby Allrod?" my father would ask, trying to be nonchalant, at least pretending to be. Big mistake.

"A boy in my class. He has a crush on me. They say he has a huge ..." My sister would crow like a rooster.

Determined as they were to not keep falling for my sister's rascal-ity, my parents couldn't help themselves.

"That's enough!" my mother would shout.

But she'd been frazzled, and my sister knew it.

"I'm too young to get preggers, right?"

"You heard your mother, enough," my father would say.

But my sister, all of eight, couldn't resist her piece de resistance.

"So why do we need a rubber?"

"Go to your room!" my father yelled.

"Why? I was just asking a question?"

"You certainly know how to spoil a meal. Now go to your room."

"How'm I sposed to learn bout the birds an' bees if you keep cen-soring me?"

My father would respond with his own rhetorical: "Do I have to raise a hand to you?"

Then, he'd stand, arm raised, finger pointing upstairs.

"Can I take my plate with me?"

Truly, my sister could try my parents' patience. Sometimes, she could try mine.

"Let her finish here," my mother would say. "Who knows what she'll do with her food upstairs?"

And so my sister would get a reprieve. Of course, to her, a reprieve would have meant being sent to her room, on her way allowing her to feed her food to the dog next door. He wasn't fussy. But it was not to be. It was never to be. And all of us knew it. It was just a ritual enacted again and again and the three of them knew their parts.

* * *

Nothing delighted my father more than a surprise visit.

At home on a weekend afternoon, or a weekday evening stressed out from his few afternoon hours at the office, he was usually in a prone position, on the sofa or in bed. But should the doorbell ring, as though he'd been lying in wait, eager for anything that might free him from feeling alone, even if he wasn't, he'd rush excitedly to the door. If it was friends or family—in those days they used to drop by unannounced—throughout the house you could hear his excited shout to my mother: "Millie! The Morgensterns are here!" Or: "Millie, it's Moe and Esther!"

I could never figure out why sometimes he chose to announce visitors individually by first name, other times as a couple via surname. There seemed to be no rhyme or reason. On one surprise visit a couple could be announced in the more formal manner; on another, the same couple might be announced by the more informal first names. One visit might elicit both. Each may have been expressed with equal exuberance, but first names were delivered with a more affectionate inflection.

My father was not fussy, with the exception of my uncle Izzy and maternal grandfather, everyone was always welcomed with enthusiasm. Even if he'd seen them the previous week, he might greet unexpected guests with such gusto, hugging and kissing them like they were long lost relatives or friends he was relieved to see were still alive. He may have been over the top in his demonstrations of affection, but he felt so happy to have an audience, to not have to deal with being alone, that he made visitors feel delighted they'd dropped by.

The closest my mother came to expressing the same degree of delight at unexpected arrivals was when one of the neighbourhood kids rang our bell, asking if I could come out to play. I was such a shy recluse that my mother may have feared for my sanity. She certainly feared my solitude. Her annoyed aura would immediately evaporate when she saw me with friends. Indeed, when I was in high school, or home from college late at night with a friend or two, even if she'd been fast asleep, she would slip out of bed to "heat something up for us," perhaps dish out some dessert. And she wasn't putting on airs. Her joy was genuine. You could tell it was genuine. Because it was so rare.

* * *

Few things made my father happier than sharing his sadness. And so he would hold court in our home, entertaining gatherings of guests of every shape and size, every personality stripe too: from the raunchy boisterous grossly overweight Ottawa aunt, to the shy straight-laced concentration-camp skinny uncle from Atlanta. A few were poor peddlers. But most were well off, made their money in women's clothing, men's or real-estate.

As shy and reclusive as I was, I savoured the semblance of joy these get-togethers brought to our home. Surrounded by a slew of friends, my father took a perverse pleasure in expressing his gloom. In some convoluted way, it made him the life of the party.

Of course others might try to express discontent about politics, their health or business. But they were no match for my father. His despair could always trump theirs. For one thing, they lacked his emotional palette, or didn't have the courage to flaunt it in public. My father had no such inhibitions. He could break down and cry at the drop of the hat, or jubilantly throw his arms around and kiss another man when he said or did something that delighted my father, even if the latter had disrupted his display of distress. He was not one to put on an act. Which made him a hard act to follow.

* * *

The mood at our Passover Seders was a cross between the friction of our nuclear family meals and the fun of social gatherings with family friends.

Uncle Izzy, my father's bachelor brother and black sheep of the family, always attended. So too my father's sister Bessy and my mother's father. Both of the latter's spouses lived in Toronto and their children were scattered across the continent. But that didn't stop the seven of us from enjoying our annual extended family feud.

Out of sheer habit, my parents would begin the meal with their usual undertone of dinner table disquiet. Unlike with other relatives or friends, none of whom frequented our home nearly so often as these three Seder regulars, my mother wouldn't feel she had to put on airs, be all smiles.

Half of what made aunt Bessy humorous were her looks: a big sway back behind with a tiny turned up nose set high between two beady black eyes. And her wide open mouth, if not babbling, then about to, her sly smile betraying her big Bugs Bunny buck teeth. Her humour didn't stem from cynicism as much as from a skewed outlook on life.

She may not have been quite as foul-mouthed as uncle Izzy, but aunt Bessy was a master of the good-natured insult. She could put down my dad for his relentless fretting and uncle Izzy for his unrepentant filching, all in the same breath: "One brother a goody goody and the other a no-good, thank god you don't have to be a man to be a mensch."

Thus the Seder's dramatic tension was set from the start. Whose mood would hold sway, levity's or gravity's? On the side of levity, my sister, me and aunt Bessy. On that of gravity, my parents and maternal grandfather. Like a swing vote on the supreme court, uncle Izzy was our family wild card. He had a wicked sense of humour, but there was little levity lost between him and my father. Nor between my father and maternal grandfather.

Yet, laced as it was with quips from my uncle and aunt, unlike the tensions at our nuclear family dinner table, this extended family friction was fun for my sister and me. And we looked forward to the festive fireworks.

Sometimes it was my sister who got it started. At the age of six or seven she knew how to stir up a shit-storm, in all innocence asking our maternal grandfather: "F'we're so special, how come god let us be slaves in the first place?"

Taken aback at my sister's precocity and not having an answer handy, the rest of the table remained tongue-tied as my grandfather jumped in with a long convoluted explanation. It took so many twists and turns my father started impatiently tapping the table: "Get to the point already, if there is a point."

Ignoring my father, my maternal grandfather kept talking, trying to compare what it meant for the Jews to escape Egypt to what the holocaust had cost him having to leave his whole life behind in the old country.

My father couldn't contain himself.

"You left twenty years before?!"

"I could see it coming!"

"Like I can see Elijah coming through that window."

My mother stepped in.

"Don't start. Both of you, please don't start. Not in front of the children."

My sister and I looked at each other, our eyes wondering why our mother's father and ours couldn't argue in front of us when our mother and father did it all the time. But then most of our parents' behaviour didn't make much sense to us. I'm sure they felt the same about ours.

The same could not be said for my father and his father-in-law.

For centuries, Sarajevo had been home to many Sephardic Jews who'd escaped oppression and slaughter in Spain. And though it may have been one of the most secure cities in Europe for Jews, my maternal grandfather never felt safe there. He never felt safe anywhere. Not as long as this world was awash in anti-Semites. And he saw them everywhere, just itching to come out of their shells, devour all who'd shed their foreskins.

Sacred Jewish teachings are suffused with stories of mistreatment of the twelve tribes. And, like most Jews, my maternal grandfather had been imbued with it, if not from birth, from the time he was old enough to read. An avid student of Jewish history and self-taught teacher of the Torah and Talmud, he savoured stories of the ancient Israelites' trials and tribulations. And he could point out every pogrom that had occurred in the past century, spout details of the Spanish Inquisition that would startle its scholars. After years of immersing themselves in the most minute details of such atrocities, the antennae of men like my maternal grandfather became so fine-tuned they could pick up evidence of anti-Semitism on other planets.

The assassination of the Archduke Ferdinand, tapping as it did into the already overflowing reservoir of his persecution complex, shook my maternal grandfather to his core, convinced him that a backlash against Jews was imminent.

What could his wife do? Fight it? Fight him? She tried to convince him he was afraid for nothing. Sarajevo was the safest city for Jews in all of Europe. Maybe safer than America. It was no good. He wouldn't listen to reason. When it came to such deep-seated prejudice, reason could find no place. It was time to leave.

He'd always dreamed of making it to America, making it *in* America. He was drawn to that mythical land like a moth to a marshmallow roast. A cousin of a cousin had emigrated to Montreal, so why not him? So he fled with his young family, first to Dubrovnik on the Croatian coast, then across the Adriatic to Italy, and from there across the Atlantic to Ellis Island. Finally, they made their way to Montreal.

Family rumour had it that he was running from the law. Doing business between the cracks of the law, he'd cut some corners that could be considered criminal and the best way to avoid the consequences was to get out of the country. Anyway, as my mother used to say, her father, like her husband, had ants in his pants.

Once settled in Canada he could never seem to get his bearings, never quite get back on his financial feet. He would blame his difficulties on having been forced to uproot himself, fleeing to save his family from the ravages of rampant anti-Semitism. Nothing legitimized his move as much as the Nazi holocaust. The fact that that hadn't begun until almost two decades after he'd fled didn't seem to make any difference to him. Chronology has no place in the annals of men whose sacred teachings hold their status of eternal victim in the highest esteem.

Convinced he was a holocaust survivor, my maternal grandfather kept a dining room full of framed pictures, names and ages of both close and distant relatives who died in Auschwitz. Having a father who was obsessed with the holocaust's horrors, my mother must often have felt like a holocaust survivor herself, one who then had to survive a pogrom survivor. For my father would not let my mother wallow only in her father's misery. He had to make his misery hers too. Thus, having actually lived through neither the holocaust or a pogrom, my mother was blessed with the burdens of both.

Fortunately, my mother's family had had money, which helped ease their way. But, having had to pay so many bribes to cross borders, by the time they got to Canada they were broke. Little by little her father built up a small business buying and selling used bottles, the recycling business almost a century before it became fashionable. But he never earned enough to really make ends meet. Finally, his wife left him.

To escape his feeling of family and financial failure in Canada, he threw himself into his study of the Talmud and Torah, neglecting his business. Both he and my father shared that tendency, my father out of depression, my maternal grandfather out of obsession.

Both my father and his father-in-law possessed psyches that were in some disarray, but by immersing himself in the Torah, Talmud and the mind-numbing ritual of repetitive prayer, my maternal grandfather not only gave himself the means to focus his diffuse anxiety, but an excuse to merge it with an already well-established collective one.

My father not only resented his father-in-law for his ability to find sanctuary for his anxiety, he also envied him for it. And this may have irked him more than the man's bogus flight from persecution. For my father had renounced the security of religion, and in so doing, forced himself to face his anxiety alone. And it crippled him.

He may have been raised in a religious household, but after his father's murder my father had grown not only into a ardent but also an angry atheist, especially hostile toward the ultra orthodox. The death of his father—the *way* he'd died—had obliterated the image of the father of all fathers for him. He felt god had failed him so fuck him and every one who believed in him.

This led to a bitter fight over my circumcision. My father had wanted to forego "the torture." My maternal grandfather had insisted it would be "over my dead body." My father's resentment turned to rage.

"When you have a son you can do what you want. Until then, mind your own business."

Once again my mother intervened. But this time, instead of encouraging a truce between the two men, she exacerbated my father's antagonism: "If you refuse to allow our son ..."

She couldn't finish the sentence. She didn't have to. The ominous tone of her voice told my father all he needed to know. All he wanted to know. And though he tried to forget it, he never fully forgave her for that threat. Nor her father for forcing the issue.

Trapped between a pogrom-scarred psyche and a holocaust survivor wannabe, my mother's life was a veritable cauldron of crazy.

In some way, my father and maternal grandfather seemed to enjoy arguing with each other. But underneath it all a strain of, if not outright hostility, extreme annoyance—even resentment—seemed to lurk, mostly in my father. It wasn't like him to disrespect his elders. But his father-in-law seemed to touch a nerve in him, a rather raw one, provoking something he might have preferred to keep under wraps: rage. I'm sure it had something to do with the truly horrific trauma he had suffered and the imagined agony his father-in-law liked to flaunt. The man's gall, cavalierly portraying himself as some sort of holocaust survivor, irked my father no end. As foolish as it might have made his father-in-law appear to an outsider, within the family, it seemed not only to diminish my father's suffering, but make a mockery of it.

Yet my grandfather was the glue that held the whole Seder ritual together, the only one to whom it meant something more than merely going through the motions. He would find the meaning hidden behind and give wonderfully detailed explanations for each ritual in the Haggadah.

Impatient as he was to get through the Passover ritual, my father knew my sister and I relished our grandfather's elaborations. And, though our favourite bedtime stories were Ali Baba and the forty thieves and other tales from the Arabian Nights, we also savoured stories from the Old Testament.

* * *

I don't know why we preferred Ali Baba over the more conventional Hansel and Gretel or Rumpelstiltskin. Maybe because it had been banned in our grandfather's house. Despite it being before the establishment of the Israeli state, as far as our grandfather was concerned Arabs were enemies. They'd sided with the Nazis during the Second World War. He didn't want their sacred stories in his house.

My sister argued that they weren't sacred. They were just stories. But for our grandfather we might as well have been reading the Koran. It was all Arab propaganda and he wouldn't have it in his house. Of course, he had never read either of those books. And when my sister brought that up, our grandfather hit the ceiling.

"I've never tasted pig's feet, doesn't mean I don't know it's not kosher! I forbid you to bring those books into the house again and that's that! Understood?"

We'd only sleep over at our grandfather's once in a rare while, and then only for a weekend. By the end of the weekend my sister and I had had enough of him, and he, of us. Had he known how we got the books he might not have only hit the ceiling, he might have hit us.

That summer, my sister and I saved our pennies. By the long Labour Day weekend we were to sleep over at our grandfather's, we figured we had enough to buy copies of both Ali Baba and the Arabian nights. We had gone to the book store with the best of intentions, but when there discovered that we were a couple of dollars short. Over the summer they'd raised their prices. We could have bought only one. But we wanted both, had been looking forward to buying both, and the ones we wanted were those with the most elaborate art work.

So it was either go back and pilfer some money from one of our parents' pocket books or swipe this pair of hard covered ones. It didn't take us long to decide. Rather, it didn't take my sister long. When it came to taking risks, she was as decisive as a child as she was as an adult. I, of course, hemmed and hawed. But when my sister slipped one of the books under my sweater, and the other under hers, I didn't have time to resist, or remember that I'd promised myself to never let her rope me into one of her hijinks again. There was no turning back now. The crime was a fait accompli. Or would be, once we managed to get away without being noticed.

But instead of choosing to be discreet, and silently slipping out of the store, my sister took the opposite tack, whispering: "Pretend we both have cramps, clutching our stomachs and the books underneath our sweaters."

Simply stealing the books was not adrenaline-inducing enough for her, she had to raise the stakes and, before I could protest, she began moaning and muttering—"I've got cramps too! We shouldn't have eaten those hot dogs! I told you we shouldn't have eaten those hot dogs! Dad's gonna kill us now!"—loud enough not only for me to hear but for anyone else who might be interested in why this pair of little kids would be half-keeled over clutching their stomachs and, as though making a beeline for a bathroom, running toward the store door. Where would this bathroom be anyway? In the streets? But that much consistency my sister hadn't contemplated.

As she was about to exit, not satisfied that we'd so easily made a clean getaway, my sister glanced back, trying to catch the owner's eye. Terrified she was going get us caught, I shoved her out the door.

Although we'd made it down the street, around the corner and back inside our grandfather's house without 'the long arm of the law' (I'd heard that phrase on Boston Blackie, my favourite radio detective series) reaching out to arrest us, I kept thinking, any moment they're going to ring the doorbell and take us away. Unlike my sister, I've never been one for rash ventures.

Perhaps only in retrospect does it appear that way, but from an early age my sister seemed to have some sort of death wish. Or might that just be how the adventurous like her strike the risk averse like me?

Anyway, back to our grandfather's Ali Baba tirade: as much as he feared for us as Jews, he ended his invective with a clandestine wink. That wink, was his way of letting us know that nothing, not even his inordinate dread of anti-Semitism, would interfere with his love for us. That absolution only made me feel worse, not only that I had initially upset him, but that my sister and I were hiding a secret from him.

Yet in some convoluted combination of atonement and turning the tables on him, from then on my sister and I began referring to our maternal grandfather as Ali Baba.

"Ali Baba might be angry if we did that," or "Ali Baba wouldn't like this," became our tongue-in-cheek way of teasing him for being so dogmatic. Only behind his back, of course. We wouldn't dare do it directly to his face.

However, little by little, we began calling him Baba, leaving out the Ali. By then he'd forgotten the book, certainly the title, and Baba sounded so much like a child's affectionate mispronunciation of the Hebrew for grandpa, we could make light of his strict philo-Semitic chauvinism and get away with it.

Still, though both Ali Baba and Baba began as double-entendres, they gradually became undiluted terms of endearment. We loved our Baba.

* * *

If in some ways my father couldn't stand his father-in-law, and resented that, unlike his own father, he had lived long enough to enjoy grandchildren, he was glad his children had at least one living grandparent, and that they looked forward to Passover Seders with him. So my father put up with him. As he put up with my father. Like a bad marriage, the two of them tolerated each other, for the sake of the children.

As it so often did, my mother's intervention at the Seder table managed to keep some semblance of peace between our father and grandfather, for a while anyway, as both, along with the rest of us, focused on attacking our food. Perhaps attacking's the wrong word. Stomaching might be more appropriate.

For, as I've mentioned, bland was the hallmark of my mother's meals. She rarely used spices, including salt, and would be insulted when my sister or I insisted on adding some. Nor was she much for other spices. Unless you consider onions a spice. Onions were in everything, from soup to nuts. Borscht with onions. Mashed potatoes with onions. Beef flanken boiled with onions. Instead of almonds and honey we got almonds with onions.

* * *

Perhaps the constant patter about other subjects—any other subject—was meant to cover up disappointment with the food. For the more bland the dish the more vigorous the banter.

Without other relatives there my sister and I could complain to our heart's content about the food's lack of taste. It was shrugged off as typical childish whining. My father would defend my mother with how wonderful it was, how we didn't appreciate what we had, and my mother would cap it off with "In Europe they're starving." The more she repeated this mantra the less convincing it became. I'm sure she knew it was a feeble defense. But it was easier than trying to come up with a fresh response to the same old whine. Or spicing up her cooking.

Of course, by the time my sister and I were teenagers they'd stopped starving in Europe, at least in the half that wasn't under Russian occupation. Why couldn't my mother, for the sake of maintaining credibility with us kids, switch her admonition to Africa or India?

Moreover, she'd refuse to let anyone into her kitchen when she was cleaning up. She didn't want us to see her saving every sliver of leftovers from our plates. She would never leave leftovers. Including those of guests. She'd either finish them as she was cleaning up or store them for later. For herself. She'd never feed her family the leftovers of others. Too unsanitary.

Yet when one of us had pneumonia, measles or mumps, all of which my mother had managed to escape, before secretly eating our leftovers, she'd soak them in salt. She did the same for leftovers from guests. No wonder she didn't salt our food. Though when my sister or I had sore throats she'd pour salt into hot water for us to gargle. She later suffered from severe high blood pressure, and little did we know that, convinced it killed germs, she was consuming so much.

* * *

Back to the Seder. If sooner or later someone had to break the food-suffering silence, who better than uncle Izzy? And so, as though continuing a conversation from god knows when with some out-of-the-blue off-the-wall no-preamble-necessary non sequitur, between bites he abruptly uttered: "I'd trade being a soldier for both my bris and bar mitzvah."

"Bite your tongue!" my maternal grandfather shouted back.

Never having fought in a war, some men feel deprived of a primal rite of passage. Hemingway, his hero, my uncle Izzy was such a man.

A fervent Marxist, he would argue with my father: "Lenin stopped the slaughter of Jews."

"And murdered millions of others," my father would respond.

When he heard that Norman Bethune, a Canadian doctor, had cared for wounded Maoist guerrillas, uncle Izzy decided to go over there and do his part. Unfortunately, he procrastinated so long that by the time he went the communists were firmly entrenched and the Korean War had started. He got as far as Hong Kong before authorities arrested him for bribing a British agent to smuggle him onto the mainland.

Flown home courtesy of the Canadian consulate, when he got back my father had to put up a bond to ensure uncle Izzy didn't try to go back. Because of this incident, and sharing the same surname, for years my father had trouble crossing the border into the U.S.

Like uncle Izzy, my mother's father also felt deprived. But, unlike Izzy, not because he'd never fought in a war but because he'd been robbed of his right to life and death persecution. How could he flaunt his credentials as a true Jew if he'd never suffered a pogrom or holocaust first hand? Thus he struggled to convince, not only others, but himself, that he didn't have to be there in body to know the pain. He felt it in his heart. As he felt all Jewish suffering. From slavery in Egypt to the Spanish Inquisition, Russian pogroms and Nazi holocaust, he'd experienced them all.

No sooner would my father mutter something about "the frimehs (ultra-religious Hasidic Jews with earlocks, long black coats and big black hats) giving us a bad name buying up all the lots in the Laurentians for bupkiss" than my grandfather would lay into him.

"It's just like you to insult the only true Jews left in this world. Atheists like you give us all a bad name."

"And charlatans like them give us a good one?"

Our Seders weren't exactly jovial banquets, the adults having a ball being together. Not with our grandfather insisting we wade through the whole Haggadah service. At least the other adults' do-we-have-to-sit-through-this-again air let them get a kick out of displaying how much they weren't thrilled. A perverse pleasure, but a pleasure nonetheless.

* * *

I've always wondered why so many who've suffered unspeakable horrors seem to survive relatively unscathed, while others, like my father, become emotional basket cases. Are the former less feeling, the latter more fragile? I don't know. All I know is that few people my father knew, including those who'd survived the holocaust, seemed as scarred as he.

However, there was one couple—one of them a cousin on my mother's side—who, in escaping the Gestapo, had to suffocate their infant son so that he would not betray their hiding place with his crying. Cradling their dead infant in their arms as they ran for their lives, they refused to drop him until they felt it safe enough to stop, bury him and say Kaddish.

Eventually caught and put in concentration camps, they seemed to have survived—even thrived—emotionally. How, I find it hard to imagine. My father did too. With most people he would share a litany of worries about his health, business and money. But not with this couple.

They'd known an agony greater than his own, a more gut-wrenching guilt too, yet they always seemed so calm and unperturbed. Perhaps that's why my father was drawn to them.

Then again, it might simply have been that, Berlin born, from wealthy families, this couple had an elegance about them. More highly educated than most of my parents' cronies, more cultured too, in some ways they seemed out of place in my parents' circle.

In any case, during their infrequent visits my father seemed a different person. Enchanted—more likely mesmerized—as if touched by a special spirit, he almost seemed at peace with himself, with his past. The silent sharing of their unspeakable histories seemed soothe both my father and this couple. They certainly savoured each other's company. Perhaps opposites do attract.

* * *

Uncle Izzy never seemed to suffer from either pangs of conscience or anxiety. He was a fatalist. And had little sympathy for my father. Anytime the subject of pogroms, concentration camps or cancer popped up, his response was: "Sooner or later we all end up in our own little Auschwitz."

Pogroms and concentration camps were subjects too painful for discussion in front of my father. Nevertheless, sometimes, when he was sleeping off a depression, out of town on business, or simply in the bathroom—he spent a lot of time in there, as did I, both finding it a soothing place to sit—these subjects did come up for discussion. Actually, the word discussion doesn't do justice to the back and forth bickering between relatives who'd suffered Russian or Polish pogroms and those who'd spent time in concentration camps. Rather than philosophical debate about suffering, life and death, the arguing would be over which was worse, who'd suffered more.

At the age of seven or eight my sister could already find the humour there. She had a wicked—one might say sick—sense of whimsy, finding—indeed, seeking out—places where the family darkness could make a masked appearance, and be magically transformed into something funny.

For instance: though in retrospect these topics may not seem amusing, she invented a game show in which contestants competed with one another to see who'd had it worse, the holocaust or pogrom survivor. The one who evoked the greater sympathy from the audience received the greater 'reparation'. How did she know about reparations at that young an age? I don't know. But she relished the word.

Along with emceeing, she'd play both parts, concocting escalating sequences of competitive horror stories. The more far-fetched the funnier. The more outrageous the more it allowed us license to laugh.

The game might go something like this: "I lost two brothers, both boiled in oil while I was forced to watch them eat their fingers like French fries."

"Well, I was forced to twist off my father's testicles with a pair of pliers then eat them raw, *before* they were cooked."

"That's nothing, I was forced to turn the tap of a gigantic glass oven and watch my whole family be baked."

Suffice it to say that it gradually got more and more gruesome. And the more outrageously gruesome the greater the laughter. We'd both be keeling over as she alternated more and more rapidly between contestants, increasingly escalating and exaggerating their horror stories. Finally, we could laugh no more. Our stomachs hurt too much. I would shout: "Stop! You have to stop!" But she wouldn't. Laughing too hard to continue in sensible sentences, her stop and go stuttering spewed out slivers of one horrific image or another, one horror story or another, until she too was in too much agony to continue.

Finally, her facial muscles worn out, she'd stop laughing, stop smiling even, sruggled to catch her breath.

Of course, in terms of sheer numbers, the holocaust clearly had it. In terms of historical stature, it was also no contest. How many pogrom movies have you seen? While you can hardly keep track of the number of holocaust hits.

* * *

From the same womb yet poles apart from his older brother—my father—always broke, always borrowing, uncle Izzy was a man who couldn't seem to earn a living. Though it wasn't for lack of trying.

Going from one pie in the sky scheme to another, his ideas, either before their time, after, or simply too farfetched for any era, always went nowhere. Like the toilet seat that could be raised merely by pressing a foot-pedal. To lower it after you finished urinating, you had to tap it twice with your toe, quickly, one tap after another, in rapid succession.

"If I could just get a spot in the New York Toilet Show I'd be rich. But to do that I need stock, not just a prototype. That means money."

My father refused to lend him any.

"I built up a business lamps and shades. Lamps and shades, that's it. You think I'm going to let you make me a fool for every cockamamie idea?"

Uncle Izzy was livid. But not one to be easily deterred, he found a distributor who agreed to front him enough money for a dozen prototypes.

Unfortunately, his target market, old arthritic men, had trouble putting all their weight on one leg while using the toe of the other to tap-dance the toilet seat back down. The young and fit also found it frustrating, for if you didn't do that double-tap just right, the seat would end up stuck somewhere between perpendicular to the toilet bowl rim and flush with it. You'd have to force it down with your hands or, if that didn't work, sit on it, and break the connection to the pedal.

Still, the distributor managed to sell all twelve prototypes before their defects put Izzy out of business. They almost did the same to his distributor. When the man threatened to sue Izzy, he was admonished: "You can't take blood from a stone."

The distributor, polite and elegant to the end, responded: "I'm neither a surgeon nor a geologist." And promptly punched Izzy in the nose.

Izzy's nose was never the same. It was probably broken, but he didn't trust doctors. So, until the day he died he had trouble breathing through it. Mostly, he breathed through his mouth. Since he'd never bothered to take care of his teeth, he had chronic bad breath. A hard man to be around. Still, I was fond of him. He always seemed to be smiling, a sort of smirk, as if he was up to something underhanded. And, usually, he was.

Uncle Izzy was my father's youngest sibling, born shortly after my grandfather was butchered. All his life my father had to look after him, look out for him, pay some of his debts.

"And this is the way you repay me?!" I'd hear my father exclaim when he had to bail his brother out of one kind of trouble or another, including jail. Don't get me wrong, my uncle never did time. He rarely broke the law, he only skirted it. And 'skirted' is the appropriate word. For, other than money, most of the messes my uncle managed to get himself into were with women. Young women. Either on the edge of being underage or just below it.

As Uncle Izzy liked to put it: "So I've got a yen for young beaver, sue me that makes me a monster? Saul, David, Solomon, all our kings, I'm in good company."

My mother might simply be embarrassed, but my father would turn red with rage. Especially if my sister or I were within earshot.

The same scenario repeated itself so often one might wonder why my father didn't just disown his brother. The simple answer may be that my father was too soft-hearted. The more complex reason: my father felt responsible for depriving his baby brother of a father. Most probably, he'd been like a father to Izzy, and felt responsible for him.

I don't know how many suckers Izzy fleeced of their savings but it was more than a few. And it didn't seem to bother him. For years my father barred him from our home. But he didn't have the heart to disown his brother for good. Not when the man came begging. A con man through and through, he didn't mind humiliating himself if that's what it took.

Often the only source of adult levity in our home, for my sister and me uncle Izzy was an antidote to our father. Single, a lifelong bachelor, uncle Izzy never seemed to need anyone. Certainly he didn't seem needy. Nothing like my father. And not toward us. He could take us or leave us. Mostly he took us to places that were fun. And let us go on rides like the Ferris wheel and roller coaster my father would never allow.

* * *

Unlike uncle Izzy, there was an underlying innocence, a purity if you will, to our aunt Bessy. With her my sister and I could talk about anything. And she had an answer for everything. An aphorism too. She had little formal education, and read nothing but the newspaper and condensed *Readers Digest* novels. Nevertheless, there was a wisdom in my aunt Bessy, an intelligence that could spot a person's strengths or weaknesses quicker than any over-schooled shrink.

A self-made woman, she earned a small fortune in the textile trade.

Some of her competitors accused her of dealing not only in black-market but stolen goods.

Once, I went with her to confront a competitor she heard was spreading such rumours. In the middle of a store filled with weekend shoppers she shouted: "If you've got a case, prove it! If not shut up or I'll sue! A son of a bitch like you may you-know-what where he eats but when I get through with you you won't have a pot to cook never mind you-know-what in!"

And she did sue one or two. After that she never heard a peep from any of them, or the police. They either had bigger fish to fry or were paid to look the other way. I wouldn't put it past my aunt Bessy to try the latter.

"They're all jealous I get a penny or two off the top, two hundred rolls that's all it takes when you pay cash up front they don't have to listen to excuses the cheque's in the mail. Mostly, I wait till a distributor's about to go belly up then buy a dime on the dollar. Better ten cents before they file than a quarter after. I give them cash they can hide and have a nose for knowing who's in trouble and won't survive and who's in trouble and will. Nine times from ten I'm right, and nine times from ten they're grateful, give me deals others can only dream of."

Aunt Bessy bought remnants, what were called piece goods, remainders or leftovers from clothing manufacturers' production line runs, which she sold in her four stores in Ontario and Quebec. Her husband minded the store in Toronto—"I make sure he's far enough he can't nag me day in and out"—while two of his brothers took care of two others. The fourth, by far the biggest, was her baby, one she ran herself with a little help from hired hands. Uncle Izzy worked for her for a while, until she found out he was stealing. For years she wouldn't speak to him.

* * *

It wasn't so much that uncle Izzy was without scruples; it's that he was oblivious to them. A fine distinction, to be sure, perhaps only fit for family members one is fond of. Especially when it involved underage skirt-chasing.

"What do you want I should ask for ID before they take off their clothes? She told me she was twenty-one I should call her a liar to her face?" That was his cavalier quip when my father bailed him out. Arrested for drunk driving and trying to bribe the policeman who'd stopped him for speeding, he was equally unrepentant.

"This is the last straw!" was a phrase my father uttered so often when referring to uncle Izzy it lost its significance.

But it never lost its significance for my sister and me. To resolve the stress of disputes with each other, we used to spoof the expression. She might start the routine off by uttering an exasperated "This is the last straw!" in a tone that, at the same time as it emulated our mother—she too used the expression, but aimed only at my sister and me, never anyone else, including uncle Izzy—mocked my father's use of it. I'd respond with "Yeah, well, this is the second to last straw!" She'd come back with "Yeah, well, this is the third to last straw!" And so on and so forth until one of us couldn't continue keeping a straight face. Soon, the other'd be in stitches too.

No matter how angered or hurt one of us felt by the other, how stubbornly either of us was intent on sticking to their feelings of betrayal or resentment, once one threw down the 'This-is-the-last-straw' gauntlet, like it or not the other had to play along, however grudgingly. It was a betrayal of our bond not to.

Worst come to worst, one of us being so angry at the other that initially we'd refuse to participate, the initiator of our it's-the-last-straw method of conflict resolution might have to keep playing both parts until the aggrieved party could no longer keep holding onto his or her anger.

The routine might go something like this: "This is the last straw." Grudging silence from the other. "This is the second to last straw." More grudging silence from the other. "This is the third to last straw." And so on and so forth until grudging silence gave way to grudging giggling.

Sometimes the peace overtures would get all the way up to the seventh, eighth, ninth or tenth last-straw before the aggrieved party could no longer maintain their recalcitrant tone and caved in, cracking up all the harder for having held out—indeed, held their breath—for so long. Finally, they just had to let go with laughter.

Should I try to stop my sister's attempts at undermining my anger at her by saying: "I'm serious," she'd respond with: "So am I. This is the seventh and last straw." It wouldn't take long before we were both howling with laughter. We could never stay angry at each other for long. I could stand my parents being angry at me. In fact, I expected it. That was what parents were supposed to do to keep their kids in line. But I couldn't stand my sister's antipathy. It would break my heart.

Oh baby bro,

Remember the way we used to make up rhymes? Crazy kid rhymes. Having a great old time laughing our heads off. Until mom or dad shouted for us to keep it down or we'd have to go back to our own beds, our own rooms.

Now, never knowing when my more militant comrades will come to kill me, to keep the fear (which I only feel at night, trying to fall asleep) at bay, I make up little kid rhymes, cozy ones, trying to soothe myself to sleep. The weird thing is I see myself as a fellow traveller. Except when it comes killing. Guess this gringa's just not far left enough.

Why is it that long distance like this, a distance filled with such longing (For what? Home? Being with my baby bro?) I'm more forthcoming than I am face to face? Well, when we're together we can just be quiet, without talking, at least without feeling we have to fill up the silence between sentences.

I always feel safe with you, I'm not being judged, there's nothing I need to say, I can just enjoy the stillness between us. I know few people, if any—I'm sure it's the same for you—with whom I can share a prolonged period of keeping my mouth shut, savour it even, without getting antsy, feeling I should say something to break the ice. With us there is no ice. There never was.

But I don't have to tell you this. I don't have to tell you

anything. You know me oh too well. I should probably just send
you a bunch of blank pages, let you fill them in. Fill me in.
Still, I hope you're listening. I wouldn't want to whine for
nothing. If I can't bitch to my baby brother to whom can I?

Love you to pieces,

M.

Whenever I was with my sister I felt uplifted by her sheer delight in the minutiae of life. Her light-hearted laughter was infectious, her goofy giggle disarming. With an innocent—almost indiscriminate—enthusiasm for every little thing and childlike openness to other people—the latter a talent that escapes me—she seemed to take delight in any new encounter, savouring the uniqueness of each.

When we were kids she would initiate conversations with anybody and everybody, anytime, anywhere. As an adult she was a little more discriminating. But not much. She could be so bubbly she'd salivate, like a little girl who'd not yet learned to not drool. Her delight would explode in bursts, often, of laughter, her face lighting up in amazement, genuine astonishment, like she'd just seen something she'd never seen before, heard something that she'd never heard, thought something she'd never thought.

Her effervescence could sometimes border on annoying. For those of us who prefer a more morose default face, her boundless enthusiasm could be taxing. You wanted to say: *Give it a rest, I don't believe it, I don't believe you.* But, try as you might not to, you did believe her. Like some born again infant in an adult body for whom every encounter was a wonder, she was that convincing, that infectious. Sooner or later she would manage to break down the wall you put up to get through your day, to get through your life.

Perhaps, to cope with and counter our parents' unhappiness she was determined to flood the world with a surfeit of hers. At least on the surface. Perhaps she didn't know which part of her happy face was real and which part wasn't. Still, people, especially men, were drawn to the buoyant upbeat way she seemed to dance through life. Maybe that was her downfall, along with her daring. Not only as a child but as an adolescent she would do anything for the sake of adventure. Yet her teen years proved to be merely a training ground, preparation for what was to follow. Parental restraint cast aside, the freedom of full-blown adulthood would give her the chance to really up the risk-taking ante.

* * *

My sister's recklessness may not have begun with my uncle Izzy, but he certainly didn't dampen her attraction to danger.

Uncle Izzy saw himself as a bon vivant, our parents saw him as a degenerate, my sister and I, somewhere in between. Once, long before we were of age, he snuck us into a strip club.

Unlike movie theatres, bars and strip clubs rarely demanded ID. So there was no problem getting my sister into my uncle's favourite strip joint.

Because a fire in a packed movie theatre had caused a stampede that crushed dozens, the province of Quebec had passed a law that you had to be at least sixteen to attend a movie. At the age of nine my sister could get in without ID. Which irked me no end.

When it came to getting me into the strip joint, my uncle just winked, told the maitre d' I was a midget. The man laughed. My uncle could pull stings if he had to. But he rarely had to. Just a wink, smile and a ten dollar bill is all it took.

Had my father found out he would have freaked. But he never did. My sister and I had been sworn to secrecy. And my sister made sure that I stuck to my oath. There seemed to be a special bond between my uncle and sister, more than between him and me. In the years since her death I've often thought about it.

* * *

Once their daughter hits puberty, the ubiquitous male appetite may pose problems for parents. With my sister, normal concerns were compounded. All of eight or nine when she'd fully blossomed, she was so pretty and precociously sexy that much older boys and men would flirt with her. And, whether conscious of it or not, she seemed to encourage them. A physically mature body supporting an immature brain can be a troublesome combination. It took its toll on my parents. Particularly the day my mother came home to discover my uncle giving my sister a dance lesson behind my sister's closed bedroom door.

My mother's mind must have been racing: if nothing untoward was taking place why the closed door? There was no one else in the house. So the music couldn't have been disturbing anybody. Suspicions aroused, she could hear uncle Izzy's voice, above the music, singing out instructions along with it: "And a one and a two and a one two three. Slow, slow, quick quick, slow. And now we dip, hold on to me tight, tighter!"

I can picture my mother, ear against my sister's bedroom door, odious images of uncle Izzy and my sister nestled cheek to cheek racing through her head as she listened to him sensually humming, savouring both the music and my sister. And when my mother heard my uncle sing "Dancing is like making love!" head aching, heart pounding, she must've had a fit.

What did my eight- or nine-year-old sister know about making love, except from fairy tales, a prince pecking the cheek of a princesses? The princess blushing. The next words that flowed from my uncle's mouth must have shook my mother.

"You have to throw your heart and soul into it, your whole body! No holding back!"

Afraid of what she'd find, my mother didn't dare do anything right then and there. How do I know all this? I arrived home just in time to hear her shouting hysterically to my father over the phone. She probably thought the music would drown her out. But my ears were against my bedroom wall, the one I shared with my parents' bedroom.

* * *

My father rushed home, a half hour after the phone call. I timed it. By then uncle Izzy had been on his merry way, whistling as he danced out the front door, my beaming sister waving him goodbye. He may have seemed oblivious and carefree, but he must have sensed something. He could hear that my mother was home—she was yelling at me—yet he didn't bother saying goodbye to her, something he would normally never neglect doing.

For my parents, mouthing the word 'molest' in front of my sister or me would have been more taboo than any impropriety that might have taken place between my uncle and sister. I doubt my father knew the word existed, let alone what it meant. It was certainly not in his vocabulary. But he was furious.

"Never again will I let that good-for-nothing in this house!" But his fury was vented solely at my mother, within the confines of their bedroom, for allowing my uncle to be alone with my sister in hers.

My mother chose to repeat "like making love," over and over for the sole purpose of rousing my father's rage to a fever pitch. She'd never liked my uncle Izzy. But she put up with him for my father's sake, "for the sake of family," as my father often put it after Izzy crossed one line or another.

But to my parents, this breach of etiquette not only crossed a line, it crushed all boundaries. Those three little words, "like making love," threw my father into a tizzy. My mother too.

I thought those words might have been innocent enough. My uncle had a way of acting out—overacting—magnifying expressive sounds, manifesting all sorts of oohs and ahs to punctuate his stories and tall tales. His idol was John Barrymore. I think he saw himself as some sort of replica. His performances often embarrassed my parents. But it was no use telling him to put a lid on it. That would only encourage him. I once heard him act out his latest young lady friend's orgasm for my parents.

But he rarely indulged in such vulgarity with my sister and me there, at least not in the same room. When it came to his brother's kids, he knew how far he could go. Still, he often tested that edge, from time to time going over it. But he knew my parents would put up with him going only so far. And he needed them. He needed us. He had no kids of his own, no other family. And with all the 'young ladies' in his life he was a lonely man, often at loose ends. You could see it in his eyes. On occasion, when it came time to leave, he'd tear up.

Though my father was an unreservedly affectionate man, his expressions of affection were limited to big warm bear hugs and paternal pinches or pecks on the cheek. Not only would my sister and I frequently get big hugs and kisses from him, but our friends would too. As adolescents it became somewhat embarrassing. Yet never was there a hint of lecherous impropriety.

My uncle Izzy, on the other hand, loved to add a little naughty innuendo to an interaction, even when there wasn't really a trace. He enjoyed stirring things up.

Even if nothing untoward had taken place between my uncle and sister, that closed door opened up a can of worms in my parents' imaginations.

Considering that my uncle had been caught in a motel in a compromising position—actually, many compromising positions according to the cop spying on him—with an underage girl didn't help. To my uncle that girl looked a lot older than her sixteen years. Indeed, my sister looked a lot older than her nine.

Considering my uncle's history and reputation with young women, you can understand my father's explosion of rage. When it came to transgressing taboos, uncle Izzy was a ticking time bomb, one that had finally exploded.

My parents were not the sort to carry on heart-to-heart or simple civil conversations with their kids. I doubt they did it with each other. While my uncle was a rake, with the scruples of a snake, and my parents feared something inappropriate may have taken place, they were reluctant to question my sister or confront Izzy. This was something they simply didn't know how to discuss. But they had other ways of dealing with it. Instead of the usual loud primal sharing of his pain, my father adopted an intense angry uncommunicativeness with uncle Izzy.

* * *

Since it was unclear whether something truly taboo had taken place and, if it did, its precise nature, for my parents, the uncertainty was all the more unsettling. Our parents never talked about sex. Few parents did in those days. Nor did they discuss other matters of intimate consequence, such as feelings. My father could emote, cry and wail but never calmly articulate what was bothering him.

My uncle Izzy, on the other hand, wasn't one to shy away from taboo subjects. In fact, he'd flaunt them. He liked nothing better than to shock, seemed to prefer it to simple, comfortable conversation. Yet, however raunchy and beyond the pale he might be, he too would never probe truly deep. He stuck to the surface. For him there didn't seem to be more to life than its veneer, more to emotions than their façade.

In any event, there was no way my parents would broach the subject of the dance lesson with my sister or uncle. For in so doing they might be forced to imply lurid details. Since sex or anything remotely related to it was just too difficult to discuss, the only way to deal with the dance lesson was to avoid it.

Besides, they were scared of my sister, afraid of implying she'd done something wrong. She could turn the table on my parents, accuse them of having warped minds.

Same with uncle Izzy. They'd gone through the routine so many times my father knew how an argument with him would go. He didn't want to give his brother an excuse to accuse him of having a dirty mind, that he should be ashamed of himself thinking so little of his brother. Of course, he did think so little of his brother. With good reason.

So the best option with Izzy was silence. Seething stone-faced silence. And my parents invoked it with a vengeance. You can't argue with it. Unless you ask what's wrong. And my father knew that, refusing to acknowledge he'd done anything wrong, Izzy wouldn't ask. And, not doing so, would be tantamount to an acknowledgment of guilt.

Indeed, Izzy never asked why the tango lessons had been terminated. Without being warned, without a cross word being uttered to him, the subject never surfaced. My father's fiercely focused silent anger had conveyed more than any tongue-lashing could. That uncle Izzy seemed to remain oblivious to how far over the line he'd stepped with my sister's dance lesson, that he had even crossed a line in his brother's eyes, only served to deepen my father's mistrust and animosity toward him.

My sister felt our parents were infringing on her privacy, her freedom to fend for herself, to find free space for herself. Her bedroom was hers. What went on there was none of her parents' business. Yet the way she smiled and swaggered when my parents avoided the subject of uncle Izzy's impropriety did nothing to allay their anxiety. At that young age, she already had a way with innuendo, one more subtle and insidious than either of my parents.

By not making a fuss the moment my parents forbade further dance lessons, my sister must have known she'd be encouraging their suspicion that something improper had taken place. Whether true or not, belief that she may have been the object of her uncle's desire had given her the stamp of a grown man's approval, certified her as a woman, a desirable one at that.

Yet, smitten by that Argentine-inspired exoticism, bitten by its erotic bug, that one tango lesson became a life-altering experience for her, with dance, and men, kindling a premature appetite for more of each. And so, a few weeks after 'the incident,' just when the tumult appeared to have passed and my parents had put it behind them, my sister decided she wanted to take dance lessons. No, she needed to.

And when my sister needed something, there was no stopping her.

Thinking it was safer for her to take dance lessons from a stranger than her uncle, my parents paid for a private instructor at Rosita and Deno's, a renowned Montreal ballroom dance studio where most of the upwardly mobile Jewish immigrants went to learn the right steps.

Now it's never been easy reading my parents' minds, but they may have thought that, in seeking lessons from a legitimate dance studio, my sister was indicating that her interest had been in the dance and not her uncle's attention. On the other hand, she may have been aspiring for more of what started with uncle Izzy, but with a younger instructor. Once again she'd managed to put my parents' minds in a bind. But what could they do? They were afraid to put their foot down. With my sister they were always afraid.

At first they fretted over her instructor, one much younger and better looking than uncle Izzy. But when Rosita informed them that this teacher had no interest in women, lived with a man with whom he was head over heels in love, I'm sure they didn't quite know whether to feel reassured or bewildered.

* * *

Perhaps it began with that rite de passage with my uncle, a premature certification of post-pubescent attractiveness, all her life my sister would be a sucker for men's interest, approval and desire.

From the age of ten my sister began pressuring my parents to let her to go out on dates. Things that most parents fretted about with their teenage daughters had already begun to panic my parents. For a couple of years they managed to keep the boys away. But when she turned twelve my parents conceded. She could go out on dates, but only with boys her own age. This posed a problem. She looked older and more mature than boys a year or two older, including those who could grow beards. As for peach fuzzers her age, forget it: she looked more like their babysitter than date.

After her first couple of years in high school, she started dating much older boys, young men, some in college, some straight out of correctional facilities. God knows where she found some of these guys. She went from staying out to the wee hours of the morning to staying out all night.

A couple of times, when she hadn't returned from her date by sunrise, my parents resorted to calling the cops. In response, my sister threatened to move out. Once, she did. Moved in with a man in his twenties. She had yet to celebrate her sixteenth birthday. Lord knows at what age she lost her virginity. I never asked. Neither did my parents. They were afraid to.

* * *

My father was a showman. From the way he dressed to the manner he expressed unadulterated emotions, to the way he gambled at cards, in business and building homes he couldn't afford, he was a flamboyant man, lived with a definite flair. In that sense he was not unlike my sister. Or she was not unlike him. Except for her seeming lack of fear.

A flashy dresser, with silk suits of every imaginable hue, from copper gold to silver grey, formal black to folksy white, my father simply couldn't pass up an excuse to have a party. The bigger the better. To celebrate my bar mitzvah and, much later, my sister's weddings, he'd spend like there was no tomorrow. But the day after that, he'd collapse in a how-to-pay-for-it heap.

Everyone with whom my father did business, including dozens of Gentile buyers from all the chain stores were invited to my bar mitzvah bash. My father did half his business by phone, as often as not from bed. Because he could sweet talk. How he could sweet talk. As a buyer once confided in me: "He's a hard man to turn down, your father, surtout when he turns on the charm. He could sell ice cubes to an Eskimo!"

He made buyers feel like part of the family, a festive part. Yet if he felt like weeping with one of them he would. It may have embarrassed me no end in my world, but it seemed to serve my father well in his, establishing an intimate bond with buyers, one I'm sure unlike they had with any other manufacturer. What he was selling most of all was himself, and his uninhibited display of emotion.

A twelve-piece orchestra played my father's ballroom dance favourites. And when that band took its break, a gypsy trio serenaded the crowd with old Russian classics, climaxing with a *kazatzka*, a rowdy Slavic folk-dance. At any wedding or bar mitzvah, all my father had to hear was that slow haunting fiddle prelude, and nothing could stop him from getting ready to kick up his heels. Often, my aunt Bessy would join him. When it came to the squatting and leg-kicking-out part of the dance, she was one of the few people who could keep up with him. But, during my bar mitzvah's first big-band break, despite my father's cajoling, my Aunt Bessy insisted it was too soon for such a strenuous dance. "I haven't digested my dessert yet!"

It turns out she'd forgot her underarm deodorant and was trying to avoid sweating so early in the evening. So my father went solo and, in the midst of dancing up a storm, enticed my sister to take aunt Bessy's place. Squat for squat, kick for kick, she kept pace with my father. By the end, it was hard to tell who was more out of breath. Whereas my father had to change his sweat-drenched suit, her dress so thin and back so bare, my sister hardly broke a sweat.

Unlike my parents, whose stoic stiff-upper-lipped smiles contradicted the lithe movements of their legs, my father and sister's unadulterated looks of delight when tangoing together could steal the spotlight from their elegant footwork. At times consumed by her own performance, my sister appeared oblivious to her partner. But that didn't bother my father. Proud of his daughter, and not afraid to show it, his was the supporting role, hers, the starring. And he would let her shine until, bowing her head ever so slightly, as though both apologizing and thanking him for allowing her her little indulgence, she'd beam at him and they'd return to acknowledging each other's moves. The awareness they were performing, that all eyes were on them, rather than inhibiting their enjoyment, enhanced it.

Where does a thirteen-year-old girl get such precocious poise? I don't know. But, when it came to the tango, she'd had it since she was ten, less than two years after she started private lessons. With more restrained dances like the waltz, she was not only at ease with each step, but with the élan that accompanied it.

Once the music started my sister and uncle Izzy went out of their way to avoid each other. But watching her dance with other male relatives and friends, my father would brag: "My daughter took to dance the way a duck takes to water," a touch of misgiving in his tone.

During the final big-band break my father insisted the gypsy trio play another *kazatzka*. And this time aunt Bessy joined in.

Over four hundred had attended the festivities. In addition to the dozens of travel alarm clocks and briefcases with my initials that I got as gifts, I received thousands of dollars in cheques and cash. But before I could finish counting my father appropriated it all. He needed the money to pay for the party. To reimburse me, he put me on his business payroll. Along with my mother. But had to take us both off when the tax man started asking questions.

I'm sure my father considered bribing the Revenue Canada guy to look the other way when he came to audit the business books. How could he not have? That was what his father would have done. And his father before him. Doing business that way was in his blood. Every fibre of his being must have been urging him to pull out his wallet and whisper: "Psst, buddy, here, buy your wife a little something she should feel special." I'd seen him do it countless times with ushers, doormen and maitre d's, anything so he didn't have to suffer the indignity of standing in line to buy tickets for shows or sports events.

When a night club was empty, he'd still slip the maitre d' a ten. Perhaps it was to guarantee that when the place was full he'd get a front table. Anyhow, it was habit. You could see that glow in his eyes, the sheer joy of being free to grease someone's palm without having to fret about the consequences. It may have been that, in exercising that old influence-peddling instinct, one handed down from his father, he'd found a way of keeping his father alive, inside him.

But when it came to the taxman, bribery was a bridge too far. Still, rather than break the law, he let his accountant help him circumvent it.

* * *

My parents had distant relatives in Poland who'd survived the holocaust but were having a hard time making ends meet. So my father sent them money every month, and eventually managed to bring them to Canada, in one case by bribing a customs and immigration official with a carton of Crown royal. This wasn't as risky as it might appear. The man was Jewish, and sometimes played cards with my father.

Yet on this occasion my father was not afraid to break the law. What he would never do for himself he often did for others. Specially if they were desperate. He understood desperation.

Chapter 3

MY FATHER'S LOVE often felt stifling. Combined with his all-consuming concern for our safety, it could be crushing. Too much love can be as debilitating as too little.

To free herself, my sister knew she had to get as far from our family as possible. And so, when she finished high school, she decided to go to college in California. My father resisted. Somehow, he sensed that would just be the beginning of her flight from family safety.

"So far from home!? So far from your family?! What's wrong with McGill? The best doctors in the world come from McGill! If it's good enough for them it should be good enough for you!"

As headstrong as an adult as she was wilful as a child, in the end what could my dad do? In some ways, her leaving home for university must have been a relief for my parents. They no longer had to fret about her relations with men. What they didn't know couldn't bother them.

Yet once my sister learned Russian, she and my father shared a secret language. It became part of their bond—a special intimacy—between them, a language the two of them could share and neither my mother nor I could understand. Often they'd revert to whispering—what they were saying meant only for each other's ears—though we couldn't have understood if they'd enunciated loud and clear.

On the rare occasions when she came home to visit, she and my father would speak only Russian to each other. When she was away, they would carry on lengthy long distance tête-à-têtes. What they talked about I don't know. Neither did my mother. Neither of us carried on such protracted conversations with my father in any language. Nor had my father and sister before she learned to speak Russian.

It may have taken my father back to a time when he'd made his father proud that he could read and write Russian so well, showed such prowess in the language of power, had given my grandfather hope that my father could succeed in the Gentile world, have a better life.

My sister was a beautiful woman. And the bond between father and daughter is often more charged than that between mother and son. Whenever the two of them were together, you could feel the spark from my father. That they spoke Russian to each other only added to the unique intensity of their intimacy.

You could single them out as a couple in any crowd, more so than my father and mother. For, unlike my parents, they would usually be holding hands, and whispering to one another. While my parents rarely talked. Unless it was to argue.

My sister and I treasured our Passover Seders as children. As adults, however, the two of us were rarely in town at the same time. When we were, the cantankerous façade that once suffused those extended family get-togethers seemed to fade. As an adult, my sister was the spark that could light a fire of undiluted laughter and joy under our expanded family gathering, put a smile on my father's face, and fresh pep in his step.

During these short visits, he was on his best behaviour, cracking the odd joke, trying as hard as he could to make sure my sister was happy to be home, so she'd come back. For me he didn't seem to bother. Perhaps he felt he could take me for granted. I'd return from time to time no matter what. He didn't have to romance me.

* * *

Initially, my sister's going off to college left me in a kind of limbo. Growing up, knowing that she was always there for me, a mediator between my parents and me, a mentor too, had sustained me.

But I now had a girlfriend to nurture me in other ways. She had three siblings, all much younger, was like a mother to them, doted on each. I savoured being part of this happy little family. We spent so much time looking after them, I sometimes felt like their surrogate father, albeit one still a virgin.

Thus, several years after I, in the eyes of my people, became a man, I decided, once and for all, to feel like one. And what better time than the day of Atonement. Don't get me wrong, I wasn't sacrilegious. As a boy, the eerie echoes of the Kol Nidre stirred chords of my people's tortured history in me. Still, when you hit puberty, your priorities can suddenly stray, take a back seat to other longings.

Since my true love's parents were ultra-orthodox, on Yom Kippur they stayed in synagogue from morning to night, while their three youngest spent the afternoon with grandparents. So, knowing we'd be safe, my honey and I rushed to her bedroom right after morning services.

When I first saw her naked, awed by her beauty, I cried. She never wore makeup or used perfume. Because she was extremely allergic, her soap and shampoo were scent free. Yet she always smelled like a bouquet of freshly-bathed newborns, even when she'd worked up a sweat on our hot summer hill-climbing hikes. In fact, the more she sweated the sweeter her scent.

Can pheromones be the key to what makes a couple click? Well, making love, her aroma was so intoxicating, like a crazed bloodhound, my nose couldn't get enough of her and, before I could mount her, like Vesuvius, I erupted.

So much for becoming a man. A lifelong pattern had been set, one which, in some perverse way, allowed me to feel faithful to my first sweetheart with many of my one night stands.

We got back to temple just in time for the Yom Kippur climax. That ram's horn sound seemed so similar to some of the noises we'd been making just an hour earlier, I glanced up to see my sweetheart, face flushed, beaming down at me from the women's balcony. It confirmed my feeling that something sacred had taken place between us.

* * *

There's something I should tell you here. Two left feet are hard to hide. Don't get me wrong, the toes on my right foot are aligned normally, equal and opposite to those on the left. But both the bone that should jut out behind the big toe on the inside of the right foot and the concave arch area that follows are on the outside, back of my smallest toe.

Confused? You're in good company. My genetic code. After faithfully carrying out instructions for my left foot, it had a memory lapse, started making another left then, mid-course, realized its mistake, put the toes in their proper places but forgot to correct the foot-bone foundation.

Puny as they were, I was less afraid to parade my privates in public than my feet. I shied away from swimming and, for sex, wore socks. Padded puffies.

When one of the women who'd bedded me—shy when it came to sex, I let them take the initiative—asked why I'd kept my socks on, I told her I had spasms of the arteries that reduced blood flow to the toes and so were always cold. She immediately quipped: "Better wear a rubber then, make sure your phallus doesn't freeze up on me." At once, it did. Yet when another new bed-mate responded to the same explanation with "Getting intimately involved gives you cold feet," I fell in love.

The only woman with whom I didn't wear socks for our intimate inaugural—where I didn't feel I had to—was my first love. But when it came to marriage with her, I *did* get cold feet.

Still, not only did she provide my earliest experience of erotic affection—my most powerful too—her parents gave me my first taste of contented family life. However, by the time I'd finished my undergraduate work, I'd been with my beloved for almost eight years, and had become too comfortable—i.e., uncomfortable—with so much contentment. Besides, her parents were pressuring us to marry, before I went off to graduate school. Unmarried, she would not be allowed to accompany me.

As part of my heartthrob's happy family, I could see what life would be like if I were to wed her. And though I regretted not having grown up in a home as joyful as hers, and was fond of her parents—of her whole family—I resented this "bourgeois imposition." More, I was angry that my beloved accepted it, refused to break with what I then considered the most stultifying of middle class conventions. How dare she defer to her parents rather than me.

But I was determined to keep my resentment to myself. When it came to domestic drama, each tied so tightly to the emotions of the amygdala their rational brains could rarely get a word in edgewise, my father and sister had always been victims of spontaneous combustion rather than perpetrators of pre-meditative pyromania. Damned if I was going to let that happen to me. Not reasonable level-headed cerebral me. I wasn't going to explode, just quietly walk away. Later, alone, I could implode.

We're all composites of unfathomable complexity, genuine rationality doomed to be second banana in the fruit salad of our psyches. Thus, I convinced myself she simply wasn't bohemian enough for me, for what I as an aspiring artist felt she had to be.

To bolster my illusion of sound judgement, I reread Rimbaud and Baudelaire, both of which helped convince me that, for an artist, not only was happiness unfashionable, it could kill one's creative juices. Contentment was the artist's number one enemy, alienation, his key ally.

Of course, I hadn't yet turned on my artist's spigot. I was going to write, soon as I finished graduate school. First I had to make sure I had some means of support. And the right female muse.

Maybe, like my sister, I was drawn to the drama of misery. After all, it was so familiar to me. I'm sure my parents wanted to see me 'settle down' and happy. Still, considering all my father had suffered, and that for so I'd long felt bad about being in such good spirits around my girlfriend's parents and so often depressed around mine, the prospect of once and for all trading my family's misery for the serenity and joy of my sweetheart's became too much to bear. I would leave both behind. Along with boredom.

One thing you could say about my sister, she never bored me. Unnerved, even alarmed, yes. All her life she'd kept me on edge. She'd kept our whole family on edge. I couldn't see settling down with one woman when I'd never been with another. I'd never know what I'd been missing.

Going away to graduate school, it was time to graduate to other women. In my naive mind, philandering was one of the perks—one of the imperatives—of being an artist. It was essential that I, as a full-fledged bohemian, sample as many women as possible. And so I became a serial lady killer, as reckless and self-destructive with women as my sister with men. By her early twenties she'd already been through her second divorce.

Had my sister's adventurousness helped determine the kind of woman I wanted my girlfriend to be? I'm sure some part of me believed that, if I couldn't be the devil-may-care bohemian I would've like to have been, I should at least have a woman who could pick up the slack. And my teen steady simply wasn't that sort. All she wanted were lots of children and to look after me. As different from my sister as any woman could be. Certainly not one to go out on life-risking limbs.

* * *

Graduate school was packed with women eager to please. One after another they fell to my sword of seduction, and soon after to my axe of abandonment, until they became a blur. Yes, I broke a lot of hearts. Not that I was diabolical, it's just that the inability of these intellectuals to exude the same simple joy and affection as my first love, and my inability to feel the same intensity of affection for them as I did for her, caused me to abruptly cut myself off from whoever I was sleeping with.

Deeply attached to my teen heartthrob, for long after I'd abandoned her I would hug my pillow, whisper sweet nothings, pretend it was her. But I was determined to tough it out and, in doing so, managed to not only break my beloved's heart, but my own.

Heart-broken or not, eventually the erotic urge would rear its animal head and I'd be off bedding a new body. This *opéra bouffe* played out over a period of decades. But my philandering stopped the day my sister died.

* * *

My father had been flattered that my sister had bothered to learn his boyhood language. But when she decided to spend a year in Odessa, his reaction was: "We ran for our lives from there now my little girl wants to go god knows why?"

"To improve my language skill."

"You and me we don't speak enough?"

"It's not the same."

"You can't trust the communists! They're worse than Cossacks! Than Tsars too! They could arrest you I wouldn't know we'd never see you again!"

He'd never shouted at her before. Never raised his voice to her. She was the one to shout if she didn't get her way.

Maybe he was afraid she'd find out what he'd done. Perhaps he didn't know for sure himself, didn't want to know, never tried to find out, was afraid she'd open a whole can of worms if she started sniffing around. Somehow it would get back to the powers that be there and he'd be persecuted—prosecuted—like Eichmann after all these years. To play footsie with the Palestinians, the Soviets might try to make an example of him. Who knows what scenarios might have roiled through his mind.

She insisted she was doing it as part of her graduate studies. In the end, as usual, what could he do but acquiesce.

My father had done everything not only to protect himself from his past, but to protect my sister and me from it. Yet one thing had always been clear: there were demons buried in our family basement, and we children were not allowed to go down there. No one in our home was allowed to go down there. Not with my father present.

Someone mentioning an atrocity in the news would trigger "Vot vee vent tru new vonder ve're nairvous," a mantra my father often uttered meant to explain and excuse his anxiety as well as change the subject. And should a visitor speak of the holocaust or pogroms in front of his children, my father would get furious. Simply to speak of the unspeakable in front of my sister and me might have sealed our fate, infected us in some way. And he may have been right.

From time to time, when my father wasn't around, my sister tried to probe into his past. But, when it came to their father's death, both my aunt and uncle would become evasive, neither of them quite clear about what happened or how. Other relatives had been more willing to speculate, but none knew for sure exactly what my father had experienced or precisely how his father had met his end.

In trying to stitch together the shards of our father's shattered soul, my sister and I could only find fragments of his boyhood ordeal. It is precisely the elusiveness of those scattered remains, our inability to pin them down, that made his past so hard to put to rest, and let it keep haunting us.

A single incident, however traumatic, may be a flimsy foundation upon which to base one family's entire edifice of unhappiness, yet the monument of sadness built upon it was anything but. All her life my sister had tried to figure out how to dismantle it, break it down, undermine its very footing, yet she'd barely managed to make a dent. The structure of our family sorrow, its stranglehold on our father, seemed indestructible. It stifled her every attempt to get out of its grip. She just had to get back to where it began.

My dear baby bro,

Talked to the Cossack's daughter today. She told me that, after the massacre, her father was a broken man. He quit the Cossacks. And became a recluse, obsessed with washing his hands, dozens and dozens of times a day. His wife had to go to work to support the family.

I found it hard to fully believe her. She seemed to be hiding something. But I decided not to push it. I could see she was getting uncomfortable, impatient too. I didn't want to overstay my welcome, at least not this time, hoping to maybe talk to her again, another time, when her husband wasn't around. He seemed uncomfortable with me, and not all that hospitable. And she kept jumping up every so often, like she'd forgotten something, another dish, tea, cookies, dates, keeping busy, going back and forth to the kitchen.

I plan to keep digging, see if some other family members can corroborate her story, or elaborate upon it. She did seem to be holding something back.

By the way, I adore this city. Reminds me of Montreal in some ways. But a lot older, and more mature. Whatever maturity means when applied to a city. It feels more lived in. More loved in. Don't know what that means either. Maybe it's just me. The city in which one is born always leaves a little something to be desired. Something one can't get away from fast enough. On the other hand, there's something so exotic about Odessa. It seems to hold so much history. So much of our story too.

More anon ... and on ... and on ...

Your loving sis ...

M.

As dogged in pursuit of the details of our grandfather's death as our dad in his efforts to avoid them, she seemed determined to not only uncover the events leading up to—but also the grisly minutiae of—our grandfather's final moments. And I feared that relentless probing might wreak havoc on her.

Well, baby bro,

Today I came across the long lost brother of the woman I spoke to last week. Living in the same city as his sister. But as far as he's concerned they could be oceans' apart. They haven't spoken in decades. He refuses to have anything to do with her. Hates her husband. But that's not the reason. Though I'm sure it doesn't help.

It seems that unlike us, baby bro, he and his sister never got along. Specially after the slaughter. His sister was proud of her father, sided with him when he insisted: "It had to be done."

According to him his father never quit the Cossacks. He just took early retirement because of emotional issues. A long time— years—after that last pogrom. He kept breaking down. But he never regretted what he'd done. If he did, he never admitted it. According to the son, he kept insisting he was just doing his duty. Doing something that had to be done. But his son resented his father's not having the guts to regret what he did, retreating instead into self-righteousness. A retired psychologist himself, he's sure that that was at the root of his father's emotional breakdown. He was ashamed of his cowardice, his lacking the courage to not take part in that pogrom, to having precipitated it in the first place.

He says he met our zeydeh, remembers him as a kind generous man with a twinkle in his eye. He had been to their house many times, always bringing them candy along with a bag of cash for their father. He remembers his father counting the kopecks and rubles.

According to him his sister has no regrets over what their father did. No remorse either. Has never had any. She knows that pogroms are no longer a la mode, so she was just going through the motions of what's now unacceptable for my sake. For her sake too, painting their father in a more pleasing light, whitewashing the whole picture.

"Though perhaps her portrait is closer to the truth than mine, employing unconscious colors, ones my father would never consciously dare confirm, to himself, or anyone else. Don't get me wrong. I loved my father. Felt sorry for him. Pity, even. Though not compassion. I was and still am too angry at him, too resentful of what he did to us to feel anything as mature and altruistic as compassion. But at least I can sympathize with patients struggling with a similar psychological syndrome."

Well, my dear baby bro, how do you like my detective work

*so far? Should I keep digging. Me thinks that if one digs deep
enough, sooner or later one finds oneself back in the same hole.
But this time one is filling it with fertile soil instead of emptying
it of its soul. Pretty deep, your big sis, huh, baby bro?*

Hugs from here ...

Your happy-go-lucky sis,

M.

My father would share his grief with any and everyone, break down in
tears at the drop of a hat. But he couldn't share his guilt. Yet the two
were inextricably linked.

Whoa, baby bro,

*After separately pressing both brother and sister, I seem to have
come away with several different stories. They may have a
common thread. If they do, I'm not sure what it is. Perhaps the
vodka made the brother veer off course. It certainly loosened his
tongue. The stuff was probably a hundred proof, if not more.
And so acidic. I tried to dilute it with enough tonic to obliterate
the taste of the alcohol. But the tonic wasn't much better, its
fruit likely as fermented as the vodka's grain, yet even more
biting and bitter. I'm sure the brother keeps it only for guests.
God knows how long the unsealed bottle had been sitting there.
Maybe vodka can't go bad, but tonic certainly can.*

*I had to stifle my regurgitation reflex, stop myself from
spitting it out. Even so, once I'd started to drink, I couldn't just
suddenly stop, not when he was savouring every sip. He might
have taken it as an insult. Come to see me as some prissy
Canadian. Still, I could only stand the smallest of sips. So I
stayed sober. Besides, I wanted to be sure I got his stories
straight. Even if he didn't.*

According to him, after the slaughter, daddy tried to kill him. Smashed him in the head, then left him for dead. He refused to tell anyone what really happened, that he had got into a fight with daddy, and lost. That he had attacked first. But somehow had been knocked unconscious. He didn't really know how. He still doesn't. All he remembers is a rock in daddy's hand and then lights out, as if someone had suddenly shut the sun. Then, just as suddenly, he woke. With a sore head. Told his parents he tripped playing soccer and smashed his head against a stone. Had a big black and blue bruise there for weeks. But he was not one to squeal. There was a certain code of the street, one the son of a Cossack above all obeyed. Can't imagine daddy trying to kill anyone, can you? Yet this old man insisted it was true.

Could it be that some of daddy's sadness stems from another source, another guilt, that he'd killed the Cossack's son? Have we opened a whole can of worms here? Maybe that's why he argued so vehemently against me going, against my coming here? Maybe he was afraid I'd find out what he'd done. Perhaps he didn't know for sure himself, didn't want to know, never tried to find out, was afraid I would.

Anyway, don't want to stir things up. Let sleeping dogs lie. Then why'm I here? Don't know, to get a sense of the city, the Russian soul, daddy's sadness. Probably same reason I studied Russian.

When you get down to the nitty-gritty, could be that to this day daddy thinks he killed the Cossack's son. If so, not sure what purpose it would serve to tell him otherwise. Most likely, like the rest of his memories of here, he's stifled it. Why stir them up again. That said, I'll keep sleuthing. Hard to stop after coming so far. Getting so far.

Your Sherlockian sister,

M.

The closest I came to confrontations resembling those of my father with the Cossack's son took place sneaking onto the École Notre-Dame-de-Glace—a private French-Canadian Catholic boarding school—hockey rink. Their ice was the best in our area, much better cared for than any public park's. And Sunday mornings most of the school's students were in church. At least they should have been. The danger was that a few budding atheists might have strayed. Nevertheless, all we had to do was climb the ten-foot chain link school fence and we'd be home free.

There was always an aura of excitement to these ventures. Not because we were breaking the law by trespassing. At worst, if confronted by adult authorities, we'd be warned never do it again. An admonishment and promise we would neither honour or obey. When it came to Catholics our conscience was clear. We didn't need a saviour to absolve us of our sins, nor a confessor to saddle us with saying a hundred hail Marys.

For us, the true danger lay in having to confront some unruly students. To belittle the ever-looming threat we felt from them, among ourselves, cavalier in our political incorrectness, we referred to these kids as peppers, a colloquial tongue-in-cheek term of faux endearment derived from what we Jews deemed their favourite soft drink: Pepsi Cola. We never used the word to their face. It was a term we only bandied among ourselves. If push came to shove, and we truly wanted to insult one of them, we would call them French pea soup. I don't know why either we or they took it to be such a derogatory term but it certainly worked like one. Especially mouthed in an angry insulting manner, spitting out the sibilant in soup with sufficient strength to spray the intended insultee with spit.

Now, such vehement racial slurring were rarely initiated by us. We were too scared. We first had to be provoked by some slur of theirs such as maudit Juif. Then and only then might we retaliate with a salvo from our arsenal of insults.

We never pronounced the p in soup. For some reason we thought it sounded more insulting that way, more French too. Of course, in French the word sou means cent or penny. So I'm not sure why we thought it sounded so insulting.

More often than not, the phrase was uttered on the run, or a split second before, followed by sporadic breathless repetitions as we raced to escape an attack. I was rarely the one who did the verbal taunting— politically correct before it was politically correct to be politically correct —nevertheless, the strongest physically of my peers, I was always the one who had to bear the brunt of the blowback to this false bravado.

So it was with a mixture of fear, dread and elation that I would scale that boarding school fence, my legs shaking so, I had trouble planting my toes between the chain links.

But what could I do? Say I'm not playing? And be called a coward. Which I was. Or worse, "You're no fun," the most fatal words your friends could foist on you. More hurtful than "maudit Juif." The latter merely an insult by your enemies, the former a hint of ostracism by your friends. Peer pressure to a pre-teen is like air pressure to a pilot.

By and large we would have the rink to ourselves. But the odd time we were caught, surrounded by a bunch of bigger French-Canadian boys, in order to avoid a collective thrashing, I'd offer myself up as our gang's gladiator if one of the goyim's gang would offer to be theirs. Thus, though emotionally the most frail, as the most physically powerful of my peers, I was pitted against the toughest of theirs. If I could prevail, my friends would get off scot-free, with nary a black eye to blemish the brown or blue hue of their optical organs.

Believe me, I didn't want to have to deal with the flailing fists of a street fight. One could get hurt that way. So, first chance I got, I would get the other guy in a headlock and hold on for dear life, till he gave up. Or my arms gave out. Fortunately, the former usually occurred first. Sometimes, my opponent would do me the favour of fainting from the shortage of blood flow to his brain. Strictly speaking, I wasn't trying to strangle him. Otherwise I would have worked on his throat. No, I didn't want my opponent to die. I just wanted him and his buddies to go away, to be left in peace, to not have to put up with all this macho swagger.

This contest could go on for hours. And it often did. To me, it was a test of wills. And patience. I was determined to bore all involved until they'd had enough. After an hour or two struggling to slow the blood flow to the other boy's brain, if I saw that my opponent was about to black out, instead of continually yelling "Give up?" I would merely let go. By then he had no fight left in him. Neither did I. And neither did anyone else. The bluster bored out of us, the male ritual was over. And both groups of boys would then go their way, satisfied that they had stood their ground, defended their territory, along with their budding manhood.

But when I got home the sense of futility of that fighting would come flooding out of me. I would lock the bathroom door, run the bath water so no one could hear me, then cry at all that callousness.

* * *

Since he never spoke of it, certainly not in front of Maya and me, I'm not sure how devastating my father's fight with Alexei might have been for him, how it might have reverberated throughout his life. Was he sure he'd left him for dead? If he was, did that add to his lifetime of dread? Or was he able to dismiss the incident as an accident, an act of self-defence? Perhaps deep down he might have relished feelings of revenge, a fight he'd fought and won for his father.

Yet when Maya discovered Alexei was alive, I thought of telling him. But my sister was adamant: she didn't want our father to know she was delving so deeply into his life. As far as he was concerned she was merely a tourist in his home town, enjoying the chance to hear and speak Russian. And though they'd so often shared the language of my father's former life, they never spoke of it. Besides, she was doing this for our sake, not for his. At his age, rather than help put his history to rest, more likely it would have stirred up an emotional hornet's nest.

Lo there, baby bro,

Today the Cossack's son told me that many years after the incident, his father confessed that he had used the pogrom as an excuse to get rid of our grandpa because he had cheated him on a deal. Not only had he cheated him, but he was also threatening

*to tell the Cossacks that Dimitri was bypassing them, doing
deals on his own, keeping them a secret so that he wouldn't have
to share the spoils with his regiment.*

*I don't know what to think. Nor do I know what difference
these slants on the story make. In making the case that Dimitri
was acting in some sort of self-defence, he appeared to be
blaming our zeydeh for his own death, at least shifting some of
the onus onto him. In the son's deranged drunken mind the line
between his father's guilt and our zeydeh's was little more than
a blur. In some sly and not so subtle way he seemed desperate to
share the dishonour, sully both sides, so that neither emerge
completely innocent.*

*The whole story's begun to smack of such seedy circularity:
the two of us blaming daddy for our misery, and the Cossack for
daddy's; the Cossack's son blaming our zeydeh for his father's
misery, and his father for his. The music goes round and round
... and comes out a cacophony of incrimination. Maybe there's
some sort of a lesson here. Maybe we should stop blaming
anybody for our misery. Maybe it's time we take responsibility
for it ourselves. What say you, baby bro?*

*Anyway, I no longer believe either the brother or sister.
Perhaps they don't believe themselves, are no longer sure what
they believe. Who wants to be responsible for their father's guilt?
Who wants to be responsible for their own? The only consistency
I can find here is that their father killed our zeydeh. Motives
don't seem to matter. Case closed. Or is it?*

Your can-opening sister,

M.

As blurred as the most brutal moments of my father's boyhood may
have become in his mind, and the lack of clarity in the Cossack's son
and daughter's, over the years, they would become clearer in mine.

My dear baby bro:

Well, after more back and forth visits with both brother and sister, and talks with other old timers, instead of corroborating what I've heard before, our Odessa history becomes more and more hazy, specially when it comes to pogrom details. Not many left from those pre WWI days. And those who are seem to have failing memories.

I don't know if those failures of memory are simply conveniences or inevitabilities of age. Unlike fine wines brains don't seem to get better with age. Specially when preserved in steady streams of Vodka. Anyway, nobody seems to remember the pogrom. Or rather, nobody seems to want to remember it. Certainly not this brother and sister, both of whom must be well into their sixties. Both are brutally honest. At least, seem to have been. Told me they don't want to go back, refuse to relive the past, above all the parts that are most painful, their father's involvement in that pogrom.

Though they deny it, I think the two of them started talking to each other, at least communicating with one another after meeting with me. There is simply too much consistency in their revised versions of what they first told me. Or maybe it's just me, putting the fragments of their failing memories together with my own hazy one.

According to their most recent biographical revisions, both brother and sister became ardent Bolsheviks as soon as they came of age. When the revolution happened in 1917 they were only in their early teens, but they were filled with revolutionary zeal, believing it to be the dawn of a new day, that, once and for all, the corrupt ways of the Romanov dynasty were dead.

All this corruption seemed to infuriate the Cossack's son and daughter even more than the murders that took place during pogroms. Young idealistic Bolsheviks, they were sticklers for law and order, integrity in government, any government.

Their biggest disappointment in their father seemed to be that, rather than upholding it, he consistently broke the law.

Anyhow, their idealism long gone, now in their dotage, they mourn what has become of the Soviet Union. Certainly they're no fans of Stalin. Not so crazy about Malenkov or Khrushchev either. They seem to look back on their father's time as a Cossack with nostalgia, a simpler time, when they still had ideals. They both seem traumatized by all the upheaval they've been through in their lives: revolutions, world wars and too many financial depressions to count.

I don't know how much more of their story I can stand. Or how much scalding hot tea. Like daddy, these people drink it just below boiling, out of a thick glass with a spoon in it to keep the glass from cracking. No sugar, of course, nor milk or cream. I've scarred my throat trying to be congenial. As if that family hasn't wounded us enough already. It's time to stop trying to get another brother and sister's story straight and get on with our own. What say you?

Your loving sister,

M.

After reading this letter, the last she wrote from Russia, the gruesome end that had always lurked behind even the more innocuous flashbacks to my father's boyhood, one that I'd been evading, that had been evading me, now came into clear focus. I could see the Cossack swords slashing away at my grandfather's blood-drenched body, over and over, like the scene had been looped.

Yet it was as if I was viewing the slaughter through the wrong end of a pair of binoculars. Not only did that diminish the nightmarish immediacy, it minimized its power over me.

Was this because I already knew that my grandfather had met a horrific end? Or was I experiencing a sense of second-hand sangfroid similar to my sister's? Perhaps her presence there in Russia, trying to piece together precisely what had happened and why, not only triggered flashes of those fatal blows, but tempered their impact on me. It was as though she too had travelled back in time, was there with me. And that bolstered me.

However, there was still so much that was missing. Suppressed for so long, family trauma can be hazy: the longer it's allowed to fester, the hazier. Survivors erase remnants of their experience, their children fill in the blanks with fantasy. So it was with the Cossack's son and daughter, so it seemed to be with Maya and me. Were we all just spinning the wheels of imaginary vehicles?

Well, imagination may be no substitute for reality, but in filling in its gaps it may go a long way in making sense of it. To tame the power of our family past over me, I knew that someday I'd find a way to put it all in writing.

What I didn't anticipate was having to do so without my sister.

* * *

She'd always loved to embellish. Even as an adult. Perhaps that's why she never seemed to get the Odessa story straight. She'd create mystery where there was none, fit fiction into her facts, and facts into her fiction, so that one could never really know what was true and what not, what was real and what not. Which is why she didn't last long as a journalist.

She'd been determined to carve out a niche for herself, a name, in the cutthroat world of freelancers. She loved being one, refused to be tied down, told where to go, what to do. She'd tried working full-time, first as a stringer for *The Toronto Star* then as a foreign correspondent for *The Toronto Telegram*, but those jobs didn't last for long. She wanted to go where she wanted, when she wanted, to do what she wanted, and liberal bias be damned. Truth too. At least in journalistic terms. On the side of the downtrodden, her stories were always slanted.

After she was fired from her last job as a journalist she followed her rebellious spirit wherever it took her: what began with Fair Play for Cuba in the early days of the revolution and continued at Berkeley during the heyday of the free speech movement at that California campus led her to march from Selma to Montgomery with Martin Luther King. Later, she joined the French student-worker barricades in 1968 Paris followed by a trip Afghanistan after the 1973 coup.

She was always doing something exciting, living somewhere stimulating, exploring the world in ways I'd never dare, exposing herself in ways I'd never do. Just knowing she was out there, eagerly sinking her teeth into life, alert to every instant of it, buoyed me.

* * *

I so looked forward to Maya's letters. But, what I looked forward to more were her rare visits, sudden unannounced middle of the night knocking at my door. I'd stumble out of bed and, without bothering to ask who's there or peer through the one way eye-aperture, pull the door open and, as if she'd just magically appeared out of some dream, there she'd be, beaming, dressed in some exotic outfit indigenous to the area in which she'd been living. I still remember that colourful campesina costume.

"A deal I just couldn't resist!"

Still groggy I asked: "What?"

"A plane ticket quarter price! Worth it to see my baby bro!" and she threw her arms around me. We spent all night talking. At least she did. I, the passive pensive supportive partner, mostly listened.

* * *

I am a somewhat shy undemonstrative man. Not so my sister. Even when she'd sent me the date and time of her arrival, spotting me at the arrival gate evoked such astonished emotion from her, as though she couldn't figure out how I found out she was coming.

Shouting my name, her arms outstretched, she would run through airport throngs and, though I was a half foot taller and fifty pounds heavier, she would somehow manage to sweep me up in her arms, lift me off my feet, swing me round and round until dizzy, we'd both fall to the floor in a heap. A happy one. She had no shame. Not when it came to expressing her love for her brother.

She simply loved me to pieces. Not that I didn't feel the same about her, I just didn't to show it.

* * *

Eventually, she grew tired of the freelancer's life. Thus began her Latin American peace corps period. In her early years there she was full of innocent enthusiasm. Nothing could undermine her zeal for organizing barrios in Bolivia, Venezuela and Ecuador, building roads and schools with the poorest of the poor. Attempts on her life from both the far left and far right only served to steel her resolve.

* * *

Eventually, community organizing became too confining for her. She then became an NGO freelancer. From all over the world, as she dashed from one war or natural catastrophe to another, from one NGO assignment to another, she kept sending me letters. She couldn't stop writing. And she couldn't stop running. Like my father, she was unable to remain in one place for too long. Rather, she seemed afraid to.

My father's moves were always within the same city. Maya rarely spent consecutive years on the same continent. I, like my mother, preferred to find peace in one place, maintain the same routine, to the point of tedium. Added to that, my love of solitude, reading and feeling myself a misfit in this world inevitably led to a desire to write, not letters, but stories like this (details ahead).

Maya's letters to me, over a decade at the same L.A. address, must have given her some sense of security. But it was only an office box number. I didn't want her to fret that her baby brother was forced to keep moving to smaller and seedier places as he slipped from eking out a living selling options on screenplays that never got produced to writing scripts that never got optioned.

* * *

How did I come to writing screenplays? Well, wishful thinking had always been a way of life for me. Especially when it came to making a living.

Since my father never talked about his boyhood trauma, yet never stopped talking about, seemed obsessed with, couldn't stop fretting over money, in my pre-adolescent mind, it had not only been the root of all evil but, more importantly, half my father's unhappiness. In fact, the two were entwined. Evil was the injury incurred grovelling for money, having to get up early to do so, the added insult.

Now, my father never rose before noon, but he did have to make a living, which obsessed every one of his twelve waking hours, and tormented ours.

And so, long before my bar mitzvah, I'd decided I'd do whatever it took to avoid having to deal with the ups and downs of earning a living. If need be I'd emulate one of my ancestors who, to stay out of the Tsar's army, poked holes in his eardrums. Deafness would qualify me for disability. But that seemed too drastic. Attention deficit disorder didn't. I already had many of the earmarks that, as an adult, would definitely qualify as a disability. If it didn't, there was always autism. But parlaying that into an adult affliction might be too taxing.

As I got older, my ideas of how to evade the vicissitudes of making money matured. If it meant becoming a monk, I'd convert. If I had to stay in school the rest of my life, so be it.

An armchair anarchist, I could have been considered a radical, had that not entailed a commitment to act. But I was too attached to the comforts of contemplation, disliked being part of a group, detested organized activity. For the most simple informal evening out, I had difficulty coordinating with a date. Committing to a time threw me into a tizzy. I led a laissez-faire life. No schedules, appointments, preparations or plans. But to remain within the safe confines of the academy I had to make one.

Thus, for my PhD, I proposed an experiment in which a selected group of African-American inmates would be transferred from violent maximum security federal prisons to minimum security white collar 'country clubs'. There, rather than continuing to rub shoulders with other armed robbers they'd have the luxury of hobnobbing with the more discreet white collar kind. Once released, having learned to skirt the laws of finance, they might have the skills they needed to stay off inner city streets, to make their way to Wall Street.

Of course, my teachers refused to take my proposal seriously, suggesting that, since I was no Thorstein Veblen, I come up with a more viable thesis. And so I did.

> *Whether inherited, divinely ordained or the ballot, power needs legitimacy. No society—above all the modern post-industrial U.S.—can survive without a shared set of faith-based, i.e., religious (derived from the Latin religare, to tie or bind together) beliefs.*
>
> *For no matter how secular a society or individual believe themselves to be, their beliefs about governance are always embedded in axioms, i.e., articles of faith which cannot be proved or disproved.*
>
> *As science replaced superstition as the ultimate arbiter of reality, the pseudo-scientific discipline of economics became the political bible.*
>
> *Though scientific paradigms shift as scientists discover facts that don't fit their previous models, economists stretch them to fit their particular political beliefs: denominations on the right worship the invisible hand of the 'free' market, left-leaners, the visible hand of government.*
>
> *To an economist statistics don't lie, whereas a lawmaker knows they do, and he must. There are simply too many variables to accurately predict the consequences of any policy. Thus politicians, like preachers, promise pie in the sky.*
>
> *Yet how many voters or their representatives carefully study the great political thinkers? Scholars who do, disagree. Moreover, specialists in one school may be relatively ignorant in others. While lawmakers and the public may be equally*

ignorant in all. Though that rarely interferes with their facades of infallibility.

With the birth of contemporary democracy in the eighteenth century, faith in the fairness of representative government became linked to that of the fairness and efficiency of the 'laissez faire market'. Real power passed from the divine right of kings to the divine right of capital and its faux-Darwinian 'survival of the fittest' dog-eat-dog myth of 'meritocracy'.

As 'one man one vote' provided the illusion of influence for those without wealth, the demands of international finance dictated the limits of both right and left. For as monotheism monopolized religion, so money has monopolized economics. There can be no other god. The overwhelming power of capital has turned class conflict into a cultural one.

Or why, in the sanctity of the voting booth, would most voters cast their ballots based more on vague belief in their most sacred values than a bigger paycheque, blue collar workers opting for union-busting Republicans, while outside it they strike for higher wages?

And why would their white collar bosses employ armies of highly-paid accountants, lawyers and lobbyists to pinch every penny they can from the government, then placate their consciences and receive kudos for their philanthropy (along with tax deductions) from the mass of poor and unemployed they've helped create by their lopsided influence over government policy?

And so, elections become a circus of collective insanity in which politicians and voters, like all fundamentalists, not only reaffirm the foundations of their faith, but curl up in a tiny corner of its security blanket. Meanwhile, the unquestioned power of capital turns class conflict into a cultural clash, more akin to a holy war than a secular battle of ideas.

Yet, since democracy, unlike it's predecessors, is inherently tragic, its promise to the secular pilgrim progress in this life, not the next, it's destined to end in disappointment even as every so often, the dashed hopes of the hoi polloi allow some

'anti-establishment' outsider to sell himself with a saviour's
swagger, whipping voters into a frenzied state of evangelical
fervour. But the greater the fervour the greater the letdown that
follows.

With citizens stranded on islands of bullshit floating in seas
of make-believe, faith and fantasy become the foundation of
American democracy as, in the sanctity of the voting booth,
based on charisma and half-baked doctrine, lay members of the
electorate keep making their leaps of faith. Believers gave birth
to American democracy, and religious zeal has been the
underbelly of its belief in itself ever since.

The faculty response? "You have a gift for glib turns of phrase. But with your penchant for repetition and lack of substance or specificity, we're not quite sure what you're trying to say. Neither, it seems, are you. You're proposal lacks focus."

Needless to say, they flunked me for being superficial. Then poured salt on that wound by expelling me for plagiarism. Forced to beat a hasty retreat from graduate school, and losing my teaching assistantship, I had to find a way to eke out a living.

Perpetually broke and having to beg for "Just a few bucks," still my uncle Izzy had always seemed so carefree. Whereas my father would get stuck spinning his wheels deeper and deeper into the sinkhole of saving his business, my uncle would simply abandon his vehicle, thumb a ride to a sunnier destination.

Rather than let money torment me as it did my father, like my uncle, I chose to make a mockery of it. I chose to make a mockery of most of my life. Or it chose to make a mockery of me. I simply didn't have the skill or will to deal with its demands any other way.

Since I'd had so many absurd adventures with women I'd met through newspaper ads, I decided why not try selling an erotic travel book to one of the big publishing houses.

All it took was the title, COMPANIONS WANTED: AROUND THE WORLD IN SEARCH OF LOVE, along with a one page sales pitch that began 'Though there is such strong demand for travel books,

194 ~ Raphael Burdman

and there are so many out there, there is nothing that gets into the intimate lives and loves of the locals like this.'

Now, some of the shenanigans with women I met through the classifieds in Montreal and Manhattan were pretty bizarre. But I knew their locales were not exotic enough to sell as a globetrotting adventure. Thus the piece de resistance of my sales pitch, the two sample chapters they required, would take place in French Polynesia and Cambodia.

That was enough to get me a $10,000 advance to cover travel expenses. But I had to keep each and every receipt, no matter how small.

Since I'd never been to either place, nor did I intend to—I detest the discomfort of travel—some of my research would have to be second hand, from other books.

Of course, I couldn't say that to them. What I could say was that I'd lived in both countries, had enough intimate encounters to fill a book, let alone a couple of chapters. Hence I didn't need travel money. But I did need to eat and pay the rent while I wrote.

A few weeks after I submitted my samples, the publisher called, said he loved the writing, I had a flair for quirky turns of phrase. A fantasy I'd been waiting to hear all my life, his words went straight to my head: elated, flying high, nothing could stop me now! I was taking the publishing world by storm! This best seller would put me on easy street!

Rapt in my mind's flight of fancy, I failed to say anything for so long—not so much as a humble 'aw-shucks thanks'—that my publisher was forced to fill the void, clearing his throat, then pausing. When that didn't evoke a verbal response from me, he seized the opportunity to inject this adrenaline antidote: "One of our editors thinks he's come across a few sentences that sound somewhat similar to those in some of our other travel tomes. I'm sure this is just a coincidence. Would you mind coming in and clearing this up?"

I was tongue-tied, the short trip from success fantasy to reality failure too abrupt for my brain. Floor falling from under my feet, ceiling closing in on my head, I started shaking.

Once more the publisher seized upon my silence, this time to politely suggest that when I came in I could meet with a couple of seasoned travellers in the two countries I'd written about. "Just to talk."

I, in my dazed state, took this to mean 'be grilled by'. Once again my adrenaline began pumping, this time in self-defence-fight-or-flight desperation. In my dizzy race to find the right response, I came up with the wrong one, shouting: "I refuse to succumb to such an indignity!" then slammed the receiver down.

No sooner had I done that than I realized I'd made a mistake. I immediately phoned back, apologized for my outburst, suggested that, since they loved the writing so much, they should buy it as a novel. Determined not to give him a chance to get a word in edgewise till I'd finished my sales pitch, I started spouting full speed.

"I could really let my imagination rip. Of course, I'd have to touch up some of the tourist bits, add bits of suspense here and there, perhaps a plot. Though when it comes to fiction I'm more of a post-modern kind of guy. Magical realism's my cup of tea too. Still, I know what a best-seller needs, and a best seller is what you'll get. Guaranteed. Naturally, for that I'd need another advance. Not much. Just enough to tide me over till I'm through touching the thing up."

No sooner had I done that than I realized I'd made another faux pas. Not only with such dim-witted double-talk, but confessing to writing a piece of fiction. Yet it was too late. He cancelled my contract, threatened to sue me for misrepresenting my work and demanded his advance back.

Pleading I'd already spent half the money, had no other source of income or any prospects of one, I promised to repay half if he agreed not to sue me. In return, I wouldn't sue him for breach of contract. Thus we'd save each other the embarrassment and cost of a court case.

I can be awfully annoying when necessary. Also, when not necessary. Eager to just be rid of me, he accepted.

It may have been a mistake to sell my writing as fact rather than fiction. But had I done that, no major book publisher would have bought it. Certainly never given me an advance. After all, I had no track record. This publisher may have loved my writing. But it was the idea that first got my foot in the door.

Now that it had been slammed shut, what could I do? Submit my work to some literary rag? Sell them as a series of short stories with the same theme? Someone might snap them up. But there was no money there. Not enough to support me. Besides, I was now on the New York publishers' shit list. It wouldn't take long to find me out.

Bottom line: with my academic and amorous adventure-writing fantasy bubbles burst, I had to find a way of feeding myself while still maintaining my anything-but-hard-nine-to-five integrity. It was time to take stock of my skills.

I had a penchant for making things up. A talent too. And I'd always fancied myself a budding novelist. But having just been black-balled by a major publishing power, this was no time to try kick-starting that career. However, there was another green pasture in which my muse could graze. One more lucrative than the literary field: film.

Since visions were the most powerful part of my psyche, I was a natural for a visual medium like movies. Moreover, L.A. was as far from New York as you could get on this continent. There I might make enough money to allow me to retire and write serious fiction.

Meanwhile, as I made concessions to the demands of commerce and a quick buck, I could fill in the blank pages of my family past, churning out screenplays based on bits and pieces of it. Thus, without having to delve too deeply into my soul, I could amass enough family vignettes for what, one day, would be my contribution to literary posterity.

To boot, given enough time and distance, my name would disappear from the New York publishers' blacklist.

* * *

Both uncle Izzy and my father lived beyond their means. I was determined to live below mine. And, in L.A., I succeeded, sleeping in a storage locker the first six weeks.

I'd finally fulfilled my fantasy of living like a monk. But without the security of a monastery or community of true believers. Nor did the pretensions of being an 'artist' soften the disgrace and discomfort of financial deprivation.

Moreover, taking a vow of quasi-aesthetic purity in tinsel-town was tantamount to taking a vow of poverty, which, in turn, was tantamount to taking a vow of chastity. Unable to afford the foreplay of wining and dining a woman, I'd been forced to revert to the self abuse of my bar mitzvah days.

Still, I'd stuck to my guns which, like my wallet, were never loaded. If I was going to make it, I'd make it writing what I felt. Hollywood looks for happy endings. My family history hadn't yet ended but, given the agony suffered by some of my ancestors, and the morose music my father conducted in our little family orchestra, unless I believed in an afterlife, a happy ending didn't seem to be in the cards.

However, I did manage to string some studios along. Or they strung me. I was too close to the material, couldn't see the dramatic forest for my family tree. Yet despite their depressing subject—most scenes taken directly from mystic memory—my visual descriptions were so strong, enough of my screenplays were optioned to allow me to overstay my welcome at these dream factories.

However, following more than a decade beating my head against the Hollywood wall, I began to burn out. After ten years there's a high turnover rate of script readers and executives, so I decided, what the hell, why not give it a shot, recycle some of my early screenplays.

In some sense I'd been writing variations of the same script from the beginning, sticking to similar themes: family history and emotion, individual guilt and letting go. In one script it was the father who'd suffered a childhood trauma, in another, the mother. Each grappled with their unhappiness in somewhat different ways, but with similar effects on their family.

To see how very different characters might deal with similar emotional scars, in one screenplay, I used uncle Izzy and aunt Bessy as the parents. It turned into more of a black comedy than family tragedy, but it was neither dark nor funny enough to get optioned.

So I went back to my forte, family calamity: a six-year-old boy in love with his twin sister has to come to grips with her death in an accident he thinks his fault. Perhaps I was being prescient, peering into the future rather than the past.

My first two agents had dropped me, saying I was stuck in the mud of family affliction. Sure, you could say I was obsessed. I still am. But what artist isn't? What is art but the expression of obsession, compulsive going over the same material again and again until, like some golem, your visions take on a life of their own?

To resurrect my career as a screenwriter, I found a new agent, a young one to whom an older writer like me—with seven optioned scripts—was a catch. It wasn't easy. Nevertheless, I convinced him to submit some of my early screenplays to the same studios that had rejected them way back when. I changed only the titles, first page, and print font.

Just one studio responded positively to my recycled material. Rather, it didn't promptly reject the submission. That took place during my drunken pitch to its exec. (Details to come.)

As I continued my descent into financial and artistic distress, I could still glean some serenity from the sea and sun. But as soon as the latter started to sink so did my spirits. And once it had set, the wind went out of my sails. I'd just lost another day of my life.

My final L.A. slide could be considered a step up thanks to a twice-a-week job teaching English as a second language. This allowed me to move from subletting the sofa of a younger screenwriter to a rundown rooming house run by a rundown alcoholic who rented out rundown rooms the size of closets, some, such as mine, without windows. Ah, the joys of upward mobility.

One toilet served all tenants, its seat invariably splattered with shit, semen, vomit, urine and god knows what else. Whatever the landlady sprayed to mask the odours emanating from this little enclave of excrement, its scent of lilacs, garlic, horseradish and onions wafted through every room like some perverted French perfume that smacked of mustard gas.

Less an L.A. melting pot than a pressure cooker, for entertainment there were daily fights between drunks. Nights were much calmer. By then most were too intoxicated to fight, additional booze more likely to lead to dozing off than duking it out.

Like my ESL classes, the rooming house was filled with an array of immigrants, mostly men. Unlike my students, most of these boarders were there illegally. Of course, I never checked the status of my students. And they never checked mine. Nor did the schools, until two students complained that from time to time I appeared to disappear, not only in the middle of the class, but in the middle of a sentence, and was silent for so long they worried I might be having some sort of seizure. Then I'd quickly recover and continue as if nothing happened. To them it was eerie, to me, just another apparition.

That I'd never explain what happened unnerved them most. Well, how do you describe a trance to a class full of people who hardly understand my language, let alone each others', a veritable tower of Babel tapestry of Iranians, Koreans, Egyptians and Latin Americans?

Sure, I could have made like Marcel Marceau, mime a headache, dizziness or feeling faint. That would have been simpler than trying to convey a vision. But, given that these trances recurred from time to time, I doubt resorting to my usual theatrics would've helped. Most likely it would have just convinced my students that I had some dangerous—perhaps contagious—disease.

On top of that I was often drunk. Or seemed to be. Between my trances and being tipsy it was hard to tell.

You see, like my father, I'm a late riser, normally, never before noon. So I don't make morning appointments. If I set my alarm my psyche reacts like it's a ticking time bomb and won't let me sleep. In fact, setting my alarm guarantees I won't sleep. As do sleeping pills. Unless I swallow enough to induce a coma. All the prescribed dose does is make me more groggy in the morning. Without the pressure of untimely appointments, my little world under my control, I need to nod off as nature intended, too tired to keep my eyes open, and wake up as naturally, when I've had enough sleep, not artificially aroused by an alarm.

Unfortunately, to get to my 8 a.m. class I had to set my alarm for 6 and drive forty freeway miles through L.A. rush hour. By the time I got to the school, having downed a flask of vodka and grapefruit juice, I was quite loaded. I rarely drink, but to get my performance juices going at such an ungodly hour demanded drastic measures. And what could be more drastic than drinking and driving—actually, drinking while driving—bumper to bumper with commuters one step from road rage?

Student complaints were enough to cause those responsible for hiring me to check into my checkered past. And lo and behold they discovered that, though I still had a U.S. social security number from my days as a graduate student/teaching assistant, my green card work permit had been expired for a decade. They'd hired an illegal alien! Not a wetback but—as the cheeky young Canadian actors and screenwriters crammed into my first L.A. apartment building referred to each other—a frostback! L.A. was full of both. Wetbacks had come to pick fruit, frostbacks to pick Hollywood's pockets.

After calling me in, neither school administrator asked me about my disappearing acts during class. I suppose they didn't want to open a can of contractual worms. Nor did they accuse me of being drunk. Their sole reason for firing me was my lack of legal status. But I suspect that both my vanishing routines and being intoxicated were as much to blame. After all, good ESL teachers are hard to find. And I was good, using my hands, face—indeed, whole body—to get the meaning of difficult words or phrases across.

* * *

My career might have taken a whole different trajectory had my invitation to a power breakfast at the Beverly Hilton not turned into a fiasco, one which began with setting my alarm, taking one sleeping pill too many, then not sleeping a wink. Hoping to impress that low level exec with my pitch for the script his studio had optioned, I decided a flask of vodka and grapefruit juice would, if not help power my performance, at least keep me from being too nervous to do my script justice. It did neither.

By the time I got to the hotel I was so drunk, every gesture of mine exaggerated, every word mouthed momentous, all I succeeded in doing was looking desperate. To top it off, in the anxiety-ridden rush to get there, I'd forgot my breath mints. And so, as I spoke, with each of my alcohol-scented exhalations inducing increasingly painful face expressions from that executive, I grew increasingly frantic, and my performance correspondingly reckless. Needless to say, not only did I not sell that script but that studio never optioned another from me.

Getting loaded to pitch or teach may wreak havoc with making a living, but driving under the influence can be life-threatening or worse. And worse is what happened. I was pulled over for zigzagging from one side of the highway to another, my California driver's licence was confiscated, as was my car.

No car, no driver's licence, facing months behind bars, what better time to flee L.A. for the kinder, gentler, greener financial pastures of monthly welfare checks to which, as a citizen, I'd be entitled back home in Montreal. Moreover, the Canadian government subsidized screen-writers.

Sure, no longer would my family be able to maintain the long distance image of me being a somebody in showbiz, a man with a big break just around the corner. No matter. In L.A. such corners are fewer and farther between than the long winding freeways that lead longshots like me from one disappointment to another.

* * *

Little did I know that disappointment would follow this dark horse home. For, to my chagrin, in Montreal I discovered that fully realized screenplays could only be submitted by producers who intended to put them into 'development'. In tinseltown, this meant getting writers to keep 'polishing' the pure untamed power of the original until it felt safe enough for the money men. No way I was going to endure that again.

However, Telefilm Canada did finance the writing of a screenplay's first draft. For that, you had to submit a short summary or extensive treatment, depending on what stage you were at in the writing process. So I sent them a short synopsis of one of my old screenplays. That it had already been written was nobody's business but mine.

* * *

My film grant evaluator looked like she was straight out of university. I may have only been in my late thirties, but she made me feel old. To begin with we engaged in back and forth banter about the movie business. But when talk turned to my synopsis it quickly turned into bickering.

Disappointing though it may have been, I'd had all this New York and L.A. experience. Who was this fresh-from-a-bachelor-of-fine-arts-in-film to fancy herself some kind of screen-writing connoisseur? I'd had at least a decade and a half head-start in the business on her and here she was treating me like some novice, has-been or, worse, never-was. Which, in a way, I was. And that hurt.

Above all when she began patronizing me: "You are indeed a brave man to try following in the footsteps of Mordecai Richler."

"My work is deeper," I said.

"Canada is such a vast diverse country, there is so much to choose from our multi-cultural menu, we have to put a limit on the number of comedic scripts we can subsidize," she responded.

That got my goat.

"You mean my work's too Jewish."

Sure, I could use a few lessons in tact. But, not only didn't she flinch at my attempt to intimidate her, she stood, looked me in the eye and ... "What we're looking for nowadays are scripts that deal with our many ethnic and indigenous cultures. If you could see fit to step out of your comfort zone, familiarize yourself with this fascinating country, instead of your navel ..."

She then turned and strutted away, leaving me stranded there, my speechless mouth open in awe, stuttering with the will to shout something after her, but unable to think of anything. I'd been bested, busted, given the brush-off. And was too embarrassed to go back and beg.

For some of us success just isn't an option. Still we stumble through life tilting at its windmills, going through the motions of getting ahead when all the time we seem to be falling further and further behind.

Nevertheless, under the pseudonym of Izzy Littlefeather, using a Kahnawake mail box number, I sent in a script synopsis in which a happy-go-lucky Iroquois, like some indigenous Paul Revere, coaxes his over-the-hill horse through the reservation shouting: "The Canucks are coming! The Canucks are coming! Hide the contraband!"

Of course, I never heard back. The only government money I could now depend on was welfare.

But that wasn't enough to support me, unless I was willing to let my parents see me living in the same squalor as in L.A. So I supplemented my income, buying rolls of fabric remnants from major manufacturers' discontinued lines of clothing then selling them to smaller sweatshops and fabric stores.

In the beginning, I couldn't afford a car, so I'd bicycle to the textile districts, go door-to-door in building after building—there were dozens —trying to sweet-talk receptionists into letting me coax their bosses into giving me swatches of the rolls of textile remnants they no longer needed. Most didn't want to bother. It wasn't worth the trouble.

Unlike my father, I was too proud to plead. So I'd stoop to self-deprecating humour, mocking the chichi Sally Ann long-hair I seemed to be. Which, in its way, was more shameful than pleading. But it seemed to put them at ease. Besides, they could see my despair, hear the inflections of desperation in my voice.

Less often than not I succeeded. But then came the hard part. Finding someone other than aunt Bessy to buy the goods. Selling only to her I couldn't make a living. Profit margins—if any—were too small. She drove too hard a bargain.

I had to move fast to find another buyer and, when successful, rent a truck, pick up the goods, pay with a postdated cheque, deliver the merchandise and collect the cash.

One Hasidic owner of several fabric stores insisted "I pay cash you don't need me I should put my name to paper. Believe me, my word's good as gold. In stone like the ten commandments you can take it to the bank."

But when I arrived with the truckload of textiles, he took a look, touched the tips of a few rolls, shook his head saying "These shmatahs are shmatahs. Not worth what I thought."

He halved his offer. Which meant I'd be getting less than I'd paid. Which meant my cheque would bounce. Which, because word I was unreliable would spread like latkes in the textile building cafeterias, meant I'd be out of business.

I started shouting. But to no avail. He wouldn't budge. Wouldn't bargain. For days I fantasized about firebombing the place.

My back against the wall, I had to resort to my last resort: aunt Bessy. This time, for some reason, she went out of her way not to humiliate me, shaking her head from side to side, pretending to drive a hard bargain, insisting "Business is business, family is family, and never the two should meet," then offering me twenty percent more than I'd asked for.

I felt embarrassed, as much for taking advantage of the pity she felt for me as that I felt for myself. But I put my shame aside.

I never told her I was getting welfare. I didn't have to. From her winks and nods I knew she knew. And would never say a word about it to my parents. Neither would I. In their eyes there was nothing sadder than a Jew sinking so low. Nor was there any way I'd tell them I was never going to get my PhD. Not after hearing my father say to friends: "Maybe he's not going to be a doctor a doctor or a doctor a dentist, but a doctor of something's better than a doctor of nothing, no?"

I couldn't tell whether it was tongue in cheek, bragging or simply an attempt to help me keep up the pretence that, on the side, like some renaissance man, I was working on my thesis and screenplays. But whether I was maintaining the illusion for his sake or he for mine, didn't seem to matter. It served our shared interests: sparing my mother. As far as she was concerned I was shipping my dissertation into shape till the day she died. Or was she mollycoddling me too?

Anyway, that I could come down off my artist's 'high horse' in order to make a living seemed to make my parents proud. At least pretend they were.

Yet once, my father asked me: "You're getting royalties they made movies from what you wrote, no?"

How could I tell him my screenplays were attempts to make emotional sense of our family history which nobody would buy? To keep him from insisting on seeing the movies from which I'd alleged I was getting royalties, I told him they were horror movies, with so much murder and mayhem he wouldn't be able to stomach them.

"And from this you expect make a living? Write a musical, something light we should laugh already we don't have enough tears in life?"

From the way he glanced at me, out of the corner of his eye, rather than looking straight into mine, I could tell he hadn't believed me, could read between my lying lines. But didn't want to hurt me by expressing doubt. He never brought up the subject again, most likely for my mother's sake as much as mine. Why burst her bubble if she believed me? But I suspect she didn't. And didn't want to burst his.

* * *

If you're going to lie, it's more convincing to use the truth. And, in a way, I *was* working on a horror story, one I've been wrestling with my whole life: my family's.

White lies and wishful thinking had always helped us get by. In my sister's case, the illusion took the form of locomotion—stress loco—as though she had to keep moving, lest she become a target, pinned down or picked off by strays, men or munitions. Besides, things were bound to be better next stop. But they rarely were.

One man led to another, one war to one more, her adventurousness became a way of escaping the lifelong care, commitment and risks of raising a family. Terrified of having kids, she was afraid of passing down the family poison: depression and fear. I've never met a more seemingly happy adult on the outside; I've never known a more forlorn one on the inside.

She knew she couldn't control her feelings, how love always left her at loose ends, and feared that if she got too deeply involved with one man, any man, he'd discover her demons and distance himself from her. Her soft heart and fragile soul couldn't handle that hurt. She was a fool for love, but would steel herself against staying with one man, find a way to break each bond, force herself to keep moving on. Oh what hurt, what havoc a fragile fearful heart can wreak not only on others, but on itself.

Hi ho, baby bro,

Once again, my usual mantra: what am I doing here? Hope you don't get tired of hearing it. I do get tired of uttering it.

Some may think there's something exciting about the way I live, flitting round the world, from one adventure to another. And I suppose there is. But it's beginning to feel like I'm fleeing one futile venture for another. More than anything, I long to belong someplace, feel at home somewhere, somehow.

Like some biblical character, born at the wrong time, in the wrong place, searching for her true home in history, her place in this mystery we call life, this wandering Jew keeps looking for the promised land. It certainly's not here. Though this is where the wanderlust started, that summer on the kibbutz.

I was all of eighteen, no longer a virgin. What excited me more than feeling part of the promised land was the fantasy of 'free love'. No more feeling guilty, slinking around behind backs. That in the holy land I'd find attitudes towards sex as liberal as those in Scandinavia sent me soaring. I couldn't wait. And wasn't disappointed. Even working in the fields.

Idealism was not only in the air, it was on the ground, in the earth, everywhere. Communal living was the wave of the future, the way of saving the world. Suffice it to say it's not the same here anymore. The idealism's long gone. Occupation's put an end to it.

Is loneliness a form of depression? Or is it something completely apart? My heart aches. Oh how I would love to know that I am loved, truly loved, for better or for worse, in sickness and in health, till death do us part. And I could feel the same about someone else.

There, I said it. Your sister's exposed herself. Sounds like she wants the white picket fence. Truth is, I'd rather hook up with a pickpocket. Someone who lives outside the law, exceeds speed limits, robs banks, burns candles at both ends. His and mine. Yes, I'm addicted to bad boys and don't know why.

Anyway, I don't want to go there. Right now I need someone to hold my hand. Literally. I feel so deprived of affection, so hungry for it, for all the love that I'm missing, that's been missing for so long.

Your lonely sis,

M.

As she aged, she began to grow increasingly dissatisfied with her life. The earlier excitement had worn thin, and so she kept immersing herself in increasingly precarious situations. The world was going to hell in a handbasket and the least she could do was ease the pain, if not her own, then that of others. The destructive wake left by wars, earthquakes, tsunamis or typhoons seemed to put her in touch with a power that transcended her own petty suffering.

Finally, after decades of searching for a battlefield in which she felt at home, she found herself in Sarajevo.

Chapter 4

Hey there, baby bro,

Bullets and bombs make such distinct sounds, both startling at first: the sounds of bullets, sharply etched, staccato; bombs reverberate like thunder, shaking the ground for miles around.

I just put a RESTLESS SOUL SEEKS SHELTER OF WAR sign on my door. Inside, of course. For my own amusement. Nobody outside would be amused. I seem to flit from one war zone to another, yet there is nothing I abhor more, nothing I understand less. All this maiming and killing for god knows what, names on a map? Maybe I'm going mad, can smell testosterone's bluster in the blood and smoke. Yet I stay, searching for islands of sanity in this sea of the insane.

The norm here is nuts, no life is safe, no life is sacred, not even the local priest who wears a helmet and flak jacket to work, putting himself in harm's way just so he can visit each and every one of his housebound parishioners, in their homes, or wherever they're taking shelter, making his daily rounds carrying food, water and fuel for those unable to venture out. He knows he's a target. But that doesn't stop him. A heroic figure here. Gives people hope. For me, men like him make being here worthwhile.

Miss you ...

Wish you were here, hah hah ...

M.

WHAT THE HELL was Maya doing in Sarajevo in the midst of a civil war, an uncivil slaughter? Was it just another stop on her world tour of catastrophes, because my mother was born there, or a bit of both? My mother was barely two years old at the time her family fled Sarajevo so she had no memory of that flight. Perhaps Maya intended to relive it for herself.

Or, as unsuspected forces may spur history, it may be that unconscious impulses, particularly when linked with historical circumstances, can propel a person toward their destiny. For, sadly, so it was with my sister.

* * *

As my then eight-year-old father had witnessed the dismembering of my grandfather, he could not yet have known that another killing, one of peace-shattering significance, was about to ricochet across Europe. For it was on that very same day, perhaps that same instant, that the assassination which triggered off the First World War took place.

Whereas in history's eyes the murder of one ordinary man, my grandfather, would be overshadowed by the assassination in Sarajevo of a more monumentally significant figure, the Archduke Ferdinand, soon so many were to die in so many god-awful ways they would dwarf the Archduke's death.

Yet in history's heartless way, the Archduke's assassination would trigger a death in my family perhaps more devastating for my father as an old man than that, when a young boy, of his father. Thus we return to yet another primal trauma, one with as much impact upon the family of man as upon one man's family.

GRAVE III

ADOLESCENT BOYS DON'T differ much in their daily habits from one nation to another, from one generation to another, but most don't become assassins.

All his life Gavrilo Princip had been a loner, not given to hanging out with cliques of other Croatian kids. And when he hit adolescence he became more reclusive. The easy interaction of others his age with the opposite sex not only escaped, but upset him. Why couldn't he engage in such simple banter? He retreated further into a shell of solitude, one which allowed him to exercise his imagination not only *vis-à-vis* the world, but with respect to the opposite sex. Long before his political dreams came to know no bounds, his erotic fantasies had found unfettered freedom.

He may have been too shy to put his erotic impulses to a more social use, but locked behind his family's bathroom door, he could safely indulge in marathons of self abuse, lying on the floor, staring up at the ceiling, one wallpapered with images of bare-bottomed infant angels, hovering over a near naked Madonna. Blasphemous? To most Bosnians, maybe. But not to his Croatian mother. She saw only sanctity in those faded pink pastel images. So it is fitting that her son would find sanctuary here, freedom to worship at his altar of Eros.

* * *

There was an unhappiness in Gavrilo Princip's home, more specifically, a sense of dissatisfaction in his father. Not that he was unhappy in his marriage. The fault seemed to lie with his status in life, the feeling that he might have made something more of himself. His discontent never seemed explicit, never clearly manifested itself in some angry outburst. He kept his cool, almost compulsively so, and prided himself on containing his emotions. He was not a moody man. Still, something was amiss in him, in his life, and his son knew it. He'd always known it. As far back as he could remember.

Perhaps it was his failure as a revolutionary nationalist, his failure as a farmer, to be anything more than the subsistence tiller of a tiny plot of land and keeper of a few pathetic animals.

From a young age, Gavrilo had sensed that one day he was going to do what his father—until family and having to eke out a living got in the way—had wanted to do with his life. But Gavrilo was never quite sure what that was.

When we're young, we want to change the world, make our mark, make a difference. Although destiny may give hints, it rarely provides a roadmap. And Gavrilo had no idea how to go about finding his mission in life, let alone fulfilling it. Until he heard his teacher speak with contempt of the Slavic nationalist Black Hand, and their youth wing, Young Bosnia. Bored with school, he was determined to drop out and join them.

He knew that, if he said that to his father, the man would hit the ceiling. So he told him that he didn't feel suited for school, wanted to set out on his own, move to Sarajevo, get a job there, doing something, anything other than farming, for which he also felt unsuited.

His father warned "Not only are you not fit for farm labour," his father told him. "You're not fit for labour of any sort. With your frail health what are you going to accomplish in life without school?"

"You didn't finish," Gavrilo said.

"Unlike yours, this body was born to farm," his father responded. "This brain too. Yours was meant for more. But you're lazy. Lack ambition."

Little did his father know how ambitious his son was. Little did Gavrilo know. But he soon would.

* * *

A few weeks before he fired that bullet, knowing what he was about to do and that the repercussions flowing from it might prevent him from ever seeing his parents again, perhaps trying to reconcile with his father before fame or infamy came between them for good, Gavrilo decided to pay his parents a visit. Hard as his mother tried to get the two of them to reconcile, Gavrilo's father would not budge.

"You too were an ardent nationalist when you were Gavrilo's age," she said.

"A lot of good it did us," her husband responded, and lapsed into stony silence.

But Gavrilo tried not to let his father's intractableness bother him. Convinced he was about to do more for his family than his father—for all Slavic families—he'd never felt so heady, so free. He could not let his father know this, but the Black Hand were training him to do something he was sure would make the old man proud.

* * *

Knowing her son's involved with Young Bosnia, as the impending state visit of the Archduke and his wife draws near, Gavrilo's mother grows increasingly fearful. Perhaps they're planning a demonstration, or something more. She can't be sure.

She's been on pins and needles for days now, hadn't slept a wink last night. For several nights. Not a full deep sleep. At best she'd doze in fits and starts, woke feeling more exhausted than before she'd gone to bed. Her other children seem to be looking after themselves. As is her husband. It's as though she's sleepwalking through life lately. Consumed with worry for her son, she seems to have abandoned the rest of her family. She hasn't said anything, explained why, still, they know. She's sure they know. They won't ask what the matter is. Probably afraid she might answer. Most likely they share the same fear.

Her husband's always been good at putting on brave airs. She, not so much. And now he seems to have taken over care of the children. Cooking and cleaning too. She's been going through the motions but, her mind elsewhere, he can see that her heart isn't in it. Her mind is elsewhere.

It's strange that such a small frail figure as her son could loom so large. As a child, he had been emaciated and sickly. As a young man he's little better. In his late teens, he is so physically and emotionally undeveloped, he could be called a boy. Yet his spiritual presence has always loomed much larger than his physical. And it is for the latter that she is afraid. His spiritual well-being may be in good hands. Perhaps, in God's. But his body?

* * *

Neither in good hands or God's, but the grip of a huge hairy fist attached to the arm of some bearded faceless hangman, Gavrilo Princip is in a nether world. Neither awake nor asleep, adrift in some hallucinatory sea, he is about to be hung, not by a rope, but this giant's hairy hand. Unlike its bearded counterpart, this hand seems to have a face. And it speaks, informing Gavrilo that, for daring to do in the Archduke, and with him the whole Hapsburg Austro-Hungarian Empire, he's been refused the right to die by the rope and, instead, is to die by the hangman's own hand. Huge. The size of Gavrilo's head. Enough to crush Gavrilo's neck.

Choking Gavrilo just enough to gag but not kill him, the hangman keeps teasing him, toying with him, until, about to lose consciousness, he wakes.

One nightmare after another, so many Gavrilo has hardly slept. He'd doze off. But no sooner would he do so than he'd be immersed in another hellish dream. Then, after just a few minutes—according to the mechanical alarm clock by his bed but an eternity in torment time—as each nightmare reached its horrifying climax, he'd wake, in a sweat. This pattern kept repeating itself, Gavrilo drifting in and out of one terrible dream after another. Or was it a different sequence of the same one? He's no longer sure. One thing he's sure of, he's had enough. He's not going back to sleep.

But he has not really slept. Not for days. Nor will he. Not until this is over. Anyway, he's better off remaining alert, rather than letting himself drift off. Dawn's about to break. He can see the slightest hint of light outside the tiny window of the cell he's been assigned by his Black Hand mentors. He stumbles up, shuffles around the barren room. Anything to keep himself from going back to bed.

A little stiff and sleep-deprived, he feels exhilarated, angry, fearful. This is the moment he's been waiting for, the moment he truly becomes a man. He's never been with a woman, at least not in a manner that might make him responsible for bringing another human being into this world. However, he's now going to be responsible for taking another human being out of it. And this will make him more of a man. As much as any who's been to war. More.

The bullets he fires will not end the life of some unknown soldier, some anonymous uniform. The man felled by his bullets will be one known to all the world. As will the one who fires those bullets. He wishes his parents could be there to watch him, his brother and sister too, beaming with pride as he coolly pulls the trigger.

His mentors have warned him. Stop dreaming. There is no room for dreaming. Daydream and you will be dead. Your mind must be on your mission, on what is outside of you, not inside. At every moment, you must be in touch with your surroundings, everything within sight of your eyes, within sound of your ears. He can hear his instructor's haranguing, all these months, his voice haunting him in his sleep.

But the only way he can fight his fear is to let his excitement surface, his imagination run wild. If it weren't for his imagination, he wouldn't have put himself in this position, wouldn't have let himself be put in this position. He had to dream of killing the Archduke before he could imagine doing it. And he had to imagine doing it over and over to get ready to really do it. And now that he is about to do it he can't seem to control his imagination.

* * *

Like Odessa, Sarajevo has been basking in a gloriously sunny summer day, one like many others. As the day progressed, a smattering of thin white cumulus clouds began to spread across the sky. Few and far between, each sufficiently sparse that, when directly in its path, they neither blocked the sun nor cast a dark shadow over the city, but seemed to amplify the sun's light, make it more harsh to the naked eye.

And now, it's so bright Gavrilo has to squint. Yet his sight seeming more acute than normal, he can read the small letters on that distant sign, the numbers underneath.

Neither too hot and humid, nor too windy and cool, the day is calm. Unlike Gavrilo. His gun hidden inside his jacket, he makes his way downtown toward the designated kill zone, right by the Moritz Schiller café. He has to get there before the Archduke's procession. But not too soon. Lurking there might make him conspicuous, though the procession route is well-known. Everyone loves a parade. And famous people. Those who are against the Empire won't be able to help themselves. Some might shout their disapproval, others hurl invectives. But slogans and signs don't do any good. They never have. Only drastic action can bring about the demise of this Austro-Hungarian Empire.

As he turns the corner onto the Latin Bridge crossing the Miljacka River, a high cumulus cloud crosses the sun, the sky dims and he starts to shiver ever so slightly. Moments later, the sun reflecting off the water magnifies its light so that Gavrilo Princip has to squint to see the sign. He's so fired up he's afraid he might lose sight of where he is. He has to make sure he's on the right bridge. Not the Cumurgia a few blocks west or the Emperor's Bridge a few blacks east.

That would be ironic, crossing the Emperor's Bridge to kill his son. The death of the Archduke might deal a mortal blow to the Emperor himself. See how he feels losing his son when over the centuries Slav fathers have lost so many of theirs. Of course, this is the Latin Bridge. Should lead right to the corner near the café where the Archduke's car slows down to make its turn, perhaps stop for a split second or two. Just enough time for him to be a perfect target.

He's got to stop shaking. He'll never be able to hit his target if he doesn't stop shaking. He's out of breath, like he's been running when he has been trying to walk as casually as he can, as if he's just out for a morning stroll, has no place in particular to be. Then it dawns on him: it might be better to walk with purpose, as if he does have some place to be, work or school, not some drifter, someone with no links to real life. Perhaps he should look eager to see the procession. He doesn't want to miss a moment of it. A faithful fawner over the Emperor and his family, of this lovely loving couple, especially the Duchess Sophie, the love of the Archduke's life, the woman for whom he was willing to risk his throne to wed.

He's enraged. The propaganda that pulls the wool over people's eyes. Diverts their attention from the real truth, the terrible toll this Empire has taken on its people. Especially the Slavs. Well, they will soon have their blinders ripped away.

He steps off the bridge leading to the Appel Quay, turns onto it. He's getting close now. The sounds of people in the streets, birds in the trees, all seem heightened and distorted. Feels like he's had one beer too many, but he's not drunk, just a bit heady, hearing things, things he normally doesn't. As though there's a background noise to life, a noise he'd missed before. Now it seems loud.

He's always been oblivious to his surroundings, doesn't know one tree, bird or flower from another. His little brother is obsessed by birds. His little sister by flowers. Knows all their names. Not he. Yet now he sees birds everywhere, never knew there were so many. Perhaps it's in their nature to know something's in the air, a storm's coming. That's how they protect themselves, migrate in winter, know where to go.

His brother told him birds can read other animals' minds. People's too. That boy is always making things up. You can't tell what's true and what isn't. He loves his little brother so. His sister too. What if he never gets to see her again. What if he never gets to see his whole family. He might have to flee the country. Forever. But he'll be a hero, a hero in hiding. People will make up stories about him. Wonder where he is, if he's alive or dead.

His eye catches something, moving, in the bushes nearby. A dog, cat or squirrel? Maybe just the wind. But there's barely a breeze. Bushes don't sway just from a slight breeze. He must be imagining it. There's nothing there. If there is, if there was, who cares. It's got nothing to do with him. No one knows what he's about to do. Least no one he can't trust. No one who'd be following him. Why would someone be following him? Hiding in the bushes. Maybe they're watching, making sure he goes through with it.

Highly anonymous and secretive, Slavic cells have been trained in teams, not only to maintain each other's morale, but to make sure each stays in line, doesn't betray their mission. These squads serve as webs of spies, each member monitoring the demeanour of each of the others. Not the best way to build trust. But on this mission, alone or not, Gavrilo Princip is the key, the one chosen to kill.

Suddenly it feels cold. The breeze off the river sends a chill through him. As he gets closer to the killing grounds, he begins to contemplate merely going through the motions. For all his bravado among his assassin cell buddies, as the momentousness of the impending act begins to hit him, along with what might follow for his family, he begins to pray that some fortuitous circumstance might foil the entire plot.

No. He's letting his fear get the better of him. Should have known it might. But how could he? He's never done anything like this before. Probably never will again. He won't have to. He'll have made his mark, be giving orders to others, coaching them on the fine art of assassination.

Someday, they'll build monuments, put up statues of me, the boy—no, the man—who began it all. They might not know why they're free. But it will be because of me. My bullets' ripples will reverberate for years. This thought sets his blood ablaze, as if he's running a fever. But he's not. He knows he's not. They warned him. Don't let it go to your head. Just do what you have to. Focus. Take deep breaths, slowly and calmly put one foot in front of the other. Feel your feet move. As though in slow motion. Do not hurry. There is no hurry. Your mind must be still, like steel, stuck on the mission, repeating each step, over and over at the same time as your eyes and ears scan your surroundings, not surreptitiously, so that you look suspicious, but calm and confident, self-contained.

He spots a small crowd up the street, his nose so sharp, he can smell the café. Stay calm, eyes straight ahead, your mind on your target. Don't look to the right, don't look to the left. Just straight ahead. Hands steady. Mind and eyes focused, locked on the Archduke, pull the trigger. Twice. Three times if you miss. But you must not miss. And you will not. If you follow instructions. The first shot is the key, the kill-shot, the smallest, hardest to hit target, the reason you've been practicing all these months. The second can be through the heart, but the first must be through the head. Keep shooting until you've seen him slump over. Cool, collected, make sure you've not missed, that he ducked.

Then walk away. Do not run. Just walk, unhurriedly, as if nothing has happened. Chaos will ensue. But not in you. You've made sure you've finished the job. There must be no movement by the Archduke. None at all. Not the slightest twitch. You must not see him squirm. Otherwise, you must fire again. Stand there serenely and fire again. Until you're sure he can move no more. Not a muscle. Not a twitch.

If you're caught, so be it. Not a word. Hold your head high. The whole Slavic world will be with you, watching you. You will not utter a word. Not one word. Or you will go from a people's hero to its most hated person. An embarrassment to your parents, your people, yourself. Keep your mouth shut and you will have nothing but respect, not only from us, but from our enemies. If you do not you will have only contempt from all.

He's but steps away from the Moritz Schiller Café now. There is no hiding. He is out in the open. For all the world to see. If he fails everyone will know. But he won't. He can't. He's rehearsed it so many times. Eyes focused. Hand steady. Pull trigger. Eyes focused. Hand steady. Pull trigger.

* * *

Everything and everyone seems to be moving in slow motion, even he, his feet inching toward the Moritz-Schiller café one slow step at a time. The small crowd seems to part for him, as though they'd been anticipating his arrival.

As the motorcade rounds the corner, for a second the sparkle of sunlight off the limo's polished steel body blinds him. And the sun reflecting off the rear window forms shadows he can't seem to decipher.

But, as the lead car gets closer to him, he steps toward it, sees the driver looking his way, staring at him. Or is he imagining it? No matter. There are two people in back of the limo, two bodies ready for burial. It must be the Archduke, with his wife waving beside him. Who else could they be? They wouldn't send decoys. No, they're too smug, have no idea what's in store for them.

As Gavrilo Princip approaches the car, mirrored in the Archduke's window he sees a reflection of himself, his hand, the gun. It's as though he's watching someone else make each move. What is he waiting for? It's the Archduke! Who else can it be? Shoot! Pull the trigger. But his finger freezes. Or is he stalling, waiting for the last conceivable second to be sure, to see the Archduke's face up close as he collapses, as his empire collapses with him?

Finally, the Archduke's face comes into clear focus as he smiles, raises his hand to wave, as though, because he knows a weight is going to be lifted from his shoulders, he's smiling and waving for his assassin. It is then, impelled by some robotic force, that Gavrilo Princip pulls the trigger, once, twice, point blank. Unlike the small crowd of people, crying out, running every which way, Gavrilo does not move. He cannot. To the objective observer, he may seem calm, resigned, ready to accept his fate rather than resist it by running. In truth, he's lost control of his legs. He needs to flee but cannot, unable to decide where or how. Not only can he not move, he cannot think.

* * *

He's spent his days and half his nights memorizing the many charts, tables and maps on the covers of his old school workbook. The one his mother brought him so he could keep a diary. But he hasn't. The days are all the same. The nights too. He has nothing to say. But he now knows his multiplication tables backwards and forwards. And every town on this tiny map. To keep himself sane he's run one crazed calculation after another through his mind.

How many Krones in a Kopeck? He can't remember. Not that it matters anymore. He'll never travel those two thousand kilometres to Russia. Never escape over the border to Odessa where, protected by Cossacks and cops paid to look the other way, Black Hand sympathizers would have put him up in a safe house. He could have stayed hidden there until, his country freed from Austro-Hungarian fetters, it was safe to come home. But that was not in the cards. His panic following the shooting made sure of that. He couldn't move. Afraid to be so far from his family. Alone. In frail health. Running from other assassins. In fear of other assassins. Surrounded by a language he didn't understand.

He should have been a better student. He could have been. But he never really liked to study. No, he was more a man of action. As his action has proved, if not to himself then to the world. Yet if he had known that the consequences would be this kind of claustrophobic solitary confinement, he might never have done it. Why did he do it? For notoriety? To free his Slavic brothers and sisters? Out of sheer boredom? Damn it. He no longer knows. Maybe he never did. The act itself evoked a feeling of pure freedom. His confinement anything but.

Shackled in his cell, coughing and spitting up blood, his tuberculosis is not taking kindly to his damp cold surroundings. Nothing to look forward to but his next miserable meal. And the next. Counting the hours. The interminable hours. No wonder he keeps having second thoughts. Yet his jailers treat him with anything but contempt. In fact, though they struggle to keep it well-hidden, from the way they speak to him, with a certain tone of respect, and the way they physically handle him, with a gentleness they never show other prisoners, he can sense a certain sympathy from them. They never try to make him cower or cause him any more discomfort than they absolutely have to.

Still, he's going crazy staring at the bare cell walls. More so at the ceiling, flat on his back, in the dark of night, exercising his erotic imagination. Fantasy is now his only freedom. Maybe it had always been so. He may have fulfilled his political dreams, perhaps his father's too, but he'll never fulfil his female fantasies. Not in this life. And he doesn't believe in the next. He's condemned to a dead end. The pleasure of playing with his privates, imagining himself the hero in some young woman's eyes, between some woman's thighs, aroused by her sighs, is beginning to wear thin.

Nights are especially awful. And are becoming increasingly so. His coughing keeps him awake. Sleep deprivation is taking its toll on his health. More than the damp cold. Together, they are lethal. His life is limited and he knows it. One thing he can be thankful for is that his sentence will be cut short, commuted by his tubercular death. He is not likely to outlive the war that his bullets have begun.

Well, thankfully, he's been spared having to fight at the front. Still, he might have survived that better than the solitary confinement of this cell.

At least his life has not been for naught. He's made his mark. History will not forget him. One bullet. That's all it took to end one life and immortalize another. His name will be indelibly etched, not only on his tombstone but in the mind of a whole nation. A whole people. His people.

He begins to cough, uncontrollably, as though the very thought of his immortality, the trajectory those bullets travelled have triggered the fit. His chest spasms feel more like a heart attack than mere tubercular coughing. This is how Christ must have felt on the cross. A stake right through his heart, his head, the pain unbearable.

How much longer must he endure? One more family visit. His mother will surely come. Afraid they will take his son's actions out on him, on the rest of the family, his father has refused to, kept his children from coming to visit their brother. But he hasn't been able to stop his mother. She's always favoured her frail son. Probably because he was so frail. How could she not take pity on such a poor physical specimen? Surely, he has made up in spirit and courage what he lacked in physical prowess. His poor health could not keep him from committing himself to a cause greater than himself. More noble too. His mother must be proud. Still, she probably takes as much pity on him as pride.

His coughing becomes uncontrollable. Blood and phlegm fill his hands as he tries to cover his mouth and nose, to keep them from the cold. But he cannot. He is going to die now and he knows it. He will never see his mother again.

GRAVE IV

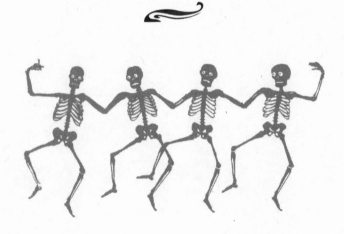

FROM AN EARLY age children take for granted they'll outlive their parents. Nevertheless, they unconsciously prepare for the trauma of losing their mother or father. On the other hand, from the time their children are born, parents live in terror of something untoward happening to their offspring. Yet can never adequately prepare for the trauma.

* * *

Hey, baby bro,

War seems to bring out the best in people. And the worst. Sometimes both at the same time. One moment I'm shocked by people's selfishness, the next, surprised by their selflessness. In cities at peace people tend to be more at war with themselves, more isolated as individuals, more insulated from each other. Here such barriers have been bombed away.

Though it's much harder to a get a really good rest down there, what with all the fidgety sleeping bodies, the snoring, along with the insomniac chit chat, I'm still better off sharing sheltered sleep quarters in this apartment building's basement than remaining alone up in my room. Find loneliness a more lethal weapon than any array of armaments.

Anyway, last night, in the middle of the night, one little boy became so sick, coughing and spitting up blood, a few in our basement bunker became concerned, not only for their own health, but for that of their children. What he had could be contagious and it might be best if he were moved back upstairs, to his own apartment.

His father had been killed a few days earlier, hit by a sniper while out foraging for food. The other brothers and sisters, five in all, between the ages of four and eight—their mother didn't seem to miss a beat when it came to baby-making—were too frightened to leave. Their mother refused to risk their lives upstairs. Nor would she agree to leave them behind—though I volunteered to look after them—so she could look after her sick child upstairs. If she and her son were to die up there what would happen to the rest of her children down here? She wouldn't abandon them to be orphans downstairs, nor would she let them risk their lives upstairs.

After a lot of arguing, her begging to keep her sick son down here, safe with the rest of his siblings, I volunteered to look after him upstairs. I have no children of my own to be concerned about, and some medical training, albeit elementary. Soon as I picked him up out of his mother's arms the little boy seemed to take to me: he stopped coughing and crying. Maybe somewhere deep down he understood it was the best option, his only option, who knows?

I promised his mother that, the first light of day, I would take him to the doctor, so she could stay with her other children. It wasn't all altruism. At that point I just wanted to get away from the group, preferred to be alone upstairs with that little boy than be contained in that claustrophobic basement. Besides, the bickering was beginning to get to me. And he's the sweetest cutest little thing. Not caring in the slightest that I'd catch what he had, I'd hold and console him. Maybe he brought the mother out in me, or the mourning at never having been one. And of course, the guilt of not providing mom and daddy with grandchildren. Good old guilt. Can we ever get away from it?

Bye for now, baby bro ...

M.

She may have been too young then to later remember, as a two-year-old having to flee her homeland because of her father's fear must have taken a toll on my mother. At least so my sister had maintained. And insisted that being under siege in Sarajevo might help her have a feel for what it may have been like for my mother in those crucial formative months.

I suggested that if she really wanted to know what it felt like to be my mother back then she should wear diapers.

She said: "I might." Then after a long pause added: "If I thought it would help me understand her. Anyway, all I'm doing is giving mom's native milieu its due, the same due I gave daddy's in Odessa. As you no doubt are aware, there were no pogroms in Odessa when I was there. Sarajevo under siege'll be a lot closer to what mom went through."

A lame last-moment attempt to placate me the night before she left, we both knew she was looking to find out not what made our mother tick, but what she herself was made of. However, by then she must have known. She certainly should have. Yet something compelled her to keep proving it.

Oy, baby bro,

Last night we seemed to be missing a mattress. I don't know if someone's stealing them or we're just not good at keeping count. Of people or mattresses. Some children sleep with their mothers, fathers or siblings. But they sometimes wet their beds. So on any given night, it's hard to know how many mattresses we might need. Above all when we have guests, i.e., neighbours from other buildings that have been bombed, shelled or simply had a close call. Too close. Their basements might be intact but they're too scared to sleep there and have family or friends in this building. Still, there's a limit to how many we can house in this bunker. From the bickering, think we've pretty much reached it.

Tonight we needed a volunteer to fetch a doctor. He lives only a few blocks away. But the shelling was so intense no one was eager to go. Some argued we should wait till morning, when the doctor made his rounds. Most agreed. I didn't. An eighty year old man with no family was sick. Very sick. He wasn't coughing, sniffling or sneezing, the usual symptoms in the dampness down here, just shivering with fever. He was in no condition to make it to the doctor. Nor were we equipped to carry him there. The hospital was out of the question. The nearest one is too far, and the shelling too intense. Besides, hospitals are targets, not only to terrorize, but to make sure enemy combatants can't get the care they need to get them fit to fight again.

Turned out that the usual volunteers were afraid to go for fear that when they returned their mattresses might have disappeared. Not that someone would abscond with them, but their sleeping spot could easily be usurped. If it weren't so sad it would be funny. Actually, it did make me smile, once I was out of there. You guessed it. I volunteered. But only after several of our more influential bunker residents agreed to guard my mattress with their lives. Mea culpa, I can stoop with the best of them. You have to stand your ground down here or some'll ride roughshod over you.

Anyway, this was the fourth or fifth time I'd volunteered to venture out like this, and didn't want to look like a hog playing hero. You have to walk a fine line down here or you risk becoming a victim of behind-the-back bad-mouthing for looking too eager or too selfish to do good.

Take care my little angel,

M.

The morning before Maya flew to Sarajevo my father had fought with her, begged her not to go.

"You haven't put us through enough already you want to put us through more? Please? Please? You know how precious you are to me. If something happened to you I don't know what I'd do. You can't see them shooting I saw on the news! Like sitting pigeons. What's the point you might as well paint a target. Do me a favour put a knife in me right now."

"I need to feel needed."

"I need you, that's not enough? Your mother needs you too. She doesn't say much, but at night she can't sleep. Sick with worry she'll toss and turn and keep me awake all night. Is this what you want? Don't you think old age we're entitled to a little peace? What kind of life is this running round the world looking for wars? Like an ambulance chaser. You want to be an ambulance chaser you should've gone into law. You want you should make the world a better place why can't you start here?"

My father could cajole buyers from the biggest chain stores, but he couldn't do the same to my sister. When catastrophe called she couldn't resist.

Merhaba, baby bro,

I get the blues most every night,
I get the blues much worse than fright,
I get the blues oh boy they bite,
I get the blues but I'm alright.

Can we blame our blues on daddy? Can he blame his blues on his? Or should our blues just be blamed on life? They begin at birth, end at death. Death's right outside the door here. Can taste it every time I leave my cozy little bunker.

It's unusual to see more than two family members together in the streets here. More makes for too much of a target. But unless the family wants to starve or freeze to death, sooner or later someone's got to get the groceries. So it's not uncommon to see a parent and child out there, or either, alone.

Some parents are like ours, so protective they won't let their children out alone. The irony is that the parent, being a bigger body, is more likely to catch a sniper's eye than the child. Yet even more ironic, the presence of a parent poses a greater danger to the child than the absence of one. Why? Well, some snipers seem to get a kick out of picking off a child in front of its parents.

But, sadistic as they may be in the role of sniper, some are still human. Perhaps parents themselves, they may have sympathy for a child out there alone, and not fire at it. Or miss on purpose, just get close enough to get the kid running scared. So sometimes the safest bet is to send your youngest out alone. But most feel too guilty or fearful.

Remember when mom and daddy would take separate flights to Florida so that if one plane crashed we wouldn't be orphans. Little did they know how we relished being orphans those four winter weeks. How we loved their surrogate, Mrs. Lipmann, so fat, jovial and funny. And boy could she cook. Those crepes Suzette, mmm, mouth's watering just thinking of them. And we could stay up late as we liked. Long as we didn't fall asleep in school. And didn't tell our parents.

Of course, we would've no more squealed that we'd stayed up late than we would've squawked she was a closet drunk. Though she must have gone through half a bottle of hard stuff a day—remember marking the Crown Royal?—she could really hold her booze. And daddy never kept track of what he had in his liquor cabinet. How could he? It was so large, all those mirrors, it was like a maze. He had such a huge stash of such a wide variety Mrs. Lipman could go from one bottle to another without being too conspicuous. Or maybe daddy knew, but didn't want to know.

Mom knew. I know she knew. Yet never said anything. Guess they both wanted to get away from the humdrum of home, wanted a respite from us as much as we wanted one from them. And for that they were willing risk leaving us with a lush.

A discreet one. Even overprotective parents have limits.

Boy what would any parent here in Sarajevo now give to have a problem as puny as an imbibing babysitter. Of course, our folks are survivors of their own siege.

Your oh too sober sis …

M.

The one place in the world Maya couldn't try to make better was our home. That probably propelled her to flee as far as she could, to places where people had good reason to be miserable. Perhaps she felt if she was doomed to being unhappy she might as well find places where it was appropriate. Misery loves company. And where better to find both company and misery than in the world of the war torn.

Oh baby bro,

Saturated with such hatred as this war is, I don't know where else I could find the kind of love I felt helping this little girl, whose hand was turning green before I drained the pus from her thumb. I used a match to sterilize the needle that punctured the skin and then that same needle to suture the wound. The little girl was screaming so loud I was scared she would damage her vocal chords. Thank god for the strong-armed women holding her or I would have botched the surgery. That little girl was one step from gangrene if she wasn't there already. She could've lost her hand. But we couldn't get her to a doctor. It was too dangerous out there. Nonstop barrage.

Can't stand to see children suffer. Can't bear their pain. Breaks my heart. Yet rather than run from heartbreak I seem to run to it. That mean I'm a masochist? Or is immersing myself in the heartache of others the only way I can seem to escape my own? Shit. That smacks of sadism. Whatever the reason, never feel as alive as I do running for my life. Just another adrenaline junkie? Don't think so. I do love the rush. But rather do without it. Yet a Mother Theresa wannabe I'm not. What I am, I'm not sure. A dilettante of despair, vicariously searching for the holy grail of love among the ruins of other people's lives?

Sure I like to help those in distress. But daddy was right, I could do that at home. But since I'm not a nurse, a qualified medical practitioner of any kind, I'd have to be a volunteer. Which wouldn't pay the rent or put food in my mouth. Here room and board are taken care of. Plus I get a pittance to put away for a rainy day. So you could say I'm here for the money. Toss in the adrenaline rush and do-gooder pats on the back and the question still remains: am I here to help or hide? Probably a bit of both.

At the moment things are calm. Writing this by candlelight, in a quiet corner of this building's basement. It's funny, no matter how wretched they are, we struggle to civilize our surroundings, tame them, make the best of the worst situations. I've set up my private little sanctuary, using a sheet as my tent to separate me from the snorers nearby. One is beginning to stink. She needs a good wash. As do we all. But between the smoke of this candle and the bar of pine-scented soap I keep by my side I can imagine I'm by some forest campfire getting ready to sleep under the stars.

If I do get desperate for the night sky I can always risk going up to the roof. There hasn't been any shelling for a few hours now. Probably trying to lull us into some false sense of security. They're sadists that way. It's got so that, unless I'm surrounded by explosions, I can't sleep. And this quiet's driving me crazy. Is it a sign of something to come, something far worse than sporadic shelling?

Some kids here seem to have copied me—or me, them, not sure which—complaining they can't sleep when it's too quiet. Guess, like me, they've grown so used to the shelling it provides some sort of solace. Hearing it, they know they're not being hit. But when it's quiet they anticipate the worst. The butterflies in the belly can be as bad as any bomb. The constant shelling probably acts as a pacifier. Some fall asleep to the sound but wake up soon as it stops. Am tempted to make my way up to the roof. But my coming and going might disturb the light sleepers.

Though others come and go all night long. Mostly it's to the nearest toilet, down the hall here. Don't know why there's one there. Perhaps for the maintenance people. Just toilet and sink, no shower. So you can imagine how it stinks down here. In there too. Some don't clean up after themselves, splatter you-know-what all over the seat. It's got so bad that if I have to go I go upstairs, shelling be damned. And if it's the middle of the night, I stay up there till morning. Don't have the stomach to come back down.

Had enough of roughing it. Sounds outrageous I know. How much rougher could it be?

Starting to get sleepy. Thank heaven for Halcion. Ciao for niao.

Love you more than life,

M.

My sister knew to keep her trips home short and time them so that she was in the middle of a project, in a hurry to get back to a commitment she couldn't be talked out of not seeing through to the bitter end. But this time was different. She'd just finished a stint helping survivors of the cyclone in south-eastern Bangladesh, was disaster and war weary, and simply wanted a rest from the world.

For the first few days my father was on his best behaviour, but after that he couldn't help himself. And the bickering between him and my mother brought back old familiar memories, ones unpleasant enough to rekindle that I've-got-to-get-the-hell-out-of-here urge. One of my favourite novels as a young man was Thomas Wolfe's *You Can't Go Home Again.* How true. For her. For me too.

Yet I too tried to talk her out of going to Sarajevo. Natural disasters were one thing, civil wars, another. Hadn't she seen enough carnage to last a lifetime? But she was determined to go. And, as usual, nothing anyone could say or do would stop her.

Halo, my angelic baby bro:

We've divided this side of Sarajevo into units that pairs of us, armed with walkie-talkies (which half the time don't work) patrol day and night, specially after shellings, seeing who needs what, giving first aid and comfort where we can.

Hit by a bullet last week. Don't panic, only a flesh wound. Grazed my thigh. I gauzed and taped it, without antiseptic. We'd run out. Mea culpa, I'm the one who's supposed to keep track of these things. Needless to say it got infected. But I'm okay now. With the aid of in-short-supply antibiotics. Felt guilty depriving others in dire need. Plan to be more careful, less cavalier.

I'm anything but when I first wake up most mornings, in an anxious sweat, a state of pure panic. Yet once I'm outside, the worse the weather the better. When it comes to war, sunny days are the worst. War seems more tolerable when it's wet. It seems obscene having to face the horror of bullets and blood under a crisp perfectly clear blue sky. Something must truly be amiss in mankind if men don't mind killing each other on gloriously sunny days.

Anyway, once I'm in motion, have managed to get my body from my basement bed to the battlegrounds outdoors, no matter how dreadful the damage that day, I inevitably feel better, am able to cope.

My saving grace? Never seem to be concerned about my safety. Feel more fear, in fact, often filled with it, when alone. Surrounded by people sharing the same imminent threat of a mortal wound, my fear seems to vanish. I do get a fight or flight adrenaline rush. But any fear inherent in it is overwhelmed by the exhilaration, and I come away from the incident with an acute sense of calm, one I never experience any other way.

The more lethal the threat the more alive I feel. Perhaps, rather than let myself become some scared little psyche, I've become some fearless little psycho.

Could Freud have been right, we all have a death wish? I do know that some love to see others die. If those who like to see them suffer are sadists, what can you call snipers aiming for a clean kill, idealists? I'm sure they get a thrill up there in the hills as they peer down through their sights, spot a target, pull the

trigger and pop, see the person fall. Don't understand fervent
nationalists any better than ardent hunters. Having a deer die
so you can put its antlers up on your wall. Can see Serbian
soldiers proudly displaying Bosnian trophy heads for their
grandchildren. They're that fanatic here. Scary.

Sayonara,

Maya

Only in war could she seem to find peace, only in natural catastrophe
some kind of comfort. She became a card-carrying soldier of misfortune.

My father would often refer to her as "My daughter, the war tsour-
ist." *Tsuris*, being the Yiddish word for troubles. He was prone to
puns, ones meant not so much to be funny as a poignant way to convey
his fear.

One *could* see Maya as a war tourist, a disaster-chasing dilettante.
And the more unsettling her circumstances, the more frequent her letters. Barometers of her innermost moods, they became an outlet for the
turmoil and uncertainty most of her associates never saw, the face
under the mask she had to wear to get her through the day in these
death zones.

Yo yo baby bro,

Going up and down here. I've been warned there's a bounty on
me, a bullet with my name on it, the name of all foreigners who
refuse to mind their own business. Imagine, me a marked
woman? Never dreamt I'd see the day. And then, of course, I
did. Many times. Too many to count. Near the end of my
Guatemala adventure, almost daily. So I should be used to
bullets by now. But I'm not. And this feels so different, so
disconnected. Then, I was building something, not only a
bakery but a co-op, one in which every campesino could play a

*part, look forward to a better life. At least that was my illusion
there. Here I have none.*

Your obsessed with herself sis,

Maya

*P.S.: Did you know they've named it after me? Panaderia
Maya. Nice ring to it no?*

The whole time Maya was in Sarajevo must have felt like that morning
seven decades before to my father, as though he was once again facing
a catastrophe, one he couldn't bear to imagine, yet in his bones felt
inevitable, one he could have prevented, but didn't. Suffused with the
sort of suffering that went well beyond fear, a paralysis of feeling, an
emotional numbness I'd never witnessed in him before, he became
more like my mother, stoic and silent, as though expecting the worst,
yet steeling himself against it, an unsettling state for a man usually so
emotionally effusive. Perhaps this was his way of facing his worst fear.

You'd think by then he'd have been used to her putting herself in
harm's way.

Jello again, baby bro:

*How you used to love that cherry and raspberry. Still have a
sweet tooth? I'm so skinny look straight out of a concentration
camp. Find eating to be a bother. Can't stomach those snipers
who've set their sights on me. On all do-gooding outsiders. As
though they discriminate. As though they can discriminate. But
this city's always steaming with one sort of hearsay or other.
Don't trust people who spread it. A strategy to scare us. Like
we're not scared enough. Though after a while you take such
threats for granted. A siege'll do that to you. Otherwise you
couldn't live. Not like this.*

Wish I'd had the guts to stay put like you. That Pascal you love quoting, 'Most of man's troubles stem from his being unable to sit alone in his room.' Well, this girl's finally solo in hers. Was going bonkers down in that crowded bunker. Yet not doing much better up here, the loneliness beginning to get to me. Like daddy, can't seem to be by myself, need to be surrounded by people, lose myself in them. How can a free spirit like me be so dependent on others? Often ask myself the same question. Too antsy to wait for an answer. Gotta swing into action, get busy doing something, anything.

It could be as inane as cutting my toenails, trimming the cuticles, pushing them back, over and over, in search of the perfect pedicure. Thank heaven for my Swiss army knife. Hard coming up with new ways to indulge old neuroses, keep them fresh, make them more intricate with age. Unfortunately, can't cut fingernails to kill time. Bitten to the bone. Good thing I'm not agile enough to reach these toes with my teeth.

Pedicure completed—can it ever be?—I scrutinize my toes, over and over, a kind of meditation, caressing them as I contemplate each cuticle. Could such compulsive perfection be an aesthetic impulse? Or's that putting too positive spin on it? Think I'm losing it? From idealism to inanity.

Once upon a time, each in our own way, we were both idealists. How wise you were to confine yourself to the realm of ideas. Because that's where rose-coloured glasses belong. On the eyes of the armchair beholder. Don't get me wrong, baby bro, I envy you. Admire you too. Ideas are their own end. Ideals too. You don't feel the need to act. You've never felt the need to act. Beginning to think that's a blessing. Half the bloodshed I've witnessed has been caused by idealists, the other half by cynics. Wouldn't say I'm a cynic, but I've seen so much bloodshed, so much cruelty, feel like I'm falling through the cracks.

I'm tired of running, baby bro, I'm tired of running. But I don't know how to stop.

Miss you, baby bro, miss you,

M.

All our father had worked for, all he had wanted in life, was for his children to have every advantage he hadn't had. Yet, whenever I visited my father's factory, I felt ashamed of being the boss's son. Saddled with class consciousness from an early age, I felt embarrassed for being born into money. Then did my best not to earn any.

But Maya did me one better. She felt regret for being born altogether, and later, for not being maimed in one war or another, at least traumatized like our father. Why should she have been entitled to such a safe and secure childhood when others had to endure such misery?

And so, after all her father's striving to give her the good life, a safe life, to protect her from adversity, she kept forcing him to face his worst fear.

> *Oh baby bro,*
>
> *Our capacity for self-deception seems unbounded. As is our capacity for denial. The one animal that knows we're going to die yet, knowing that, we can still get out of bed in the morning, make our way through the day like we're going to live forever. Of course, our knack for denial's not limited to our own deaths. Killing others we use it to give guilt the slip.*
>
> *Anyway, fed up with men. War'll do that to a woman. Not that I wasn't fed up with them before. But all these mortars are fired by men. Still, I seem to be drawn to these macho types, guys with too much testosterone, for whom sex is a means to ego gratification as much as erotic satisfaction. For them one woman's never enough. These guys haven't the slightest idea what love means, unless it's a kind of narcissistic mixture of vanity and self-loathing. All about conquest, I'm not sure they can distinguish between the two. Do I sound bitter? You bet I do. Though it's hard to imagine settling down, I'd be willing to settle for one man. Yet I keep choosing these wild and wooly ones. Well, excuse the expletive, but I've had my fill of these fuckers.*
>
> *Here I go moaning and groaning again. If it's not about*

war it's about men. Well, in my wounded mind they're linked. Unlike you, baby bro, most boys are born brutes. Biologically, they're hunters, if not for animal meat then females in heat. Can smell them a mile off. The hills are full of them, making death a way of life here. Wouldn't take much to turn me into a cold-blooded killer.

Truth is, I wake every day dreading I might die. That this may be the day one of those bastards get a bead on me, blow my brains out. And this morning, out to buy something for breakfast, a stray bullet struck a wall just inches from my head.

All I remember thinking is that they missed. I'd rolled the dice and it came up double sixes! Just dawned on me that the plural for dice is die. Anyway, the instant I heard that explosive staccato sound I jerked backward. I'm so used to it I'm not usually startled. But this time I was. And it saved my life. I know bullets travel faster than sound. So how could I have heard the bang before the bullet. Beats me, some kind of sixth sense I suppose. Live like this long enough and you develop a strange inexplicable ability to anticipate.

Ta for today,

M.

Maya kept putting herself into increasingly precarious situations. Her addiction to war zones mirrored my father's penchant for getting himself financially in over his head. Both were ways of diverting themselves from more debilitating torment.

Yet she had not taken into account that, trapped inside her living quarters, though she might not have been facing imminent death there, she couldn't simply escape outside, go for a stroll or run. Unless she wanted to have to run for her life.

Life was not a game you could play at your whim in a city under siege. Death was always at your doorstep, the moment you stepped outside. Under such conditions she was forced to face herself more frequently than she would have with serene circumstances outside. I could see that. Why couldn't she? And why couldn't I convince her?

Hi dee ho, baby bro:

Here I go again about men. Most are looking for adventure. Most are carnivorous killers no matter what their façade. Try as they might to tame their testosterone-tainted impulses, even those posing as pacifists can't escape their macho bent.

 But this pacifist seems as sweet as a man can be. Effeminate in a sort of transcendent way. Like you, he's a difficult man to describe. At first I thought he was gay. When I found out he wasn't I fell. Head over high heels. I'd fallen for him at first sight, but wouldn't confess those feelings to myself till I was sure he wasn't bent. Or, if he was, it was towards women, preferably older ones, like me. Yet it's precisely for that reason I'm reluctant to sleep with him.

 He's so much younger than I, we have fun together now, but I know there's no future as a couple. So why subject myself to the heartache? I've had enough of those to last two lifetimes. Unfortunately, I've only got one.

 And today was such a crazy day. Are there any other kind here? I was caught in a crossfire on the outskirts of the city. The danger, it seems, is not always from on high --those creeps shelling from up in the hills-- but from the 'good guys' down here, and their completely futile return fire. The shots seem to ricochet, echo and reverberate so that you can't tell where they're coming from, who they're aimed at. It all seems so random. I'm less afraid when I can spot the shots. Specially at night. Like fireflies, at least I know where they're coming from.

 Though the soldiers down here are supposedly on 'our side' you can't be sure it's not some nutcase. Perfect cover for some kill-crazy psycho. And there are plenty, believe me there are plenty. After such a long siege with constant shelling some start to go stir crazy, myself included.

Of course, I'm not the kind of nut who kills. But this siege is taking its toll. I can imagine myself running through the streets shouting "Stop it! Stop it! Stop it!" Beginning to feel like a firefighter surrounded by arsonists. After a while nowhere seems safe. Not even sleep. Yet I'm so used to it, it's hard to imagine living any other way.

My world's become a mightmare,
Macho men everywhere,
Puffed up balloons of hot air,
Twisted balls beyond repair.

Can you tell I'm cracking, concocting stupid rhymes without reason? Well, that's how far your sister's sunk, little pun-poems make her smile.

Smooches,

M.

I'd fully expected Maya to come back unscathed. She'd escaped the grim reaper by a hair's breadth so often before, I took for granted she'd do so again.

Oh, baby bro,

I've spent so many sleepless nights in this cellar, don't know how I stand it. The shelling used to help me sleep. Now, nothing does. Who're they shooting at in the middle of the night? Think they're doing it just to keep us awake. A form of torture to unnerve us. And it's working.

Inside here, eruptions mirror the explosions outside. There are no enemy combatants in this basement, least none that I we know of. Still, civil strife abounds. Civil war light I like to call it. Petty arguments over who'll sleep where and when, who's disturbing the peace with their snoring, who stinks, needs to wash before bunking down. Though we're all on the same side—I think we are—from all the bickering lately you'd be hard-pressed to tell.

Some complain they can't sleep with people coming and going at night. "If you're going to go, go, if you're going to stay, stay!" I heard one woman shout, at her husband. Think she was talking more about their stormy marriage than disruption of her sleep.

Thank heaven I'm single. Otherwise I too might take it out on my husband. Instead, here I am dumping on you. Hope it doesn't make you feel like some doormat, wiping my feet all over your face. Remember we used to do that with snow, pretend our hands were feet, our mitts, boots, fall down in fits of laughter rubbing snow all over each others' faces? Getting sentimental in middle age.

You take care,

M.

———————

Oh, baby bro,

Another day, another damn night without sleep. Another what am I doing here moment to share with you. Bet you're getting tired of me second-guessing myself. Probably something I should keep to myself. But I've got to vent with somebody. Aren't you lucky I'm willing to lift the veil of falsity for you? Maybe those few Muslim women here are onto something, not having to flaunt their happy-go-lucky face all day, even if it makes them targets.

This morning, mortars were hitting right near this building, or it sounded like they were, certainly much more than sniper shots. This little Bosnian boy, named Babic—I call him Ali Baba—insisted on going to school. Nobody was going to stop him. He was going to school. All of six or seven yet he can talk like a nine- or ten-year-old. At least that's what my neighbours tell me. A born politician, they say. As if we don't have enough of them already.

He kept insisting he should be allowed to go to school. And wouldn't listen to reason: that there is no school now. He said that by showing he was not afraid, maybe others would follow. It was only fear that kept kids out of school. But if someone stopped being afraid, if he stopped being afraid, maybe others would stop being afraid too. It's parents who're keeping their kids out, keeping the schools shut. And it's parents who're doing the fighting. It's up to the kids to show courage. If they start going to school maybe the shooting will stop. And he wanted to be the first to try.

Now this is obviously naive. In the eyes of an adult. Yet, as he kept trying to convince his parents to let him go, simply wouldn't take no for an answer, there was no kicking, crying or screaming like other kids his age might indulge in. Nothing but persistent logical insistence. He kept countering every argument from his parents, or rather, from his mother—his father is a man of few words—with a calm argument of his own. No histrionics, just mature reasoning and pleading.

The little bit of heaven peeking through all the hell here is not just the precociously well thought out little boy's genuine bravery, bravery that was anything but bravado, it's the way the way the mother and boy interacted, respected each other's arguments—respected each other's attitudes—that so moved me. That so astonished me. Neither one tried to use emotion or willpower to manipulate the other. These two, mother and son, actually talked to each other, and listened, as equals. Rare enough between adults. But between parent and child? It so touched my heart. You had to be here.

I know some highly-educated parents back home try to always reason with their kids, try to teach them to reason, psychologize to the nth degree, often end up manipulating each other. But that's not what I'm talking about here. These parents are not highly educated. The father's a part time plumber, the mom a cook, with several other kids. Yet there was something between her and her son. Something I never would have seen if war hadn't thrust us together in this basement.

So there are a few fringe benefits to this war, the odd taste of heaven in this hell. Maybe heaven's not all it's cracked up to be. And hell's not half as bad. Or you have to taste hell, to appreciate heaven. You're the philosopher not me.

Take care, baby bro,

M.

For me, a good book about war's as good as being there. But reading Maya's letters brought me too close for comfort.

Like me, my sister feared being afraid. But her antidote was the opposite of mine. She had to face the fear, feel it, throw caution to the wind rather than be careful; take chances she didn't need to.

A pacifist by nature, a coward by choice, I don't need the excuse of armed conflict to cower. I cower because I am. I cower therefore I am. *Contremisco ergo sum.* My sister refused to cower. And paid the price.

Was she driven to such perilous places so that she could peel back the layers of her psyche? Peer into the hidden recesses of her soul? Be forced to strip it bare? Or was this simply her way of shielding herself from doing so? I've asked myself this again and again. And have yet to come up with a satisfactory explanation. The most disturbing? She was driven to self-destruction.

Bottom line: I don't know. I doubt if she did. What I do know is that she was as outgoing and unselfish as anyone I've ever known, as gregarious as I am reclusive. And, face-to-face, I've never laughed so much and so hard with anyone as with her.

Still, these letters are so brooding and self-absorbed, collectively they seem like an in-progress suicide note. I know she was in the middle of a war. But what better place for black humour? Her letters had so little of it, it scared me. She was losing her sense of humour. And with it her way of coping.

Oy, my dear dear baby bro,

Today I witnessed another horror. I don't know how many more I can take, before the horrors take me.

The shriek that came out of this man when his son was shot, so loud and long, so high-pitched and piercing, it was like he'd been shot too. But he hadn't been. As he turned to step toward his son, who'd been knocked several feet away by the bullet, the father's knees were shaking so they couldn't keep him upright and he collapsed. Wailing in agony like some unearthly animal, shrieking his son's name again and again, he crawled over the boy, as if to shield him from further sniper fire. But it was futile. The boy was already dead.

I'd taken cover as soon as I'd heard the first round of shots. But instead of doing the same, this man decided to run for it, pulling his young son—he couldn't have been more than five or six—along with him.

Hope I never have to see another drop of blood. Unless it's my own. Speaking of which, it's that time of the month. The safe period. Should find myself a local lover. I'm sure that some Serb hunk would like nothing better than to screw a Jew. God, think I'm becoming as sick as some of these Slav sons of bitches. Makes me want to cry.

Your mad sad sis ...

M.

The shorter Maya's letters to me, the more concerned I'd become: at what she might have left unsaid; at what she seemed to have left unsaid. But then came a couple of longer ones.

Oh baby bro,

Remember when we were kids I used to stick my fingers in my ears, scrunch my eyes shut so I wouldn't have to see what I didn't want to see, hear what I didn't want to hear. Well, surprise surprise! it doesn't work anymore.

Last night I listened to this Muslim woman struggle to describe how Serbian soldiers knotted leather thongs around her husband and sons' necks, then forced them to watch as they repeatedly raped and tortured her and her ten-year-old daughter.

In the woman's scarred voice I could hear echoes of her daughter, husband and sons begging, crying, screaming for the soldiers to stop. But (here, the gut-wrenching bitterness of her words underscored by her caustic facial contortions) that only seemed to spur on the sadistic Serbs.

However, should the father or any of his sons try to shut his eyes or turn away from the atrocity being inflicted on mother and daughter, the noose around his neck would be tightened till, choking, he'd be forced to 'pay attention'.

My tears tinged with rage and a forlorn sinking feeling, I could hardly bear hearing the woman howl pleas of "Don't hurt my children!! Please don't hurt my children!! Kill me! Please don't hurt my children!!" as she laboured to explain how the soldiers forced her and her daughter to watch them mutilate and murder the father and sons.

The little girl blacked out. The soldiers, consumed by their cutthroat orgy, didn't bother to revive her. This, a year later, her broken spirit still barely able to speak, lugging her body like a burden she wished she could be rid of, the girl's mother took to be Allah's last-minute mercy!

How can we continue living in this world knowing what we know, what we refuse to admit we know, what we keep ourselves from knowing?

Your heartsick sister,

M

———————————

Oh baby bro, my dear dear one and only,

I don't know how to say this but I seem to be coming apart at the seams.

Though it's not usually my way of dealing with these doldrums, seeking help never has been, sometimes I just want to run into the street and scream, loud, for all to hear: "Help!" But I seem to have the wherewithal to wait until I'm outdoors and there's a series of explosions, or a flurry of gunshots. Then, by cupping both hands over my nose and mouth like I'm about to sneeze, I can muffle the sound for myself. I don't want anyone to think that I'm actually shouting for help, though of course I am. Believe it or not, simply shouting a loud, hard, but muzzled "Help!" seems to help, lowers the level of panic to a more palatable level, probably drops my blood pressure a few points.

But my doldrums are getting worse by the day. I don't know why anybody would want to be here.

Seen several fathers shot in front of their sons and several sons in front of their fathers. The same for mothers and daughters, mothers and sons, fathers and daughters, both parents and children, every conceivable permutation and combination of catastrophic cruelty you can imagine, a veritable smorgasbord of excruciating family suffering. Sometimes both parent and child are shot at the same time in coordinated sniper fire, but usually it's one immediately following the other by the same sniper, more often than not with the child being felled first.

I've heard that some snipers take bets as to who can take down the tiniest target, the master sniper being the one who, to make the challenge most daunting, can kill an infant cradled in its mother's arms without hitting the mother. The aim? To leave her in shock, holding her dead baby. How callous can men be, how cruel?

This is not really a war nor simply a slaughter, but a sheer exercise in sadism, in unadulterated evil.

Your sweet loving insane sis ...

I could always count on my sister to taste every bittersweet morsel of life without succumbing to its vicissitudes. Now she was letting me down. Part of me was angry, another, sad, still another, scared.

Despite her bravado and cheerful surface charm, I'd always known she was fragile, her perch in life precarious. And now she was teetering. I had to do something to keep her from slipping off the edge, if she hadn't already done so.

But what could I do, fly halfway across the world, play surrogate father crying for his little girl to "Come home! Please come home! It's too dangerous to play outside here!"

I never ran short of excuses for not having to leave my comfort zone. Hoiwever, if the turmoil of that war had begun to unhinge my sister, what might it do to me? I knew I didn't have what it takes to console her there. Even less, to come between her and her chosen manner of martyrdom. To get her out of there I'd have to convince her she'd feel better back home, and we both knew she wouldn't.

No matter, I should have got up off my ass and gone to her, instead I sent her this note: 'I love you. You know how much I love you. Please come home.'

And she responded as succinctly: *Love you too. But home? Where is home? I have no home.*

Chapter 5

THE PHONE CALL came in the middle of the night. Maya was missing. She had not been to her apartment, its basement shelter or her NGO headquarters in several days. No member of the NGO that she was a part of—including the most free-spirited—stayed away all night let alone days at a time without first, perhaps with a knowing wink and nod, notifying someone in their unit they might. Perhaps she'd been kidnapped, was being held for ransom. It was not unheard of. But there were no such demands. The suspense went on for days, her disappearance a mystery.

I said nothing to my parents. In fact, afraid that my father might sense something in my voice, I avoided speaking to him the whole time she was missing. Whenever I did speak to him the first thing he would ask was: "Hear anything from your sister?"

Diversionary weather or state of his health small talk would simply make him suspicious. When it came to my sister his ears were like lie detectors. No matter how I tried to hide it he would sense the slightest quiver in my voice. Trying to cover up with clichés like 'No news is good news' or an innocuously evasive 'No, not really' and I'd trigger off an alarm.

"What do you mean 'No, not really?' What're you trying to say 'No news is good news?' Why you talking in circles? What's happened? Tell me what's happened?"

So I avoided my father, kept the news to myself, hoping against hope it was all a mistake, she'd shacked up with some other NGO-nik. For days I couldn't sleep. No matter how many tranquillizers I took. I might nod off for a minute or two, then wake up in terror.

* * *

Finally, I got the news.

My sister was dead! Shot through the skull!

How could it have taken so long to confirm she'd been killed? Well, there were disputes over jurisdiction. Wishing to be seen as still having their hands on the civilian pulse of the city, each ethnic police faction struggled to keep itself relevant. Alleged allies against the Serb forces besieging the city, there were constant sectarian fights between Muslim and Christian police, as well as their military and paramilitary units. Add in criminal gangs of black market gun runners and it was sometimes hard to tell whether the civil war was taking place within the city or between those in it and the Serbs besieging it.

Unless it was clear, with numerous witnesses, in a spot known to have been shelled—how many spots weren't?—until the cop units in that area were convinced it was a casualty of war, they tried to treat each killing as a possible homicide. One never knew when someone within the city could use the cover of war to commit murder. Moreover, with communications crippled by the chaos of war and the morgue overburdened with bodies, it was not hard for a corpse to get lost in the tragicomic crossfire. That my sister was a foreigner also complicated things. All sides wanted to make sure their asses were covered.

After I got off the phone, I began to hyperventilate, shaking so much, I lost control of my limbs and collapsed to the floor. I wasn't sure where I was, that I'd heard what I'd heard. I didn't want to believe that I had. Not only was I unnerved at the news, news that I must have known was bound to come sooner or later if my sister kept chasing wars around the world, what scared me most was knowing I would now have to inform my father.

I swallowed so many tranquilizers to sleep that night I was lucky to be alive in the morning. At seven a.m. I was on the phone with our family doctor. At ten the two of us were at my parents' door. As my father opened it, spotted the doctor standing beside me, he started shouting: "Something's happened to my Maya! Oy God something's happened to my Maya! Something's happened to my little girl!"

With anguished ear-piercing shrieks, he began trembling uncontrollably, arms crossed, pounding himself with his fists.

In shock, my father required repeated sedation. The doctor suggested he be hospitalized, but my father wouldn't accept it. In reality, incapable of making sense, he was like a child, in the midst of a tantrum, oblivious to anything but his misery. Between gasps for breath, he couldn't put a sentence together without breaking down, wailing, beating himself with his fists.

As the tranquillizers took effect, his loud cries would begin to fade into soft moans, and he'd just lie there, a pathetically feeble old man, drooling like some simpleton, until finally he'd fall asleep. But not for long. As soon as the sedative began to wear off, he would wake and, his voice still hoarse from howling, his body bruised from self-inflicted beatings, his hysterics would begin again.

We'd tried giving him pills, but they weren't fast-acting enough and he'd begin pleading for more, screaming—"It's not working! Put me out of my misery! Please? Put me out of my misery!"—and grabbing for the bottle. Terrified I would hurt him or he'd have a stroke, I had to wrestle the pills away from him, pleading with him to stop fighting me. As the pills began to work, and wrestling with me had worn him out, he'd give up begging for more and begin pleading for mercy, from God, from me, from my mother.

It was impossible for me to keep trying to sedate him with pills when he was like a wounded animal. So, at all hours of the day and night, our doctor had to come to give him an injection.

The scene was always the same. In the midst of variations of my father's plea-bargaining mantra, "I don't want to live, doctor! I don't want to live! Please, doctor, I don't want to live!" the doctor would have to feign an attempt at injecting my father. My father would fence him off shouting: "I want to die! I want to die, doctor, I want to die! Please, doctor, I want to die!"

The doctor would then fake a second lunge forward then, my father now wailing "Kill me, doctor!! Kill me! Kill me! Please kill me!" follow up with a quick third thrust and, like some extremely skilful swordsman, finally strike my father with a sedating injection. Within seconds my father was out. From loud histrionics to sudden sleep, with no tapering off in between.

But the doctor couldn't afford to keep coming, and we had to hire a burly male nurse.

In stark contrast to my father, my mother went numb, and silent, her agony exposed only by sporadic streams of tears. She'd been used to my father's over-the-top ups and downs. But now there was nothing but despair so deep she was in no condition to deal with it.

* * *

But eight or nine days, it took what seemed like weeks with dozens of calls back and forth to get Maya's body home. Neither my mother or father were in any condition to handle the retrieval so I had to put my grief aside and talk my way through all kinds of red tape—both that of my government and the one in Sarajevo—then make all the funeral arrangements.

Reluctant as the Bosnian authorities were to deal with the death of a foreigner, at first they'd informed me that my sister may have been murdered by a former lover, later, that she may have committed suicide, finally, that she'd simply been in the wrong place at the wrong time.

All the long-distance to and fro between embassies, other authorities and me, the confusion of language and information had begun to resemble a game of broken telephone. But what details I could glean of the circumstances surrounding her death along with the desperate tone of her last letters made me wonder if she'd committed suicide. Venturing out in the middle of a snipers' onslaught in what was called 'dead-eye alley,' she may have wanted to die.

Heartbroken, I too wanted to die. Without her there was a void in my life I couldn't bear. How could she not care what her death would do to me, never mind our parents? Was she that desperate? How could I not have got off my ass and gone to her?

* * *

I thought it best that my father be allowed to fully exorcize his anguish at the funeral, so we didn't over-sedate him. But that might have been a mistake. For at the cemetery, each moment seemed to be followed by one more nightmarish than the previous, my father, howling in incomprehensible anguish, clutching at the casket, clinging to it. His nurse and I had to struggle to hold him back

"Mr. Blittstein," the rabbi said, stepping between my father and the coffin. "Remember her as she was. You don't want to see her like this, remember her as she was."

"But she'll be lonely! We can't bury her lonely! We can't bury her lonely!"

He was fighting so hard his nurse and I had to use all our might to restrain him, all our wits and words too. Finally, whether from exhaustion or grief or blends of both, he seemed to black out. I say 'seemed to' because, though his nurse and I had to bear most of his weight, it wasn't all of it. Conscious or not, my father's knees hadn't completely buckled. As much as anything, we were helping to maintain his balance, keeping him from keeling over.

In a rush to get the ceremony over with before things became unmanageable again, the rabbi indicated that I should say the Kaddish instead of my father.

"My father would never forgive me if I let him miss saying the Kaddish."

"Your father is in no condition, you'd be doing him a favour sparing him. You were so close to your sister, I promise, the Lord will approve."

The rabbi's approval was all I needed.

* * *

I couldn't tell if it was because he blamed himself for blacking out or that I'd said the Kaddish instead of him, but after the funeral my father stopped speaking to me. Not that he spoke much to anybody. Maya's death had induced a distress so deep my father could do nothing but grieve, every waking moment.

Alone, or surrounded by others, at home, or in public, though he seemed to find no catharsis in crying, no consolation either, his tears were endless. His weeping might peter out for a few moments—months after my sister's death, maybe for a few minutes—but soon it would start again. The short pauses between fits of convulsive weeping were moments, not of relief, but of biological necessity, brief interludes his body needed to allow him to keep wailing.

* * *

For months my father wouldn't look at me, acknowledge I was there, let alone that we both bore the same unbearable burden, shared the same unspeakable sorrow.

Finally, I could no longer stand it. For the umpteenth time, I pleaded with him. "Talk to me! Blame me for saying the Kaddish instead of you, for Maya's death even, anything, you're doing her a disservice! She wouldn't have wanted us to live like this! She wouldn't have wanted *you* to live like this!"

"Like what?" he finally responded.

"Like you're dead too!"

"I wish I was, don't you?"

"I'm mourning for her! You're mourning for yourself! And dragging us down with you!"

My father started flailing at me with his fists, shrieking: "You had to encourage her to go! Why did you encourage her to go? You didn't have to encourage her to go!"

"I didn't encourage her!"

"You didn't discourage her! If it wasn't for you! If it wasn't for you! It should have been you! It should have been you! Why wasn't it you? It should have been you!"

To stop my father from flailing at me with his fists, I resorted to the same tactic I'd used as a teenager to keep an opponent from hitting me. But instead of getting him in a headlock, I got my father in a bear-hug and held on tight as he feebly pounded away at my back. Gradually, either from physical or emotional exhaustion, I wasn't sure which, he stopped hitting me. I kept holding him close, hugging him, not only to make sure he couldn't hit me again, but to try and heal his hurt, mine too. And he acquiesced, allowing himself to be hugged, hugging me back. Then, clinging to me, his face in buried in my shoulder, his muffled weeping so feeble I could barely hear him.

* * *

That night, desperate to do something to deal with my guilt and grief, I wrote my sister a letter:

> *My dear dear Maya,*
>
> *I should have gone to the airport to see you off the morning you left for Sarajevo. Instead, though he was reluctant to let you go, I let dad drive you. I didn't want to watch him break down, try to stop you from going. I knew you could handle him better than I. You always could. I would just get in the way. Besides, I was afraid that if I'd gone to the airport, I might have ended up like dad, pleading for you not to go.*
>
> *Because mom and dad got married so late in life, they always seemed old to me. So I knew they'd one day die. But, because I thought you'd always be there for me, that didn't bother me as much as it might have. What did bother me was trying to imagine the world without you. I couldn't. That gave me the shivers.*
>
> *And now I'm shaking so I can barely read what I'm writing, and the tiny pools of tears are making the rest all the more illegible. Well, you always claimed you could read between the lines of my letters, let's hope they're not too blurry now. If absence can make the heart grow fonder, death can break it.*
>
> *There is so much left unsaid, so much left to share. A piece of me has been stripped away, a slice of my soul. That is love,*

258   Raphael Burdman

*that is loss, that is the darkness that others can't see, even those
closest to me. Nothing can heal the hole you left in my heart. I
love you more than you can know, miss you more than you can
imagine.*

Your oh so sad baby brother,

W.

To make sense of Maya's life I had to make sense of her death.

But the profusion of phone calls only confused me: one informed
me there were rumours she'd been a deliberate target of assassination;
another, that civilians, specially those with armbands identifying themselves as NGO nurses' aides, were prime targets. Putting two and two
together, I couldn't help thinking she'd deliberately placed herself in
harm's way.

Yet, amidst a prolonged flurry of shots, one of which was certain
to hit her if she stood, she'd suddenly sprung to her feet. Did she regret
being so reckless? Was she trying to make a run for it? Or was that
merely part of her panache, her way of showing she refused to let some
sniper force her to run and hide with every pah-pah-pah-pah-pah-pah
series of rapid-fire rifle shots?

Perhaps she couldn't stand feeling she was letting herself follow in
our father's footsteps, cowering as his father was killed, and for the rest
of his life feeling like a coward, fearing like one.

* * *

It's hard to capture a complete picture of my sister from the few letters
I've salvaged. They don't really do her justice. But they're all I have. I wish
I'd saved more of her earlier letters. They were so upbeat, filled with
relish for her role as shit disturber for the wretched of the earth. She'd
found her niche. I was jealous, envied her even. Maybe that's why I didn't
save her letters. And, with a whole lifetime ahead of us, I just didn't
think mementoes mattered. The past didn't seem worth preserving.

Besides, my sister was so enthralled by her present, so focused on her future, clinging to her letters made me feel lame.

But, strangely enough, once seeds of doubt about her life and work began creeping into her letters, I started saving them. She was older then. As, of course, was I. Maybe that's why. However, as my income kept shrinking, so did the size of my living space.

I'd accumulated so much stuff, unlabelled boxes of a mishmash of memorabilia, writings from my youth, letters from my sister, photographs, paintings, books and rejected manuscripts that were costing me an arm and a leg to keep in storage. Except for a few precious folders of photographs and letters, ones I was able to find without having to wade through dozens and dozens of cartons, I decided to jettison all my mementoes.

It was a crazy impulse. One that seemed more like something my sister might do than I. Chalk it up to a foolhardy impulse toward freedom, to the illusion of it too, that I would suddenly discard so many precious attachments. Perhaps it is the same sort of impulse that led my sister to let herself die. To free herself from her past, from feeling imprisoned by it, from her present too. One crazy moment, one untamed urge, and all the tensions of one's life—all the tenses too—are put to rest. And the ramifications can never be reversed.

Had I only anticipated that every word from my sister would become so dear, that they'd be all I'd have left of her voice.

* * *

When news of Maya's death spread our family received letters and phone calls from all over the world: lovers that were, lovers that wanted to be, fellow NGO-niks and friends, male and female, all pouring out the pain of her loss. How could she have felt so forlorn when she was in the hearts and minds of so many?

For most of my life, just knowing Maya was there for me, would always be there, made me feel invincible. Immortal even. That we shared the same baggage—our parents—linked us in ways impossible with anyone else.

How could I ignore Maya's continually putting herself in harm's

way, forcing herself to face death every day? Well, I'm sure when moun-
taineers set out to scale Everest they don't expect to die. Nor do their
families expect them to. Yet the life and death thrill is an essential as-
pect of the adventure. At least, that's what I told myself.

Who was I to interfere with her adventurous life? She wasn't asking
for help. At least not in so many words. And though she did seem to be
losing it in Sarajevo, I was serving as her sounding board, letting her
get stuff off her chest. Moreover, letters tend to bring out the introspec-
tion in us, exaggerate our insecurities.

But none of this consoled me. Or convinced me otherwise. I felt I
should have gone to her. The guilt kept tightening its grip on my grief,
and would not let go. Moreover, my father never gave me a chance to
fully exorcize my agony. I was too busy coping with his.

After he died I felt free to unleash mine. And unleash it I did.

* * *

Why is it we're allowed—even encouraged—to share laughter, but crying
in company's a no-no? Tears of joy are okay, but tears of sorrow taboo.
Perhaps the few days following a funeral, a few weeks, maybe months
—even a year—but then it's cheer up, Charlie, time to paste on that goof-
ball grin again.

Well, I ask you, what would life be without its wistful melodies,
music, without its minor keys? How sweet the sadness. Rather than
suppress my life's most heart-wrenching memory, I surrender to it, let
its melancholy serenade me. For in it there lives so much love. And lest
I forget that love, let it fade and die, when it comes to those wrenching
moments, that wretched monument to the cruellest of misfortunes in
my family chronicle, I can never grieve long and hard enough.

Lighting a candle in the dark, I rock back and forth, chant, scream,
wail for all I'm worth, whole hog, no halfway measures, praying like a
pious Jew, beating my chest till it's black and blue.

Sometimes I recall the lunatic high-pitched howling that accompanied my sister's black humour and, for a moment, my wailing turns
to laughter.

Yet some hurts laughter cannot heal. Whereas crying can be so cleansing, not only of one's sorrow, but one's soul. And the release in lamentation, as great as any joy.

If I didn't mourn with such fervour for my sister, how dear could she have been to me? Could I have cherished her half as much as I do?

GRAVE V

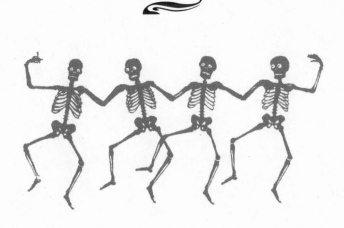

Chapter 1

I WAS APPROACHING middle age when my daughter was born. Why so old? Well, when each of the long term partners preceding my daughter's mom discovered they were pregnant, it dawned on them that, given my many idiosyncrasies and the likelihood I'd never be a breadwinner, they couldn't imagine being locked up with me the rest of their lives. I couldn't imagine doing life with them either. But, more, I couldn't stomach the idea of abortions.

I may be a progressive libertarian lefty, but in my heart, though I detest the term and politics associated with it, I'm—please forgive me—pro-life. Nevertheless, a talent for self-deception coupled with a capacity for denial allowed me, acting attorney for foetus and father, to voice my vehement objections.

Of course, not wanting to permanently tether myself to either of these women or they to me, I didn't really want to convince them. Thus, I wasn't very convincing.

Still, I would love to have had more children but that meant my daughter's mom putting up with me. A moot point because, months after giving birth, she left me. The consolation prize? I became the primary parent.

With a little help from my mother, daycare and the increased welfare benefits to which I was entitled as a single parent, I was now able to relegate my textile business to the back burner and, no wife with whom to bicker, start writing serious fiction.

* * *

For the first four years of her life, my daughter with me full-time, grief seemed to take a backseat to joy. Moreover, after my father passed away it was as though, freed from his all-consuming despair, my mother began extricating herself from hers. I'd lived with her the first twenty-two years of my life and never really knew her. Rather, I knew her mostly as morose and silently suffering, struggling to survive our stress-filled family.

The easy-going contented person she became was one I never knew—one I could never imagine—growing up. Of course, I was no longer living with her. And she'd always had a smile for those outside our family. Maybe now that we weren't sentenced to round-the-clock sharing of the same sad cell, she'd begun to see me as a fresh face. And I felt the same.

My daughter and I would spend prolonged stretches with her. She basked in just being around my little girl.

I'd never seen my mother happier than she was her last years. She seemed to savour being mistress of her emotions, of her life. I treasure our long walks, talks, holding hands like long lost lovers, my mother clutching mine, as though she was afraid to lose me. My one regret is that I didn't get to know her this way sooner.

* * *

From time to time I did long for someone to share my daughter with me but, since she'd been living with me full time, I was rarely lonely the first four years of her life, didn't miss or mourn my sister as much.

However, when my daughter suddenly decided she wanted to live with her mother, though I was reluctant to relinquish custody of her, and knew that not having all those years with her growing up would leave a hole in my life I'd never fill, I felt she'd be better off with two loving parents than just one.

A social butterfly, my first wife had remarried. Whereas I, a recluse, was content to be home alone with my little girl. A contentment she obviously didn't share.

* * *

At the airport, the moment my daughter's hand left mine to join that of the smiley Air Canada stewardess, I felt lost. With sinking heart I watched as they made their way up the passenger ramp. Then, just before boarding, my daughter turned toward me and, beaming, with one last wave disappeared into the Vancouver-bound plane.

For weeks I couldn't stop crying. Well, my daughter wasn't dead; she was simply in another city, in good hands living with her mother and devoted stepfather. At least that's what I told myself. But nothing could stop the tears. Afraid to get into bed at night, terrified of getting out of it in the morning, I lost my appetite for everything, including eating.

Thinking I might be able to write my way out, no sooner would I sit down to than, overwhelmed by anxiety, I'd immediately spring back up.

Only with the bedcovers over my head could I find the slightest relief. But it was too stuffy to stay under there for more than a minute or two. And as soon as I came up for a fresh breath, I'd again be encased in anxiety. Thinking it might provide both refuge and more breathable air, I'd try burrowing under just a sheet. But there was no security without my blanket. A sheet didn't feel weighty—nor did it keep it dark—enough to let me feel sheltered.

Stringing several sheets across a circle of chairs with a tall floor lamp in the middle, my daughter and I used to pretend we were Indians, in our tepee hiding from the bad black-hatted cowboys. How can you hide in a tiny tent? And how can being stuck in one be safer than behind some bushes outside? Well, if my little girl felt protected in our warm little wigwam, why should I disillusion her? Now, here I was, burrowed between the sheets. Who could tell me I shouldn't feel more secure?

Anyway, there was light at the end of that initial tunnel of despair. My daughter would spend parts of her school vacations with me, and her mom and stepdad never seemed to mind my visits, no matter how long or numerous.

Whenever I showed up to spend a few days—which sometimes stretched into weeks—with my daughter, they welcomed me as part of the family, albeit with a touch of tongue-in-cheek—"You invite him to lunch and he brings his luggage"—followed by a wink and warm hugs. From time to time, I probably did overstay my welcome. But I loved being near my daughter and, even if I envied it, part of her cozy family.

Then, one evening, violence intervened.

* * *

I've always been reluctant to unleash my rage, terrified I might kill someone. Once, I nearly did.

In-between tenants, my sister's ex-husband had offered me a chance to escape my Montreal writer's rut for a rent-free four-week respite in the basement of his Northern California beachfront bachelor pad. I couldn't pass it up.

The last weekend there, my first wife showed up for a visit. Not with me. But the shmuck upstairs. A surprise arrival, neither my brother-in-law nor I had any warning.

I could tell it was she by the ecstatic intensity of her high-pitched howling, her signature sound during sex. I've never heard anyone make such a commotion about coming. If not in spirit, in volume it equalled the fits of anger that emanated from my last wife. However, the latter made no sounds at all throughout intercourse. I could hardly tell she was there. And maybe she wasn't.

Anyhow, years before, while my first wife and I were still together, she and my brother-in-law had had an affair. Behind my back. Now, years later, when it should have been water under the weather-beaten bridge of wedded bliss, out of the blue, there they were, at it again.

Unable to just sit there silently seething, to protect my knuckles in case I needed them, I pulled on a pair of wool gloves, slipped upstairs and, without knocking, charged in to find the two old flames, naked, fondling in front of a blazing fireplace.

Before he could say a word, I started pummelling my sister's ex. Screaming, my ex ran from the room. My sister's ex fought back, hitting me with a hard left to the lip and a right to the respiratory system by way of the belly. I buckled, began to fear losing this battle of nitwits. He was shorter and slighter than I but, most likely due to more testosterone, much tougher than I'd thought he'd be.

To protect myself from his fists, I grabbed him in a headlock, holding on for dear life as he bucked like an enraged bully. Gradually, I managed to get him against the front door and, with a free hand, kept trying to turn the handle. But it was too close to the door frame and my wool gloves made it so slippery that I couldn't get enough of a grip to get the door open.

And thank heavens I couldn't. Because I was hoping to shove him over the balcony railing, anything to stop him from pummelling me. Had I succeeded, he might have broken his back, been brain-damaged or dead.

Eventually, we both ran out of gas. He stopped bucking, I let go and, without saying a word, slipped back downstairs.

In some unconsciously convoluted way I blamed my brother-in-law for my sister's death. If he hadn't been a womanizer, they'd have remained married. And she might never have gone to Sarajevo. But I was more angry with my ex. How dare she sully the precious memory of my sister. To say nothing of her priorities as a parent, trading time with her husband and daughter for a tryst with a two-timing son of a bitch.

I considered telling my ex's husband. But why break up their home, one that seemed happy, and good for my daughter. For all I knew he knew. And didn't care. Or sucked it up for the sake of the marriage. If so, he was a better man than I.

I stopped speaking to my ex for over a year. But, in the end, I had to give in, break the silence. In order to see my daughter.

* * *

Days before my daughter's twentieth birthday, her mom died. A year later, her stepfather. She was devastated. Having just graduated university, she decided to move back to Montreal, to be closer to me, her only remaining family.

Chummy as I'd been with her late parents, fond of them too, in some perverse way I was heartened to have my daughter's undivided paternal devotion. And I wasn't about to easily let go of it.

* * *

Months after my sister's death the Bosnian authorities sent back a suitcase full of her belongings. Her clothes were so colourful: wools, cottons and leather from all over the world; shawls, skirts, slacks, blouses and dresses she'd amassed in her travels; an array of clothing and jewellery that belonged in some indigenous fashion show.

For years I kept them in my closet. Afraid I'd lose the last links to my sister other than her letters, I was reluctant to give them away. They were my comforters.

I know I should have given them to my daughter. They were the same size, same temperament too. And that terrified me. Specially when she talked of following in her aunt's footsteps.

I'm not really a superstitious man, at least I don't think I am, but I couldn't help feeling that handing her my sister's belongings might help seal my daughter's destiny. Maybe the fear we all feel for our loved ones, especially our children, is a kind of fatalism. My father felt it to a pathological degree. And now it was emerging in me.

After nearly two decades, it was time to come to terms with Maya's death. It was time to come to terms with mine. But I remained stuck in limbo. And Maya's clothes stuck in my closet.

Chapter 2

ONE SUNNY MID-WEEK morning, my daughter phoned to tell me she was coming over after work to talk. From the tone of her voice I knew what she wanted to talk about. And so I steeled myself.

Loneliness may be the most debilitating of human emotions. Men will do anything to avoid having to deal with it, even kill. Others. Or themselves. Perhaps it was to lose himself in something larger than his lonely little self that the man who shot my sister joined the Serbian cause. And, with that license to kill, he'd made me more lonely than I could ever have imagined.

Now my daughter was going to follow in my sister's footsteps. I couldn't let that happen.

Then in my late sixties, I'd had a couple of brushes with death: kidney failure caused by prostate cancer. And though up to then I'd gone out of my way to not let my poor health make me dependent on my daughter, I decided that when she asked how I was doing, I'd cut right to the chase: I didn't want to die alone.

Then I started having second thoughts: Had I become as needy with my daughter as my dad had been with his?

With third thoughts I came full circle: I'd tell her that I'd like to talk about my funeral. Plan for it. Perhaps then she'd get the point.

But what was the point? That I'd become a desperate man, a lonely man and, as I neared death, needed my daughter near me? Or was I simply trying to avoid having to deal with that dread of such doom?

All this stress caused me to feel a slight fever. I knew it was fear, but couldn't fight it. I didn't want to fight it. So I took to my bed. Besides, being under the weather might be a good strategy.

The trouble was, once my daughter danced though my front door, I stopped feeling so feverish, my gloom and doom began to dissipate. Seeing her always seemed to soothe me. She had such a calming presence, a commanding one too. But not in an aggressive way. Just a quiet self-assured composure. Unlike her fidgety fear-filled father.

I knew I should tell her how wonderful it was having her there. That would be honest, and more mature than moaning and groaning. Yet some perverse part of me felt compelled to stick to my plan. Head her off at the pass.

—Tell her that the closer you get to your seventh decade the more you realize you don't have that long to live. The more you realize you don't have that long to live, the more you fear dying. The more you fear dying the less you want to live. And the less you want to live the more you contemplate suicide. Your life has become a kind of dead-end syllogism. In fact, knowing you're going to die soon has made you want to die now.

—*Now?*
—Not right this moment.
—I didn't think so.
—But soon.
—You're afraid? my alter ego asked.

And my other alter ego responded:

—I don't fear death as much as I do the uncertainty of living with it. Will today be the day? Tomorrow? Two weeks? Two years? Ten? The suspense is killing me. Each time I phone for an ambulance I think, this is it. Thank heaven, this is it. I'm finally going to shuffle off this goddam mortal coil. But within days I'm back home from the hospital. Destiny keeps teasing me. For god's sake, destiny, give me a break.

Fed up, my benevolent alter ego intervened.

—They say misery loves company. Well, you love her company. And to show it you want to share your misery with her?

But my selfish spirit persisted:

—Maybe you should tell her you miss your sister more now that you're near death than you did when you weren't.

—No, you promised yourself you'd never use your sister's name in vain. It would be doing a disservice to both her and your daughter.

—Shit, she's right here and you're running both sides of the conversation in your mind.

I've always managed to live in a reality mostly of my own making. But my sister and daughter could usually snap me out of my world into theirs. My heart a stethoscope for hers, I've always doted on my daughter, hung on her every word. Yet here I was stuck in my head. Fear—not wanting to hear what I didn't want to hear—was keeping me in bondage to my brain.

Finally, staring at me like I was having one of my trances, which, in a way I was, my daughter snapped me out of it.

"So-o- ... how are you dad?"

"I'm tired of waking up with a knot in my stomach, an ache in my heart, a longing and loneliness I can't live with. I no longer want to live with. Knowing my future is now relatively short and close-ended rather than long and open-ended is tantamount to having no future. Now that the end is near I'm lonely. And you're the one person in this world I feel close to."

To let that sink in, I paused. Then, about to continue, I realized her mouth was moving. She was talking about splitting up with her boyfriend. Telling me *her* troubles!

—So that's why she'd come! Or was that just a ruse, to divert me from what she really wanted to talk about?

Well, it wasn't. And hearing her was breaking my heart. All I could do was nod sympathetically. When she finished, there was a long pause. I felt I should say something. But I had no words of wisdom, none that wouldn't sound like clichés.

Relieved I hadn't heard what I feared, I just hugged her, held her for I don't know how long.

Regretting that, like my father, I'd been so preoccupied with myself I hadn't sensed my daughter's sadness when she first showed up, I resorted to rhetorical consolation: Is there any love as intense and unconditional as that of a father for his young daughter? I'd never doted on anyone as fiercely as I did mine. That kind of love never loses its lustre. My daughter's troubles always made me forget about mine, took precedence over them.

But, as she deftly slipped out of my hug, took a step back from me, I stopped basking in my little make-believe breather. From the way she was staring at me I could tell the shit was about to hit the fan. And it did.

It turned out that the rupture of her relationship with her boyfriend was the catalyst that pushed her over the edge. She'd tried to get her man to join her, but he had a teaching career to think of, and was afraid if he took time off he'd lose his tenure track. He wanted to marry and have kids. And my daughter just wasn't ready.

I'd known it was coming; nevertheless, when she told me she'd decided to volunteer for an NGO near the embattled Ukraine-Russian border, I freaked, reacted just like my father had with my sister.

"If something happens to you …"

"Nothing's going to happen to me."

"That's precisely what my sister said."

"I'm not your sister."

"And you're not going to follow in her footsteps. We haven't suffered enough for one family?"

"I'm not doing this to make you suffer. But now that I have no more ties …"

"No more ties?!"

"You know what I mean."

"Please, don't put me through what my sister put me through, what she put my father through."

"You'd rather I sit here watching you try to out-grieve him?"

She stopped, game me an apologetic look.

"I'm sorry, dad. She's meant as much to me as to you. In some ways, more."

"You never met her?"

"You made her into martyr I lived with every minute I was with you!"

"I didn't know how to deal with her death."

"So you dumped your despair on me."

"That's a terrible thing to say."

"It's true."

"I gave you every ounce of affection ..."

"You smothered me with it."

"And you're still suffocating, that's why you have to go so far?"

"Sarcasm doesn't cut it here, dad."

"What do you want me to say? Sometimes I'd look at little you, feel so much love, and then it would hit me. It would just hit me. Out of the blue. My sister would never get to see you. And you'd never get to know her. Believe me I didn't want to saddle you with my sadness. I knew what my father's did to me. To my sister too. But I couldn't help it, couldn't hide it."

"I needed as much of your heart as she had. I still do."

Taken aback, I didn't know what to say. Astonished by her own words, neither did she. So we just sat there, hesitantly staring at each other, as though a can of worms had been opened that could be hard to close and the best thing we could do was to catch our metaphorical breaths.

With a sigh, she took my arm, helped me sit up and slide my legs over the side of the bed, then sat right beside me, a bit too close for comfort when she looked me in the eye, yet oh so comforting when she put her hand on mine.

"Dad, did you ever think that maybe I've been as disappointed with my life as you've been with yours?"

"I'm not disappointed, just tired. I want your permission to let myself die. With dignity."

She burst out laughing.

I'm not sure if it was shock, simple surprise or a reflexive defense mechanism to protect herself from suddenly feeling the weight of having to care for her feeble old father. Still, I couldn't help smiling. She has such a wonderful raucous laugh, a lot like my sister's.

"Dad, don't take this the wrong way, but dignity is not a word that belongs in your vocabulary."

"Look, I've been crawling this earth more than two thirds of a century, and if I haven't managed to find much happiness heretofore, I'm certainly not likely to from here on. I'm tired of getting up day in and day out just to go through the same old motions. I know what's coming, a feebler more infirm me followed by a long bedridden good-bye. I want to spare myself that suffering, spare you too, by leaving this world before I'm too crippled, infirm and not of sound mind."

She looked at me as though I was nuts.

"What makes you think you're of sound mind now?"

"Age appropriate for an old fart with metastatic prostate cancer."

"Those androgen deprivation injections have stopped it from spreading?"

"For now."

"Now is all we have."

"If I die now, if you let me die now, I can leave you a little money. If I don't I'll eat up what little is left of your inheritance."

"How much?"

"A hundred thousand."

"Okay, go now."

"I knew I could rely on you."

"Sometimes I feel sad and lonely too. Does that mean I should do myself in?"

"Bite your tongue."

"Back at you. No one wants to hear this shit. No one needs to. Certainly not me. As a father, you're supposed to keep your depraved feelings to yourself, not unload them on your daughter."

"That would be dishonest, and doing you a disservice."

"Do me a favour. Do me this disservice.

"I come from a terminally unhappy family. Raising you, I tried to hide it. Now I no longer hide can."

"You're alone too much. Solitary confinement is considered cruel and unusual punishment, even in prison."

"A writer needs his solitude."

"Then stop complaining about it."

"I'm not complaining. Who's complaining?"

"What do you call playing this woe-is-me I-don't-want-to-live any-more card?"

"Kvetching."

Her mood seemed to suddenly shift. She stood up, started pacing in front of me like some predatory animal, or perhaps, prosecuting attorney.

" I'm not responsible for your happiness. Or your unhappiness for that matter."

"I didn't say you were."

"Not in so many words. All my life I've felt guilty for abandoning you, for choosing to live with mom when I turned four rather than you."

Just a few seconds earlier I'd been on offense, now, all of a sudden, she was. How quickly she could turn the tables. She always seemed to have the upper hand. Even when I felt I should have it. And before I could respond she resumed her offensive.

"You want me to provide you with a made to order family so you won't feel so alone. But where was my family when I needed it? You couldn't stay together for my sake now you expect me to stick with someone for yours?"

"Hugging my little girl, holding her little hand, cradling her in my arms and singing her to sleep, those were the best moments of my life."

"You live a self-absorbed life, a completely selfish life. If you got out there and did something for somebody else it might make you feel better."

"At my age you want me to become a social worker? Or better still, volunteer fireman. Always wanted to be a fireman, from the time I was knee-high to a hydrant."

She took a deep breath, let out a long sigh.

"I'm glad we had this little chat, dad." Her tongue-in-cheek tone took me aback as she got up to go. Panicked, I was about to blurt out 'Please don't go!' but stopped myself.

Still, I knew that as soon as she left I was going to feel much worse than I did before she came. Then, in spite of the trepidation I'd felt at what she was going to tell me, I'd experienced my usual excitement at the prospect of seeing her. A lot like how I used to anticipate my sister. Anxious elation. I never knew what to expect from either of them. Yet I always looked forward to both of them. Now all I had to look forward to was my daughter's absence. The letdown would be unbearable.

However, with all my talk of dying, I'd been able to divert her from making her decision to go to Russia a clear fait accompli. And I think she was glad I did. Or she wouldn't have let me do it. Certainly not so easily.

I'd planted my flag of opposition, and she of intransigence. For the moment there was peace. Persist with my pleading and she'd only get fed up with me. Whereas, if I backed off for now, I'd live to fight her another day. Maybe some *deus ex machina*—a truce between the Ukraine and Russia—would come to my rescue.

She glanced at her watch.

"Got to run."

She hugged me and, before I could say another word, rushed out.

* * *

But our little truce didn't last for long.

From all the years of fear my school principal was calling to complain to my parents about me, long after I'd finished graduate school I'd still get butterflies in the belly every time the phone rang. After my sister's death the phobia became much worse.

The phone ring became an alarm bell, igniting memories of the long distance call informing me my sister was missing. And, since my daughter began talking about following in my sister's footsteps, my tel-electro-acoustic transducer jitters had become a full-blown panic disorder.

So when that sound jolted me out of sleep, my heart started fluttering like a dying bat. I picked up the receiver and, after my shaky "Hello," heard my daughter say: "I'm not coming over to break the news because we'll just get into another argument. And I'm in no mood to argue. Or put up with your pleading. If need be, I'll simply hang up."

My heart still thumping, I calmly told her she wouldn't need to. Whatever she chose to do she had my blessing.

I could hear her inhale, hold her breath. She'd been taken aback, as had I, by my words. After a few seconds of silence, in an excited upbeat tone, she told me she'd officially joined Builders Without Borders and was being assigned to help with casualties in Eastern Ukraine. She'd be based in Donetsk, a city she insisted is less subject to shelling than the rural areas of Donbass, a no man's land between Russia and Ukraine.

The shock felt no different than that nightmare news from Sarajevo. And sent my fear of losing the last near and dear I had left surging.

I knew that what my sister had wanted to be but hadn't discovered it until too late was what had inspired my daughter to become an emergency trauma and triage nurse. Now, following in my sister's war-torn footsteps, the link between aunt and niece was about to transcend time.

* * *

While the lure of adventure to a young woman is understandable, might there be a darker side to putting yourself in perilous places, one that may harbour something akin to a—dare I say it—death wish? Could that dark side have been as much of a magnet for my daughter as it had been for my sister?

After putting the receiver down, the sinking feeling my daughter was destined to die in Donetsk became too much to bear. The years of grief over my sister's death turned into a torrent of fear for my daughter.

Feeling like I was already mourning her loss, overwhelmed by the grief welling up inside me, I swayed back and forth between vertigo and nausea, unable to decide which I was going to do first, faint or throw up.

I stumbled over and grabbed hold of the top of the closest chair and just stood there, struggling to get a grip on myself. But I couldn't. Fear I was going to lose my only remaining flesh and blood kept surging inside me.

I'd often contemplated suicide. The next best thing to doing it. It gave me a sense of freedom: there was a way to put an end to suffering in this life. But fear of feeling worse in the next always stopped me.

Now, shaking, unable to control my panic, feeling I was about to slip off a cliff, something my uncle Izzy once said seemed to offer salvation.

He took great pride in his way with words, fancied himself a writer, one who'd simply never got around to putting pen to paper. I remember being startled the first time I heard him utter the expression "If life gives you lemons, make lemonade. If it gives you sadness and self-pity, reach for a razor blade."

My father had money, at least compared to my uncle, but he didn't enjoy his life as much as my uncle did. Or thought he did. And never let my father forget it. His callousness had scared me. How could one brother be so cruel to another? More incomprehensible: how could one brother put up with such unkind words from the other?

* * *

Struggling to identify a carotid artery in my shaving mirror, my eyes slowly scanned the skin of my neck, carefully scrutinized the spots where I might make my incisions.

First I would cut my left carotid, then quickly do the same to the right. But, as I stared at my reflection, I realized I hadn't shaved in days. Showered either. On top of that, my T-shirt was full of spaghetti sauce stains. I didn't want to die looking like some bum, so I decided that, before slitting my throat, I should at least shave. Once I'd finished shaving, I thought I should shower. When discovered, I didn't want my body to be sweaty and foul-smelling.

After showering I felt so much better, had such a sense of accomplishment that I decided I should go out looking like a million dollars, dressed in my finest: pink silk shirt, grey suede sport jacket, black tuxedo trousers and sky blue Spanish boots with a white silk scarf suavely wrapped around my neck. Unlike the rest of my outfit, the scarf would have to be added immediately after I'd severed the second carotid artery, before I passed out.

As a cadaver I'd certainly be making a fashion statement, a kind of corpse haute couture. But having to wrap the scarf around my neck in such haste, I might not have time to get it just right. And it had to be just right. Too loose, and it would look like a rush job. Which it would be. Too tight and it would like I was trying to strangle myself after botching the bloodletting. Which, hopefully, I wouldn't. I wanted my daughter to think I went out calmly and coolly, that my death was not a hasty decision, but a carefully contemplated mature choice.

Then again, if I did tie my scarf too tight, it might serve as a tourniquet, stanch the bleeding, then what? I might not die, have to face my daughter, a pitiful fuckup who couldn't even succeed at suicide. Worse, soaked in blood, my scarf would turn red. That would clash with my shirt. My daughter had given me both for my sixty-ninth birthday. I couldn't sully gifts I so cherished. I should've stayed in my grungy pyjamas. But I didn't want to change again. Not after shaving and showering.

Out of inherited habit I've usually bawled my way out of misery. But the closer I get to greeting the Grim Reaper the more frequently I lapse into howls of laughter.

And, staring at myself in the mirror, I did, so long and hard the laughter turned to tears. *Ridi Pagliacci.* Laugh clown laugh. Behind the torn curtain of tragedy lies the impervious screen of comedy.

I simply couldn't go through with my suicide. How selfish it would be of me. What it would do to my daughter. I *had* made her a substitute for my sister, mourning her as though she was already dead instead of sharing her excitement as she embarked on a new phase of her life. Well, I could never cramp my sister's spirit, I certainly wasn't going to stymy my daughter's.

So, dressed in my funereal finest, I called her, invited her out to dinner during which I never mentioned the moments that led up to my invitation. Why spoil what turned out to be one of the most delightful evenings we'd shared as adults.

The one thing we argued over was the bill. As I grabbed it she reached for her purse, insisted she'd pay.

"It's the least I can do for upsetting you."

"How can you say I was upset when I acquiesced so easily, couldn't have been more calm, cool and collected?"

"Which to me indicated you were anything but. That you were so shook up you couldn't even argue. Soon as I put down the phone I had second thoughts, was going to come over. But that would have been playing right into your hands. So I stopped myself. I shouldn't have dropped a bombshell like that over the phone."

"Or in person."

She laughed, that long raucous laugh I love so much.

I shoved the bill over to her.

"Here. Pay."

And she did.

* * *

As a rule my daughter would drop by at least once a week, usually after work, unannounced. I loved that upbeat element of surprise. Of course, it had its downside, since more days than not she didn't show up and I had to deal with the disappointment.

However, knowing it was too soon for her to show up again, the first day or two following each visit I simply enjoyed basking in its afterglow. By the third or forth day, as memory of the previous rendezvous began to fade, anticipation of the next would begin to build. To soften the possibility of a letdown, after the clock cuckooed five, I'd begin finding reasons why on this particular evening she was unlikely to appear.

Normally, not wanting my daughter to feel pressured by a needy parent, I'd wait for her to initiate contact. But now, nearing the third week without her looking in on me, not hearing from her, I became concerned.

Did she feel that, after resisting so vehemently, I'd only given her impending adventure grudging rather than gung-ho approval? Maybe I needed to make a more concrete gesture of encouragement, one that would leave no doubt in her mind. Or, for that matter, mine. Something

I'd been meaning to do for a long time. But that was too heavy to hit her with over the phone. I needed a more casual excuse for calling.

Thus, following her "Hello!"

"I feel bad for letting you foot our last dinner bill, I want a chance to atone, this time *my* treat," were the first words out of my mouth."

She confessed that she hadn't dropped by because she felt bad too.

"For what?" I asked.

She hesitated, then responded: "For not letting you pay." Accompanied by a nervous laugh.

Usually her laughter was raucous and unadulterated. So I was right: she'd been avoiding me. And I knew why. At least I thought I did. Well, after this meal I'd make up for it.

* * *

Next evening, once we'd ordered our dinner, I said: "Of course, the reason I invited you was not only to atone for letting you pay last time."

"You knew I'd see through such a flimsy excuse."

"That I did."

"But you were worried you hadn't heard from me."

"That I was."

"I'm sorry. I did feel guilty for not getting in touch but ..."

Before she could bring up what I thought she was about to and turn this meal into mouthfuls of mea culpas from me, I cut her off.

"I don't blame you. But there's something I wanted to share with you. At home. I've been thinking of it for a long time and decided now's the time."

"A surprise. I love surprises."

Yet she seemed anything but ebullient.

Our appetizers arrived, and she immediately shifted her focus to the food.

"Umm ... that looks yummy."

Feigning enthusiasm wasn't like my daughter, wasn't like her at all. And though we both tried to seem blasé, there was an ill-at-ease undercurrent to the rest of this dinner neither of us could seem to abate. I was so anxious I could hardly eat. My daughter didn't seem to be doing much better.

The one person in the world with whom I could make small talk and I was tongue-tied. And she, usually a bubbling fountain of conversation with me, had to force herself to utter the odd word. We could both taste the silence, but were afraid our verbal knives might be too blunt to try cutting through it. The whole dinner felt like a blind date gone bad.

That I was keeping something from her was a given. That she'd try to tease it out of me should have been too. But she didn't.

Could she know what I had in store for her and didn't want to spoil my surprise? Or worse, didn't want any part of it. Maybe the whole idea was a mistake. But I'd wanted to do this for so long and, like it or not, now was the time.

* * *

At home, initially seeing my daughter in one of Maya's outfits, I was shocked. My sister seemed to come alive in her. Not only did she share the same sparkle in her eyes but she had a similar pizazz to her body, a bounce, like she was ready to boogie, had so much life in her she could hardly contain it. It broke my heart.

Somewhere, in the slippery recesses of my psyche, I might have been hoping that handing her my sister's clothes and jewellery would put a stop to my daughter's following in Maya's footsteps. But seeing her standing there, a veritable facsimile of my sister, I knew it would only reinforce her resolve.

In fact, for a few moments, it felt as though in bringing my sister closer to life, I was moving my daughter closer to death. But her smile snapped me out of it. Along with her words.

"Thanks, dad. You don't know how much this means to me."

"You know how much this means to me."

"I do," she replied, "I definitely do."

I'm not much for eye contact, avoid it at all costs. Whether it's discomfort with the degree of intimacy involved, not knowing how long to let it last or who should blink first, the longer I look the more lost I feel, until finally, I'm forced to escape the elusive islands of the other's eyes for the firmer ground of their feet.

A fleeting eye to eye is the best I normally do, even with my daughter. But this time my eyes gripped hers. And hers, mine. This long-hidden exotic wardrobe had allowed my daughter and me to share a tangible taste of my sister's spirit. And neither of us wanted to let it go.

Finally, my daughter broke the spell.

"Now I've got a surprise for you."

"Uh oh."

"It's good news."

"You're not going."

"To Donetsk."

"Why don't I like the sound of that?"

"How does Gaza sound to you?"

"Like you're going round in circles."

"I *was* having trouble making up my mind."

"You sounded so decisive on the phone?"

"I was."

"What happened?"

"Initially, I chose Russia because that's where zeydeh was born. But your hysteria ..."

"At first, maybe, but when you phoned it was final, have I ever sounded more calm and accepting?"

"Defeated is more like it."

"I can't fool you."

"After I put the receiver down, I felt completely deflated, as if the spirit had been sucked out of me."

"I'm sorry. I didn't mean to do that to you."

"I deal with you better when you're full of fight."

"I'll do my best."

"But I realized that in Russia I don't have ties to either side. Whereas in Gaza I do."

"You're a Jew!"

"Can you think of a more morally appropriate reason to go?"

"Than having an identity crisis?"

"It doesn't bother you what's been done to Palestinians?"

"It bothers me. Believe me it bothers me. But my protest days are long gone."

"Well mine are just beginning."

"What're you going to do, slingshot Gaza stones 'gainst the Goliath on the other side? I did that as a student in the sixties."

"Against the Israeli occupation?"

"The Vietnam war."

"And the U.S. got out."

"And then got into Afghanistan, Iraq and god knows where else. Politics is power grubbing, trading one pie in the sky pipe dream for another. A pox on all their bullshit houses."

"You don't distinguish between the victim's rhetoric and that of the victimizer?"

"One day a victim, the next a victimizer, so history goes."

That got her angry enough to shout: "To hell with history, we're the victimizers now!"

"Tribal guilt, you'll get stuck there!" I shouted back.

"Like two million Palestinians!"

"I'm not concerned about two million Palestinians, I'm concerned about you! You want to turn me into a basket case?"

"You've done a pretty good job of doing that to yourself."

"I'm a firm believer in passive resistance."

"Like Gandhi? Or Linus, in *Peanuts*?"

"The latter."

As she began to give me her exasperated there-you-go-being-facetious-again look, I tried to head her off at the pass.

"You accuse me of being a basket case what do you expect?"

"This is not about you."

"Anything to do with you is about me."

Aware how bad that sounded, I quickly tried to make amends.

"With you there's an emotional investment, a caring I can't feel for anyone else. In fact, your problems are more important to me than mine. *You're* more important to me than I am."

"That's the nicest thing you've said to me in a long time. Even if sad. And untrue."

"You calling me a liar?"

"A white one."

Once again, as though she was playing a musical chairs solo, whenever our banter took a breather, she slipped over to another seat, each one a little closer to me. Or so it seemed. It was hard to judge since the chairs were such a standing-room-only hodgepodge.

You see, though no one but my daughter ever visits me, to make the homely little hovel I call home feel homier than it otherwise might, I've filled it with chairs, so many it's hard to move. Others cast them out, I take them in and, like stray cats, give them a home.

Each four-legged piece of furniture I rescue has its own personality. Crammed into this tiny space, my crazy quilt of chairs not only clutter, they clash.

After all, how does a one-piece plastic miracle of moulded mass production, so pristine in its sheer whiteness, go with a threadbare Louis XIV art deco imitation, one with a screw loose in one leg? Or an all-wood Adirondack garden chair go with a four-wheeled Aeron office model? A pink perforated plastic beanbag with a blue all-leather butterfly?

To the fashion maven they may not fit together. But as long as they get along I don't care. Surrounded by an ever-present audience of empty seats in such a wide variety of styles, some suffering from severe wear and tear yet asking nothing of me other than, every once in a while, I sit on them (in the case of Louis Quatorze, carefully) I don't feel quite so old and alone.

Most people have pets because they're easier to get along with than other human beings. More predictable too, providing furry love and affection at one's beck and call without the responsibility of having to reciprocate if one doesn't feel like it.

Well, I prefer chairs to pets. In a sense, they are my pets. You can love a chair, be grateful for its presence, its potential as a resting place, yet only take a load off your legs when, eager to savour the bosom of your warm bottom, it's willing to bear the full weight of your body.

So, as long as I'm still breathing, no furniture section of the Sally Ann is safe. Nor is any neighbour's castaway. I'll be there on garbage day. In between too.

So many chairs to choose from may be an invitation to keep moving. No wonder my daughter couldn't sit still. Perhaps, filled with nervous energy, uncomfortable in one chair, she kept trying to find another more to her liking. With each of her incremental advances toward me feeling like, in our contest of wills, she was gaining ground, I was determined to stand mine, i.e., stay glued to the same seat.

If I moved away from her, she might take it as an insult. While advancing toward her might be construed as countering her move toward to me, a nonverbal 'How do you like them apples?'

Of course, she could also see my migrating toward her as a concession, which I wasn't ready to make.

As though she'd been reading my mind, my daughter startled me out of my own.

"Dad, you've got to get rid of some of these chairs. It's like a crazy person lives here."

"You don't feel comfortable on one there's always another."

"At least this one with the loose leg."

"It's one of my favourites."

"Then fix it."

"I like it the way it is.

Exasperated, she shouted: "It's dangerous!"

"Don't sit on it!" I shouted back.

With one's nearest and dearest it's often easier to argue over nothing than something. Still, she had a point.

Anyway, I knew that all the chairs in the world wouldn't keep me from feeling lonely after she left. She leaves such a vacuum in her wake, the letdown's unbearable. Thus, when she sprang up again, terrified she was going to leave, I was about to apologize, beg her to stay, but all she did was slide over to another seat, stare at me like *she* was about to apologize. But I was wrong.

"You know, maybe somewhere in the deep recesses of the twisted psyche I inherited from you, I thought that if I first told you I was going into a war zone and then changed it to a concentration camp ..."

"Spare me the radical rhetoric."

"What else can you call it?"

"Occupied territory."

"If that makes you feel better."

"And what'll you do if Hamas finds out you're a Jew?"

"You watch too much status quo cable, dad."

"You want to placate your conscience, how bout Indians and Eskimos ..."

"They're referred to as First Nations and Inuit now, dad."

"Mea culpa, I stand politically corrected. Still, we stole their land, why not start here?"

For a second she seemed stumped, didn't know what to say.

"You have no answer."

"I don't need one."

"You think you can get in and out just like that?"

"I'm not going to get in and out. Anyway, there's no war there."

"At the moment."

"And it wasn't a war."

"No, what was it?"

"A one-sided slaughter."

"Well, that's reassuring."

"Something I hope we'll never see again."

I knew I had to oppose her, give her the satisfaction of rebelling not only against the occupation, but the inertia I feared she might have been afraid she inherited from me. Bottom line: I was not simply relieved she was not going to Russia, I was glad she'd chosen Gaza. Had the guts to take a stand. But I just had to ask: "What's your solution, two states?"

"One."

"My parents would turn over in their graves."

She looked at me, smiled, then leaned over and hugged me, whispering: "Your sister would be proud."

* * *

After she left, my mind was all over the map. When does despair become a death wish, and a death wish suicide? Masked though it may be by the inner needs of conscience, the outer demands of ego or the thrill of taking risks, if you put yourself into situations where the dice are so loaded against you you're bound to die, what else can you call it?

If my father's depression led my sister to take her last dangerous leap, would *my* despair lead my daughter to take hers? And should this unthinkable happen, would I have the guts to take mine? The guts not to?

Chapter 3

MY DAUGHTER'S DETERMINATION to follow in my sister's foot-steps convinced me it was time to come to terms with my sister's death, confront my sister's killer. But I wasn't sure how to go about it. Besides, I'm a dreamer. It's a lot safer and cheaper to dream. And I couldn't help indulging in all sorts of vigilante-justice fantasies. They let me exorcize some anger and anxiety without actually endangering my ass. Easy chair aficionados like me don't like to jeopardize their derrieres.

You see, not only do I detest travel, I'm claustrophobic, agoraphobic and, worst of all, phobophobic: afraid of being afraid. Yet in these revenge reconnaissance missions I'm always on the move, seeking justice for my sister, scouring Sarajevo for her killer, actively taking my demon bull by the horns instead of simply sitting back and suffering.

Lying on my living room lawn chair, I was doing just that when I heard a voice whisper these two words: "American Sniper." I'm not a religious man and, though I don't believe in him, when god talks, I pay attention. In this case his words were emanating from my computer. I'm not much for action flicks, nor am I influenced by advertising, specially insidious ads like the one that popped up on my computer screen. But the words "American Sniper" made my head snap. And so I went to see the movie.

From time to time I like to see what blockbusters are breaking box office records, which screenwriters are making the killing I never managed to make.

What a gruesome immoral film. Feeling sick, I left before the end,

292 ~ Raphael Burdman

decided to console myself with a giant burger, next door, at my favourite fast food joint.

The back of that eatery is one wall to wall mirror. Adjoining it, my preferred booth, where I can sit facing the wall and still survey the whole scene. Glancing at that glass wall is like looking at a mural, one that transforms the raw unframed reality of an oh so ordinary restaurant into an artful tableau. Sitting there, it dawned on me that Maya might have used her compact mirror for more than safely peering round corners, perhaps to make war seem less perilous.

As that thought flashed through my mind, the guy in the booth behind mine began bragging about the number of bodies he'd bagged as a sniper in the siege of Sarajevo. Oscillating between some Slavic-sounding language and a patois of English, French and that exotic tongue, his accent was so thick I couldn't make out every French or English word but, between his "pow pow pow pow!" histrionics and lament for the good old days, I got the gist.

We were back to back, so I couldn't see his face but, rage roiling up inside me, I wanted to smash it. Feelings that followed that dreadful phone call from Sarajevo came flooding back. Suspended somewhere between anger and anguish, I started shaking, barely able to contain my desire to spin around, lunge and choke the bastard to death. But, by his thick neck and hint of black hairs sprouting from his huge shaved head I could tell he was both much bigger and younger than I. The skull and cross bones on the back of his scalp made him more menacing. In stark contrast to the man sitting opposite him who, with a full head of blonde hair and boyish face, seemed almost cherubic.

Watching the back of the braggart's head bob this way and that as he babbled on and on about his exploits in the Serbian army, I tried to stop seething, get my breathing under control, talk sense to myself. Why give him the satisfaction of making a scene when I could do to him what he did to others, perhaps to my sister? An eye for an eye, true biblical justice.

But how to go about it? I'd never fired a rifle, never held one. A pistol either. Where do you buy them? At sporting goods stores? Would

I have to register as a gun owner, give my name? Or do I go to a gun show, pay cash, leave no paper trail?

Safer to simply shoplift the weapon, leave no smoking gun. No, stores have 360-degree camera surveillance. I'd be caught before I could kill him. Well, that was a chance I'd have to take.

I'd follow him for a few weeks, get to know his routines, drive out to the middle of nowhere for target practice. Couldn't chance going to a rifle range, leave loose ends connecting this sniper to that one. I'd need a silencer, so he wouldn't hear the shot, have a chance for a reflexive split second duck. The shot must take him by surprise. And give me time to get away. After shooting him, I'd dispose of the weapon, dump it in the St Lawrence, making sure to wipe off all prints. Better still, from the moment I stole it, to target practice and the actual assassination, I'd wear gloves, leave no fingerprints in the first place. No, that might make me stick out. Christ, was I embarking on a life of crime in my old age? Or merely losing my mind?

I was so furious I couldn't think straight. But fortune had given me a golden opportunity to avenge Maya's death, free myself from the grip of fear, guilt and grief. I couldn't let it slip away. No more a passive participant in my pain, by taking vengeance I'd be an active survivor.

My heart was pounding, my head too. I couldn't catch my breath, thought I was going to have a stroke. Then the goon got up to leave, along with his buddy.

Afraid to stare—didn't want my eyes to catch his, or his catch mine and see the rage there—I tried to get a quick faux disinterested glance at the sniper. I needed to remain anonymous, not the slightest hint at what was in store for him. My bullet had to come out of the blue.

No. If he died instantly, without knowing what hit him, had a chance to wonder why, what good would it do? I'd be deprived of his suffering, his missing the imminence of his end. Let him slowly bleed to death, remain alive long enough to know he'd been hit. By a sniper's bullet no less. He hadn't got away with his guilt. It had finally caught up with him, followed him to this country, to a restaurant, right to his home.

But now he was getting away. I had to pay my bill and get out of there, quick. I tried nonchalantly waving to the waitress, but my hand was shaking, out of control. I immediately pulled it down and, still trembling, managed to slip it into my back pant pocket, pull out my wallet and shake a bunch of twenties onto the table.

One would have covered it. But I couldn't take a chance. I'd intended to drop two, but these new bills are so thin they're hard to separate, specially when you're in a hurry: the two guys I was tailing were now out the restaurant door.

I told myself don't act frantic. Stay cool, calm, cavalier . You're an old man. Act your age. You've been around the block a few times. Hurry. But don't hurry. At least don't look like you're hurrying. But you can't let that bastard get away.

My knees had been giving out. I knew that sooner or later I might not be able to walk. Of course, sooner or later I'd be dead. Then I definitely wouldn't be able to walk. But it wouldn't matter. Unless I was a Zombie. But what was the point of being a Zombie if you couldn't walk?

These thoughts flashed through my mind as I stumbled out of the restaurant. I and caught sight of the brute—with his black and red blazer he was a hard man to miss—just a short distance away. Keeping my distance, I followed the two to their car. An old Corvette. The motherfucker drove a muscle car!

I had to run several red lights and stop signs, but my old VW bug managed to keep up with his Corvette. There was no way I could remain completely out of range of his rear view mirror without turning off my headlights. But that was too risky, and might have made me more conspicuous. Anyway, a Corvette's not hard to keep track of, specially one that's chrome yellow, with modified tail lights across the top of its trunk.

Finally, on a modest street, filled with small nondescript bungalows, the Corvette pulled into a driveway and came to a stop beside a house that stood out from the rest, not in size or shape, but in color: painted yellow, top to bottom, including the roof. This thug was nothing if not ostentatious.

About ten car lengths back, I pulled to the curb, turned off my headlights and watched as the sniper jumped out of the driver's side, rushed round to let the young blonde guy out, embraced him then planted a quick kiss on his forehead.

I started to laugh but, as the house door closed behind the two men, the laughter turned to tears. I kept sobbing for I don't know how long. I'd lost track of time. That bastard mouthing off had been like a gun to my head, a knife to my heart.

I switched on the engine and started to slowly drive away. As I passed their house I was tempted to stop, jump out and throw a rock through the living room window. But that might give him a heads up, force him to start looking over his shoulder. And I didn't want him to have a hint what was in store for him. Or did I?

* * *

The summer after my sister was shot, thinking it might be a way for me to deal with her death, I took some LSD. Rather than spiritually uplifting visions, the acid opened up a Pandora's box of anxiety. My mind went blank, my body berserk. Pent up with physical panic, I couldn't lie down without having to immediately spring back up to a sitting position. The only way I could sleep prone was under heavy sedation, in the hospital.

Once I got out, it took me months to come down. And I began having long recurring visions in which it was I who triggered both the First World War *and* the Bosnian civil conflict. How's that for megalomania? Evidently not stopping my sister from going to Sarajevo was insufficient for my conscience. It had to bear the whole burden of history that drew my sister to her death.

Anyway, the morning after following those two Serbs, I woke so upset I took it out on my bathroom wall. Thus the bruised knuckles and dents beside the door.

There was no way to know if that Serbian son of a bitch was the one who shot my sister, but at least the perpetrator of my family's pain now had a real face. No longer was it some anonymous entity, nor was Maya simply a casualty of war. She'd been murdered by one man. If not this one then one just like him. I now had a killer in my sights, a chance for real closure.

He had opened a can of worms that was now eating away at my insides. I hadn't been able to finish my Super Burger in the restaurant, and after that hadn't eaten anything for days, at least nothing I could hold down. I was going to waste away if I didn't do something, and soon.

I'd drive by their house at least once a day, often twice: first in the afternoon, then again at night. I knew their routines. Or lack thereof. Neither of these guys seemed to have a job. Or, if they did, their hours were erratic. More often than not the Corvette was parked in their driveway. Maybe they worked out of their home, were on the phone or internet all day. They only seemed to leave their house in the evening, for dinner, the same time each day, but always at a different eatery.

Maybe they worked for Michelin, rating restaurants. Or feared being followed. By someone other than me. Some former rival from the civil war. Anyway, after tailing them for several weeks, my appetite returned. And I started eating at the same places as they. Why not get in a good meal while keeping an eye on them, kill two birds with one stone?

Now if it were the same restaurant every evening, it would be easy to explain my presence: we shared the same favourite. But spotting me at a different one each night would seem more than a coincidence. He was bound to wonder what was up. Well, let him. I'd pretend to pay him no mind, never look his way, just focus on my food. An eager eater, I hoped to make him uptight. I had every right.

So much for no foreshadowing. I simply couldn't resist.

* * *

At the next restaurant to which I followed them, after finishing their meal, the two of them got up and started strolling my way. I began to panic. The exit was in the other direction! When they reached my table they stopped, just stood there looking down at me, waiting for me to say something. When I didn't, the bastard took a step back and, like a bullfighter executing a pass, made an elegant motion for his sidekick to slide into the booth opposite me, then slipped in beside him.

Now they were both facing me, there was no avoiding their eyes. Above all, the sniper's. If the eyes were a window into this asshole's soul, this was not going to end well: an opaque pair of black marbles, dark, but with a sparkle that reflected the soft restaurant light so harshly it made my stomach squirm. Determined not to let this son of a bitch intimidate me, I slugged it out eye to eye.

Still, his bad breath began to get to me. With the wrong wind, I can recoil at the scent of an onion a half mile away. Half a table width, it was making me nauseous. Best to break the ice before his breath broke me.

"You two look familiar. Have you been following me?"

Wouldn't you know it, the jerk took my touch of tongue in cheek literally.

"Funny, Slobadan and me we was just asking the same question us."

"Actually, Radovan he was the one asking the question him."

"Your car it is old one. Yet it keep up with our new one pretty good no yes?"

"Why you are following us you?"

"Old man like you he not looking for the sex no yes?"

"Radovan and me we are not interest."

"We are happy couple."

"I've been wondering what to do about you."

"What you mean what to do about us you?" he asked.

"Not us. You."

"I do not know you."

From an early age I sensed that there was no room for two wilful children in my family. Watching my sister storm through life, intimidating my mother with her histrionics, I was determined to take a more tranquil path, less a participant in our household turmoil than an observer. Let my sister do the shouting. She could always manage to stir up a storm. Even in death, she was a shit-disturber. I could clearly hear her voice, shouting: "Stop using me as an excuse to wallow in self-pity! I may be dead, but you're not! Stop living like you are, in limbo, longing for what you've lost! It's time to make some noise!"

Her voice seemed so loud I was sure the two goons could hear. I had to do something before they did. These men didn't matter. They were just excuses for me to act, to once and for all exorcize my anger and anguish, see where it went once I allowed myself to vent. The time had come to resurrect both my father and sister's histrionic spirits, keep them alive.

But before I tell you what happened next, let me backtrack a moment, with an excerpt from something I wrote for the L.A. storefront synagogue I joined while a screenwriter down there. Feeling lonely, unmoored and struggling to stay emotionally afloat on that enormous freeway of a city, I thought it a good way to find female companionship along with a taste of the sanctity and sense of community I once felt in prayer with 'my people'.

Needless to say, it didn't work out. Too many singles on the prowl for one synagogue. The women hampered tribal bonding with the men and the men traditional bedding with the women.

> To find the solace I once found in the synagogue as a child, I've again started dropping in on my tribal muse. Doesn't mean I've suddenly started believing, certainly not in that all-powerful Old Testament persona non grata. But I do believe in the healing power of plaintive wailing. And if the pretence of a prime mover is what it takes to elicit such profound and powerful impulses, who am I to rain on that parade? I'm just happy to march in step with the band.
>
> Because laughter and tears, like life and death, are two sides of the same tragic-comic coin. According to Arthur Koestler, they spring from the same source. The basic three beat breath of laughter being: huh, huh, uh; out out in; exhale exhale inhale. The basic beat of crying, the opposite: uh, uh, huh; in in out; inhale inhale exhale. Oom pah pah. An awkward inner waltz.
>
> The truth and power of Hebrew prayer, like our body's spontaneous decision to laugh or cry in reaction to the dilemmas and contradictions of Creation, lies not in literal translation of the liturgical words but in their emotional utterance, the chant, from the primal depths, as expressive as laughter, but more often close to tears. Tears turned to music.

Opera moved my father so. Whenever he'd hear Puccini's *O Mio Babbino Caro* or *O Soave Fanciulla* he'd break into tears. Both he and my sister knew how to belt out their feelings. And now, it was my turn to take the stage. Blood boiling, stomach roiling, hands shaking, at the top of my voice, so loud, high and clear all could hear, like the great cantors of old I chanted: "You killed my sister!"

Suspecting that sooner or later I'd be confronting Maya's killers, that we were destined to meet, those words, like Zola's 'J'accuse!' in the Dreyfus affair, must have been locked somewhere in my psyche, ready to explode. As soon as the sentence left my mouth I felt such relief.

The gorilla's face changed colors so quickly—from slightly pink, to orangey yellow to dark red, like a stoplight that had gone haywire, couldn't decide what signal it wanted to send. I'd caught him off guard. He knew he'd committed murder, probably too many to count. He just didn't know who, where or when it would catch up with him, if ever. Perhaps he feared the International Criminal Court in The Hague but never a little old man like me would come after him.

So, faced with the most unlikely of Grand Inquisitors for his conscience, the most implausible of avengers for his evildoing, his double take was understandable. As were the few seconds the two of them were tongue-tied, glancing at each other, at me, then back at each other before the bruiser uttered "What?" as though, stuck in his throat, he had to cough the word up.

"You murdered my sister. If it wasn't you it was one of you it might as well have been you."

The couple at the next table abruptly stopped arguing with each other to listen to us. To counterpoint my voice rising to a fever pitch the lug lowered his to a half whisper.

"You are crazy old man no yes?"

"If I am I have good reason."

"We kill your sister?"

"Not we, you."

"You *are* crazy old man."

"You were a sniper in Sarajevo."

"I was soldier."

"And you shot my sister. In the head!"

Aware my voice had again risen to a highly agitated state, I abruptly shut up. But it was too late. The waitress who'd been glancing our way, strolled over.

"Is everything all right here?"

"We old friends. Go banana too loud how much we love this restaurant we come again next time not at different table us."

She smirked, and walked away. Once again the thug lowered his voice to a half whisper.

"I do not know you crazy old man. I do not know your sister. I fight in war, the war it is finish."

"Not for me."

The dope dropped his hand onto mine. I started to slip it out from under his, not abruptly, as if flinching, and giving him the satisfaction of a clear statement of discomfort on my part, but slowly, almost nonchalantly. But before my paw could escape his, he'd somehow managed to tighten his grip, at the same time twisting my metacarpus so that we were now palm to palm, as though shaking hands. Don't know how he did it.

I was once at a dinner for a producer who'd optioned one of my screenplays. The host was the editor of an L.A. newspaper, a man who did coin tricks. I was sitting next to him at the table, was aware he was trying to divert our attention with all the chatter and hocus pocus with his hands, and I'd still managed to keep my eyes glued to the coins on the table. Yet presto, he'd made certain coins appear and others disappear and I couldn't for the life of me figure out how he'd done it.

"I do not want fight with you me."

"Then apologize."

"Apologize?"

"Say you're sorry."

"What your sister she do in my country her? You are not from my country you."

"She was helping care for civilians. Civilians you were shooting at. Civilians you shot."

"You never fight for your country?"

"No."

"Then you do not know what a soldier he know, what he have to do."

From a semblance of shaking hands, the nutcase and I had now graduated to some sort of wrist-wrestling. When I was young I used to be able to beat my peers. For a Jewish boy, I was strong. But now I was an old man. And my arms were weak. Yet I somehow managed to hold my own. Most likely the big lug was not trying too hard, his way of being friendly, affectionate even.

From time to time I would try to pull away but, just as my hand was about to slip out, he'd tighten his, squeezing my fingers so hard they hurt, then, to get a fuller grasp of my hand, he'd briefly loosen his, and before I could pull away he'd again get me in his grip.

Not only was he much younger than I, he was obviously much stronger and clearly conveying that to me. Every so often, to emphasize a point, he'd tap the hand of mine he was holding with his other hand then, as though trying to assure me I was in the hands of someone who meant me no harm, who had never meant me any harm, who had never meant anyone any harm, he'd let his other palm lie gently on mine, with a consoling tender touch. It seemed so out of character, I assumed it was his way of smooth-talking me.

"No one he like to kill. A soldier he do what he have to. I happy I no have to kill no more. War it is ugly. But now it is over. The war it is over. We do not wish to be your enemy us. I do not wish to be your enemy me. No one he want to fight war. But we have to we do. I no like it more than you me."

"Then why were you bragging about it to your buddy here?"

"I no brag. Maybe I tell him story. You listen. It is not your business to listen. Why you listen? And then you follow. Why you follow?"

"This is a free country. What the hell you doing here anyway, hiding?"

"At home I am hero."

"Then why the fuck aren't you there?"

"You curse to Slobodan you make Slobodan angry. We go now us. You go now too. And you keep to follow us we call police."

"Call them. I'll tell them you're a couple of war criminals. If they can't haul your ass before a judge, put you in jail for war crimes they should at least send you back to your country."

"This our country now."

"You people purposely targeted my sister!"

"Who tell you this? Why they tell you this? Why we would to do this?"

"To scare her away. To scare others like her away. Because she was there to help civilians, civilians you *shot*!"

From there things again escalated and, emboldened as my anger rose into road rage, the sort I hadn't experienced since I'd left L.A., I lunged at the asshole and ended up in a wrestling match. However, you couldn't really call it a match. I certainly was no match for this man.

As a boy and young man, the headlock used to be my lethal weapon of choice. But before I'd managed to get the slightest grasp of this goon's head, like some enraged bull, he'd shaken me off, clasped *my* head and squeezed it so hard it hurt.

Satisfied he'd inflicted me with a sufficiently severe headache, he then spun me round into a half nelson. And that's when tragedy began to turn to farce.

To try to get him to let go, at least to inflict some damage upon him, I started frantically flailing at him. But it was futile. His physique resembled that of a silver-back mountain gorilla, both in the ratio of the length of his arms to the rest of his body and in their strength. Those arms, a lot longer than mine, were holding me up off the ground at a distance from him as if I was an infant who might pee on him.

As a boy, I used to wet myself, mainly when immersed in my parents' past. Tiny trickles, not quite enough to become an embarrassment. Perhaps a vestige of an animal instinct, unconsciously marking my parents' past as mine. Reclaiming it for them too.

But now, so many decades later, thanks to an enlarged cancerous prostate and the stents implanted to drain my bladder and keep my kidneys from failing, I'm doomed to a more mundane but embarrassingly abundant urinal incontinence.

Still, no matter how fashionable the ads for Depends, I refuse to wear diapers. When I have to go I have to go, pronto, without delay. And once I start there's no stopping, can't put it on hold, couldn't, even if my life depended on it. And at that moment, though it might have, and I had to, I simply wasn't going to give this guy the satisfaction of thinking he'd made me wet myself or worse, watch me soil his shiny black boots and further inflame him.

Yet I felt anything but scared. Enraged, yes. Fearful, no. Pumped with fight or flight juice coursing through my veins, I felt better than I had in months, maybe years.

Simply put, I was sick and tired of those lousy little parasites of anxiety having a great old time dancing around inside me while I, their host, was paralyzed, afraid to move, lest I upset my guests. Well, no longer would I let them put me on pins and needles.

Our short unchoreographed twist and shout tango climaxed with us each back in our respective seats, again holding hands. Rather, his was gripping mine. That short war had culminated in another prolonged hand-held truce, disrupted by the restaurant manager's high-pitched "Gentlemen, you'll have to leave. Now. Unless you'd rather I call the ..."

"You no need cops you. We no need cops us. No one they need cops here, yes, no?" These last two words, aimed directly into my ear, loud and clear. "We just friends we like to play rough, us, yes, no?" Once again these last words spit straight into my auditory canal, this time more like a warm whisper, a wet one too.

The goon was salivating! On me! Not only could I hear his heavy breathing, I could feel it! He must have been pumped too! Perhaps I'd scared *him*, though he'd didn't seem like someone who could be scared by a little old fart like me. But I'd certainly unnerved or upset him. And that gave me some satisfaction. Still does.

By now the entire restaurant had become our audience. And the three of us didn't seem to care. In some ways we'd been playing to them as much as to each other, as if they were a jury of our peers, with whom we were trying to curry favour, clear our consciences.

To show the show was over, the clown bowed to the nearby tables of diners. His sidekick slipped out of the booth and followed suit. Then, half facing me and half the rest of our audience, as though trying to bring closure to this case, the son of a bitch dramatically shoved out his hand for me to shake.

"Friends?"

I didn't take it, left his hand dangling there in mid air.

"We make peace with our enemy why we cannot peace with you my friend?"

"I'm not your friend."

"You are not my enemy. Look, I do not wish to be angry with you old man. I sorry for your sister. I true sorry for your sister. I sorry for what happen to her I do not know her I do what I have to. If I shoot her I am more sorry."

"I sorry too," the other said.

"We are both sorry us."

At that I started sobbing.

"Here my card, you want talk, call to me, we talk more okay?"

I nodded agreeably, assuming I'd never call. After all, what did we have in common? In one way, nothing, in another, a lot. But I'd gone as far as I could. As far as I should, having been given a chance I never would have expected. I looked up at him, tears still in my eyes.

"If I speak so loud you think I boast I sorry for to make you to suffer. I sorry for what I say. Maybe for what I do too. I think more what you say, what I say too me."

I stood, he reached out and, reluctantly, I reciprocated. We shook hands, all three of us. A number of diners clapped.

Chapter 4

I USED TO marvel at how Maya managed to get her way by making a scene, usually in the form of a temper tantrum. My father, show-master of sympathy that he was, relied on heartbreaking sobs rather than scare tactics. While my mother, mistress of muted martyrdom, milked silent suffering. As loud and clear as my father's noisy histrionics, and as effective in evoking pity, but a type tinged with a bitter taste.

I seemed to fall somewhere between parental cracks.

Well, in old age I was finding my niche, escaping the closet of quiescence.

Up to then, except with my daughter, I'd been a sub-rosa scene-maker, kept my theatrics to myself, behind closed doors. With the Serb, I'd come to appreciate the joy of making a public spectacle of myself. The goon had brought out the exhibitionist in me. I now had carte blanche to kick up a fuss. Following in my father's footsteps never felt so good.

* * *

Heading home from the restaurant I was buoyant, a little lightheaded. Like I was drunk, yet in full control of my faculties. In some small yet significant way, taking part in my own little war crimes tribunal seemed to help the vise gripping my chest come loose. I was driving in a different gear, as though on cruise control, which my car didn't have.

Yet I'd been mourning for so long I found it hard believe this ebullience would last. (Spoiler alert, it didn't.)

In the first years after Maya's death I'd never once dreamed of her, at least not while I was asleep. Then I began having frequent night-mares of her, ones in which she hadn't died, just chose to disappear, without informing my parents or me, and felt no remorse for all she'd put us through. She just had to free herself from her family is all she'd say, refusing to elaborate. Each time I'd try to probe further she'd lapse into a stony silence: her eyes colourless, her skin cold to the touch, she seemed like some corpse, one that, though it may have been buried for decades, hadn't aged, had simply hardened.

Unlike the witty affectionate person I'd known, in these night-mares she was so distant and uncaring, I found it hard to accept it was her. This was not the sister I'd missed so much, the one I'd mourned so profoundly. She'd insist she was. "Get used to it," her response to my refusals to reconcile her with my real sister.

How could the fond warm memories I have of her become the cold aloof phantom of my nightmares? Perhaps she was trying to question why, in spite of her self-destructiveness, I continued to mourn her. Perhaps I'd been trying to ask myself the same question. All these years, had I been angry at her for abandoning me but unable to admit it, afraid to, lest my animosity interfere with, confuse—even dissi-pate—my sorrow? Worse, had I been afraid of feeling guilty for think-ing ill of her, for being resentful toward her? Or was I reading too much into these nightmares? Well, I certainly wasn't ready to suffer anger with my grief, outrage with my love.

Maybe that detached dark shadow of my sister had been trying to tell me it was time to get on with my life, move on from mourning, put her to rest. If so, I wish she hadn't been so brutal.

I kept asking myself how a woman who so loved life, who attacked it with such gusto, with such style, could simply let herself die. Our psyches may be nothing but pits the bottoms of which can never be truly plumbed yet, like some deranged grave digger, my sister was de-termined to unearth the remains of our ancestral terror. And in the end, she may have succeeded.

As these thoughts roiled through my mind, I heard a voice, com-ing from the back seat. I glanced up at my rear view mirror.

Little more than laser-like outlines of a disembodied shadowy figure, I couldn't see the source of the voice, not in any detail. I wonder, does mutilation follow a loved one into the next world? If so, can dread of the sight of a spirit whose skull has been shattered by bullets loom so large in the mind of the left-behind beholder that only the voice is allowed an afterlife? For I could clearly hear hers, as vital as when she was alive.

"Stop looking in that mirror! You can't see me!"

"Maya?!"

I started to crane my neck.

"And don't turn around or I'll disappear."

As bossy as ever. But with me, she knew she had to be.

"It's been so long ..."

"In heaven it's always forever. Nothing to do but bask in our disembodied being, every soul wholesome and happy. I keep asking myself: Is this what I risked my life for in Sarajevo?"

In her previous incarnation, she'd speak so rapidly, as though she was afraid she'd forget what she had to say if she didn't get it all out right away. It was like having a visitor who won't take off her coat because she had to be elsewhere soon. But once you got used to it, it was quite charming. There was a bubbliness to her being that had more hallmarks of childlike enthusiasm than adult impatience.

Prone to carry on monologues then, this appearance was no different. But I didn't dare interrupt, just kept driving, afraid to do anything that might make her disappear. No different than when she was alive.

"You may not believe it, baby brother, but the pain of being human down here is nothing compared to our plight up there. Of course, there's no up or down in the afterlife. Everything is everywhere, and nowhere, always the same, ever changing. Never having died, at least not that you're aware of, I'm sure you don't know what I mean. You can't. Nor can I explain it. You have to experience it. But there's no rush."

She may have been in her usual before-afterlife hurry, but I wasn't rushing, driving ever so slowly, hoping the slower I drove the longer it would take to get home the longer she'd be there with me. Yet, transported, for a few moments I forgot where I was, what I was doing, i.e., driving, when I spotted a car coming straight at me. I was on the wrong side of the road!

My late sister shouted: "Look out!"

I swerved just in time to miss the oncoming car. But I could hear its angry honking as I sped to get away from the scene.

"You trying to die?"

"I wasn't paying attention to the road."

"So you can be with your big sister forever."

My awkwardness quickly turned to anger.

"The clairvoyant corpse."

"You do have a death wish."

"Every morning I wake with grave disappointment to find I'm still among the living. No sooner do I stop feeling anxious—start feeling something akin to cheerful, carefree, light-hearted, even happy—than I'm abruptly consumed by fear. The more sunny my spirits the greater the dread that dark clouds will descend."

"It's the romantic in you."

"Dwelling on yesterday, dreading tomorrow, I feel like some sort of ghost, my body a nuisance, some pet I feed and clean up after, all for the sake of keeping memories of you alive."

"You've got to stop."

"I know."

"It's annoying. Cloying too. With all the blissful boredom up there, the only thing that keeps me from going out of my disembodied mind is the hope that before you die you'll stop being a testament to cloistered living. Get out of your comfort zone, go somewhere, do something, stir things up, learn to love life and all its misery. And stop fearing death! It's a blast! It's what comes after that's a bore."

Then she evaporated, a whoosh in both my ears.

The rest of the way home the silence was deafening. Literally. Not only had Maya's voice disappeared, I couldn't hear anything, neither the sound of my engine or other traffic. I rolled down my window, shoved out my hand, could feel the wind, but couldn't hear it. It scared me. Had Maya's vocal apparition damaged my eardrums?

During those moments of deafness, it dawned on me that, in grieving so for my sister, I'd let myself become a surrogate for my father, keeping his grief alive long after he'd gone to his grave. Now I was determined not to take it with me to mine. Gradually, my ears began to clear and, as I stepped out of the car in my driveway, the silence disappeared. I could hear! Hallelujah!

And what I heard were the faint faraway voices of my parents. And equally dim distant memories.

As I stepped through my front door and turned on the light, I was stunned to see my parents, in flashy multi-coloured mismatched nineteen-twenties borscht belt burlesque outfits, shoes and knee socks of comically different lengths, baggy knee pants and garishly-coloured suit jackets several sizes too large, performing a routine that reminded me of those my sister used to do, trying to amuse the toughest of audiences: my mother.

Like a lot of little girls, Maya had a penchant for performing. Had my parents pushed her, she probably could've been a child prodigy, one who might have stolen scenes from Shirley Temple.

But once she hit a premature puberty, her performances stopped. She became less playful, more serious. Preoccupied with appealing to the opposite sex, she lost her innocence to lust and good looks.

My phantom father stared at me, then, step by exaggeratedly slow careful step, trying not to not trip over his outsized shoes, he inched closer and closer, looking me up and down as he did. In the end, he was so close, we almost touched. I was afraid to move lest, in touching him, I'd overstep the limits of my trance, and my parents would suddenly vanish.

He kept scrutinizing me head to toe, trying to make sense of me, as though I was the apparition not he. Finally, he took a step back, nodded toward me with the side of his head as he turned to address my mother.

"The boy thinks he's had it hard."

"Did he ever have to get his hands dirty waited on hand and foot our Little Lord Fauntleroy?" my mother asked in a high singsong soprano I'd never heard from her before.

"Fauntle boy."

"Roy, boy, what's the difference?"

As Jolson's voice in the *Jazz Singer* must have amazed audiences experiencing their first talkie, so was I bowled over not only seeing, but hearing my parents. But when I tried to join in the verbal jest fest, before I could get a word in my parents immediately raised the velocity and volume of their repartee.

"He thinks he hears us."

"The boy hears what he wants to hear."

"He always did."

"Deaf in one ear."

"Dumb in the other."

"Always thinks he's missing something."

"A few marbles maybe."

"He loved marbles."

"A collection he wouldn't share."

"Even with his sister."

"How come he's not still mourning for *us*?"

"He doesn't miss us."

"Good thing we don't miss him."

"One of the benefits of being dead."

"Who knew it would be such fun?"

And then they disappeared, poof, just like that.

Unlike their wicked nether world words, alive, my parents never said what they thought of me. Of course, my mother had her collection of clichéd exasperation: "It pays to have children. Next time you want something you'll whistle." And my father, mostly a no-comment man when it came to me, a time or two popped up with "We spoiled you," or "You're spoiled." But nothing more elaborate than that.

Did they ever wonder what I thought of them? Did they think they should care? I doubt it. It was not in their lexicon.

While there was more than an undercurrent of cruelty in their kibitzing, a callousness I'd never before felt from them, I'd never seen the two of them so in tune with each other, having such a good time together.

To cope with woe during their lives, zaniness was not a tool my parents possessed. So I was delighted to discover they'd developed it after they died.

* * *

In college, I used to keep a copy of Kierkegaard's *Fear and Trembling* in my back pocket. An intellectual stance that went with my Birkenstocks, it also helped serve as a way to seduce women.

The irony is that the angst I, in my early post-adolescence, pretended to embrace, I could not seem to free myself from later on in life. What was once a philosophical posture, a pretence assumed by any incipient intellectual worth his salt, became all-pervasive in me. And I resented it, blamed it on my parents.

My last shrink, a Freudian fatalist, began our initial session by laying out his fundamental philosophy, his sales pitch to each new patient, a mantra he'd obviously memorized.

"Deep down, all children resent their parents for bringing them into a world in which they must suffer and die. But take heart. Heaven awaits us all. Hell is only for the living. After death, all suffering stops, no more ups or downs, just an even-keeled oblivion. What's more heartening, sooner or later our universe will die too. First, all animate entities will disappear, then all inanimate, then all else, including time. In eternity's eye, all will have been but a blink, in God's, perhaps just a wink. So, embrace your mortality. That of your late loved ones too. Let it comfort you to know that, though you can no longer enjoy their earthly companionship, they bask in that ultimate state of bliss: extinction."

Words of wisdom from the esteemed school of crackpot psychiatry. The closest he'd come to making some semblance of common sense was his insistence that the only place we really live, the only reality we truly have, is the present. This moment is all that matters.

Yet for me, to be human is to be in a constant state of mourning, for the continuous passing of the present, of everyone and everything. Moreover, remembering can be as present and powerful as any other experience. Aging like fine wines in the cellar of our unconscious, all the more precious for having passed, memories may assume a transcendent place in our psyche's pantheon.

And with the passage of time even the most unhappy reflections may become soft spots engraved in our hearts. If we can fully face them, feel them in all their anguish, the most painful recollections become precious, even profoundly pleasurable.

For mourning loved ones, reliving priceless moments with them, is not only remembering, it is resurrecting. Only the love of the living can keep the dead alive, grant them a true afterlife. Should we let go of that love, that life, and not only deprive ourselves of a taste of eternity, but them too?

In the afterlife memory of my parents has granted me, resentments of my youth have been have been replaced by love. If I could admire Kierkegaard for his sensitivity to the human condition, why could I not appreciate my parents for their sensitivity to theirs? So they couldn't eloquently articulate it. They lived it. In a rather messed-up manner. One all the more moving for being so frailly human.

Perhaps giving in to a grown man's hysterics, like giving into a child's tantrums, merely encourages him. But what can one do, blame the victim?

As a boy that's precisely what I did, feeling bitter whenever my father broke down. I should have been more sympathetic. But my hostility outstripped my compassion. Perhaps I was angry that he'd saddled me not only with his tormented presence, but his traumatic past too.

I loved him dearly. But I resented his bleak moods, couldn't accept his sadness, looked down on him for it. When I grew up I'd find a way to be happy. Life would be great once I was old enough to get out of the house, be on my own. I was so much wiser than my dad.

Oh the arrogance of youth, the ignorance too.

Before my sister's death I couldn't understand my father's lifelong grief. After, I not only understood it, I experienced it. And I can see that his deep fear and sadness sprang from the same well as his unfettered love and affection. Without one my sister and I might not have experienced the other.

So maybe a melancholic like me should count myself lucky I have the courage to stay nailed to the cross the tickled pink are afraid to face.

Anyway, we're all hostage to our families. And, as in Stockholm syndrome, sooner or later we come to appreciate our captors.

Postscript

WELL, ONE FOOT in my grave, one foot in my sister's, I've been hiking the hills overlooking Sarajevo—the summits from which snipers snuffed out the lives of so many in the city below.

While muted, the colours more Mediterranean and the architecture more Moorish than I'd imagined them to be, Sarajevo reminds me of Montreal. Of course, my hometown has never been bombed, had any of its buildings riddled with bullets, but for me there's a bleakness to both cities. The source of so much family sorrow, perhaps the similarities are only in my mind.

Yes, not only am I in Sarajevo, I'm volunteering with the same NGO as my sister! I may not be dodging bullets but, strange as it may seem, I'm having a ball, feeling better than I have in years, teaching English and screenwriting to young Mid-East refugees. Who better to tutor aspiring screenwriters than a failed script tease? He knows the pitfalls.

Initially none of my students could carry on the simplest conversation in English. However, a couple of kids could spout phrases from Hollywood blockbusters they'd watched over and over. The two of them hope to make it to Hollywood, to make it *in* Hollywood. How can I break their innocent little hearts? Hearts already broken by the murderous havoc in their home countries.

Telling them about my sister's life and death has helped forge a bond between us. One teenage boy came up to me after class, confessed he'd been having nightmares about killing the soldiers who'd slaughtered his brothers during the Syrian civil war. He asked if I'd come to Serbia to wreak vengeance upon my sister's killer.

Taken aback, I told him that, though it crossed my mind from time to time, I was here to bring closure to my sister's loss, honour her in some way.

And it was true. I knew I could never track down the actual sniper, certainly not one who'd confess to Maya's murder. People here have tried to put the war behind them. And most Serbs still have loyalty to their soldiers. Besides, I'd had my fill of vengeance fantasies. Or so I thought.

* * *

One evening, the sole witness to my sister's murder phoned me, said she'd heard I was in Sarajevo and had something she'd like to show me. We agreed to meet at the Moritz Schiller café.

She turned out to be a lovely soft-spoken middle-aged American. A nurse during the siege, she married a Bosnian, settled here in Sarajevo and became a Serbian citizen.

Amidst the initial niceties, she appeared as excited and anxious as I.

"How did you know I was here?" I asked.

"Your sister's NGO."

"I should have guessed."

"I felt so angry. Not only at what he'd done to your sister, and trying to kill me, but the whole sordid siege. I needed some closure. And he seemed to be the key. I spent years searching for him, ready to forgive and forget. Indeed, eager to do so. But he refused to admit remembering anything about the incident. Insisted he shot soldiers, not civilians. Not an iota of regret. Or a sliver of guilt. All the scumbag did was exacerbate my anger."

She reached into her hand bag, pulled something out, handed it to me. It resembled one of those grainy black and white 'wanted' posters you see on post office bulletin boards.

The guy was old, and ugly, with long scraggly white hair and beard. He couldn't have been very young when he killed my sister. Certainly no naive gung ho gun crazy kid. No. He must have been a middle-aged monster.

"Took it myself. Had it cropped into a facial close-up."

"He let you?" I asked, astonished.

She smiled, shaking her head from side to side.

"Enraged, he tried to grab my camera. But I was too quick. I turned and ran. He chased after me, down the stairs, onto the street. Lucky for me he had a slight limp, which slowed him down. And I work out four times a week. But as I was unlocking my car door he caught up with me, tried to grab my camera. I screamed. A passing pedestrian, a woman closer to his age than mine, came running to my rescue. She must have been a neighbour, one he knew knew all about him, because the bastard immediately backed off, turned, bowed to her then limped away. I thanked her, slipped into my car, switched on the engine and drove off. You might find it useful. Anyway, I have the negative. However, I'm thinking of discarding that too. Putting the war behind me. Perhaps this will help you do the same."

As she wrote down the man's name, address and drew a little map for me on the back of the picture, I tried contemplating what I would do should I fail to get him to confess and apologize. I'd fantasized for so long, gone through so many of the motions. Well, I was now too old to care what happened to me.

As though reading my mind, she looked at me and, flaunting the picture while at the same time emphatically withholding it from me ...

"I'm letting you know who he is, where to find him, but you've got to promise not to do anything crazy."

"At my age?"

"If anything were to happen to him, I don't want it to come back and bite me."

"Don't worry, it won't."

"I have your word?"

I hesitated, then nodded, somewhat half-heartedly. She nodded back, much more vigorously than I, handed me the picture.

* * *

After driving me back to my apartment building, the woman and I just sat in her car, engine idling: I, reluctant to leave the last person to see my sister alive; she, seemingly hesitant to part with me too. As though so much had been left unsaid, yet neither of us ready to say more, the awkwardness of her silence matched mine.

As I slowly stumbled up my building stairs, stopping after each step to steel myself for the next, rage again began roiling up inside me. This made it more difficult than usual to catch my breath.

Since my legs lack the strength and my knees the flexibility to navigate the hills surrounding Sarajevo or the stairs where I live, I've begun using a cane. I've learned, to be effective, it must always be one step ahead of me. And so it was, not only on those stairs, but in my head, beating the sniper to death.

I'd thought I'd left that anger behind me, found closure in my own little war crimes tragicomedy. Yet, my mind wouldn't stop racing. My cane wouldn't do. I didn't have the strength. And forget about guns. I'd be so shaky I'd probably miss. Even at close range. Besides, if, after that American Sniper incident, I hadn't had what it takes to actually go out and get a gun instead of merely fantasizing about it, I certainly wasn't going to do it here. I'd never get out of Sarajevo alive. I didn't care about dying, but not before seeing my daughter again.

Anyway, I could rent a car, run him over. At night. No witnesses. But that would mean getting blood on the bumper, if not skin or hair DNA. To say nothing of denting the car body with his.

Once in my apartment, exhausted, I plopped onto the sofa, pulled out the grainy sniper photo, kept staring at it. If a woman who spoke the man's language—according to her he spoke no English—couldn't get a confession, come to some sort of reconciliation, how could I expect to? And I knew I couldn't do anything to him. The woman had been so accommodating, I couldn't betray her.

Still, as visions of me punching the fucker in the face churned through my head, my hand morphed into a fist, scrunching the photo into a ball. I fired it against the wall, watched it bounce off the yellowed plaster and come to rest a few feet in front of me.

Too wired to sit, I sprang off the sofa and, like a crazed Peg Leg Bates, the tap dancer famous back in the early fifties, kept alternating between stabbing the ball with my cane and foot, desperately trying stomp its image into oblivion. Like some cockroach, the crunched photo seemed to take on a life of its own, rolling this way and that each time I tried to put it out of its misery.

Finally, my left knee buckled. In agony, gasping for breath, I stopped, and another stream of thoughts started surging through my head.

How could I have not tried to get in touch with the sole witness to Maya's murder as soon as I got here? Instead, I let the woman take the initiative.

Well, if I'd told myself I was coming to confront Maya's murderer or have the woman who witnessed it re-enact all the gory details I might never have come. Perhaps I was hoping that just getting to Sarajevo, volunteering with the same NGO as Maya, would be enough to bring closure.

Still, the whole time we were together that morning I never mustered the courage to ask what it was like to be there, how the woman managed to avoid being shot and my sister didn't. Truth be told, preoccupied with the sniper's picture and the raw feelings of rage it elicited in me, I was afraid to hear anymore details of Maya's death. I could only handle so much anger at one time.

But now it felt like an evasion. On both our parts. And made me wonder why this woman had bothered to get in touch with me in the first place if it were futile for me to confront my sister's killer? Why burden me with his whereabouts? Was it to share the burden, perhaps unburden herself?

And why, the instant I shut the car door, had she sped off? It was as though she hadn't wanted to give me a chance to ask what more she had on her mind, or reveal what else I might have on mine.

Well, now that Maya's killer had a face, I needed a clear picture of her killing, or I'd never find closure. I had to know, did she, in fact, commit suicide or, seeing no choice, simply let herself die?

* * *

The next few days I kept trying to call the woman. But each time I picked up the phone something stopped me, something more than my usual procrastination. I didn't want to impose on her, thought I should give her a bit of a breather. Or maybe I wanted to give myself one, let our initial encounter sink in. Finally, I couldn't stand it.

I phoned the woman and she agreed to drive me to where Maya had been shot. As her car curbed to pick me up, a crack began to appear in the monotonous mass of grey cloud, and a sliver of brilliant sun spotlit her through the windshield.

Stepping into her Skoda I couldn't help quipping: "You part Sarajevo clouds like Moses the Red Sea."

She was all smiles. As was I. A stranger in a strange land, one charged with so much significance for me, the long hours between classes left me at loose ends. Back home I wasn't much better off. With my daughter a world away in Gaza, lacking her visits to look forward to, the isolation became intolerable, enough to force me off my agoraphobic ass, trigger this trip to Sarajevo. Now, seeing this charming woman again, hearing her voice, I felt buoyed.

"So ... how've you been? Keeping busy?" she asked as we drove off.

"There's only so much sightseeing a man can stand. Especially without seeing the one that matters most."

"I've been meaning to ask you, why didn't you get in touch with me before?"

For an instant I was taken aback, tongue-tied too.

"Th-the ... authorities I talked to were never quite clear how many witnesses ..."

"Just one," she abruptly interjected.

Not wanting to sound antagonistic, add to the touch of unexpected tension now in the car, I took my time, made sure my tone would be gentle.

"Why didn't you try to get in touch with us?"

"It never dawned on me your family might have wanted me to. During the 'incident' (her inflection a faint attempt to resort to the nurse's clinical detachment) I was focused, oblivious to fear. Then I fell apart. A delayed reaction I'd seen before in others. And the authorities, well, they'd seen it before too, so often, they were blasé. I was anything but. As they were going through their token questions, pretending to take notes, I started mumbling and shaking so, they just let me go. And I never heard from them again."

At last, we arrived near the scene. As I stepped out of the car, I started shivering, as though I had not dressed warmly enough to cope with the chill in the air. But with the sun out, I was over-dressed. And it didn't take long before I started to sweat, as much from fear as from trying to keep up with the woman as she marched toward the spot, her mouth keeping pace with her feet.

"It's not far. Just ahead. But I'd rather not park there. Guess I'm superstitious, afraid someone will take down my license number, try to blow my car up. I know it's not rational ..."

I'm sure she could hear my huffing and puffing, and she wasn't uncaring or cruel, but she seemed so eager to get where we were going or to get this over with, I didn't have the heart to ask her to slow down.

Suddenly, she stopped.

"This is the spot."

Still huffing and puffing, both sweating and feeling chilled now, I kept opening and closing my coat, fiddling with the buttons like they were worry beads as she began to describe the scene.

She'd been on an adjoining street, one not in clear line of sight of snipers up in the hills. But the instant she heard shots she took cover. Once certain the shelling was not on her street but the one intersecting it, she slipped toward the corner, listened as one shot after another ricocheted off metal and concrete.

Often, bored with no one to shoot at, snipers would pick non-human targets on which to practice. Or randomly spray bullets at any and everything to terrorize the neighbourhood.

Pulling her compact out of her fanny pack, she used its mirror to peer round the corner, straining to discern the sniper's target. It was my sister, crouched behind an old Skoda.

"Most of us were familiar with our counterparts in other organizations. Especially those who patrolled the same neighbourhoods. Sarajevo was a small town that way. I didn't know your sister terribly well, but I did admire her spunk. And spirit. In fact, I was quite fond of her.

"Though it was our duty to go door to door, make sure no one in the neighbourhood was sick, short of food or medicine, she shouldn't have been out on that street, not at that time of day.

"Sarajevans knew that certain streets were less exposed to snipers than others that there were routes you could take to get from one place to another that would minimize your chances of getting shot. But your sister was not one to take the long safer way. She was always in a hurry."

Shaking her head from side to side, she stopped, gave me a sad glance, then continued.

"I shouted to her that I was going to use my mirror's reflection to catch the sniper's eye, divert his attention long enough to give her time to make a run for it. When she didn't respond, I assumed she'd heard me, and kept holding my compact mirror out there. But it didn't work. This sniper wouldn't be distracted, kept firing all around the car."

The woman paused, her face flushed with anger.

"Those bastards loved toying with their victims, scaring the be-jesus out of them. I shouted for your sister to stay where she was. That I'd get help. Soldiers or cops to shoot back, help her get away. But she didn't respond. Maybe the contradictory messages confused her. Perhaps she was too preoccupied with shielding herself. Or she couldn't hear me. Amidst all the rifle shot reverberations, close and distant, there never seemed to be complete silence.

"She too had a walkie talkie. I don't know why she didn't use it. Maybe it wasn't working. Half the time these contraptions conked out. Or she didn't want to be caught where she wasn't supposed to be. She'd been warned about her reckless cowgirl ways.

"Finally, to make sure she could hear me, I stuck my head around the corner and shouted for her to stay where she was when ..."

The woman stopped, took a deep breath.

"She sprang up shouting ..."

Shaking, I clenched my eyes shut, trying not to hear what the woman was describing. Trying not to see either. This was one vision I could not bear. But, however muffled and distant I'd managed to make her words, they hit me so hard, it felt as though I too had been pierced by a bullet.

After the woman's disturbing depiction of Maya's death, she paused. I opened my eyes, saw that hers were filled with tears.

"As a nurse, a first responder, I should have run to her, tried to stanch the bleeding, check for a pulse. But the bullets had pierced her skull. I knew she couldn't survive. She couldn't have survived."

The woman stifled a sob.

"He started firing at me. I immediately pulled back around the corner. For a while he kept shooting. Then stopped."

She paused again, then, in a plaintive tone: "I knew he was just itching for me to try to comfort her."

"There was nothing you could've done."

Unable to let go of the other's gut-wrenching gaze, we clung to each other with our eyes, found succour there, solace too. Finally, she broke the silence.

"I radioed for help. It seemed like hours before the authorities arrived, in full battle gear. But it was too late. It had been too late the instant your sister was shot. Still, I feel guilty. All these years, I still feel guilty."

"So do I," I whispered, "so do I."

She reached out her arms, and we hugged.

* * *

Back at my apartment building, promising to stay in touch, the woman and I bid each other a prolonged goodbye. As I shut the car door, about to switch on the ignition, her hand hesitated, she turned to me, and waved. I waved back, then watched her slowly drive away.

As her car disappeared into the distance, the woman's description of my sister's death hit me. Transfixed by the vision, I could see Maya, hear her as, fed up with cowering behind that parked car, her lust for freedom inflamed, she confronted the firing squad of her fears, sprang up shouting: "Screw you, you sick Serbian son of a bitch!" Then, like she'd lost her marbles and was hell-bent on finding them right then and there on the streets of Sarajevo, she started doing the *kazatzka*.

Yes, it's true, Maya went out with a dance. Was she deranged? I don't think so. Determined, definitely. Foolhardy, maybe. Enough was enough. It was time to stop running. If she had to go, she'd go with a bang. And she did.

For a few seconds of unfettered freedom, tempting fate for a moment of transcendent bliss, she let it bring her down. But whether meditating in a monastery or submitting to sniper madness, from the most tranquil to the most turbulent, she had to taste every facet of life. And, in the end, she had to taste death too. An ecstasy of despair equal to any joy.

Now off to Gaza, dance the *kazatska* with my daughter there!

GRAVE VI

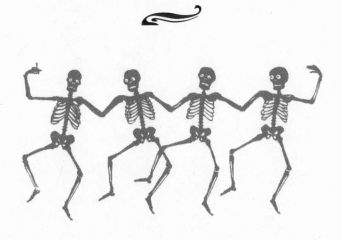

FOOL THAT I am, fool that I was, I'd begun to look forward to an upbeat ending to this saga. However, hidden deep beneath our lucky-to-be-alive veneers of delight lurks a dread we can't shed no matter how much we smile: our death sentence, and those of our loved ones.

Yet I never could have imagined a grief greater than that which I felt for my sister. That grief would not only get the better of me, it would get all of me.

I wanted to bury my daughter in Gaza, where she was killed. All the Israeli authorities wanted was to get rid of a hot potato. Against my wishes, her body was fast tracked back to Montreal. It happened so quickly, I didn't have a chance to fight.

Still, I was determined to have a private little funeral, just my daughter and me. But to bury her next to my sister, I had to deal with the funeral home which owned that cemetery. This meant purchasing of one of their complete interment packages which included choice of hard or soft wood casket, small, medium or large chapel, gravestone size (flat or upright), number of limousines and special folding chairs for the seven days of mourning at home.

I just wanted a simple burial. No limo, chapel, folding chairs or fancy casket. Just my daughter and me. Like some rigid restaurateur, the funeral director was adamant I stick to the menu. A la carte picking and choosing was discouraged.

"However, we have packages to suit every pocket book."

I stared at him, couldn't believe he was serious. But from the way he stared back I could see he was. Since he held a monopoly on Jewish burials in the city, I threatened to move my sister to a Gentile cemetery, my whole family (the plot included my parents) too.

But he didn't buy it. Didn't even blink. Blasé in a way only someone who'd been through this sort of scene before.

325

Too distraught to sustain a confrontation, I started to weep. "All I want is to be with my daughter. I can't cope with this."

Handing me a handkerchief embossed with the funeral home logo, he offered to enrol me in their abject elder's program, a charitable arm of the Jewish Hospital of Hope, intended for those who'd outlived their peers, lost touch with relatives or reality. If he'd decided I was sufficiently old and non compos mentis to qualify, who was I to argue?

Not when they introduced me to the lovely young social worker who would take over all the arrangements, shepherd me sympathetically through every phase, even chauffeuring me to and fro the funeral. For all I recall she may have showered, shaved and dressed me.

* * *

In a tiny V.I.P. R.I.P. reception room meant for guests to meet, greet and mingle with the family of the deceased before the ceremony, one visitor after another would knock, my angel of mercy would open the door, discreetly whisper I was too upset to see anyone at the moment then graciously inform them she'd be glad to convey their sympathies.

During the small chapel ceremony, I slept. Perhaps I'd passed out from all the stress, lack of food and sleep or plying myself with too much tequila. I just couldn't cope with having to listen to the house rabbi make his pro-forma speech. And I was in no condition to make one of my own.

I must have started snoring because my caregiver elbowed me, shushing me out of the side of her mouth, just as the pallbearers were about to pick up the casket.

The funeral home had hired a few beefy young men. For all I knew, they could've been distant cousins I'd never met. The only one I recognized was my daughter's former boyfriend.

Outside, watching him help carry her casket to the hearse, the irony that her breaking up with him had led to her demise wasn't lost on me. Neither was the morbid twist that my daughter, a Jewish girl in Gaza to help care for victims of the Intifada, would be struck down by an Israeli sniper.

I started to laugh. Guests stared at me. But I couldn't stop. Was it to keep from lashing out in anger, racing over to beat my daughter's former boyfriend's brains out? Her death was not his fault, my sister's or mine. It was another Jew 'doing his duty'. After my daughter was buried, I'd take my revenge. At that thought, my laughter turned to howls so loud they might have been heard a block away.

At the cemetery, my caregiver took my hand, helped me out of the limo then, linking her arm in mine, gently led a reluctant me (if I didn't witness her burial I could still make believe she wasn't dead) toward my daughter's grave site.

Unlike during my sister's burial, I didn't have to suppress my grief to deal with my father's. I was the father now. Wailing like a wounded animal, everything a blur, my sight distorted less by tears than my brain's inability to make sense of my surroundings—to accept where I was and why—I struggled to find my footing on the slippery slope of sanity. But I could hardly feel my feet, let alone firmly plant them. Only the strong arm of my guardian angel—at times supporting half my weight—kept me from collapsing.

Yet I must have blacked out, because I don't remember my daughter's casket being lowered into the ground, covered with earth and the ceremony coming to an end. All I recall is being afraid to leave her, of re-entering a world without her.

As my guardian angel slowly guided me back toward the cemetery parking lot, like some out-of-his-mind mystic, I couldn't stop muttering the Kaddish. And despite her support, I kept staggering like some drunk, struggling to put one foot in front of the other. If it wasn't so sad, I could have been mistaken for a clown, clumsily trying to coordinate with his caregiver and recalcitrant cane.

Not far from the cluster of parked cars, I realized I was part of a cortege: nearest to me, were four of my daughter's closest friends, along with a couple of my sister's high school acquaintances. The latter had so aged I hardly recognized them.

Never having met before, they and my daughter's bosom buddies seemed to have gravitated to one another. In her world travels, my sister had lost touch with, outgrown her high school cronies. Yet perhaps sensing themselves in these much younger girls, they'd been drawn to them as they had been to my sister. Or it might have been more, some hidden force, the shared deja vu shock of a friend's premature death.

I remember feeling something strange when my sister was killed. Before I knew she was missing or murdered. As soon as I stepped outside, though it was mid-day, and there were only a few cumulus clouds, the sky seemed darker than it should have been. The feeling was as eerie as those that preceded flashbacks to my parents past. But without images. I didn't attach any significance to it then. Only in retrospect did I realize that I must have been sensing my sister's death.

I stopped, stared, shocked to see flickers of her in the way her friends dressed, the way they looked.

I'd last seen them together at my daughter's going-away party, all smiles, full of girlish giggles, getting more bubbly with each drop of Dom Perignon. A confusion of feelings swept over me: waves of comfort, followed by fear. Something was wrong with this picture. For a few seconds I felt sure my daughter would spring out from behind her pals shouting "Surprise!" Then reality hit. The spark who'd given us all so much joy was gone. For good.

One sentence after another streamed through my mind, but when it came to my mouth, words failed me. Yet babbling what may on the surface have seemed to be bits and pieces of wholly inappropriate gibberish meant to avoid painfully intimate exchanges, turned out to be my inept way of opening the shattered highway to my heart. For when I was finally able to respond with a full sentence, out popped: "I miss Maya so much I just want to die!"

Yes, my daughter was named after my sister. And at that moment I was consumed by grief for my daughter. However, the presence of my sister's high school acquaintances probably playing a part, I could have been mourning for both of them. Who knows how deep the well, how strong the source of our sorrow?

My agonized exclamation evoked tearful hugs from each of my daughter's friends. And for a few moments I experienced some relief. Then, the embraces over, watching them walk away together, I felt lost, alone, with no one I was truly close to, who knew me well, who I really knew. I wanted to slink into the shell of my funeral limo, be driven home and die.

However, since my daughter's murder had made headlines, a hodgepodge who hardly knew her, my family or me had showed up. Some I hadn't seen in years, even decades. Some I'd never seen at all or, if I had, didn't recognize them.

I tried to maintain some kind of equilibrium, but they kept testing me, trying my patience. And it was hard for my pert ninety pound protector to handle the hordes. I couldn't walk more than a few feet without one of them getting in my way, trying to get close to the star of the show, trying to show they were close to the star.

The presence of a couple of journalists, photographers and TV cameras didn't help. I hadn't had to talk to the media vultures at home. My guardian angel had been superb at keeping them at bay there. And they weren't so crass as to try questioning me right before, during or after my daughter's burial. But that didn't stop them from getting their coverage. Plenty of lay interlopers were willing to act as their surrogates, be interviewed, get in the picture with me, toss in their sad two cents.

To me, they felt like voyeurs, twisted peeping Toms come to witness the tragic power of parallel fates.

Versions of "I'm so sorry. How are you holding up?" would evoke grudging nods from yours truly.

One guy had the gall to lean over and whisper: "We're gonna plant a few trees in her name."

When I was a kid, cash to plant trees was a popular way for diaspora Jews to support Israel. In return they'd receive a framed certificate. My parents' walls were plastered with them, manifestations of pride in helping 'our people' make a desert bloom. As though Palestinians hadn't owned olive and orange groves.

Do I sound bitter? You bet I do. This bastard taking a cheap tongue-in-cheek shot at me. In high school his smile had been a smirk. It still was. Why do these creeps come out of the woodwork when they're least wanted?

I was about to take a swing at the guy but was too weak. And he was much bigger than me. However, I did feel a rush of adrenaline that

330 Raphael Burdman

might have stood me in good stead. They must have been reading my body language because his wife pulled him away and my guardian angel, me.

I can't imagine how someone—even a schmuck like him—could have been so callous? Maybe he didn't know what he was doing, what he had done. Surely no one could be that dumb, so oblivious. Or am I giving him more credit than he deserved? He *was* that dumb. Even so, delivery of his words could have been distorted, the sound of them made worse not only by my grief, but by my impression of him as a kid.

Whenever I bump into boyhood acquaintances I haven't seen since way back then, I always get the feeling that they're seeing—even treating —me like I was at that time. Wonder if they feel I'm doing the same.

Perhaps we never truly outgrow childhood and adolescence. Could adulthood merely be a façade we learn to foist on that immature psyche? Or does it merely shift its shape, an aging façade of wisdom foisted by nature upon the lingering fool of youth?

Then again, sometimes our ears hear what they want to, what they need to. I knew there was no way I could continue coping with my grief. Anger seemed a more manageable emotion. And this creep had provided me with a convenient scapegoat.

In fact, my cortege seemed to have furnished me with an endless supply. So, rather than see them as obstacles, I started to take them as opportunities. To vent.

Besides, by then I'd had it. For as though not wanting my agony to end, the closer we got to the parking lot, the more eager members of this death march—most of them strangers to me—became to horn in with their pro-forma sympathy.

I've got nothing against being cordial, kind, considerate. But when you're feeling grief, rage, love—even gratitude—the whole gamut of emotions at once, surface niceties can seem like a slap in the face.

I've always found maintaining a civil veneer taxing. But these people didn't deserve my bitter twisted tongue. Having lost all armour against the cruelty of this world, why should I have inflicted more on them? Well, all I can say is that my daughter's murder snapped something in me.

I certainly wasn't going to break down sobbing like my father, give those news cretins trophy shots of me crying for the cameras.

In my unhinged state, rather than suffer the slings and arrows of civil concern, it was simpler to slip from sorrow to seething. Lost in severed links of love, struggling to hold on to what was left of them, what was left of *me*, I couldn't keep from diving off the deep end. Anger acted as both armour and weapon against my grief. Instead of feeling attacked by it, I used it to attack.

Why didn't I use the presence of all these people and the media to protest the plight of the Palestinians as my daughter had tried to do? Do something positive with my pain? Well, that kind of political outburst would have just fallen on deaf ears. And the news vampires would just cut it. Of course, I wasn't that calculating. And was in no condition to make a cogent case. I'd be too easy to shrug off.

Besides, a couple of Palestinian activists had tried to get in touch with me, showed up at my home. But I'd been in no mood to make a martyr out of my daughter. And my guardian angel had made sure that they, like the media, couldn't get to me there. Yet now they were here. I could tell by their keffiyehs, and fervent faces, a couple of college kids slowly slinking toward the cameras and mikes.

I too was enraged at Israel, wanted to punish all these diaspora Zionist dandies for the death of my daughter—punish myself too for letting her go. At the same time I was proud of her.

However, no matter how just the cause, I was in no more mood to listen to political rhetoric than clichéd consoling. Nor to put up with the sudden pushing and shoving, Jews pushing the Palestinians away from the news mikes, the two kids shoving back. The last thing I wanted was for my daughter's funeral to turn into a battle between true believers. If this was to become some kind of circus, I'd be the ringmaster.

Elbowing my way through, I inserted myself between the Jews, Palestinians and news people.

Once there, unable to tell if he was trying to console me for my daughter's death or for the presence of the Palestinians, to one Jewish stranger's "We're so sorry. Is there anything we can do?" I whispered, right in his ear, so close, each word like a kiss, each sentence leaving a little saliva behind: "When the worst happens—the worst that *can* happen —what can be more liberating? Sublime! Transcendent! Soul of steel! I'm Superman! Not even kryptonite can kill me now!"

Comic relief was not a tool my parents knew how to use to cope with their grief. With mine tearing me to pieces, the only way I could keep psychosis at bay was to bring out my big guns, blow har-har holes through my anguish *and* anger.

I remember that pseudo-sympathizer looking stunned at my sarcastic curve-ball quips, giving me sheepish grins and shrugging me off with a pained 'Same-old-Willie' smile, as though he knew me. But he didn't. Nor did he want to. And I felt the same towards him.

When another poseur insulted me with another "What can we do for you?" I snarled right in his ear: "With nothing left to lose, no reason to live and no one to feel bad if I bump myself off, I'm determined to die of natural causes, savour every ounce of agony, till the cancer kills me. Yes, it gives me great comfort to know that, after me, this family will suffer no further grief. Fate will have taken its final toll. My family will be no more."

Whether I was merely thinking what I thought I was saying, actually saying it or something else, I'm still not sure. I was ranting, so most likely they couldn't make sense of what I was saying. But, thinking I was so shook up I might have some sort of stroke, yet unable to stand listening to my nonsense, some felt compelled to soothe me with their sad tales.

How long can you pretend you're listening, like you like listening when, resentful others aren't truly interested in tuning in to you, hearing what they have to say gives you a kind of vertigo, you start to feel anxious, your attention wanders, you lose the thread, your reason for being there, your reason for being period?

Like a dentist cruising for cavities, I'd try focusing on the talker's teeth. You can tell a lot about a person by the condition of their cuspids. Most people have bad breath. Above all those who talk too much. Their mouths tend to get dry. You can spot the type, desiccated flakes of white saliva outlining their fat lips.

Grandchildren galore, gold stars of David dangling under their double chins, arrogant Israel-uber-alles attitudes etched on their bloated Botox faces, their offspring settled safely in the suburbs, why should they have cared if my world had become a bottomless pit of pain?

Was it that my sister's, daughter's and my unconventional way of life made us pariahs among peers of our past? Or was it the burden every politically incorrect Jew harbours when confronted with the black eye of Israel? No, it was not conscience clashing with some deep-seated ancestral chauvinism, it was bitterness that the naive adolescent Zionist pride I'd once held, my nostalgia for tribal tradition, the comfort I once took in synagogue, family Seders and the Yiddish my parents spoke at home had brought me so much grief.

From feelings of utter loneliness to heartbreak to anger to obnoxious absurdity to bleak buffoonery wasn't a great stretch for me. Who knows, black humour might have helped bridge the gap between them, felt like a safe blend. Or maybe just a means to mask them all. It didn't work.

There's a fine line between playing the fool and being one, between compensating for an overwhelming feeling of forlornness and keeping intimacy at bay. Cross them at your peril. And, crippled by an all-consuming agony that no amount of chatter could cure, cross them I did.

I'm not making excuses for my behaviour. Or maybe I am. Does it matter? Sooner or later we lose everyone we love. Then we lose ourselves. A man can only bear so much misery before he does himself in. Until then, what can he do but laugh, cry, scream, go crazy with grief, struggle to stay sane with seemingly senseless shenanigans.

Assuming that, as Marx wrote, 'History repeats itself, first as tragedy, then as farce,' perhaps the only way to cope with life's unspeakable afflictions is to make a mockery of them, become some kind of buffoon. Surrounded by madness, saddled with unbearable sadness, wit won't do, it comes from the head, weeping, from the heart. Whereas silliness stems from the whole wounded soul.

Could it be that we're all fools, mere court jesters before god? If so, I've been doing my best to entertain the bastard.

GRAVE VII

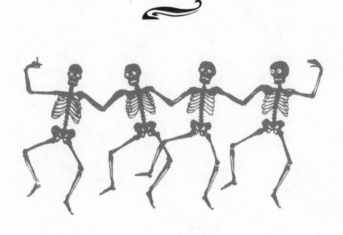

Israeli authorities today announced the dismissal of all charges against the soldiers who, during a Palestinian demonstration against the closing of the Kerem Shalom cargo border crossing with Gaza last June, shot and killed Canadian citizen, Maya Blittstein, daughter of William Velvel Blittstein.

In delving into the circumstances surrounding this story, this reporter has discovered that, months after her Montreal burial, Mr. Blittstein decided to have his daughter's body exhumed and cremated. When cemetery officials failed to talk him out of it, they sent the city's chief rabbi.

"It's against Jewish law," he told Mr Blittstein.

"I don't give a damn about Jewish law! I want to do my daughter justice!" Mr. Blittstein responded.

"Take legal action. But let her rest in peace. For her sake and yours," the rabbi pleaded.

But Mr. Blittstein was relentless. Having had time to process what had happened and why, he'd concluded that was what his daughter would have wanted.

Claiming he was in an unstable state of mind, the cemetery sued to stop him. With no family members to contest Mr. Blittstein's decision, cemetery officials were forced to acquiesce.

Upon his arrival at Ben Gurion airport, customs authorities questioned him about the urn he was carrying. He told them he was going to scatter his daughter's ashes in the Dead Sea. As a Jew, they could neither deny him or his daughter's ashes entry.

Mr. Blittstein then took a taxi to the Eretz border crossing into Gaza where he informed Israeli guards he was going for a brief visit with his daughter's former associates. He intended to remain there only long enough to allow them to pay their respects to his daughter before returning to scatter her ashes in the Dead Sea.

Not wanting to revive an incident that might have given Israel an international black eye, the head of Gaza border security agreed to give Mr. Blittstein a day pass.

After conversations with former colleagues of Ms. Blittstein, this reporter has learned that, before leaving for Gaza, her father had taken an intensive nurse's aid course in Canada. However, once he'd arrived in Gaza, he realized his cancer had progressed to the point where he had neither the time nor energy to do anything but execute an appropriate end to his mission: scatter his daughter's ashes where she had died.

Her Palestinian co-workers insisted on being there to honour her. But without placards or shouted slogans. Just a silent march of remembrance. At a safe distance from the border.

Mr. Blittstein agreed that *they* could stop as far from the border as they felt comfortable. Or as close.

According to Israeli authorities this reporter has spoken to, days after his Gaza entry, Israeli border guards spotted "this old man" (Mr. Blittstein) head covered by a black and white Kefiyeh, "clutching some kind of manuscript and container" against his chest as he lead a small group of young women toward the Gaza cargo border crossing into Israel at Kerem Shalom.

The soldiers issued repeated loudspeaker warnings not to proceed any further. Twenty metres from the border fence the group finally stopped. But Mr. Blittstein did not. Instead, he flung the cover of the container to the ground and, little by little, with each slow step forward, scattered its ashes. He then dropped the urn and started to do, what to the soldiers, seemed like a little dance, as he reached inside his jacket pocket.

An inquest into Mr. Blittstein's death has not yet been completed but one anonymous Israeli source has informed this reporter that when he reached inside his jacket, fearing he may have been harbouring a gun or about to detonate a bomb (neither were found) the guards had no choice but to open fire.

However, as soon as they realized he'd pulled what turned out to be a matchbook from his jacket pocket, they immediately stopped shooting. But it was too late. The unbound manuscript pages scattered as Mr. Blittstein dropped to the ground.

The Palestinians who accompanied Mr. Blittstein told this reporter that he'd planned to set fire to his manuscript, scatter it along with his daughter's ashes. They'd tried to convince him not to. His daughter had expressed such pride in her father's writing, felt sad he'd never had the success he deserved.

Mr. Blittstein insisted it was time to abandon his artist's ego, let the winds of fate carry the ashes of his tragic family history away with his daughter's.

This reporter has since learned that, following Mr. Blittstein's death, the same New York publisher who, more than four decades before, had demanded his advance be returned and threatened to sue Mr. Blittstein for misrepresenting a much earlier work, decided to publish his scattered manuscript. Just before leaving for Israel Mr. Blittstein had mailed him a copy, which included this epitaph:

> *I would love to have been more of a mensch, my life to have been a heroic journey, one more worthy of my family history. If you're born a genius you're doomed to do great things. That's what geniuses do. But if you're born mediocre, as most of us are, to achieve anything at all is worthy of, if not a Nobel, at least a booby prize.*

When this reporter asked the publisher whether, without all the publicity surrounding Mr. Blittstein's dramatic death, he would have bought the man's book, he replied: "How could any publisher worth his salt ignore the work of a man who sacrificed his life to immortalize his family's."

Somewhat startled, I asked if he thought this an authentic memoir. Without hesitation he responded: "His long ago pieces were fiction masquerading as fact, this one, fact masquerading as fiction. Of the two, I ask you, which is more true?"

Acknowledgements

I would like to thank Nan Gregory for her feedback on an early draft of the manuscript, and Chris Allen for his fine tuning of my final draft. Most of all, I would like to express my gratitude to Judith Ramos Cheifetz Moore for sticking with me through oh so many early drafts, providing detailed editorial insights on each. I could not have done this without you, Judith.

Also, thanks to Rafael Chimicatti for his patient feedback and suggestions culminating in his wonderful cover design. Finally, to Guernica editor and publisher, Michael Mirolla, my gratitude for sticking with me through so many edits and revisions, most of which were wisely suggested by him.

About the Author

Raphael Burdman, author of the Chalmers Canadian Play Award-winning *Tête-à-tête* published and produced in English, French, Flemish and German in Canada, the U.S. and Europe, has written for the Canadian Broadcasting Corporation, National Film Board, Caravan Stage, Los Angeles Actors Theater and independent film companies. He's also produced and directed documentary film and video in the U.S. and Canada and taught at the City University of New York as well as Douglas College in British Columbia. Born in Montreal, he now lives in Victoria.